AN AMISH
SECOND CHRISTMAS

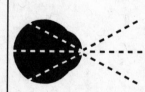

This Large Print Book carries the
Seal of Approval of N.A.V.H.

An Amish Second Christmas

Beth Wiseman,
Ruth Reid,
Kathleen Fuller,
and Tricia Goyer

THORNDIKE PRESS

A part of Gale, Cengage Learning

GALE
CENGAGE Learning

Farmington Hills, Mich • San Francisco • New York • Waterville, Maine
Meriden, Conn • Mason, Ohio • Chicago

GALE
CENGAGE Learning·

Copyright © 2014 by Elizabeth Wiseman Mackey, Kathleen Fuller, Tricia Goyer, Ruth Reid.

Thorndike Press, a part of Gale, Cengage Learning.

Thorndike Press® Large Print Christian Fiction.

The text of this Large Print edition is unabridged.

Other aspects of the book may vary from the original edition.

Set in 16 pt. Plantin.

LIBRARY OF CONGRESS CATALOGING-IN-PUBLICATION DATA

An Amish second Christmas / by Beth Wiseman, Ruth Reid, Kathleen Fuller, and Tricia Goyer. — Large print edition.
    pages ; cm. — (Thorndike Press large print Christian fiction)
    ISBN 978-1-4104-7522-0 (hardcover) — ISBN 1-4104-7522-0 (hardcover)
    1. Amish—Fiction. 2. Christmas stories, American. 3. Christian fiction, American. I. Wiseman, Beth, 1962– When Christmas comes again. II. Reid, Ruth, 1963– Her Christmas pen pal. III. Fuller, Kathleen. Gift for Anne Marie. IV. Goyer, Tricia. Christmas aprons.
    PS648.A45A56 2014b
    813'.01083823—dc23   2014036023

Published in 2015 by arrangement with Thomas Nelson, Inc., a division of HarperCollins Christian Publishing, Inc.

Printed in the United States of America
1 2 3 4 5 6 7 19 18 17 16 15

CONTENTS

■ ■ ■ ■

WHEN CHRISTMAS
COMES AGAIN

BETH WISEMAN

■ ■ ■ ■

To Karla Hanns and Joan Main

GLOSSARY

ab im kopp: off in the head; crazy
ach: oh
bruder: brother
daadi: grandfather
daed: father
danki: thank you
Englisch: the English language; a non-Amish person
gut: good
kapp: prayer covering or cap
kinner: children
mamm: mom
mammi: grandmother
mei: my
mudder: mother
nee: no
Ordnung: the unwritten rules of the Amish
Pennsylvania Deitsch: the language spoken by the Amish
rumschpringe: running-around period when a teenager turns sixteen years old

wunderbaar: wonderful
ya: yes

CHAPTER ONE

Katherine Zook fell into step with two *Englisch* women who were crossing the parking lot toward the Bird-in-Hand market. Normally, she would avoid the chatty tourists, but the tall man with the shoulder-length, salt-and-pepper hair and a limp was following her again.

"It's a lovely day, isn't it?" The middle-aged woman walking next to Katherine was a little thing with short, red hair and wore a blue T-shirt with *Paradise, Pennsylvania* on the front. Her friend had on the same T-shirt, but it was red.

"*Ya,* it is." Katherine glanced at the dark clouds overhead. There wasn't anything lovely about the weather. Frigid temperatures and the snow had just begun to fall again. She picked up the pace and hoped the women would speed up too. She looked over her shoulder, glad they were gaining some distance on the stranger. She'd first seen him a week ago, loitering outside the Gordonville Bookstore, and she hadn't thought much about it. Then when she saw him at Kauffman's Fruit Farm and Market, she'd thought it was a coincidence. She'd also spotted him outside Paradiso's when she'd stopped to pick up a pizza as a treat for the children. But this was becoming more than a fluke.

Katherine could feel the women staring at her, but she kept her eyes straight ahead and hoped they weren't about to ask a string of questions. *Do you have a telephone? Can I take your picture? Is this where you do your shopping? How many children do you have? Are your people Christians?* And Katherine's personal favorite: *Do you know where I can get an Amish pen pal?*

It wasn't that she held ill will against the curious *Englisch* tourists, but she often wondered what their reactions would be if the situation were reversed. They'd most likely run from her or summon the police.

"Ma'am, can I ask you a quick question?" The redhead spoke loudly, as if Katherine might be hard of hearing, making it impossible to ignore her. She looked over her shoulder again, but she didn't see the man anymore. She stopped a few feet from the entrance when the two women did. "*Ya.*

14

What can I help you with?"

"I-I was wondering . . ." The woman blushed as her eyes darted back and forth between Katherine and the other lady. "My friend and I were wondering . . ." She pulled her large, black purse up on her shoulder. "We — well . . ."

Katherine waited. She was anxious to get in and out of the market, then back on the road. She'd left her two youngest *kinner* home alone. Linda was old enough to babysit five-year-old Gideon, but he could be a handful even for Katherine. She pulled her black coat snug, looking forward to a brief reprieve from the weather once she got inside the market.

"Do Amish women shave their legs?" the woman finally asked. Luckily, she hadn't spoken as loudly as before.

This is a first. Katherine closed her gaping mouth and tried to find the words for a response. Before she could, the other *Englischer* spoke up.

"And . . . you know . . ." The woman was a bit taller than her friend with short, gray hair that was slightly spiked on the top of her head. She raised one of her arms and with her other hand she pointed under her arm. "Do you shave here too?"

The first woman touched Katherine lightly

15

on the arm. "We can't find the answer to that question online, and it's been an ongoing argument during our book-club gatherings." She stood taller and smiled. "We only read Amish books."

Does that fact make it okay to ask such questions? Katherine considered telling the women that they were very rude, but changed her mind. She folded her hands in front of her and glanced back and forth between the ladies.

"Only when I've planned for my husband and me to be alone. But he died six months ago, so . . ." Katherine smiled and shrugged. *That will give you something to tell your book club.* Both of the women's eyes went round as saucers. "Have a *wunderbaar* day," Katherine added before she walked into the market. She looked back once to make sure neither of them had fainted. She didn't know any Amish folks who used the word *wunderbaar,* but the *Englisch* seemed to think they did, so she was happy to throw it in for good measure.

She held her laughter until she was inside the store. On most days, it was a challenge just to get out of bed in the morning, much less to find humor in anything. But as she made her way to the back of the market, she thought about Elias. Her husband would have gotten a chuckle out of Katherine's response. *I miss you, Elias.*

She dropped off some quilted potholders for Diana to display in her booth. Katherine tried to make several per week for her *Englisch* friend to sell. The market in Bird-In-Hand catered to tourists mostly, and Diana had a permanent booth. Katherine and a few other local Amish women provided Diana with items to sell. And occasionally, when Katherine had time, she and Diana would sneak away and grab lunch and then split a dessert. They both suffered from an insatiable sweet tooth. But those times were getting more infrequent since she bore the entire responsibility of caring for the family.

Making small craft items used to be more of a hobby for Katherine, but now that money was tight, Linda and Mary Carol had been putting in extra hours sewing, knitting, and crocheting. Katherine hadn't told the children that they might have to sell their house, or at least part of the fifty acres that surrounded their home. That would be a last resort because the land had been in her family for three generations. She grabbed the last thing on her list, and as she made her way to the checkout line, she caught sight of an *Englisch* couple walking hand in hand. She missed having someone to bounce the important decisions off of. Her oldest, Stephen, was sixteen and trying hard to assume the role of head of the household, even though it should have been a time for him to be enjoying his *rumschpringe.*

As she made her way toward the exit, she saw the two women from the parking lot. The ladies actually bumped into each other as they scurried to avoid Katherine, but Katherine smiled and gave a little wave before she walked out the door.

She stuffed her gloved hands into the pockets of her coat. The snow was beginning to accumulate, and the wind was biting. It was colder than usual for December. Somehow, Katherine and her children had managed to get through Thanksgiving, but this first Christmas without Elias was going to be hard.

When she felt the tears starting to build in her eyes, she forced herself to think about the two *Englisch* women, and it brought a smile to her face. She was going to bottle that memory and pull it out when she felt sad, which was most days.

As she hurried toward her buggy, she tipped the rim of her black bonnet to shield her face from the snow, but every few seconds, she scanned the parking lot for signs of the tall man with the gray hair. Katherine didn't see him.

She stowed her purse on the seat beside her and waited for two cars to pass before she clicked her tongue and pulled back on the reins. She said a silent prayer of thanks when the snow started to let up. John Wayne was an older horse, and like so many others that pulled buggies in Lancaster County, he hadn't fared well at the racetrack. And as a result, he was no longer any use to his owner. Elias had paid a fair price at auction, and John Wayne had been a good horse for a lot of years, but these days the winters took a toll on the animal.

Katherine could still remember when, years ago, she and Elias let Mary Carol name the animal. They'd assumed their oldest daughter must have heard the name on television — maybe at an *Englisch* friend's house. Katherine and Elias had limited visits to the *Englisch* homes when their *kinner* were young since the *Ordnung* encouraged their people to stay as separate as possible from outsiders. But in Lancaster County, it was impossible to avoid the *Englisch* completely. Their district relied on the *Englisch* tourists to supplement their income. With each new generation, there was less land available for farming. More and more, Amish men and women were working outside their homes. The women in their district enjoyed having a little extra money of their own. "Mad money" was what the *Englisch* called it. Katherine had no idea why. But then, the *Englisch* seemed to get mad about lots of things.

It was several years before Katherine found out that John Wayne was the name of some kind of gunslinger. But by then, it was too late to change it. The name had stuck.

She picked up speed to get ahead of another car in the parking lot, and she was almost to the highway when she caught sight of the strange man again. He was standing beside a blue car, staring at her. A shiver ran up her spine. As she passed by him, she allowed herself a good, long look, tempted to stop and ask him why he was following her. But that wasn't always safe with the *Englisch*. Katherine was wise enough to know that there were good and bad people everywhere — even in her small Amish district — but the bad seemed to settle in around the *Englisch*. It was just simple math. There were more of them.

When Katherine locked eyes with the stranger, he hurried into the blue car. Would he follow her? She didn't know who he was, but something about him was familiar.

She turned around several times during her trip home, double-checking that he wasn't behind her. Thirty minutes later, she pulled into her driveway. She got John Wayne settled in the barn before she hurried into the house. She called out to Linda as soon as she walked into the living room. After she hung her bonnet and coat on the rack by the door, she pulled off her gloves.

"Linda! Gideon!" She edged toward the stairs and was relieved when Linda answered. "Up here, *Mamm.*"

"Is everything okay?" she asked from the landing.

"No!"

Katherine sighed as she started up the stairs. Out of her four children, Linda was what her friend Diana described as dramatic. Since no one was crying, she assumed no one had gotten hurt, always a good thing. "I'm on my way up."

"You're not going to be happy!"

Katherine picked up the pace. *I'm already not happy. What now?* She opened the door to Linda's bedroom, and when no one was there, she moved down the hall to Gideon's room.

Linda threw her hands up in the air and grunted. "I don't know what you're going to do with him." Linda stormed past Kath-

21

erine before she could ask her why she
hadn't kept a closer eye on the five-year-
old, but right now, she needed to have a
talk with her youngest.

She sat down across from Gideon's bed
where the boy was playing with his shoe-
laces. Stephen disliked having to share a
room with little Gideon. He would definitely
not approve of these new drawings on the
walls. Their home was plain. Everywhere
except this room. Stephen had begged for a
few luxuries when his *rumschpringe* began,
and Katherine had given in since he seemed
to be taking his father's death the hardest.
Posters of hot rods and musicians on the
wall, a battery-operated radio by the bed, a
pair of earbuds on the nightstand, and a
magazine with a fancy automobile on the
front. Katherine didn't like all these things
being in the same room with Gideon, but
she was choosing her battles these days.

"Gideon, we've talked about this. You cannot draw on the walls." Katherine rubbed
her forehead as she eyed her son's artwork
and recalled how she'd just repainted this
room a month ago. Diana had told her that
drawing pictures on the walls was Gideon's
way of expressing his grief. Katherine
hadn't been sure about that, but today's
imagery proved Diana was right. However,

this was not a time for scolding. "What made you draw this, Gideon? We talked about where *Daed* went, remember?"

Her son hung his head for a few moments before he looked up at her with his big, brown eyes. He brushed his blond bangs out of the way. His hair needed a trim but it would have to wait. Maybe Stephen could do it.

Gideon started talking to her in *Deitsch*, but Katherine interrupted him. *"Nee,* when you're at home, talk to me in *Englisch."* It was Gideon's first year of school, so he'd just started learning *Englisch* as a second language. "It's *gut* practice for you."

"Daed is in a box in the dirt. I saw him put there." Her son pointed to his large drawing on the wall. An outsider might not have recognized it as a coffin in the middle of a bunch of stick people, but Katherine did.

"Nee." She leaned forward until she was close enough to gently grasp Gideon's chin, lifting his eyes to hers. *"Daed* is in heaven with God and Jesus and your *mammi* and *daadi."* Why was Gideon so fixated on thinking his *daed* was in the ground? From an early age, all of her *kinner* had been schooled about the Lord and taught the ways of the *Ordnung.* "Only *Daed*'s body was buried.

23

Daed's soul went to heaven."

For the hundredth time, Katherine tried to explain this to her son, frustrated that the other children had accepted this as truth by the time they were Gideon's age. But maybe it had been easier for the others because they didn't have to apply it to the death of their own father.

"Mom!"

Katherine stood up and got to the bedroom door just as Linda blew into the room carrying a box wrapped in silver paper with a purple bow. Her face was red and her teeth chattered.

"You don't have to yell." She touched her daughter's icy cheek. "Were you outside?" She nodded to the box. "And what's that?"

"I saw a man in the driveway. By the time I got outside, he was in his car driving away."

Katherine rushed to the window in time to see a blue car going down the road. She rested a hand on her chest.

Linda joined her at the window. "This was on the rocking chair on the front porch." She handed the box to Katherine and smiled. "It has your name written on it." Her daughter bounced up on her toes. "Your first Christmas present!"

CHAPTER TWO

Mary Carol didn't think she'd ever get tired of kissing Abraham Fisher. She just wished that she didn't feel so guilty about it. Everyone in her house — except maybe Linda — was still mourning the loss of their father. Mary Carol heard her mother crying softly in her room sometimes. Stephen wouldn't say much to anyone. And Gideon had taken to drawing all over the walls, something he'd never done before. Mary Carol missed her father so much it hurt, but she was trying to give herself permission to find happiness again. And she was doing that with Abe. She'd known him all her life, but they'd only been dating for a few months. He'd just recently gotten baptized, something she hoped was the first step in what would lead to a marriage proposal.

Abe kissed her again, then pulled away. "I can tell you're distracted."

"What?" Mary Carol twisted the tie of her *kapp* between her fingers and tried to still her chattering teeth. Now that she was in her *rumschpringe,* they were spending more time together, but this was the first time they'd come to the abandoned farmhouse off Black Horse Road. Mary Carol was afraid the structure might collapse on them, but it was much too cold to sit in the buggy. The battery-operated heater in Abe's buggy had quit working earlier in the day.

Abe reached for her hand and squeezed. "You're feeling bad about being happy."

She'd done her best not to let it show. "Sorry."

"It's okay. I can just tell when your mind goes somewhere else." Abe blew a cold fog as he spoke.

Mary Carol snuggled up against him on the couch. The blue-and-red-checkered fabric was faded, and the cushions sagged in the middle. The house had been vacant for years, but from the looks of things, they hadn't been the only ones seeking privacy and a little relief from the weather.

"I wonder who else is coming here." She pointed to an empty Coke can on a TV tray next to an old tan recliner.

Abe got up and walked to the chair. "Maybe this has been here for a long time."

He lifted the can and smelled it. Mary Carol giggled.

"Do you think smelling it will tell you how old it is?" She stood up and walked toward him.

"*Ya,* maybe, smarty-pants." He grinned as he tossed the empty can back and forth, his teeth chattering like hers. "Let's look around."

"Not upstairs," she said quickly. "I'm already worried the second floor is going to fall in on us, or we're going to step on a loose board down here."

"Nah." Abe pushed back the rim of his straw hat. "These old farmhouses were built sturdy, probably by *gut* Amish folks."

Mary Carol hugged herself to keep warm as she followed Abe into the kitchen. "*Nee,* Mr. Porter lived here until he died, and he wasn't Amish."

"I know, but he was in his seventies. I heard *mei daed* talking about this house once. He was telling *mei mamm* about three men who were staying here, but he stopped talking when he saw me, and I didn't hear the rest. But I think he said it was about a hundred years old. So it could have been one of our ancestors who built it before Mr. Porter lived here." He pointed to an electrical outlet to the right of the sink. "Mr.

Porter probably had it wired for electricity." Abe opened one of the cabinets, which was empty, then he shuffled sideways and opened the rest.

"Ew," Mary Carol said when she saw the skeletal remains of a small mouse. She took a step back, and Abe came to her and wrapped his arms around her waist.

"I was warmer when we were on the couch." He towered over her as he pressed his lips to hers. In thirty years, would kissing Abe still give her this heady feeling?

She eased away from him and shivered. "It's much colder here in the kitchen."

Abe pointed to the window above the sink. "When I was looking in the cabinets, I felt the cold air blowing from here. Needs caulking around the panes." He latched onto her hand and they returned to the living room. The only furniture was the couch, the recliner, and the tray. She wanted to see the second story, but one of the steps was missing a piece of wood, and part of the handrail was broken off about halfway up. They were about to sit when Mary Carol noticed something in the corner of the room.

"Look." She pointed to a roll of silver wrapping paper, a reel of purple ribbon, a pair of scissors, and some tape. "Someone's been wrapping Christmas presents." She sat down beside Abe on the couch. "Maybe we shouldn't be here."

Abe cupped her cheeks in his hands, and she decided not to worry about it. After a few more minutes, she eased away. Abe's breathing was ragged, and she could feel her heart pounding. These were indicators that it was time to stop. She wondered how many other couples — *Englisch* or Amish — had made out on this very couch. "I probably need to get home."

Abe took a deep breath and blew it out slowly. "*Ya,* probably so." He stood up and offered her his hand. Mary Carol trusted Abe not to go too far with her, but it was getting harder and harder to keep tabs on his roaming hands. Sometimes she was tempted to give herself to him, but she'd made a vow to God that she would wait until she was married. She was only eighteen, but that was a fine marrying age. Mary Carol planned to be baptized soon, so maybe Abe would ask her before too long. Her parents had been eighteen when they got married. But every time she thought about a wedding, she thought about her father. Maybe it was too soon to be thinking about celebrating such things.

A blast of cold air met them when Abe

opened the front door, and they rushed to the buggy. Mary Carol had told her mother she'd be home in time to help with supper. She hoped she wasn't late.

Katherine sat down on her bed and stared at the gift. Luckily, Linda had gotten distracted shortly after the package arrived and hadn't pestered her about it.

She turned up the lantern on her bedside table and took a deep breath. What if this man was a threat to her family? It was an additional worry she didn't need.

She slid the purple ribbon from the package, then slowly peeled back the silver paper to reveal a saltine cracker box. She gave it a gentle shake before she turned it end over end and listened to the contents shift. *A strange choice for a gift box.*

The box opened easily at one end. She peeked inside before she dumped it on her bed. Photographs. Dozens of them. All of Elias. And a few of Katherine and the children.

She tried to blink back the tears that rushed to her eyes. There was a photo of Elias at an auction not long before he died. Another was of Katherine and Elias outside the pizza place. She picked up a snapshot of Elias holding Gideon and could no longer stave off her tears. She brought it closer to her face, and it took her a minute before she realized it had been taken just two days before the accident. She quickly glanced at the rest of the pictures, but fear was catching up with her other emotions. She unfolded a yellow piece of paper that was mixed in with the photographs.

Katherine wiped her eyes and put on her reading glasses. The penmanship was shaky, barely legible.

I know pictures are not allowed, but following the loss of a loved one, photographs can bring much comfort. I think the bishop — and the Lord — would think it's okay for you to have these. I hope they will bring you a little bit of happiness.

I'm leaving this on your front porch because I haven't gotten up the nerve to talk to you. I don't know if you're even going to want to talk to me, but I know you've seen me around. I'm not a stalker or anything. I won't cause you any troubles. I'm just an old man with a borrowed camera that enjoys taking pictures of your family. Or I should say, our family.

I will be at the coffee shop on Tuesday

morning at nine o'clock if you would like to meet. The coffee shop where you and Elias used to go sometimes.

Katherine held her breath as she reread the last couple of lines.

Kindest Regards,
James Zook

Katherine was a little girl the last time she saw James. Even back then, he walked with a limp, although she didn't know why. Like the other Amish men in their community, he'd grown a long beard following marriage, and Katherine remembered him being a deacon in the church. He no longer had a beard, and his dark hair was now long and peppered with gray.

She stood up and paced the length of her bedroom, trying to decide what to do. Part of her wanted to meet Elias's father because it would give her back a piece of her husband. But why had the man disappeared all those years ago? And why was he sneaking around? The thought of him taking pictures of the family was disturbing. And why were so many taken shortly before her husband was hit by a car?

James Zook had abandoned his wife and

only son over thirty years ago.
Katherine's knowledge, no one ha
from him since. Had he been livin₁
here in Paradise?

She sat down on the bed and fli₁
through each picture again. Whatever
intentions, her father-in-law was right ab
one thing. Pictures were not allowed
their people, but seeing them made her fe
something she hadn't felt in months: com-
forted.

CHAPTER THREE

Katherine arrived at the coffee shop early and ordered a black coffee. As she waited at the table, she prayed that the Lord would bless her with the right words today. Elias had rarely talked about his father, but his departure had left scars. Over the years, the pain had been mostly replaced by anger and resentment. She wasn't sure her husband would approve of this meeting. She'd chosen not to say anything to the children. Not yet.

James came in the door and walked directly to her booth. He stood in front of her for a few moments before sliding into the booth across from her.

Katherine cleared her throat. "Hello." She noticed right away that he and Elias both had the same nose, long and narrow. Her husband had also been blessed with incredible blue eyes that he had obviously inherited from his father. The most noticeable difference between Elias and his father were

the lines of time feathering across James's face, and whereas Elias had been gifted with a lovely set of straight teeth, this man's bottom teeth crossed in the front.

"Am I late? I hate to be late." His eyebrows drew together in an agonized expression, his eyes fixed on her as he waited for her response.

"Uh, *nee.* I-I don't think you're late." Katherine's stomach churned. "Would you like some coffee? You have to order it at the counter."

"I don't drink coffee, but *danki.*" He folded his hands on top of the table. Katherine noticed a stain on his wrinkled blue shirt. He wasn't wearing a coat. She studied his face, noticing he looked a bit disheveled and needed a shave.

"Do you still speak Pennsylvania *Deitsch*?" Maybe Elias's father had left his family but resumed his Amish lifestyle within another district.

"I remember a few words." His face split into a wide grin. He was missing a couple of teeth toward the back. "Did you like the pictures?"

Katherine swallowed hard, wishing her stomach would settle down. *"Ya,* I did. *Danki."*

"I have lots more."

"Mr. Zook . . . why didn't —"

"Just James," he said as he sat taller. "We're family."

Katherine took a deep breath and wondered if Elias was watching from heaven. "Why didn't you make yourself known to Elias before he died? And why the pictures?"

James's eyes darted around the room as he blinked his left eye a few times. Then he locked eyes with her. "I'm being followed, so I can't be too careful."

Katherine looked around the small coffee shop, then back at him. "Who is following you?"

He tapped a finger to the side of his face. "I'm not sure. But I think it's the FBI. That stands for Federal Bureau of Investigation."

"Uh, *ya*. I know." She recalled a horrific crime that had occurred in the area when she was very young. Even though her parents had kept the details from Katherine, she remembered hearing that the FBI was in Paradise. She took a sip of her coffee and kept her eyes on him.

"I used to be one of them. That's why I don't drink coffee. Got burned out on it." He leaned back against the booth and folded his arms across his chest. "I'm privy to a lot of top secret information, so they keep a tail on me. But I have no intention of telling them what I know until I'm safely behind the pearly gates." He leaned forward and folded his hands atop the table again. "How old are you?"

Katherine tried to find her voice, relieved that Elias wasn't here to see his father like this. "I'm, uh . . . thirty-eight." She forced a smile. "James, can you tell me why you're taking pictures of my family?"

He sighed, and Katherine got a whiff of his breath. She struggled not to cringe. She prayed that James wasn't dangerous, just crazy.

"I came here to see Elias, but I was nervous to meet all of you." His eye fluttered again before he went on. "I took a bunch of pictures in case Elias sent me packing, figuring I'd at least have pictures to look at sometimes." He shrugged. "But that car hit him not long after I got here." Frowning, he started counting on his fingers. "Six or seven days. No . . . actually it was twelve days after I got here. Possibly a week." He sighed. "It could have been three days."

Katherine wasn't a drinker, but she'd seen Widow Kauffman adding brandy to her coffee on more than one occasion. Katherine didn't think that sounded like a bad idea right now. She took another sip of coffee as she wondered what James had been doing for the past thirty years. "So, are you living here in Paradise?"

"For now. The Lord sent me here. The same way He sent me to Michigan to work with the FBI." He hung his head for a few moments before he looked back at her with sad eyes, one of them beginning to twitch again. "We can't question the Lord." He shrugged and grinned. "Why would we, right? He's God." Then he chuckled. Loudly.

Katherine moved her eyes about the room. Two elderly couples on the other side of the shop chatted, not seeming to notice James's outburst. Katherine nodded. "*Ya,* you're right. We don't question the Lord's will." She paused. "James, did you continue practicing our faith after you left here? Did you live in another Amish community?"

He stared at her with a blank expression. "Of course not."

"Oh, it just wondered me if you might have."

Leaning forward, he put his palms flat on the table and spoke to her in a whisper. "They don't take Amish people at the Federal Bureau of Investigation."

"*Ya.* Of course not." Katherine smoothed the wrinkles from her dress. "James, I need to ask you not to take any more pictures of me or *mei* family. It is very unsettling. And can I ask you to please stop following me? I'm happy to meet you here for coffee from time to time."

He leaned back again and waved a hand in her direction as he grunted. "No worries. I won't be here long." He shook his head. "To tell you the truth, I thought I would have been gone long before now. But our Father extended my stay."

Katherine hoped she didn't have to get the *Englisch* authorities involved. "Where are you staying?"

"I'd rather not say."

Katherine inhaled a slow, steady breath, and as she released it, she willed herself to stay calm and sympathetic. She had a great-aunt who was mentally ill. "Okay. But you will stop following me, right?"

"I will."

Katherine drank the last of her coffee. "I should go now. It was nice to see you after all these years." *Forgive the lie, Lord.* "I'm sorry you weren't able to visit with Elias while he was alive."

"I didn't really care for that funeral your people threw for my son."

Katherine's breath caught in her throat. She tried not to think about the funeral and how difficult it had been to say good-bye to Elias's earthly body. "You were there?"

"Only at the grave site, and I stayed under the patch of trees at the back of the cemetery. I couldn't hear what was said." James frowned. "But it was clear that there wasn't near enough fanfare for my son. No flowers or music."

"Have you forgotten that Amish funerals are plain? We don't do those things."

James stood up. "I know. I have to go now." He scanned the room. *Looking for federal agents?* Katherine kept her seat, just in case he tried to hug her. Instead, he put a gentle hand on her shoulder. "I wish that Elias was still here."

Her eyes clouded. "Me too." Katherine forced herself to stand.

"Don't worry. I won't hug you. I know your people don't like that."

She nodded, thankful that he spared her the awkward moment.

"Hey. It's almost Christmas, huh?" He smiled. "A celebration indeed." After he looked around the room again, he turned and left. Katherine stood there for a few moments, then she walked out the door and saw him on the sidewalk. *He must be freezing.* She watched him for a few moments and tried to fight the strange feeling settling over her. She called out to him. He turned around and walked back to her.

"I can't stay at your home if that's what you are going to ask me. And I'm not ready to meet my grandchildren either."

"I, uh . . ." Katherine stared at him, tongue-tied for a few seconds since neither of those thoughts had crossed her mind. Inviting him to her home was out of the question, but she had a lot of questions for James Zook. "Would you like to meet here next Tuesday?" She could bring him some of Elias's things. A coat, for starters.

He walked a few steps closer to her, and a smile lit up his face. "I know you're not going to like this, but . . ."

Katherine tensed when he threw his arms around her, and her initial reaction was to push him away. But then he rubbed her back, the way a parent lovingly rubs a child's back, and he said, "Elias loved you very much. He talks to me in my dreams sometimes. He understands why I couldn't be with him when he was growing up. But I gotta say, I sure am excited to go see him after Christmas." He eased himself away. "He said they are really going to roll out the red carpet when I get there."

Then he abruptly withdrew from the hug. "See you Tuesday." He turned and headed

41

down the sidewalk.

Katherine tried to ignore the rush of grief that came over her. And then she made her way slowly toward her buggy.

CHAPTER FOUR

Mary Carol waited as Abe put batteries in the new heater. He had also brought a heavy blanket for them to use at the old farmhouse. She huddled beneath it on the couch while Abe got the heater set up on the floor a few feet in front of them. Everything looked about the same as the last time they'd borrowed old Mr. Porter's house, except now six Coke cans were on the TV tray by the chair.

"Can you feel the heat?" Abe put a hand in front of the blower.

Mary Carol nodded. It wasn't very powerful, but it was better than nothing. Abe joined her on the couch and she raised the cover so he could get underneath it.

"I missed you," he said as he cupped her face and kissed her. As much as she enjoyed these Saturdays with Abe, she was becoming more and more distracted from her effort to keep things from going too far. As he eased her down on the couch, he lay beside her. "And I love you," he added, his breath ragged, his hand traveling. She gently pushed him away and sat up.

"I love you, too, but . . ." She bit her bottom lip as she lowered her chin. "I feel like we're doing something wrong."

Abe sat up, got out from under the blanket, and wrapped it around both her shoulders. Then he kissed her on the cheek. "I don't want to do anything that makes you feel like that."

Mary Carol was trying to decide if he was upset or mad. She'd only known one girl who had gone all the way before marriage, and not only had Lena regretted it right away, she'd also gotten pregnant. They were quiet as the heater hummed, blowing a warm breeze their way.

"I just want to hold you." Abe wrapped his arms around her. After awhile, she invited him to share the blanket with her again, and they resumed kissing. But it took even less time for Abe to start breathing hard as he pulled her closer.

"I can't," she whispered as her body reacted to his touch in ways she didn't understand. "I'm scared."

"Don't be. I won't do anything you don't want me to do." Abe trembled, and Mary

Carol wanted to trust him, but she wasn't sure she could trust herself.

"No," she said in a louder voice, but she didn't push him away as she closed her eyes and returned his kisses.

A noise from upstairs made them both jump, and when they heard footsteps, Mary Carol gasped as she squeezed Abe's arm. "What do we do?"

They both stood up, shedding the blanket, and moved quickly toward the door, but they were still a few feet from it when they heard a man's voice. "Hey!"

Mary Carol turned around when Abe did, and as the old man walked toward them, she held her breath. He walked with a limp and wore tattered jeans and a blue shirt. His hair was matted on one side like he'd been lying down. He stopped in front of Abe. He squinted his eyes and leaned forward. His left eye seemed to have a mind of its own, or was he winking at Abe?

"What's going on in here?" The stranger's voice was gruff. He held up his first finger, then poked Abe in the chest. "I don't know what you're doing down here, but I'm sure I heard that girl say no." He glanced at Mary Carol. "Are you okay?"

She nodded, but her feet were rooted to the floor. The man took a step back as he eyed them both. His left eye blinked randomly. "Sit down. Both of you." The man pointed to the couch as he backed into the recliner by the TV tray.

Abe cleared his throat. "We're sorry, sir. We didn't know anyone lived here. We'll go."

Before Abe even had time to take a step, the man pointed to the couch. "Sit."

Mary Carol glanced toward the door, and she hoped Abe would grab her hand so they could make a run for it. But instead, he walked to the couch and sat down, and once Mary Carol found her feet, she followed. Abe didn't even realize he'd sat down on his straw hat.

The man rubbed his chin, squinting again. "Did you know that in sixteenth-century Naples, people were hung for kissing? I'm going to guess you probably didn't."

Mary Carol looked to Abe, whose eyes were wide as he shook his head. "No, sir. I didn't know that." His voice trembled when he went on. "Please don't kill us."

"Wait here." The man abruptly rose from the chair and limped toward the kitchen. Mary Carol pictured him returning with a gun. But before he'd even gotten out of the living room, he turned around to face them. "I have a soda every four hours. I do this because I enjoy it. And because I can." He paused and studied them for a few seconds. "Wait right there."

"Let's go," Mary Carol said the moment he was out of sight. She tugged on the sleeve of Abe's black coat.

"What if he comes after us? What if he has a gun or something?" Abe looked at Mary Carol, then toward the kitchen as the man walked back into the living room carrying three cans of Coke.

"I have over a hundred guns, but I'm not planning to shoot anyone." His teeth were crooked when he smiled. "Not today anyway." He handed a soda to each of them. "Who are you people?"

Mary Carol swallowed the lump in her throat. "That's Abe Fisher. I'm Mary Carol Zook." She turned to Abe, but she wasn't sure he was breathing.

The man popped the top on his soda and took a long swig. Mary Carol opened her cola too. Despite the circumstances, the Coke was a treat. Her mother never bought sodas. She took a sip and swallowed, enjoying the tingle from all the bubbles.

"Are you any relation to Katherine Zook?" The man shivered as he talked, but every few seconds he took another gulp of Coke.

Mary Carol nodded. "*Ya.* I'm her daughter."

"Ah, yes." He pointed a finger at her. "I thought you looked familiar, but sometimes you all look the same in those clothes."

Mary Carol reached for the string on her *kapp* and twirled it in her fingers. Then she glanced at Abe before looking back at the man. "Do we know each other?"

"No." He finished the soda, crushed the can, and put it next to the others on the tray. He pointed a finger at Abe. "The next time this girl tells you no, what will you do?"

Abe sat taller. "I-I will listen to-to her."

Mary Carol hung her head as she felt her cheeks heat up. When she looked up, she saw the man's teeth chattering. She picked up the brown blanket from where it had fallen on the floor and offered it to him.

"Danki." He quickly covered himself with it, and she returned to the couch.

"Do you speak Pennsylvania *Deitsch*?" She took a sip of her cola. Abe hadn't opened his.

"A little. My name is Paul, by the way." He slapped himself upside the head and rolled his eyes. "I mean James. My name is James. And I don't live here. I'm just borrowing the place, if you know what I mean. Kinda like the two of you, I guess." His left eye started to twitter again. "So, tell me about your life."

48

Mary Carol glanced at Abe and waited for him to go first. "I-I am the son of John and Elizabeth Fisher. We are —"

James grunted loudly. "Not *you*. Her." He pointed to Mary Carol. "I want to know about you."

"Uh . . ." She wasn't sure what he wanted to know. The man couldn't even keep his own name straight. "I have a sister named Linda who is twelve. I have two brothers named Stephen and Gideon, and they are sixteen and five."

James raised his eyebrows. "And?"

"And you know that my mother is Katherine." She paused. "How do you know my mother?"

"I don't really know her. Go on. What else?"

"Um . . . my father was Elias. He passed on six months ago." She locked eyes with James. "I miss him very much." She glanced at Abe again, but he was tapping one foot and turning the full can of Coke over in his hands. She hoped he didn't plan to open it anytime soon.

" 'A time to weep, and a time to laugh,' " James said, pausing to sigh. " 'A time to mourn, and a time to dance.' "

"Ecclesiastes," she said softly.

James nodded. "Yes. And the Beatles." He

scratched his chin. "Or was it the Byrds?"

Mary Carol had no idea what beetles and birds had to do with the Scripture verse.

"Can we go now?" Abe put his unopened can of Coke on the couch next to him. "Are you going to tell our parents you found us here?"

James shook his head. "Kid, you aren't the sharpest tool in the shed, are you? Why would I tell your parents when I'm not supposed to be here either?"

Abe scowled as he stood up. "Come on, Mary Carol. Let's go."

She slowly lifted herself from the couch as she studied James. There was something about him that seemed familiar. She was thankful he'd come down the stairs before she and Abe did something they would have regretted.

"I'm the most interesting person you'll probably ever meet, but go ahead and leave if you want."

Abe picked up his squashed hat from the couch and motioned to Mary Carol for them to move toward the door, but she sat back down.

"I'd like to hear about you," she said as she set her soda can on the floor near her feet.

Abe glared at her. "Come on, Mary Carol.

Let's go."

James folded his arms across his chest and glared at Abe. "Well, you can't leave her here with me. I'm a stranger. So you might as well sit back down."

Mary Carol looked up at Abe, then said in Pennsylvania *Deitsch,* "Let's just stay a little bit longer."

Abe huffed, but he sat down beside her.

James pulled the blanket snug, then smiled. "Before I begin, let's pray together."

Mary Carol chewed on her bottom lip, but finally nodded. Abe lowered his head when she did.

"Dear Heavenly Father, please bless these children." James paused, and when Mary Carol glanced up at him, she caught him eyeing Abe before he shook his head and continued. "And help young Abraham to behave like a gentleman."

Mary Carol bit her lip again and stifled a grin. Abe didn't look up, but she could see his face turning red.

"I pray that Mary Carol and what's-his-name will walk the right path and stay on track toward a life that pleases You. I pray for Bonnie. You and I know why. And I pray for a chocolate cake, that someone will bring me one. Loving Father, I will see You soon. Amen."

Mary Carol opened her eyes, not sure what to make of this man. But for the next two hours, she and Abe listened to him talk about his life. And James had spoken the truth earlier.

He really was the most interesting person she had ever met.

CHAPTER FIVE

Mary Carol shivered as Abe guided the buggy toward her house. A light snow was falling.

"Well, you can call him interesting all you want," Abe said as he picked up speed. "But he's *ab im kopp.*"

"*Ya,* he might be a little off in the head." Mary Carol recalled the stories James told. "But I still find him interesting, and I like him."

"He told me to shut up twice." Abe shook his head.

Mary Carol laughed. "That's because you interrupted him twice. My favorite story was when he told us about staying at the White House."

Abe turned onto Mary Carol's road. "*Ya,* but I don't believe any of it. I don't think the president's wife had a sister that no one knew about named Bonnie, or that she made him chocolate cakes every week." He turned to her, eyes wide. "And I'm sure I don't believe that he saved eighty-six lives while he worked for the FBI. Tall tales. He's an old man who likes to tell stories."

Mary Carol smiled. "I like him." She'd laughed more than she had in a long time.

"We are going to have to find somewhere else to go on Saturdays so we can be alone."

"Didn't you hear me tell him that I would see him next Saturday? He seemed happy about that. And I'm going to surprise him with a chocolate cake."

Abe pulled back on the reins until the horse slowed to barely a trot. "You meant that? What about us? Don't you want to spend time by ourselves?"

"Abe, we need to be smarter about the time we spend alone. The last couple of times have been close." Mary Carol didn't want to hurt Abe's feelings. She knew he loved her, and she loved him too. But they'd been treading in dangerous waters the past few weeks. "There will be plenty of time for us to be alone after the holidays. Christmas is in a couple of weeks, and James was excited that we were going to visit him again." She shrugged as she looked out the window of the buggy. "You don't have to go if you don't want to."

Abe grunted. "*Ya,* I do. I'd never let you

go there by yourself." He pulled into Mary Carol's driveway. "He doesn't like me though."

She smiled, tempted to agree with him. But James had been very nice to her. When Abe stopped the buggy near the gate in the front yard, she looked around to make sure her mother or siblings weren't outside, then she leaned over and quickly kissed Abe good-bye.

"See you Saturday?" she asked, still smiling.

Abe frowned as he nodded. "*Ya,* I guess."

"I love you."

"I love you, too, Mary Carol." He hung his head, sighing before he looked back up at her. She'd known Abe for so long, sometimes she felt like she could think his thoughts. He was about to apologize. "I'm real sorry if I did anything to upset you. I never want to hurt you. Not ever."

"I know. I just think maybe things were moving a little too fast." She was thankful for their new friend. Today, for a couple of hours, she hadn't thought about her father, about how much she missed him. But as she got out of the buggy and hurried through the snow to the house, she knew any sense of joy she'd felt would turn to guilt when she saw her mother. When Mary

Carol was around her family, it seemed wrong to be anything other than sad.

Katherine stayed quiet while her oldest son voiced his opinion about Gideon drawing on their bedroom walls. "It's bad enough that I have to share a room with him, but now you are *letting* him draw on the walls?" He waved a hand toward Gideon's stick people and coffins. Just that morning, Gideon had added more people . . . and another coffin. When Katherine had questioned her youngest son about the extra coffin, he'd just shrugged.

"Your *bruder* is having a hard time coping with your *daed*'s death, and he is just expressing himself." Katherine wanted to ask her oldest son how he was coping. He'd closed himself off from everyone. He hadn't gone to any of the singings on Sunday afternoons since his father died. And sometimes he refused to go to worship service.

"*Ya*, well. I wish he'd find some other way to do it." Stephen shook his head, then began to walk out of the bedroom.

"Stephen, can you wait a minute?" Katherine didn't want to bring this up right now, but the boy was out of the house so much, she needed to catch him while she could. "I'm sorry to have to ask this, but would you please find some time in the next few days to winterize the pipes in the basement?" She considered it a small miracle that a pipe hadn't burst, given that December had been colder than usual. If Stephen handled the pipes, it would give her time to give Gideon a trim.

Stephen turned and before he was out of earshot, she heard a faint, "Fine."

Katherine was tempted to follow him, but maybe this wasn't the best time to get him to open up about his dad's death and the added responsibilities.

She went to her own bedroom where she'd laid out all the items she planned to take to her father-in-law. She still wasn't sure if she was doing the right thing by befriending the man who'd hurt his own son so deeply, but it was the holidays, and she was going to do what she could for him. She picked up the brown coat she'd bought Elias only two Christmases ago, and she buried her face in it, breathing in his scent. Fighting the urge to cry, she gathered up some of Elias's shirts, two pairs of shoes, and some other toiletries that she thought James could use. She packed them in an old red suitcase that Elias had used when traveling to out-of-town auctions.

She wondered if James was homeless, and

it worried her where he might be living since he wouldn't tell her. *But how does he have a car and how does he afford to put gas in it?*

An hour later, she walked into the coffee shop. James sat at the same booth they'd sat at a week ago. He wore the same clothes. Katherine put the suitcase on the floor next to him.

"I put together a few things for you. They were Elias's. I thought you might like to have them."

"Why?" James stared at her, a blank expression on his face.

"Because I . . . well, I thought you might want them." She looked down at two cups of coffee already on the table. "There's a coat in there too." She touched the white plastic lid on top of the Styrofoam cup. "Is this for me?"

"Yeah." He picked up the cup in front of him and took a large swallow.

Katherine tried to recall if she'd told James she drank her coffee black. She didn't think so, but as she took her first sip, she was glad he'd guessed right. "I thought you didn't like coffee."

James laughed. "Are you kidding me? I love coffee."

Katherine tapped a finger to her chin. "Um, what about your time as a federal agent? I thought you said you got burned out on coffee."

His expression went flat. "Oh dear." He pushed the cup as far as he could to one side of the table. "You're right."

Did he even remember their last conversation? "If you want the coffee, you should drink it." She wondered how he'd paid for it.

"I hope there is coffee in heaven." He shook his head. "I've asked the Lord about that a dozen times, but He doesn't ever tell me."

Katherine wondered if establishing a relationship with James was going to be worth it, but she pulled the cup back in front of him. "Drink the coffee. It will warm you up."

He stared at her for a while, but eventually he took another sip. "I had another dream about Elias this past week. On Thursday, I think. No . . . wait. It was Friday." He shook his head. "No. It was last night." He pointed a finger at her. "He said you aren't handling his death very well with your youngest son. You need to do something different. He told me what you need to do." He picked up his cup of coffee, put it back down again, then pushed it to the side.

Katherine was startled that James was bringing up something he'd have no way of knowing — or maybe it was simply a coincidence. She had cherished the few dreams she'd had about Elias over the past six months, but was her husband really trying to communicate through James? She doubted it. *I'll humor him.* "And what am I supposed to do differently?"

He scratched the top of his head. "For the life of me, I can't remember what he said."

That figures.

"So, how are you handling Gideon's grief?"

Katherine was surprised that James remembered his youngest grandson's name. "I'm letting him express his feelings by drawing on the wall. It seems to help him."

James burst out laughing. "Boy howdy. He's pulled the wool over your eyes. He probably just likes to draw on the wall. What does he draw?"

Katherine stiffened, clenched her jaw, and reminded herself who she was dealing with. "He draws stick people standing around a coffin, and he doesn't understand how his father's body is under the earth, but his soul is in heaven." She sat quietly for a few moments, but when James didn't say anything, she said, "He added an extra coffin to the drawing yesterday."

James rolled his eyes, the left one fluttering for a couple of seconds, and pulled his coffee back in front of him. "Well, it doesn't take a brain surgeon to figure that out, about the extra coffin."

"Well, I'm no brain surgeon, so maybe you can explain it to me." Raw curiosity brought on the question that she was sure he couldn't answer.

James took several gulps from his cup. She could see the steam rising from the opening of the lid, and she wondered how he wasn't scorching his mouth. "The extra coffin is Gideon's."

"What?"

James sighed. "The boy is afraid that he is going to die and that you'll bury him in a box too. If you keep letting him draw on the walls, he'll probably draw more coffins. One for you, then his brother and sisters. The kid is afraid of dying and worried everyone else he loves will die too." He grimaced. "Wow. You've got four kids. I'm surprised you didn't figure that out."

Katherine forced herself to ignore his last comment. She wondered if maybe he was right. Was Gideon afraid of everyone around him dying, himself included? "That might be true. But he doesn't understand that his father isn't actually in the ground, that he is in heaven. So even if he is worried his family might die, he doesn't understand what we believe."

"Then you're not explaining it right. Like Elias said, you need to do something different."

She let her hands fall into her lap, then clenched them together. "I've explained it to him the same way I did with *mei* other *kinner,* and all of them had a *gut* understanding about heaven by the time they were Gideon's age."

He drummed the fingers of his left hand on the table as his mouth twitched from side to side. Katherine finished her coffee while he pondered the situation for a minute. She jumped when he slammed his hand on the table.

"Okay. I know what you should do."

Katherine waited, but James just stared at her. At this point, she was willing to try anything to help her youngest. "Is it a secret, or are you going to tell me?"

He frowned. "Tell you what?"

Katherine took a deep breath. How could anyone be so all-together one moment, but totally lost the next? "Are you going to tell me what I should do about Gideon?"

"Oh, sure." He nodded. "I'm going to assume that the boy has been taught the basics, about Jesus, that He died for our sins, and so on." He raised an eyebrow.

Katherine nodded. She was skeptical that a man like James could tell her anything helpful. A nutty man who had spent very little time raising his own son.

"Kids are visual little creatures. They have to see something to understand it. Gideon saw his father lowered into the ground, so he needs to *see* heaven too."

Katherine brought a hand to her chest. "I don't want him to *see* heaven. He's only five."

James grunted. "Good grief, woman. Hear me out. He needs to see it in his mind's eye as clearly as he saw his father's body go into the ground."

She looked at him and nodded slightly. "How do I help him to do that?"

"We all see heaven differently. Gideon's heaven won't look like the pictures you find in books about this subject. He won't envision it the way your other children do, or the way any other person on earth does. Gideon needs to see and feel all the beauty and love in heaven, and you need to walk him through it until that light shines brightly, until he can see his father enjoying life in our Father's house."

Katherine tried to hold her tears at bay. "I don't know how to do that."

James smiled. "Yes. You do. Now . . ." He reached over and patted her hand. "I have to go. I will see you here next Tuesday at the same time. And I will be praying that you bring me good news about Gideon."

Katherine had no idea how James got out of bed and dressed himself without getting lost in his home, or wherever he was living. How in the world did he keep track of his days? The man could barely hold on to his own thoughts. But his explanation about how to help Gideon had left her speechless.

He picked up the suitcase she'd brought him, gave a quick wave, then walked out of the coffee shop. And this time, he wasn't limping.

CHAPTER SIX

Mary Carol knocked on the farmhouse's front door as she and Abe shivered on the porch. James opened it dressed in a pair of black slacks being held up with suspenders, and he was wearing a long-sleeved blue shirt. Clothes just like her father and most Amish men in their community wore. And he'd gotten a haircut. He stepped aside so they could enter, and she handed him the chocolate cake.

"Bonnie, you shouldn't have," James said, holding the cake. "But your chocolate cakes are the best, and you know how much I will enjoy this."

Mary Carol glanced at Abe before she turned back to James. "Um . . . I'm Mary Carol, not Bonnie."

James put the cake on the TV tray by the chair, then he popped himself in the side of the head, hard enough that Mary Carol cringed. "I'm so sorry! Of course you are.

You're Katherine's daughter."

She looked at Abe in time to see him roll his eyes.

"Do you feel like company right now? Or we can go. I just wanted you to have the cake."

James sat down in the worn recliner. "I would like for you to stay." He looked at Abe, frowning. "So I guess you have to be here also. Sit. The both of you."

Mary Carol sat down, and after a few seconds, Abe did too.

"Tell me, Mary Carol, how is your brother Stephen?" James crossed one leg over the other.

"Stephen?"

He smiled. "Yes."

"Um. He's okay, I guess." The truth was, Mary Carol worried about Stephen. He had detached himself from everyone, but people handled grief in different ways. "He's having a hard time with our father's passing. We all are, but Stephen stays to himself most of the time. He didn't cry at the funeral either."

"Hmm . . ." James stroked his clean-shaven chin. "Sounds like Stephen is keeping his emotions bottled up. Someone needs to pop that cork." He pointed a finger at her. "And that person is you. You need to get Stephen to open up to you."

She shook her head. "*Ach,* you don't know my *bruder.* He was cranky even before our father died. He snaps at everyone, yells at our *mudder,* and refuses to go to worship service sometimes. I'm not the one to talk to him."

"Okay." James looked at Abe. "Then you do it."

Abe stiffened on the couch next to her. "Huh?"

"You heard me. You talk to Stephen. Get the boy to talk about how he is feeling. Maybe he'd be more comfortable talking to you." James scowled again. "Although I don't know why." This time it was James who rolled his eyes, and Mary Carol tried to hide her grin.

"I'm, uh, not really very close to Stephen. He's a couple of years younger than me, and we've never hung out or anything."

"Do you ever think about anyone but yourself?" James clicked his tongue, shook his head, then locked eyes with Mary Carol. "What do you see in this guy?"

She smiled as she elbowed Abe. "*Ach,* he's a *gut* man. You just have to get to know him."

"Fine. I will talk to Stephen," Abe said.

"Wonderful." James clapped his hands. "I

bought some plates today." He stood up. "And some forks. I prayed and prayed that someone would bring me a chocolate cake." He looked up. "Thank you for that, Lord." Then he picked up the cake. "I'm going to get us all a piece of this."

"He is crazy. We shouldn't be here," Abe whispered.

"I told you before, I like him." Mary Carol giggled. "But he doesn't like you. That's for sure."

"Are we going to have to come back here again?"

She shrugged. "I don't know. I'd like to. I think he's —"

"I know," Abe said. "You think he's *interesting*. I just hope he isn't dangerous or anything. He might go nuts, kill us, and bury us in the backyard."

Mary Carol slapped him gently on the arm. "Don't say things like that. He's just an old man whose memory is failing."

Abe raised one eyebrow. "That's an understatement. He's out of his mind."

"I'm going to try to find out more about him."

James walked into the living room and handed them each a plate with a wedge of cake.

"You're not limping," she said as he

headed back toward the kitchen. He returned with his own slice. He set it on the TV tray and turned to them, looping his thumbs in his suspenders.

"Ain't that the craziest of things? I've limped for my entire life, since I was a boy. I'm missing a bone in my leg." He stood even taller. "And I feel better than I've felt in years, since before I got shot." He walked to the chair and sat down.

"Shot?" Abe had just put a large piece of cake in his mouth.

"Yes, shot. In the head." James took a bite of his cake. "By a bad guy."

Mary Carol wondered if this could be true. Maybe that's why he was a bit . . . off. "That's terrible. When did that happen?"

"When did what happen?" James frowned.

"You just said you got shot," Abe said loudly.

"Kid, I'm forgetful, not deaf." James shook his head as he stabbed at another piece of cake. Mary Carol decided to let the shooting incident go.

"You've told us stories about your job with the FBI, but you haven't told us about your family. Do you have children? Maybe grandchildren?"

James put the empty plate on the tray. "I had a son." He paused with a faraway look in his eyes. "I really loved him. But that's all I have to say about that."

She wasn't getting very far in her effort to know him better. "When you were telling us stories about your FBI adventures, you never said how long you were employed with them."

James hurried to the window. "Did anyone see you come here? Someone might be following you, trying to find me." He turned to Abe. "Did you see anything? They are usually in a red car, which is mighty ridiculous since everyone knows you don't use a red car to follow someone."

"I didn't see any red car following us," Abe said.

"Keep an eye out for them. Two men. One of them, the older one, is always wearing a black suit. The younger guy is always wearing a white jacket." He walked back to his chair and settled into it. "I don't know who trained them. I see them everywhere. They blend in about as well as a tiger swimming in the ocean."

Mary Carol smiled when she pictured that, even though it was an odd comparison. "We will keep an eye out for them."

James nodded. "Good. They aren't dangerous, just pesky." He snapped a finger. "Hey, did I tell you about the time I got shot in the head?"

Abe spoke up. "You started to, but you didn't finish. What happened?"

James sighed. "Well, it was a really long time ago. I was in a witness protection program. I had to leave my family behind for their own safety."

"I thought you were an FBI agent," Abe said as he glanced at Mary Carol, grinning.

"Kid, try to keep up." James narrowed his eyebrows as he stared at Abe and shook his head. "First I was in protective custody, then moved to the witness protection program. Six years later — or maybe two or three — the feds begged me to become one of them."

"I'm sure they did," Abe said.

"I'm not sure you're sure of much of anything." James pointed to Abe. "But yes, that's what happened. I didn't want to join them at first. I was raised in a home that didn't believe in violence of any kind, and I knew that I might be called to handle dangerous situations that could lead to me using a gun."

"Did you ever kill anyone?" Abe took off his straw hat, still a little misshapen from his sitting on it the other day, and placed it on the couch beside him.

James stared long and hard at Abe, and

Mary Carol was afraid to hear the answer. She wasn't sure she could be friends with someone who had taken another person's life.

"Don't you know that you're not supposed to ask a person something like that? Just like you never ask a soldier if they killed anyone in battle."

Mary Carol swallowed hard. That sounded like a yes to her.

James looked at Mary Carol. "Don't look so scared," he said softly. "I've been blessed. I never killed anyone. I was directed onto that path to save lives. Eighty-six to be exact."

She smiled. "Tell us more."

James broke into a story about how he saved a sixteen-year-old boy from committing suicide. Mary Carol listened, but her mind was somewhere else. *Stephen.*

Katherine wasn't one to spy on her children, but she was curious why Abe had come to see Stephen. As she passed by Stephen's room with freshly folded towels in her arms, she slowed down and listened.

"I don't want to talk about this." Stephen's voice was so loud that Katherine almost opened the door to make sure everything was okay between the boys. But as she tucked the towels under one arm and reached for the doorknob, she stopped.

"I know you don't, but you gotta face your grief. Mary Carol is really worried about you."

"I knew she put you up to this."

Katherine held her breath.

"Mary Carol didn't put me up to this. A friend suggested that I talk to you."

"Who?"

Katherine stayed still and listened.

"It doesn't matter," Abe said. "The point is, it might help if you talk to someone. And if it's not me, then maybe you should talk to someone else."

"I ain't talking to no doctor, if that's what you're suggesting."

It got quiet, and Katherine heard Abe's voice, but she couldn't make out what he was saying.

"Get out of here, Abe! You have no idea how I feel!"

Katherine latched onto the doorknob, but before she turned it, her grieving son went on.

"I hurt! I hurt every day. It's a kind of pain that I don't even know how to explain. But I'm the man of the house. I can't be crying all the time. And that's all I want to do! I just want to run into my mother's arms, bury my head on her shoulder, and cry. I want her to rub my back and tell me that everything is going to be okay! I'd be just like a big sissy baby! So get out of here, Abe."

Katherine dropped the towels on the floor, turned the knob, and rushed to where her son was sitting on the bed. Both boys froze at the sudden interruption. Stephen huffed and started to rub his forehead. She inched closer to him, motioning for Abe to let himself out. Stephen wouldn't look at her, just kept rubbing his forehead and looking at the floor. She saw the muscles in his cheeks shift, obviously from him clenching his teeth. "Stephen." That was all she said, and when the boy stood, she swiftly pulled him into her arms. When he tried to push her away, a fierce strength overtook Katherine, and she held him firmly until finally, he buried his head against her shoulder. At first he just held onto her tightly. Then she heard what sounded like a hiccup. His body heaved as he released the breath in his lungs and a torrent of sobs followed. She found it impossible to focus on her own pain while her son was in such agony. She continued to hold him, patting the back of his hair and telling him it was all okay.

She was thankful for whoever it was who

had encouraged Abe to talk to Stephen. She would pray for this person.

And thank you, Abe, for having the courage to follow through on the task.

CHAPTER SEVEN

Katherine was ten minutes late to the coffee shop, and she prepared for a verbal lashing from her father-in-law, but instead he broke into a big smile when she joined him at the table.

"You have the light," he said.

"What?" She took off her black bonnet and put it on the booth beside her, then she tied the strings on her *kapp.*

"Let me rephrase that. You've always had the light, but today it is shining extra bright. I think you have good news."

Katherine smiled back at him. "*Ya,* I do. I think my family is starting to heal."

James pushed one of the coffee cups toward her. She took a sip and nearly spit out the hot liquid. "What is this?" she asked, wishing she had a glass of water. It wasn't coffee. It was . . . sweet.

"The waitress asked me if I'd like to try the vanilla latte, so I figured, why not?"

"But you didn't try it. I did."

"I never touch that whipped-up stuff." He waved his hand dismissively.

She wasn't sure how to politely refuse the drink, so she moved it to the side.

"So, does part of that healing have to do with Gideon?"

"*Ya,* I spent some time with him a few days ago and we talked about his vision of heaven. I told him I imagined heaven was full of all of our favorite things and people. It was fun to hear him describe what his heaven would look like. Lots of games, trees with candy instead of leaves, children playing tag and hide-and-seek. I told him to imagine his father was there, waiting for him." A warm feeling washed over her. "He spent the next few days drawing his heaven on the wall. Then last night he told me I could repaint the wall if I wanted to. I think I'm going to wait a little while before I do that. Every time I see that wall, I smile." Katherine realized that working with Gideon on this had made her truly happy, something she hadn't felt in months. "He seems to be getting better. And I'm grateful to God for that." She held up a finger. "*And,* we had another breakthrough. Apparently, someone encouraged Abe — that's my daughter's boyfriend — to talk to Stephen.

Remember, he is my sixteen-year-old son?"

James was still smiling. "Yes, I remember."

"Well, whoever suggested this might have saved my son's life. Stephen finally opened up to me. Some of the things he said . . . well, they were hard to hear." Katherine looked down, then back up at James, whose smile had faded. "Stephen admitted to me that he had been having thoughts of killing himself. His grief over his father's death was worse than any of us realized. We all miss Elias, but Stephen's grief was manifesting itself in a dangerous way. The good news is that he agreed to talk to a grief counselor."

James put his hand on hers. "This is the best news." He smiled. "And just in time for Christmas next week."

"We know that this is a process and things won't be fixed in a day, but at least he'll talk to someone and maybe the counselor can help him work through his feelings. I also called the bishop and asked him to talk with Stephen soon. It's important for Stephen to have a strong male role model, especially at his age." They were quiet for a moment, their hands still touching. "Speaking of next week, on Christmas Day, we will be having worship service and a large meal. And as you probably remember, we celebrate Christmas for two days. Most years, on Second Christmas — the day after Christmas — we visit shut-ins and elderly friends who might not have family nearby, or whoever we would just like to spend extra time with during this blessed time of year. But this year, we have decided that on Second Christmas, we will stay home and share memories about Elias." Katherine moved her hand out from under James's and gently laid it on top of his. "Would you like to come to our home on Second Christmas? I think it's time the children meet their grandfather."

James blinked back tears. "And hear about my son? About all that I missed?" He dabbed at his left eye, which hadn't twitched once. "And meet my grandchildren?"

Katherine nodded. "Would you like that?"

James squeezed her hand. "It would be the best gift a man could receive."

She gently took her hand back and smiled. "*Gut.* Then it's a date." She grabbed her cup and took a sip, forgetting that it wasn't black coffee. After getting over the initial shock of sweetness, she had to admit it tasted pretty good.

James watched her and then nodded toward the cup. "Not as bad as you thought, huh?"

Katherine smiled. "Might take some getting used to, but I like it better than I thought I would."

He swiped at his eyes again. She was doing the right thing. She could feel the Lord's approval shining down on her. And Elias's.

Mary Carol couldn't thank Abe enough for talking to Stephen. She smothered him in kisses as he drove them to James's house the following Saturday.

"*Danki* so much. Whatever you said to Stephen, it helped him open up to *Mamm*. He has an appointment to talk to a doctor who helps people with grief. And we're thinking maybe all of us might go."

"Aw, I didn't do much. But I'm loving my reward." He grinned before he returned one of her kisses.

"I know you're not thrilled to be visiting James again, but next week is Christmas. He probably doesn't have anyone to spend the day with, so I at least wanted to visit him today to wish him Christmas blessings." She nodded toward the backseat. "And to give him another cake."

"*Ach,* just admit it. You like the old guy."

She pulled her coat tighter, hugging herself. Paradise was having a hard winter so far, and the temperature today wasn't supposed to get above freezing. She was glad that they'd left the small heater for James. And he'd mentioned that a friend had given him a coat.

"*Ya.* I do like him," she said after a moment. "Who knows if anything he says is true. But there is a kindness about him that seems genuine." She paused and sighed. "He's familiar. I wonder where I would know him from."

"I don't know." He turned the horse onto the gravel road that lead to the farmhouse. "Who does your *mamm* think you're making the cake for? Have you told her about James?"

"*Mamm* left early this morning with Gideon so she didn't see me baking. I've been lucky about that both times. I don't want to lie, but I know that once *Mamm* finds out, she's going to forbid me to go there since he's a stranger. And *Englisch.*"

"*Ya,* you're probably right."

"*Mamm*'s been staying up late working on quilted items to sell at the market. I know it's because we are short on money, even though she won't admit it. But she did say that the bishop was insistent that she use the community health fund for any grief counseling any of us might need. We're lucky we have a lenient bishop."

After Abe tethered the horse, Mary Carol

jumped out of the buggy, grabbed the cake pan, and they trudged through the snow to the farmhouse. James opened the door before either of them knocked. He wasn't well-groomed like last time, and Mary Carol wondered if he'd forgotten that he had invited them over today. He was wearing a wrinkled white shirt, his hair was flattened on one side, and he was barefoot and shivering. But he stepped aside so they could enter.

"Goodness, it's cold in here. Where is the little heater we left for you?" She scanned the living room. All the empty Coke cans were gone. "And what about the blanket?"

James walked to his chair and sat down. "What heater and blanket?"

"Did you maybe take them upstairs so you would be warm when you slept?" Mary Carol was still holding the cake.

James shook his head. "No. I don't know what happened to them. Is that chocolate cake?"

"Yes. Should I put it in the kitchen?"

James nodded. Mary Carol walked to the counter and set the cake down. She wondered what else James ate. She peeked in some of the cabinets, and just like last time, they were empty. She walked back into the living room and sat down on the couch beside Abe. They were all shivering.

"James, do you have food to eat?" Mary Carol gave him a quick once-over. He had a small belly and didn't appear to be under-nourished.

"Oh yes. Lots of food." He pointed to the kitchen. "And sometimes I eat out."

Mary Carol made a mental note to bring something more than cake next time. She doubted James had money to eat out. "Do you have plans for Christmas?"

He sat taller, ran a hand through his hair, and smiled. "Yes, I do."

Mary Carol doubted that was true either. "That's *gut.*"

They were all quiet. James's left eye twitched again. He was rubbing his fore-head.

"It was a *gut* idea for me to talk to Mary Carol's brother Stephen. I think it helped." Abe took off his hat and set it on the floor.

"I know it helped." Mary Carol waited for James to comment, but he just kept rubbing his forehead. "James, are you okay?" she asked after a moment.

James put his hands in his lap. "Some days my head hurts. Other days it doesn't." He scowled. "I think I got shot once."

Mary Carol was going to have to get her mother involved after the holidays. If *Mamm* knew how this man was living, she could contact the *Englisch* authorities for help. Mary Carol wasn't sure who to call.

She glanced at Abe, then said, "We can't stay today, James. But we wanted to bring you the cake." They both stood up, and James did too.

"I love cake. Chocolate cake. Thank you for bringing it to me." He walked them to the door. Abe extended his hand to James.

"Merry Christmas, sir."

Mary Carol held her breath as she waited to see if James would shake Abe's hand. She smiled when he did. Then she hugged James. "Merry Christmas," she said.

He gave a quick wave and closed the door behind them.

"We're going straight to the market," Abe said once he got the buggy going. "I've got enough money to get him a few things."

Her heart swelled at Abe's generosity.

Mary Carol opened her purse and dug around. "I have fourteen dollars. That will buy a little bit."

After they loaded up at the market, they went back to the farmhouse and knocked on the door. When James didn't answer, they left everything on the front porch. A new heater in the box, blankets, and as much nonperishable food as they could afford.

"He's not in there." Mary Carol was peeking in the living room window. "Do you think he's lying down upstairs?"

"Probably."

They knocked one more time, and when there wasn't any answer, they headed back to Abe's buggy.

God, please make sure that James eats plenty today and that he stays warm.

CHAPTER EIGHT

Christmas morning, Katherine knew that she wasn't the only one feeling the void, but they were all going through the motions in an effort to remember the reason for the season. As she'd done in the past, she had colorfully decorated gifts and placed them around the house. She knew a few plain families who put up a Christmas tree, but it was kept secret from the bishop, and mostly it was for the benefit of relatives who weren't Amish. Katherine had never put up a tree, but she did have holiday candles, sprigs of holly, and festive bows on the mantel.

"Do you like the gloves, Gideon?" Katherine had handmade all the gifts this year. In the past, she and Elias had shopped for one store-bought gift for each child, but that wasn't practical this year. In addition to farming, Elias had worked for a construction company part time, but they didn't have much of a nest egg built up.

Gideon put the gloves on his tiny hands. *"Danki, Mamm."* Katherine giggled to herself at Gideon's new haircut. Stephen had kept his word and wrapped the pipes in the basement with some foam that Elias had in the shed. He'd also surprised Katherine and trimmed his brother's hair. Gideon's bangs were noticeably crooked, but she decided to let them be instead of fixing them. Delegating some of her responsibilities meant some things weren't going to be done up to her standard, and she was going to have to be okay with that.

Stephen kept the fire going, and generally, things were going better than Katherine would have predicted a month ago.

And James Zook got credit for speeding up the healing process. Despite his odd ways, memory loss, and bizarre stories, he seemed to have a gift — an ability to understand the human spirit better than most.

Mary Carol ripped through her gifts with lightning speed, and Katherine knew it was because she was in a hurry to spend part of the day with Abe and his family. Katherine had invited Abe to tomorrow's Second Christmas. The smile on her daughter's face had been a gift in itself.

"Slow down, Mary Carol. You have plenty

of time, and the meal is keeping warm. You can head to Abe's right after we eat."

"I love everything!" Linda said loudly as she put on a black sweater Katherine had knitted for her. Katherine had asked Linda if she might need to talk to the counselor, but Linda had frowned and told her no. "*Daed* is in heaven. And I miss him, but I know he is with Jesus having fun." Linda's maturity surprised Katherine, but she was thankful for her daughter's positive spirit. Katherine could learn a thing or two from her.

After lots of hugs, they made their way to the kitchen, and once everyone was seated, they bowed their heads and prayed silently. Katherine looked up just as Stephen pointed to the sweet potatoes. "*Daed*'s favorite. And you didn't put the pecans on top."

"*Nee.* But I will if you all want me to," she said while she grabbed the potholder to handle the hot dish. Her children shook their heads. Elias had never liked nuts.

"I'm just glad you always make the paprika potatoes too," Linda said, "since those are my favorite."

After Katherine had served Gideon, she held up the potholder. Her hand burned because a portion of the material had worn thin from years of use. She normally wouldn't consider pulling one out from the stash to sell at Diana's booth, but she thought about it for a moment. *Why not? It's okay to do for yourself sometimes, Katherine.*

Most of the families in their district enjoyed a traditional meal of turkey, dressing, potatoes, peas, casseroles, cranberry sauce, and way too many desserts. Katherine's family was no exception. Katherine and Mary Carol had been cooking since early that morning while Linda kept an eye on Gideon. Despite the knot that kept trying to form in her throat, it was a blessed day.

After the dishes were washed and put away, she brought the box of craft items to the kitchen table. She lifted up a pretty sage and burgundy potholder and turned it over in her hands. Yes, this would do. She smiled, surprised at how much she was looking forward to celebrating Second Christmas tomorrow. And following a good night's sleep, she awoke with an unexpected bounce in her step.

"You're next, Linda. What fond memory of *Daed* do you want to share?" Katherine asked.

Linda clapped her hands a few times from

89

where she was sitting on the floor. "I have a *gut* one! Remember when the family played volleyball? Me, Mary Carol, and *Mamm* were on one team, and *Daed,* Gideon, and Stephen were on the other?"

Stephen laughed. "That was so unfair. Gideon was only four. That's the only reason you girls won."

"*Nee,* we won because we were better than you!" Mary Carol said, nudging Linda's shoulder in a loving gesture.

Linda laughed. "You're just not used to losing to girls, Stephen."

While the kids continued to tease each other, Katherine snuck a glance at the clock on the mantel. She hoped James remembered to be here at noon. She'd already put the homemade bread, chowchow, jams, and jellies on the table. She'd poured a glaze over the ham and was keeping it warm in the oven, and green beans were simmering on the stove. She was planning to make a batch of brownies, but for some reason they were almost out of their powdered cocoa. She'd just bought the canister a couple of weeks ago. She'd have to ask Mary Carol about that later.

Stephen would be the most excited to see the large bowl of potato salad in the refrigerator. Katherine added bell pepper to her potato salad and Stephen loved it. *Elias loved it as well.* She wondered if he was watching them from heaven, listening to them recall their favorite memories of him.

She eased herself off the couch when she heard a car coming up the driveway. The last time they'd met, she had questioned James about where he'd gotten the car and how he put gas in it. He'd told her, "I got it the normal way people get a car. I bought it. And I put gas in it so it will run."

She watched him park and walk around to the trunk. He took out a large box. Katherine's heart started to pound as he got closer, and she could see that inside were smaller wrapped gifts. She didn't want her children having any more worldly items than necessary. There were enough electronic gadgets lying around with Stephen and Mary Carol in their *rumschpringes.* And where did he get the money for presents?

She forced the thoughts aside, deciding to focus on the bigger issue. Her *kinner* were about to meet their grandfather. She'd never heard her husband speak poorly about his father in front of the children, so she was hoping the *kinner* would welcome this new family member into their lives.

Mary Carol couldn't believe her eyes when

her mother escorted James into the middle of the living room. He was carrying a box full of wrapped gifts and looking spiffy in a long-sleeved maroon shirt that was freshly pressed, black slacks, and shiny black shoes. He had on a brown coat that was similar to the one her father used to wear.

She grabbed Abe's arm. "What is he doing here?" she whispered.

"I don't know," Abe said as he kept his eyes on James. "Your *mamm* must know him."

Mary Carol locked eyes with James after he set the presents down. She noticed that once again, he wasn't limping, nor did his eye flutter.

"Hello to all," he said as he looked at each of them.

Mamm walked to his side, smiling as she gently touched his arm. "Children, I'd like for you to meet James." She paused as she looked around the room. "James Zook."

Mary Carol realized that she'd never asked James his last name.

"Isn't that the name of your father's father?" Abe whispered in her ear.

She nodded. "I'm sure there are a lot of James Zooks in this area." Even as she made the comment, it struck her why James had always seemed familiar. Finally, he looked at her and smiled broadly. She wanted to run to him, to throw her arms around him, but she was already going to have some explaining to do later.

"James is your grandfather," *Mamm* said after a moment passed. "He is going to have dinner with us. So I trust you will use your best manners." Her mother's expression turned from joyful to stern, which led Mary Carol to wonder if her mother knew James as well as she and Abe did . . . well enough to know that anything might come out of his mouth.

Her mother made introductions. Mary Carol swallowed hard and wondered if James would acknowledge knowing her already. But he just smiled and shook her hand.

"A pleasure to meet you."

Her palms were clammy from this unexpected situation, but a warm feeling settled over her to know that James was her grandfather.

"Your mother told me that you would be sharing memories about your father today, so I've brought gifts for each of you with that in mind." He smiled as he took presents out of the box, handing one to each of them. Even Abe. Mary Carol was as nervous as she could be. James looked and sounded perfectly normal. But she knew how quickly he could change. And how long had her mother known him? Should Mary Carol call him *Daadi* now?

Once everyone had a gift, *Mamm* sat down on the couch next to James while everyone else found a seat. Mary Carol noticed the way her mother was biting her lip and glancing around the room. Maybe she knew James better than Mary Carol thought.

"Young Gideon, why don't you open your present first." James sat taller, his palms flat on his knees.

Please, God, keep him on course.

Mary Carol's little brother tore the silver paper from the small package, then opened the box and pulled out a baseball.

"That was the first baseball your *daed* ever had," James said. "When he wasn't much older than you, he became quite the baseball player. A big group of kids used to play ball at the Stoltzfuses' place."

Gideon turned the ball over in his hands. *"Danki . . ."* He looked at their mother. "What do I call him?"

Mamm looked between James and Gideon. "Um . . ." Her eyes landed on James. "What would you like the *kinner* to call you?"

James smiled. "If I remember correctly,

the word for grandfather is *daadi*. But Katherine, if you would prefer for the youngsters to call me James, that would be mighty fine also."

"Can I call him *Daadi, Mamm*?" Gideon asked from where he was sitting on the floor. Mary Carol realized that Gideon hadn't known any of their grandparents. Their mother's parents had died six years ago — the same year and within a month of each other. And their father's mother had passed right before Gideon was born.

After *Mamm* told Gideon that was fine, Linda lifted her present above her head. "Me next!" She brought it to her lap, ripped the paper off, and pulled the lid off of the shoe box. "Look! Look!" She held up a yellow flashlight. "Was this *Daed*'s when he was a boy?"

James nodded. "I borrowed it the night I left. And I've had it all these years, along with a few other keepsakes."

Mary Carol was sure they could have heard a pin drop in the room. Everyone was wondering the same thing. *Why did you leave your family?* But Mary Carol had spent enough time with James to know he probably didn't understand what he was doing back then. Maybe her mother knew. She was trying to speculate how *Mamm* had found their grandfather. *At the farmhouse? Did they write letters over the years?*

After an awkward moment, Stephen asked what everyone was thinking. "Why did you leave when our *daed* was a boy?"

Mamm cleared her throat. "Those are conversations for another day. Today is for sharing memories of your father. Stephen, you go next."

Stephen's box was small, but his eyes lit up when he pulled out a pocketknife.

"I'm afraid that wasn't your father's, Stephen," James said. "It's mine. But I'd be honored for you to have it, to maybe pass down to your own son someday."

Stephen held up the knife. *"Danki."*

Mary Carol gave her box a little shake before she untied the purple ribbon. She recalled seeing the wrapping paper and other items the first time she was at the farmhouse. Inside, there was a children's book with three ducks on the front.

"Your grandmother used to read that to your father. It was his favorite. At least it was back then. He was probably Gideon's age." James got the faraway look in his eyes again. "Maybe you can read it to your children one day," he added.

Mary Carol thanked him. *"Mamm,* open yours," she said.

"Let Abe go first." *Mamm* walked to the fireplace, warmed her hands, then turned around to watch Abe.

James had warmed up a little to Abe, but Mary Carol was still nervous about what he might have given Abe. *A hangman's noose to warn him not to kiss me, maybe? A lump of coal? A bag of switches?* She stifled a smile as she thought about different possibilities. Abe's box was larger than all the rest.

Abe lifted a straw hat from the box. "Did this belong to Elias?" Abe asked with some eagerness in his voice.

Mary Carol held her breath when she saw James scowl. "No."

He didn't elaborate even though everyone in the room was waiting. A moment later, he said, "In case you ever sit on yours or something."

Everyone was quiet, but Abe actually burst out laughing and thanked him. James winked at him.

"I guess I'm the last one." *Mamm* slowly unwrapped her present. It was a box small enough to fit in her hand. She opened it and then pulled out a key. "What's this?"

James stood up and put his hands in his pockets. He wasn't wearing any suspenders today, but he had on a black belt. "It's the key to my heart. For bringing me to your home to meet my grandchildren. I am a blessed man."

"Thank you, James. We are happy to have you here, and glad that you're a part of our family."

They all watched James open two presents that their mother had placed in front of him, and he thanked her repeatedly for the two sweaters she'd knitted for him.

"Is everyone ready to eat?" *Mamm* clapped her hands together the same way Linda did when she was excited.

"Uh, actually . . ." Abe's face turned bright red as he moved toward Mary Carol. "I have something to ask Mary Carol."

"What is it?" She tried to read his expression, but his face just turned a darker shade of red. Mary Carol had been disappointed in Abe's Christmas gift to her. Well, that wasn't entirely true — the quilt his mother made her was beautiful. But it wasn't a personal gift from him. Before she had time to guess what he might be doing, he left the room and returned with a gift bag.

"I wanted to give you this yesterday at *mei* house, but I wasn't finished with it."

Mary Carol had given him several things she'd made by hand, so she wasn't surprised to find inside the bag a beautiful oak box that he'd carved for her. But she was surprised when he dropped to one knee.

"Open the box," he said.

With shaky fingers, she opened the beautiful box and pulled out a piece of paper that read, *Will you marry me?*

She looked at Abe, then at all her family members. As her eyes filled with tears, she thought about her father. But this was a season of hope for all of them, and as she gazed into Abe's eyes, she was certain that she wanted to be with him for the rest of her life.

"Yes," she whispered. Then she looked at James. He rolled his eyes, and Mary Carol laughed out loud.

CHAPTER NINE

Katherine was at the coffee shop a little early, surprised that James hadn't arrived. She decided to be daring and ordered a vanilla latte.

It was nothing short of a miracle that James had behaved so perfectly during their Second Christmas celebration. She'd been worried about her children meeting him since she never knew when he might turn into one of his characters and talk about his federal agent days or tell one of his tall tales. It was bound to happen eventually; she should sit down with all of the children before their next family gathering.

Thirty minutes later, she finished her drink and left. Worry was burrowing into her heart as she thought about where to even look for James. And how easily he could slip out of their lives, the same way he'd slipped in. What if she never saw him again?

By the time she got home, she'd worked herself up even more, picturing him lost, cold, or hungry. She'd asked him if he'd wanted to stay overnight on the couch after the big meal on Second Christmas, but he said he already had plans. Katherine was sure he didn't, so she'd prayed that he would have shelter, warmth, and food.

"What's wrong?" Mary Carol asked when Katherine walked into the house. She took off her black cape and hung it on the rack.

"James — I mean your grandfather — is always at the coffee shop on time. We've been meeting there on Tuesdays. Today he didn't show up, and I'm worried." She untied her black bonnet, brushed specks of snow from it, and hung it next to her cape. "I don't think he has a home. I don't know where to find him."

"I know where he is."

"How could you possibly know where he is?" *Mamm* put her hands on her hips. "Mary Carol, what's going on?"

"I'll explain on the way."

Katherine found Linda and asked her to keep an eye on Gideon since Stephen was at work. Linda rolled her eyes but dutifully complied. Her two youngest children didn't start back to school until the following week.

"He stays at the old Porter farmhouse,"

Mary Carol said as they directed the buggy onto the road. Katherine listened to how her daughter had been spending her Saturdays and how she and Abe had gotten to know James.

"I never lied, *Mamm.* I told you I was spending the day with Abe, and that's what I was doing."

Katherine sighed. "You didn't tell me because you knew I wouldn't approve of your visits with an *Englisch* stranger."

Mary Carol hung her head for a few moments. "He tells all kinds of stories, *Mamm.* Do you think he's . . . you know . . . crazy?"

"I don't know. Something isn't right with him, but sometimes he makes more sense than all of us."

Mary Carol gasped as Katherine guided the buggy up the driveway of the old Porter place. Katherine slowed the buggy, unsure whether to keep going.

"There's a red car. Did James tell you that two men in a red car have been following him?"

Katherine pulled back the reins. "*Ya,* but I didn't believe him."

"What should we do?" Mary Carol asked when Katherine brought the buggy to a stop in front of the house.

"I'm going to check on him. You wait here."

"*Nee.* I'm coming too."

Katherine didn't argue as she tethered the horse, then they both hurried across the packed snow toward the door. She knocked. When no one answered, she knocked harder.

"James's car is here."

Katherine knocked again.

"Why do you think he has a car but no real place to live? I've asked him, but he always changed the subject."

"I don't know." Katherine had asked him the same thing several times.

Finally, the door opened, and an older man, who looked to have many years even on James, greeted them. He was a tall man in a black suit.

"Hello, Katherine. Hello, Mary Carol," he said as he stepped aside so they could go into the house.

Katherine grabbed Mary Carol's arm and held her in place. "How do you know our names?"

The elderly *Englisch* man smiled just as another man wearing a white jacket appeared beside him, extending his hand to Katherine. "I am Dr. Reynolds," he said. "I am James's caregiver."

Katherine kept one hand on Mary Carol's

arm, ignoring the doctor's gesture. "And this is how you let him live?" Mary Carol had filled Katherine in on the conditions inside the old Porter place.

"Please come in," the man in the black suit said, not responding to Katherine's comment. "We know you have questions, and the time has come for us to give you answers. My name is Weldon Bartosh. I've been a friend of James's for a very long time."

Katherine still didn't move.

"Come on, *Mamm,*" Mary Carol said softly.

The two men stepped back even farther, and Katherine and her daughter went into the living room.

"Where is James?"

Dr. Reynolds sat down in the recliner. "Please, have a seat on the couch. I will explain everything to you. James is upstairs napping, so this is a good time for us to chat."

Weldon remained standing as Katherine and Mary Carol sat down.

"James has an inoperable brain tumor. I am his physician, and as Weldon told you, he has been a friend to James for many years."

Katherine brought two fingers to her lips,

unsure what to ask first. She decided to ask Dr. Reynolds the question heaviest on her heart. "Is he dying?"

"Yes. I'm sorry to say that he is. And his dying wish was to see you and his grandchildren. We knew that James would come here, regardless of his condition, so when Agent Weldon told me he intended to follow him, I offered to join him. James and I have been friends for years. My wife died last year and it does me good to have a purpose again." Dr. Reynolds smiled. "We bring him hot meals in the evening, and even though he rarely changes his clothes, he has a closet full upstairs."

Katherine swallowed hard as she glanced at Mary Carol, whose jaw was on the floor. Katherine was still processing the fact that James was dying. "How long does he have . . . to live?" She reached for Mary Carol's hand and squeezed.

Dr. Reynolds looked at Weldon, then back at them. "We honestly didn't think he would live this long."

Mary Carol sniffled. "Is he crazy?"

Dr. Reynolds grinned. "I'm sure he's told you some stories that might make him appear crazy, but no, that is not his diagnosis. His unpredictable behavior is a result of the tumor growing on his brain. You may have also noticed some unusual physical mannerisms, like his eye twitching."

"Or that his limp sometimes goes away?" Katherine said.

"I'm actually unsure what caused his limp to disappear. Especially since he'd had that his entire life."

Maybe God relieved him of the limp, Katherine thought.

Mary Carol was dabbing at her eyes. "He told us he'd been shot," she said. "We didn't think that was true. I guess now I'm wishing that's all it was instead of hearing that he's dying."

"Oh, he *did* get shot," Weldon said. "But that isn't what's causing his confusion."

"When?" Katherine asked as she sat taller. "Why?"

Weldon sat down on the arm of the couch farthest from where Katherine and Mary Carol were sitting. "Back when James was living here in Paradise, he witnessed a horrific crime," Weldon said. "After safely fleeing the scene, he went directly to the police station. He was shaken and fearful. Rightfully so." Weldon paused and hung his head for a few moments. "James led the police back to the scene, and based on evidence in the house and James's descriptions, they had a pretty good idea who he'd seen. These were some bad fellows." He looked back up. "And once they explained this to James, he was afraid for his family. The police escorted him home, and he gathered a few things. His wife and son were running errands at the time. We put him in protective custody that same day. We encouraged him to leave his wife a note, but he just kept saying to hurry, that she wouldn't understand. We needed him to be safe until the trial. Then he'd be free to return home. Or so we thought. And we did a pretty good job keeping his identity a secret. But on the day of the trial, despite the security we had for him, someone shot him going up the courthouse steps. They must have assumed he was our key witness. I wanted to pay a visit to his wife, to let her know he'd been injured, but she didn't have a phone, and if the criminals had gotten to James . . ." He shrugged, shaking his head. "We just couldn't take a chance that they might be following us, so we didn't notify her. By then, we knew it was a large ring of delinquents we were dealing with, part of the Philadelphia mob. After he recovered, James went into the witness protection program."

"Witness protection?" Katherine took a quick, short breath before she brought her hand to her mouth. Questions were forming faster than she could organize them, but the words wedged in her throat. She felt light-headed, but she didn't move or say anything.

"We assumed he would want to bring his wife and son into the program, but he insisted that he would be the only one to go, as long as we could guarantee their safety, which at that point, we thought we could. If he had waited any longer, I don't know if we could have. It was important to James that his son be raised in this Amish community. And as I said, the goal was to only keep him until the trial ended and all the bad guys were locked up. James didn't realize — nor did we — that when he left, he wouldn't return for decades."

"Why didn't they all just move to another Amish district?" Mary Carol's voice cracked as she spoke. "Maybe in another state?"

"We offered that to him. We told him that all three of them could start over in a new place with new identities. But he remained fearful that the criminals would find him, and he wanted to be far away from his family if they did."

Katherine dabbed at her eyes.

"The trial was postponed for a while, but eventually justice was served and the crooks went to jail for life with no chance of parole. We didn't get the entire criminal ring, but we at least captured two of the men responsible for the murder that day in Lancaster. The third man remained on the loose."

Weldon was using words that Katherine had never heard, but she was pretty sure that he was saying that the criminals would never get out of jail. She recalled the time the FBI had been in Lancaster County. A shiver ran the length of her spine.

"James made the ultimate sacrifice for his family, and only a few of us know how he suffered by not being able to see his wife and son. He wept for days when he heard his wife had died."

Katherine shook as she tried to stop the tears rolling down her cheeks. She squeezed Mary Carol's hand even harder.

"What — what did he see on that day, the crime?" Katherine's voice trembled and she stole a look at Mary Carol, unsure if she wanted her daughter to hear these details.

CHAPTER TEN

Mary Carol waited for an explanation from the *Englisch* man, feeling nervous and sick and scared. She held tightly to her mother's hand. Her father had rarely mentioned Mary Carol's grandfather over the years, and the little bit of family history that Weldon was filling in was bittersweet.

Mr. Bartosh sighed. "He told us that he was strolling down a side road toward a grove of pecan trees. It was a pretty day. He was not far from here, across the lane, when he said he saw the front door of this house burst open and a man run out into the front yard, a look of sheer terror on his face. Three men rushed out onto the front porch, one holding a shotgun. The young man was shot five times in the back. James said when the man fell in the front yard, the three men had a direct line of sight to James.

Mary Carol gasped. "Here?"

"Yes. Long before Mr. Porter lived here,

three men lived in this house. They were involved in some shady transactions and more or less hiding out in your Amish community. This place is pretty secluded, and we found Amish clothes in the house. Apparently they tried to dress the part anytime they traveled away from the house. One of the guys had even grown a beard. After James witnessed the murder, he ran from the scene. It's a miracle he got away from those men. It benefited him to know the woods and surrounding area so well. Somehow he lost them and made it to the station. He admitted that at least one of the men had gotten a good look at him, so we encouraged him to shave his beard and cut his hair, which he did.

"When I first met Paul — I mean James — I saw signs of a man who had obviously grown up in a peaceful environment, who witnessed something so horrific and upsetting, it changed him and he never was the same again."

"What about his wife and child — my *mammi* and *mei daed*? Couldn't this mob group have come after them?" Mary Carol asked in a shaky voice.

Mr. Bartosh lowered his head and was quiet. When he looked up, he grimaced and shifted his weight. "This is where we messed up. We wanted these thugs to get word that Paul Johnson was the man who witnessed the shooting — that he was an Amish man from Ohio visiting friends. We gave him a whole new identity so that he could never be traced back to Lancaster County, so that these men would never find James's wife and son. It was all in an effort to get him back here when it was all over. We knew that the media would eventually find out that Paul Johnson was our key witness. We thought we could keep him safe through the trial until everyone was behind bars." He paused. "That's when the mob in Philadelphia got involved."

Mary Carol had no idea what a mob actually was. She looked at her mother, but *Mamm* shook her head.

"It's a criminal organization. These men would do anything to get to James before he testified and implicated their involvement, so we changed his name once more and relocated him. Again. To Michigan this time, where he lived as James Shelton in a small apartment."

"When it was all over, why didn't he come back?" Mary Carol asked.

"It wasn't all over until a year ago. Remember I said one man was still on the loose? Well, that last man was found living in a nursing home in Colorado. He'd been using a different name all those years. That man was taken to jail like the others, also with a lifelong sentence, but he died soon afterward. James was bitter about that for a long time — that the last holdout got to live almost his entire life as a free man, enjoying his family, while James had been ripped from his wife and child at such a young age. But it was then that James felt it was finally safe to come home. He was making travel plans to surprise his son when Dr. Reynolds diagnosed him with a brain tumor."

The doctor cleared his throat. "James gets very confused sometimes, and he often forgets to take his medication. On the days he remembers, he can be fairly coherent. But even with his pills, he has a hard time due to the pressure in his head."

Mary Carol recalled the headaches James would get. "So he isn't crazy? This tumor in his head makes him tell the tall tales about being a federal agent?"

Dr. Reynolds looked at Mr. Bartosh, and the older man took over. "James stays confused, hopping from one identity to the other. But it's all true. He lived it." He paused as he locked eyes with Mary Carol. "And I assure you . . . James *was* a federal agent. A very good one."

Mary Carol couldn't speak, and her mother just stared.

"It seemed a stretch since I know your people are pacifists," Mr. Bartosh said. "But James knew he couldn't go home and he had an inborn desire to let justice prevail at all costs. He was a young man, around twenty-five, when this all began. He worked hard and saved his money. Then he went on to college, got a degree in criminal justice, and landed a job in law enforcement. To hear him talk about it, he was able to completely separate from his Amish life and become this new man who used the law to right the wrongs of others.

"Six years later, he looked me up, and eventually he came to work for us. It was his mission in life to find the one man left who had been involved in the shootings. And he did. So he was now free to return home to his family."

Dr. Reynolds spoke up again. "James insisted on staying at this farmhouse even though we wanted to put him up at the same bed-and-breakfast we've been staying at since we arrived. We keep an eye on him, even though he hates that we followed him here to Lancaster County."

"We were friends for a long time," Mr. Bartosh said before he looked at her mother.

"I couldn't stand the thought of him dying alone if you rejected him."

Katherine thought about how differently things could have turned out for all of them if James hadn't shown up. But she was having a hard time understanding why these men would spend months of their lives following James, no matter how strong their friendship.

Weldon chuckled. "He's quite capable of giving us the slip when he really wants to. We lost track of him for eight days last month and were really worried about whether or not he was taking his medications. He did fairly well after his initial diagnosis, but he started getting more and more confused and needed someone to check on him daily, so that's where Dr. Reynolds came in. The doctor had known James for years through other circles, and he offered to take over his case and monitor his care." Weldon paused, the hint of a smile on his face. "You know, he was a handsome devil in his younger days, but he never remarried and always said that there would never be anyone like his beloved wife, Sarah."

"Is he —" As much as Katherine wanted to care for James, she had her children to think about. She'd been nervous on Second Christmas. "Is he a danger to himself or others?"

Weldon shook his head. "No. He just stays confused, and that will most likely get worse as the tumor grows."

"We were worried that he wouldn't get here in time to meet all of you, but he has surprised us." Dr. Reynolds's smile was genuine. Katherine believed the man truly cared for James. She silently thanked God for putting these two men in her father-in-law's life.

Katherine recalled James telling her that he would be called home soon. "Can we take him home to live with us for however long he has left?"

Weldon glanced at Dr. Reynolds, then back at Katherine. "We were hoping you would."

Katherine marveled at the wonderful way the Lord worked.

Mary Carol put her head on her mother's shoulder. "I wish *Daed* would have known all of this."

Katherine put her arm around her daughter and pulled her close. She thought about the dreams James had told her about, his conversations with Elias.

Smiling, she said, "Somehow I think your

daed does know."

Weldon cleared his throat. "There is one more thing. James has some classified information we need. Do you know anything about this? Has he mentioned anything to you? During one of his rants, he said that you were the keeper of this classified information, but it's always difficult to know when James is creating his own version of the truth."

Ah. Now things were making more sense. She didn't doubt that these men cared about her father-in-law, but he also had something Weldon wanted, which explained why he had taken time out of his own life to follow James for months.

Katherine recalled the key James had given her. Her father-in-law had said it was the key to his heart, but had he entrusted her with something else? The more she thought about it, she realized that the key resembled the one to her own safety deposit box in town. She decided to keep her answer vague for now so as to avoid telling a lie. "James told me he was the keeper of top secret information, but he never said what it was."

Weldon sighed.

Katherine thought about this great man who'd given so much of himself to keep his family safe. She planned to take care of him for the rest of his life, however long that might be. But first thing the next morning, she was going to her bank on the off chance that the key he'd given her was to a safety deposit box.

Weldon stood up and reached into his pocket. "Take this card so you'll always know how to reach me. And can you please let me know if you come across anything that James might have stashed away for me?"

Katherine took the card and nodded.

"Do your people use — uh, regular doctors?" Weldon blushed a little.

"*Ya.* We do."

Dr. Reynolds stood up and gave Katherine his business card. "You'll want to have a doctor monitor his medications and probably check on him at least once a week. I can make sure his medical records are transferred here. And he really shouldn't be driving." He shrugged. "We didn't have any luck getting him to give that up, but maybe you will."

"We will help him pack his things and bring him to your house tomorrow if that's okay," Weldon said. "He keeps everything upstairs — the heater, the clothes we got him, and even his food. We eventually bought a small refrigerator for the upstairs bedroom." He shook his head. "We hate him living here, but he insisted. We figured it was better than him sleeping in his car, which he'd done in the past. He doesn't know it, but we're actually paying Mr. Porter's granddaughter rent on this dump."

Katherine's mind was still reeling, but she just kept nodding.

"I have some errands to run in the morning," she said. "Can you bring James to our house in the afternoon?"

"Sure." Weldon extended his hand. "I wish you all the best." He smiled as he shook Katherine's hand. "Gonna miss that man. Please keep us informed. If possible, we'd like to come back . . . uh, when the time comes."

Katherine and Mary Carol walked to their buggy. The sun was shining off the freshly fallen snow, and Katherine thought it was brighter than she'd ever seen it.

The next morning, Katherine arrived at the bank in town just as they were opening the doors. Mary Carol was unhappy that she had to stay at home, but Stephen was working and Linda had stayed overnight at a friend's house. Someone had to watch Gideon. Her young one had a cold and didn't

119

need to be out in the weather.

It took less than a minute for the bank clerk to confirm that Katherine's key was for safety deposit box number 2042, and Katherine was an authorized user. On shaky legs, Katherine followed the woman into a large vault. Even though Elias had kept a safety deposit box for property deeds and legal papers, Katherine had only been in the vault one time, and that had been when the bank called her after Elias died and asked her what she wanted to do about the box. She'd purchased a safe to keep at home.

After the woman left her alone in the vault, Katherine fought the urge to cry. So much had happened, and she wished she had her husband to lean on. She put the key in the lock and lifted the top. There were two envelopes inside. Katherine's name was on one, although Elias's name was scratched out. The other envelope had Weldon's name written on it. She opened her envelope, knowing that it was originally for her husband. She started to sob when she saw how much cash and savings bonds were inside.

"Oh, James . . . ," she whispered. She wouldn't have to worry about getting good medical care for James, and she was never going to have to worry about taking care of her family. Enclosed was a letter.

Dear ~~Elias~~ Katherine,

If you're reading this letter, I've most likely passed on, or I'm well on my way. I'm told by my doctors that my mental capacity will continue to deteriorate. I thought it best to write to you while I am still somewhat in control of my faculties — and it's hit or miss these days. But by now, you probably know my story, or at least I hope you do. I pray that the legacy I leave behind for my grandchildren will be one of honor and that I won't go down in history as the guy who abandoned his wife and child.

Katherine sniffled as she turned the piece of paper over to continue reading.

There is another envelope for Weldon. You might meet him. If not, here's the address for where to send his letter.

Katherine scanned the address.

Please do not open the envelope addressed to Weldon. It's classified information, and I trust you to get it to him. BUT — AND THIS IS VERY IMPORTANT — if you are in possession of this envelope and I'm still alive, PLEASE do not give this to Weldon until I die. That's all I can say about that.

And if it's not too much to ask, could you please get word of my death to a woman named Bonnie? She wasn't a love interest or anything. Only your mother, Sarah, held my heart. But Bonnie was a special person in my life at a time when I needed a friend. Here is her address, and on the outside of the envelope, you'll need to write this code in the bottom left corner so that the letter will actually get to her. 3891055574-HHG461.

Katherine brought a hand to her chest as she read the address.

The White House
1600 Pennsylvania Avenue NW
Washington, DC 20500

So, I think that's it. I love you, ~~Elias~~ Katherine. So, as the song says . . . I'll be seeing you.

~~Dad~~ James

Katherine held the letter to her heart for a while before composing herself and then walking out of the bank.

CHAPTER ELEVEN

James surprised them all by staying around much longer than predicted — long enough to see Mary Carol and Abe get married in the fall. He was in a wheelchair by then. Katherine couldn't help but smile when she recalled the blessing James said aloud before the wedding feast. Over a hundred people were at Katherine's house — as was tradition — for the ceremony and grand meal afterward. James whistled to get everyone's attention. Katherine had told him that everyone would pray silently, but James had insisted on reciting his own version of thanks to the Lord.

"Thank You, God, for this glorious, wonderful, superb, outstanding day! Please bless this couple and encourage them to name their firstborn James. Now, over the lips and through the gums, look out tummy, here it comes!"

Katherine smiled at the memory as she

watched Gideon sitting on the edge of James's bed. Her father-in-law spoke in a whisper, his eyes barely open.

"Not only is it beautiful where I am going, but there's always chocolate cake to eat." James paused and looked across the room. "Katherine, you should ask Mary Carol for her recipe, by the way. Hers are the best." Katherine looked over to her daughter who wore a sheepish expression and shrugged. "But the best part, Gideon, is that your father and grandmother are there waiting for me, and I can't wait to see them."

Gideon looked at his grandfather with an expression that seemed older than his years. "Sometimes I'm sad that my *daed* isn't here anymore."

James was quiet for a moment. "When I was gone all those years, I missed your dad something fierce. I thought about him every day. Prayed for him too. Even though he isn't here with you, he still loves you very much."

Gideon hugged James and then made his way over to Katherine's lap. Stephen, Mary Carol, Linda, and Abe were gathered around James. Each of them had privately said good-bye to him earlier in the day. But even though they knew what was coming, it didn't stop the flood of tears. Abe was sobbing even more than the rest of them. Their family doctor had been by that morning and said it wouldn't be long now. Katherine was so thankful to God that James was cognizant of them all as he prepared to take his final breath.

But now, as Christmas approached, they would be saying goodbye to another loved one. A miracle of sorts who'd breezed into their world and changed the way they all looked at life. And death.

Katherine was having a hard time holding back her tears, but she knew that this was a time for celebration. James would finally be reunited with the son and wife he'd left behind so many years ago.

"Tell *Daed* we all say hi," Gideon said softly.

James closed his eyes and nodded. Katherine had turned her small sewing room into her bedroom. There was barely enough room for a twin bed, but she didn't mind. She'd given James her bedroom so that they could all gather here with him for prayers each day. Katherine was sure James had seen and done things that would shock her and the children, but the man had stayed strong in his faith his entire life. She held his hand, hoping he could feel all the love they had for him.

As the clock neared eleven, she encouraged her children to go to bed. And she told Mary Carol and Abe that they should go home.

"He is sleeping now. These things can drag on," she whispered as James snored.

Reluctantly, they all did as she asked.

After the door closed behind them all, Katherine grinned. "I can tell when you are fake snoring." It was something he did when he didn't want to talk or be bothered. "But you are stuck with me right now."

Her father-in-law opened one eye and gave her a weak smile, then he slowly opened the other eye. She had to lean close so she could hear him. "I didn't figure you'd want them in here when I took my last breath. I might turn purple or have saliva dribbling down my chin."

Katherine smiled. "Do you realize the joy you have brought into our lives?"

He squeezed Katherine's hand. "You've made this old man very happy. Thank you for sharing your family with me. I have so much to tell Elias . . ." His voice had weakened so that his words were barely audible. She relaxed in the chair next to his bed and held his hand. They sat this way for an hour.

Then suddenly she heard him try to speak again. She stood and gripped his hand.

"They're here," he said, and a broad, luminous smile spread across his face. His eyes grew wider and he focused on the corner of the room.

"It's been a long time. Sarah . . . Elias . . . Take me home."

And he closed his eyes for the last time.

Katherine sat there for a while and prayed. Then she slowly lifted herself from the chair and eased her hand from James's. She kissed him on the forehead before she walked to the dresser drawers and pulled open the top drawer. She took out the envelope with Weldon's name on it so that she could mail it first thing in the morning, along with a letter to a woman named Bonnie that she'd written the day before.

She held both envelopes to her heart.

"Go in peace, James Zook." She smiled. "I'll be seeing you . . ."

Katherine was in the living room, looking out the window, when Mary Carol arrived for a visit. James's burial had been earlier in the week and the family was still adjusting to his absence. Katherine was also still getting used to the fact that her sweet Mary Carol was a married woman and living somewhere else. "What's going on, *Mamm*? Are you okay?"

"I'm fine, just received some news this afternoon that made me smile." Katherine was still holding the letter she'd gotten earlier. She looked at her daughter. "Do you remember your *daadi* mentioning a woman named Bonnie?"

"Yeah, Abe and I didn't believe for one minute that the first lady's sister was baking him chocolate cakes. I know that Mr. Bartosh confirmed most of *Daadi*'s stories, but he never said anything about the White House or a woman named Bonnie."

Katherine chuckled. "No, he didn't. But maybe we should have thought to inquire about Bonnie. I mailed a letter to the White House, to Bonnie, after your *daadi* passed on, just like he asked me to. I was doubtful I'd get a response. But I got a letter in the mail today. From the White House." She handed the piece of stationery to her daughter. Mary Carol stared at it with wide eyes for a second before she looked up at Katherine. "No way."

Katherine smiled as she waited for her daughter to read the letter.

Dear Ms. Zook,
    Thank you for your letter informing

me about Paul's passing (James, as y
know him). He was an incredible ma
someone I'm proud to have called
friend. I know that it blessed his life in
mensely to finally be with his family. It
all he ever talked about during his tim
at the White House, how someday he
would get home. He was a great source
of strength to me during a difficult time
in my life, and I would like to think that
in some way, I had a positive influence
on his life as well. He will be greatly
missed.

Sending you blessings at
this difficult time.
All the best,
Bonita (Bonnie) Morgan

"*Daadi* always said Bonnie was the former
first lady's sister, but that no one knew. Do
you think that's true?"

Katherine was wondering the same thing.
"I don't know. Everything else he told us
turned out to be true."

"Maybe that's what *Daadi*'s letter to Mr.
Bartosh was about."

"I don't know. I didn't open the letter
because your *daadi* asked me not to. Mr.
Weldon was your *daadi*'s friend, but he was
also after some information that James

wouldn't share." Katherine walked to the window in the living room, thankful for the bright sunlight. "Maybe it had something to do with Bonnie, or maybe not. But either way, your *daadi* was indeed friends with a woman named Bonnie at the White House."

Mary Carol read over the letter again. "I wish we knew for sure who she was."

"Well, maybe one day we can ask James about this ourselves. But not anytime soon, the Lord willing." Katherine's heart was still heavy at having endured another funeral service for someone she loved. But Bonnie's letter lifted her spirits, and it seemed to do the same for Mary Carol.

She grabbed her daughter's hand and led her to the kitchen. She pulled out the new canister of cocoa and smiled. "I know the perfect thing to do in remembrance of your *daadi*."

Mary Carol beamed. "Chocolate cake!"

READING GROUP GUIDE

1. James tells Katherine that Gideon must "see" his own heaven to understand where his father is. Have you ever done this, visualized what your idea of heaven is? If not, take a few minutes to do so.
2. Each family member expresses grief in a different way, as is the case in real life. Who could you relate to the most and why?
3. After James witnessed the crime, he chose to stay away from his family in an effort to keep them safe. Would you be able to practice such unconditional love if it meant that you might not see your loved ones for a very long time, possibly forever?
4. What were your thoughts about James — in the beginning, then later toward the end of the story?

Did you believe his tall tales? Did you think he was crazy?

5. At the end of the novella, Katherine keeps her promise and mails the envelope from the safety deposit box — without opening it. What do you think was inside the envelope? Was it really classified information? Can you speculate as to the contents?

ACKNOWLEDGMENTS

Karla and Joan, you've been with me on this journey from the beginning. You even set up my first radio interview six years ago. What an amazing journey this has been, and I'm blessed to know you both. It's an honor to dedicate this story to such fabulous women. ☺

To my wonderful husband, Patrick — I'm your Annie, and I always will be, lol. You're the best, and I love you with all my heart.

Natasha Kern, thanks for all you do. What a wonderful agent and friend you are. So glad to have you on my team. xo

Many thanks to the folks at HarperCollins Christian Fiction. You all ROCK! It's a privilege to work with all of you.

And, as always, God gets the glory for every story I write, but without the support of family and friends, it would be a challenging journey sometimes. Thank you!

ABOUT THE AUTHOR

Award-winning, bestselling author **Beth Wiseman** is best known for her Amish novels, but her most recent novels, *Need You Now* and *The House That Love Built,* are contemporaries set in small Texas towns. Both have received glowing reviews. Beth's highly anticipated novel, *The Promise,* is inspired by a true story.

■ ■ ■ ■

HER CHRISTMAS
PEN PAL

RUTH REID

■ ■ ■ ■

To my sister, Joy Droste Elwell, a great friend, beautiful sister, and wonderful baker. Your house is always full of laughter and loads of good food. Thank you for all the cherry pies you made just for me. I treasure the times we can get together!

GLOSSARY

ach: oh
aenti: aunt
boppli: baby
bruder: brother
daed: dad
danki: thank you
Englisch or Englischer: a non-Amish person
fraa: wife
grossdaadi: grandfather
gut: good
haus: house
hiya: greeting
jah: yes
kaffi: coffee
kalt: cold
kapp: prayer covering
kinskind: grandchildren
kumm: come
mamm: mother
mariye: morning

mei: my
nacht: night
narrisch: crazy
nau: no
nett: not
Ordnung: the unwritten rules of the Amish
sohn: son
wedder: weather
welkom: welcome

CHAPTER ONE

Joy Stolzfus tossed the basin of dirty water from the foot-washing service over the porch banister. The tradition of humbling herself before God and the members of her district during the foot washing was good for the soul, but Joy couldn't think of anything but the loss of her parents in last year's fire.

Meredith came up beside her and laid her hand on Joy's shoulder. "Are you doing all right?"

Joy forced a smile. "The fire was a year ago today. It doesn't seem possible."

"I know."

"I still think *mei* parents must have left the oil lamp burning for me. If Henry hadn't been late driving me home . . ." Joy touched her throat. Dry with a lump the size of a bar of lye soap.

"No one knows what caused the fire."

The bishop had tried to reassure her of

that too. But the memory of flames shooting out the window where the lamp table sat led her to believe otherwise. Maybe the cat had knocked the lamp over as Joy's sisters thought. Still, her parents couldn't be saved. A section of the roof caved just as more help arrived.

The screen door snapped and several other women brought their basins outside to empty. The women chatted about the upcoming annual quilting bee, which served to jump-start Sugarcreek's fall tourism sales. Joy's thoughts drifted back to her mother who had looked forward to the all-day frolic every year.

Meredith took Joy by the arm. "Let's go to the kitchen and get a glass of water."

Her friend always seemed to know exactly what she needed. Entering the house, Joy scanned the sitting room where Henry had been standing, but didn't find him. He must've gone out the back door with the other unmarried men. She followed Meredith into the kitchen.

"Are Lois and Sarah holding up all right?" Meredith removed a glass from the cabinet.

"We had a *gut* cry earlier today and we spent some time reminiscing about *Mamm* and *Daed.* I suppose it's *gut* for the soul."

Meredith handed Joy the glass of water. "I

think you should focus on Christmas. Isn't October when you start planning what you're going to serve for the Second Christmas sleigh ride?"

Joy nodded as she raised the glass to her mouth. The long drink brought a cooling relief to her sore throat. *"Danki,"* she said. Then added, "For everything, Meredith."

Her friend reached out and patted her arm. "Your parents would be proud of how you've taken over the bakery. But I don't think they would want you to stuff yourself in a hole and become a recluse."

"I haven't done that." Joy tapped her thumb against her chest. "And I'm *nett* a recluse. Maybe a workaholic, but that isn't all *mei* fault. Sarah isn't interested in the bakery, and Lois isn't able to spend time in town with a new *boppli.* Besides, I do get out of the kitchen. I have to wait on customers at the bakery, don't I?"

Meredith smiled. "There's the spunk I've missed all week."

She had spent a lot of time alone this week, praying and preparing for the fall feast and communion service.

"Well, *nau* that your mood has lifted, I have some news to share."

"Oh?" Joy expected with the way Meredith was smiling that she was about to share engagement news. Her friend and Walter had courted almost as long as she and Henry. Only, she and Henry hadn't spent much time together since she started going into the bakery at four a.m. to prepare the daily specials. Lately it seemed whenever Henry would stop at the house to sit on the porch swing with her, she either had already gone to bed or would fall asleep sitting on the swing with him.

"Your Henry must be ready to propose," Meredith blurted. "I overheard him talking with *mei bruder* about the acreage for sale across the pasture from us." Her voice rose with enthusiasm.

"He did?" Joy covered her mouth to catch her gasp.

"You and I both know when a man is looking for property to build a *haus* — he's looking to wed." Meredith opened the cabinet next to the sink and removed a glass.

That certainly was the case with her sister. Matthew put a down payment on the farm the same day he proposed to Lois.

"I've got so many goose bumps, *mei* arms feel like a plucked turkey." Joy rubbed her arm. "Henry's been acting a little strange lately. Even tonight he avoided direct eye contact with me."

Meredith refilled the glass with water and

handed it to Joy. "He was watching you all right, the entire time you were washing *mei* feet."

"Danki." Joy sipped the drink.

Henry hadn't always understood why Joy spent so many hours at the bakery. Occasionally he even accused her of preferring to spend time at the bakery over being with him. But learning the ins and outs of running Sugarcreek's only bakery left her feeling like she had been stuffed into a pressure cooker and was about to blow. And even though she was a proficient baker, she had to learn how to manage a business. Things her parents did every day, like maintaining the proper amount of inventory on the shelves and knowing when and how many supplies to order.

"Maybe he'll ask you tonight? He's driving you home, *jah*?"

Joy shook her head. "I waited for him to ask all week but he didn't. Sarah and I drove together, but she's already secured a ride home with Abram." Joy smiled. "Maybe if I leave *nau,* Henry will follow to make sure I arrive home safely."

"You be sure to share the news with me tomorrow."

"Jah, I will." Joy hand-pressed a damp crease in her dress. It hadn't fully dried

since she sloshed water on it earlier. *Vain.* Here she was concerned about her appearance when the foot-washing ceremony had ended only minutes ago, but she worked out the wrinkles as best she could. "I look all rumpled, don't I?"

"*Nay,* you look fine." Meredith placed her hand on Joy's back and nudged her toward the sitting room.

The bishop's wife, Martha Byler, stopped Joy on her way to the door. "How are you doing?" She frowned. "I sure miss your *mamm.*"

"I do too." Joy looked away from Martha's tearful eyes.

Lois approached, cradling Stephen in her arms. "Are you going home so soon?"

"*Jah,* I have to open the bakery in the morning."

"I was just telling Joy how much I miss your *mamm.*"

"Excuse me," Joy said, reaching for the door handle. She stepped outside into the cool breeze and pulled her shawl tighter around her shoulders. She should have thought to bring her cloak instead. The sun was fading into the horizon and the temperature was plummeting.

Joy meandered toward the buggies while keeping an eye out for Henry. He wasn't with the unmarried men who were grouped near the barn. She proceeded down the row of buggies where she had tethered Candy.

She located Henry's horse tied one horse over on the opposite side of the rail. Drawing closer, she recognized his voice coming from the passenger side of his buggy.

"You can lean on me," he said.

Joy shot under the railing, startling the horses nearby.

A woman's giggle stifled.

Joy reached them as Henry was helping Priscilla Byler into his buggy. Joy clamped her teeth over her bottom lip and whirled around.

Henry's footsteps tromped at her heels. They reached Candy at the same time.

"It's *nett* what it looks like. She twisted her ankle."

Joy untied her mare from the post and boarded the buggy. She would regret anything she said right now.

"Her *bruder* asked if I would see her home."

Without a chaperone? Joy bit back voicing her thought and reined Candy away from the other buggies. Once she rounded the tree-lined bend in the country road, she looked back as the Detweilers' farm disappeared behind the crimson canopy of low-hanging maple leaves.

The road ahead blurred. Joy was still sobbing two miles down the road when she reached the house. She unharnessed and fed Candy, then trudged across the yard to the house. At least she was alone. But Lois and Matthew wouldn't be long — baby Stephen had been coughing most of the evening. Joy went upstairs to the room she shared with Sarah and pitched herself on the bed. If it wouldn't raise questions with her sisters at this late hour, she would bake. Instead, she pulled out a pen and pad of paper from the lamp table drawer and wrote a letter to her cousin. Even though Emily couldn't offer much support ten miles away, Joy still poured out her heart into the letter, which was the next best thing to baking.

She finished and extinguished the lamp flame before her family returned. When Sarah entered their shared room, Joy pretended to be asleep. As much as she hated to admit it, she hoped Henry would appear outside her window. She lay awake half the night waiting for the tap of pebbles against the glass, his way of beckoning her outside so they could talk.

By the time the bakery opened the following day, Joy had the display case chock-full

with a wide assortment of apple pie turn-
overs, cookies, brownies, and sweet breads.
She even mixed up a new peppermint-
frosted sugar doodle, which she offered to
the early-bird customers to sample. Yet even
receiving rave reviews from her customers
didn't take her mind off of Henry.

Joy reached under the counter for the
cleaning bottle, then misted the display case
with the watered-down vinegar solution.
She wiped the finger smudges off the glass
as the bell over the door dinged.

Joy lifted her gaze fully expecting to see
Henry. Her heart deflated a little more each
time the door opened and it wasn't him.

"*Gut* afternoon." Sarah strolled into the
shop.

Jah, it was well past noon all right. Joy
tossed her cleaning rag onto the counter.
She had given her sister plenty of leeway
since Sarah didn't enjoy working at the
bakery, but Joy needed a reprieve.

Sarah pulled an apron from the wall hook.
"Anything I should know?" She glanced
about the room as she tied the strings
around her waist.

"I suppose you could make another pot of
kaffi. I sold almost three pots. *Nau* that it's
colder outside, everyone wants something
warm to drink."

151

Joy headed to the kitchen area. She packed an assortment of everything she had baked that morning into a pastry box, making sure not to cram the items together. Maybe on her way to the post office to mail the letter to her cousin, she would run into Henry at the hardware store. He always enjoyed her cookies.

"You baked all that this morning?" Her sister eyed the package.

Joy nodded. "I wanted to try some new recipes for the Christmas season." She tied twine around the box.

"You must've been real upset with Henry to make all that."

"What did you hear?"

"Priscilla twisted her ankle — or pretended to — and Henry volunteered to take her home."

"Well, they are neighbors," Joy said.

"*Jah,* and Priscilla could have ridden home with her parents."

"If she injured her ankle, she wouldn't have wanted to wait until the bishop and Martha were ready to leave. You know they stay at the service gatherings until the end."

"Still, Henry should have been more considerate of your feelings. Doesn't he remember that yesterday was the anniversary of our parents' death?"

She could almost hear the *tsk-tsk* in her sister's mind. It wasn't anything that Joy hadn't mulled over last night and most of today. She clipped the end of the twine and picked up the box. "I'm off to the post office."

"Who are you sending those to?"

"The hardware store is on the way to the post office, so I thought —"

"*Nay,* please tell me you're *nett* going to give those to Henry."

"He samples all *mei* new recipes." Joy pivoted toward the door and snatched her cape from the wall peg. "I'll see you at home tonight."

That wasn't a good reason, and she didn't dare turn around and acknowledge her sister's sigh. Truth be told, she wanted a reason to see him. He'd been indifferent toward her over the past week, and during yesterday's service, he hadn't even spoken to her until after she found him with Priscilla.

Joy untied her mare from the hitching post, then climbed up on the bench. By the time she reached Gingrich Hardware, her stomach had knotted tighter than the twine on the box of sweets. No matter how much she tried to convince herself that Henry had merely offered a neighbor a ride home, the

153

past blared at her. Prior to Henry courting her, he had courted Priscilla. She broke his heart and almost soured him completely about falling in love again.

The traffic was lighter than usual as Joy merged onto Main Street. It was normal for tourism to taper off after summer, but not usually to this extent. Where were the visitors? The fall colors always brought sightseers to Sugarcreek — the bakery too. Joy stopped at the hardware store and tied Candy to the post in the designated buggy parking area. She pasted on a smile as she entered the store.

Mr. Gingrich looked up from sorting bolts in a bin. "*Gut* afternoon, Joy. May I help you find something?"

"*Nay, danki.*" She craned her neck to peer down the row.

"If you're looking for Henry, he asked for the day off." The store owner continued sorting the bolts. "He's helping put up firewood at the bishop's place."

"*Danki.*" Joy's lips quivered. Unable to hold her smile, she turned around and rushed out of the building. Within seconds, she had the horse untied and was down the street. Once she reached the post office, she grabbed the letter and box from the bench.

Joy hadn't expected to mail the box, but

she had some extra money and her cousin would enjoy them. She jotted a note on the back of the envelope asking her cousin for feedback on the cookies. Joy had nibbled on so many they were beginning to taste the same. She untied the twine and slipped the letter inside. Although she asked for Emily's opinion of the treats, hers wasn't the one Joy desperately wanted.

CHAPTER TWO

Noah Esh glided the sandpaper block along the wood grain of the oak cabinet, then wiped it with tack cloth to remove the fine sawdust. Applying the satin finish on the set of kitchen cabinets wouldn't take long, but if he didn't receive the stained glass by tomorrow for the window panels on the cabinet doors, he'd miss his deadline. He'd already checked the mailbox twice and the beveled glass hadn't arrived. Maybe he shouldn't have given his *Englisch* customer so many choices. Next time he wouldn't show samples of stained glass that he didn't have in stock.

Noah applied the first coat of the glossy pecan stain to the cabinets. The strong fumes overwhelmed his senses. One day he would cut another window opening in the shop to create better air circulation. He set the rag on the worktable, deciding to take another walk to the mailbox. Once outside, he drew a deep breath. The crisp October air caused his lungs to spasm and he coughed.

Finding a crumpled package jammed into the mailbox alarmed Noah. The last time he received one in this mangled condition, the glass was broken. He piled the other mail on top of the package and headed back to the shop. He carefully cut open the box. Instead of finding beveled glass, he found baked goods. Noah flipped back the lid. Stolzfus Bakery. Sugarcreek, Ohio.

Not the contents he was expecting, but his empty stomach reminded him it was past noon. He removed the letter, peeled back the wax paper, and snatched a frosted cookie with tiny bits of peppermint sprinkled on it. The peppermint practically melted in his mouth. He hadn't eaten something this tasty since his grandmother passed away.

Noah filled his cup with coffee from the thermos and selected another cookie. The chocolate one tasted better than most he'd had. He took the package along with his cup of coffee over to the corner of the shop, sat down in the rocking chair, and unfolded the paper.

Dear Cousin Em,
  My life is in shambles, my heart is ach-
ing so. I just had to talk with you, even
if you're ten miles away.

Noah stopped reading. Cousin Em? He
flipped the lid once again. The smeared ink
made it impossible to read the name on the
package. The address wasn't much clearer.
Fieldstone Drive. He turned the box to get
a better look in the window light. It was his
road all right. But after closer inspection, he
made out a squiggly mark that must be an
S for south. He lived on the north end.
  Noah chewed the remaining cookie in his
mouth and swallowed hard. How would he
explain the opened box? And how would he
find . . . Cousin Em if he couldn't read the
name or address on the package? The cookies were too good to let go to waste.
  Noah grabbed another cookie from the
box. Although guilt pricked his conscience,
he was curious as to why the sender felt as
though her life was in shambles, so he
continued reading.

  . . . I found Henry helping the bishop's
daughter, Priscilla, into his buggy. Ap-

parently, she injured her ankle and Henry was kind enough to drive her home.

"Kind!" Noah shook his head.

I probably wouldn't be so worked up if I wasn't hurting so badly over missing Mamm and Daed. I'm not sure Henry even remembered they died this time last year. I hadn't seen him all week . . .

"Ah, *jah.* He was with the bishop's daughter all week. Why else would he take the girl home?" He flipped to the last page and scanned down to the bottom.

> Warm wishes,
> Your Cousin J.

"Has anyone ever told you, 'J.' that you're naïve? A good baker though." He bit off a piece of the cookie and kept reading.

Several cookies later, Noah refolded the letter. All ten pages. The woman was a wreck. In parts of the letter the ink was tearstained. Whoever this Henry was, he was no good for her, especially if he forgot the date of her parents' deaths. Noah had a notion to set her straight. He wished someone had opened his eyes to Ruby. Had he known Ruby was thinking about jumping the fence to become *Englisch,* maybe he wouldn't have fallen so hard for her. This Henry sounded like a sneak too.

Noah stood, tucked the woman's letter back into the envelope, and set the box of cookies on the table. This had been a nice break, but he needed to get back to work.

Joy set the bowl of butter beans on the table next to the red potatoes as Sarah poured milk into the glasses, and Lois placed the baked chicken dish on a potholder in front of Matthew's place setting. She and her sisters worked in harmony to get the meal prepared before Lois's husband came in from the barn.

Sarah put the empty pitcher of milk in the sink. "You never said how Henry liked the cookies the other day."

Joy sliced the loaf of sourdough bread. "He wasn't at work."

"I saw him chopping wood at the Bylers' when I took a food dish over," Lois said. "The bishop's been sick since the gathering the other *nacht.*"

Joy stopped the knife partway through the loaf. "You saw Henry there today?"

Lois nodded while stirring flour into a

saucepan of chicken broth.

Joy continued slicing the sourdough bread. "So, was Bishop Byler feeling better?" Despite not liking the idea of Henry spending more time around Priscilla, Joy cared deeply for the bishop and his family. He and Martha provided a great deal of support after the fire. Joy and her sisters couldn't ever repay them for all they'd done to help.

Sarah leaned closer to Joy. "Have you talked with Henry since the foot-washing service?"

Joy shook her head.

"Something's up. Henry took Priscilla home early that *nacht.*" Sarah raised her brows. "That would've given them two hours — alone," she muttered under her breath.

"I don't know that for sure."

Sarah shrugged. "He had to have been there when the bishop came home. How else would Henry know the bishop needed help with his firewood?"

"They're neighbors." Joy ignored Sarah's raised brows and spoke to Lois. "I made a new peppermint cookie. I might make them for the Second Christmas sleigh ride."

"Did you use extract?"

"That and I crushed some peppermint candies and sprinkled them on top."

161

"Sounds delicious." Lois glanced at the door as Matthew and their five-year-old son, Philip, stepped into the kitchen. She set the dish on the table and met them at the door. "You're wet," Lois said to her son as she helped him remove his coat. "Is it raining?"

Matthew hung his hat on the hook. "It just started." He went to the kitchen sink to wash. "The rain will bring more leaves down," he said to his wife.

"Better tonight than tomorrow. I want to do laundry in the morning." Lois made Philip sit so she could tug off his boots, then she nudged him toward the hallway. "Go wash so we can eat."

Joy wasn't able to read her brother-in-law's expression, but Lois was frowning. The harvest was over. Joy couldn't imagine why Matthew would be concerned about the leaves falling, or rain for that matter. Maybe it had something to do with the possibility of the rain turning into sleet.

Matthew dried his hands on a dish towel, then took his place at the table. "Did I hear you say something about peppermint cookies, Joy?"

"I made a batch the other day," she said, taking a seat next to Sarah. "But I didn't bring any home." Since Matthew found out he was diabetic, Joy tried to make sugar-substituted treats for them to eat at home.

"There are oatmeal cookies still in the jar."

"Nay, danki." Matthew bowed his head once Philip returned from washing up and everyone was seated at the table.

Joy's silent grace wasn't so much about the food as it was for direction concerning Henry.

Matthew carved the chicken. "How was business today?"

"About the same." Joy placed a spoonful of butter beans on her plate and passed the bowl to Sarah. As the only man in the family, her brother-in-law had become the financial overseer even though Joy and her sisters ran the bakery. He had only recently started inquiring about the daily operations. Before he only seemed interested in what repairs needed attention.

"Were there many tourists?"

"Not like last year." Joy glanced at Sarah. "Did you have many customers after I left?"

"A few. But I don't think you have to bake anything in the morning if that's what you want to know."

Joy baked every morning so the baked goods were always fresh. Although most days she didn't overbake, as she had every day since the foot-washing service. The conversation at the table muffled as her thoughts drifted back to Henry. She wanted to ask Lois more about seeing Henry at the Bylers', but would wait until they were alone.

Little Philip was the first to clean his plate. "Can we go back out to the barn?"

"In a few minutes," Matthew said. He glanced at Lois. "Bessie will probably deliver tonight."

"I get to help," Philip said. Every day that week, he had raced to the barn after school to see if the calf had arrived. The longer it took his father to finish eating, the more her nephew squirmed in his chair.

Matthew winked at his wife. He was probably teaching the child patience because everyone was finished when Matthew took another serving of butter beans.

Joy smiled at her nephew. One day she hoped to have a child just as eager to help deliver livestock.

Someone knocked on the door, and Lois stood. "I'll get it."

A moment later, Joy's pulse quickened at the sound of Henry's voice in the foyer. She padded out of the kitchen as he was asking if she was home.

Joy smiled. "Hello, Henry."

"Hi." He looked down at the floor the instant their eyes met. He shuffled his feet the same as the first time he'd come to court her.

Lois returned to the kitchen.

He motioned to the door. "Could we sit on the porch?"

"Sure." She grabbed her black cape and followed him outside. It wasn't raining hard, more like a drizzle, but the swing bench was wet. "Maybe we should go back inside."

"*Nay.* Let's just stand." He cleared his throat. "I'm *nett* staying long."

"Oh. I thought you might stay longer since we've hardly seen one another all week."

Still not looking her in the eye, he sighed. His shoulders lifted then fell. "I think I'd like to see other people." He looked at her a moment, then off into the darkness. "You're always at the bakery anyway."

She tried to inhale, but the weight of a boulder lodged in her chest. "When you say other people you mean Priscilla, don't you?" She closed her eyes when he didn't respond. "Are you saying you don't have feelings for me anymore?"

"I still do." His dark eyes met hers. "I'm confused." He looked away. "You've been preoccupied with the bakery so much lately."

"I've worked at the bakery for years, ever

since I was a young girl just learning how to bake."

"I know." He shuffled his feet. "But you changed after your parents died. You became consumed with the bakery."

"You said you understood. You said everyone handles grief differently. Don't you remember?" Her words wheezed out.

"Joy, I don't want to hurt you, but so much time has gone by . . . we don't even see much of each other anymore."

"Did Priscilla really hurt her ankle?"

"*Jah,* she could hardly put any weight on it."

She couldn't bring herself to ask if he was still at her house when her parents arrived home.

"I should probably leave. I have some deliveries to make for the hardware store early in the morning."

Joy stepped closer. Close enough that if he reached out his arms, she would be in them. But he didn't. Nor did he take her hand into his as he had multiple times in the past. Instead, he turned and trotted down the steps.

Her heart sank. He walked to his buggy without taking so much as one last glimpse over his shoulder.

■ ■ ■ ■

The following morning Joy prepared enough jelly-filled pastries to fill the bakery display case. She was cleaning the countertops when the bell above the door rang. Mrs. Yoder, one of her longtime customers, ambled into the store.

Joy set the rag down and sprang from behind the counter. "It's nice to see you today," she said, pulling out a chair for the elderly woman. "Did you enjoy your walk?"

"It didn't rain so I can't complain." Mrs. Yoder removed her winter bonnet and placed it on the table. "What do you suggest?"

"The pastries, muffins, and bread I made today." Joy pointed out the blueberry pastries on the left, the strawberry ones on the right, and the chocolate chip muffins on the second shelf. She gave Mrs. Yoder a few minutes to decide and poured a mug of coffee.

The woman eyed Joy. "I don't understand why you're *nett* married. *Mei* grandson needs a *fraa.*"

This wasn't one of Mrs. Yoder's lucid days. Her grandson married last wedding season. But anytime Joy corrected her, it seemed to confuse her more. Joy set the mug of steaming coffee on the table. "Be careful, this is hot."

"I'd sure like to see him marry before I die." She lifted the mug to her lips with shaky hands and took a sip. The woman's eyes held a twinkle.

"What else can I get for you?"

"What did you bake today?"

Joy listed everything again as though she hadn't already been asked. Once Mrs. Yoder made her selection, Joy placed the strawberry pastry on a dish and served it as Meredith entered the bakery.

Her friend eyed the display case. "I see you had another busy morning. You haven't talked with Henry yet, have you?"

Joy glanced at Mrs. Yoder, then waved Meredith around the register and into the kitchen area where they wouldn't be overheard. "He stopped by last evening."

"And?"

"He wants to court other women."

"What?"

Joy shrugged. "He's confused."

The doorbell jingled. Joy lifted up to her tiptoes and craned her neck toward the front of the store. Sarah. Her sister greeted the customer with a warm smile and eased behind the counter.

"Sarah's here. I'll tell you about Henry later."

"Maybe you can walk back to the Quilter's Corner with me *nau* that your sister is here."

"*Jah.* I have to go to the post office anyway."

Sarah slipped out of her cape as she entered the kitchen. She hung it on the wall peg. "So what do I need to know?" Her sister never sounded enthused about being at the bakery. Unlike Joy who loved sampling her own creations, Sarah avoided sweets and often complained that she smelled like a fudge brownie after working all day.

"I can't think of anything special," Joy said, removing her apron. "I shouldn't be long. I'm going after the mail." She removed her cape and bonnet from the hook and put them on. "Mrs. Yoder may like more *kaffi.* She'll probably try to fix you up with her grandson."

Meredith frowned. "Sometimes she comes into the Quilter's Corner and wants to buy material — for her husband."

"*Ach,* dear. He's been dead at least ten years."

Meredith nodded. "You can't tell her though. I did once and she practically chased me into the storage room. Wagging *mei* own scissors at me."

"That must have been a sight." Joy smiled, picturing the scene. She stepped outside, tying the ribbons under her chin. Normally the town buzzed with traffic this time of the year. Autumn always brought an influx of tourists and a nice spurt of business. But after yesterday's hard rain, the trees were bare and the pavement was littered with red and yellow leaves. Joy glanced up at the blue sky. "We won't have many more nice days like today before winter."

"You're probably right. The women at the quilt shop were complaining the other day about how poor tourism has been this fall."

Joy nodded. "It's been slower at the bakery too." They strolled along the sidewalk.

"So finish telling me about Henry."

"He said I work too much." She glanced at a storefront's window display of men's and women's shoes, then stared at the cracks in the sidewalk. "I think he might want to court Priscilla again."

Meredith sighed. "I wondered if that was why he gave her a ride home the other *nacht.*"

"I'm twenty-four and have probably lost *mei* only chance to marry." Joy gazed upward.

Meredith weaved her arm around Joy's elbow. "He's *nett* the only unmarried man in our district."

But Henry was the one Joy planned to marry. She steadied her focus on the hardware store a block ahead. Somehow she had to recapture his attention. She won him once by baking him cookies . . . *"Jah,"* she said, determination growing in her voice. "That's what I'll do."

"What are you talking about?"

Joy smiled. "I'll win him back."

They slowed their pace the closer they came to the hardware store, but Henry didn't come outside to greet them as he usually did.

"He's probably *nett* working today," Meredith said.

"He was chopping wood for the Bylers when I stopped by the store the other day with cookies. I wanted him to try the new peppermint ones. But I sent the box to *mei* cousin instead." They crossed the street and continued to the fabric store.

Her friend paused at the door. "Maybe we can get together later and sew."

"Jah, maybe." She really hoped to be sitting on the porch swing with Henry later.

"I'll *kumm* over after supper if I can," Meredith said over her shoulder before disappearing behind the bolts of fabric.

Joy walked two more blocks to the post office. The bakery didn't get much mail, flyers mostly. She sifted through the postcard advertisements, a restaurant supply catalog, and the monthly water bill. An envelope addressed to: COUSIN J. AT STOLZFUS BAKERY caught her eye.

CHAPTER THREE

Curious to find out what her cousin thought of the new batch of cookies, Joy tore open the envelope.

Dear Cousin J.,

This wasn't her cousin's handwriting. Emily's penmanship was nearly perfect and this chicken scratch was barely legible. Joy scanned to the bottom of the page.

Sincerely,
The man from the cabinet shop

Her stomach roiled. Why was this man writing to her? She read from the start.

I wanted to write to let you know that your box was delivered to me by mistake. You asked if the cookies were good. I confess, I greatly enjoyed them.

You could have used less peppermint

flavoring in the frosting, but I liked those the best. (The brownie was a close second.)

As for your dilemma with Henry, he isn't much of a *bu* if he left you at the service in order to drive another woman home. Maybe she did hurt her ankle, but why would he leave with her without telling you? Or asking you to ride along? Something else is going on. You sound like a nice girl — young and kind — but naïve.

I suggest you forget him. You'll only be wasting your time if you don't.

Sincerely,
The man from the cabinet shop

Joy snorted. Henry wasn't a waste of time. Her mind whirled with thoughts of what she planned to tell the man about his suggestion. She shoved the letter back into the envelope and marched toward the bakery. *Too much peppermint in the frosting . . .* She didn't know too many cabinet-making bakers or males who baked, for that matter. His letter was certainly slanted against women, calling her a nice but naïve girl.

Joy entered the bakery through the back door and slipped into the office. She pulled out the water bill, piled the junk mail into its designated area, then opened the top drawer and removed a piece of stationery and a pen.

October 16

Dear Cabinetmaker,
   Obviously, you don't have an ounce of decency. Don't you know it's poor manners to open a package that doesn't belong to you? You not only opened it, but you ate the contents and read the letter. What's more, you dole out advice as if you know me.
   I'm not some naïve nice girl wasting my time. Henry and I planned to marry more than a year ago. You, on the other hand, are so narrow-minded you probably have never been in love.

Sincerely,
J.S.

   As Joy copied the return address from his letter, she paused. North Fieldstone Drive. It made a little more sense. Her cousin lived on the south end. Still, he could have given the package back to the mail carrier. She finished addressing the envelope. In a rush to send off her response, she sped out the door without checking on Sarah.

Her heart fluttered as she approached the hardware store. Henry was placing a close-out sign on the rack of rakes and hoes.

"Getting ready for winter already?" She eyed the snow shovel rack next to the garden tools.

"It'll be snowing before long. I heard we might get freezing rain tonight."

Joy glanced at the sky. Cloudless and blue, it hadn't changed since her walk to the post office earlier. "Christmas is only a couple of months away. I'm looking forward to the sleigh ride . . . are you?"

He shrugged. "I suppose."

"I made some new cookies that I'm thinking about serving — on Second Christmas. They're peppermint."

"That's nice." He rearranged shovels, placing a smaller one in front of the larger one.

"I brought some by the other day for you to sample, but . . . you weren't working." *Here anyway.*

"Peppermint sounds interesting."

A flutter filled her chest. "I might make another batch on Monday." She would've suggested tomorrow, but Friday was his normal day off. Saturdays he spent making special deliveries, and since this wasn't their service Sunday, she didn't expect him to spend the day visiting her when he said the other night he wanted to court other women. "Would you like to try them?"

"You shouldn't go to all that trouble for me." He rearranged more shovels according to size.

"It isn't trouble." She wrung her hands. "You know how much I like to bake."

"*Jah,* I'm aware of that," he said dryly.

Dead space lingered between them.

He moved toward the door. "I better get back to work."

"*Jah,* I have errands to run." She meandered down the sidewalk and peeked at the department store's fall clothing display for women's fashions. The fancy sweaters and coats were nothing she would wear. She was merely loitering. Many times after saying good-bye in the past, Henry would run down the block to catch her and ask if he could see her later that night.

Waste of time . . . The cabinetmaker's words echoed in her mind. She lifted her chin and proceeded to the post office.

Joy tied a knot in the thread once she completed the last stitch of the block. Working under the flicker of lamplight strained her eyes. She preferred window light, but she'd promised Meredith she would help make a lap quilt. One of Meredith's jobs at the Quilter's Corner was to display on the wall the new fabrics and patterns for the upcoming season. The *Engischers* bought more material when they had a visual to follow, or at least that was what the store owner had told Meredith.

"I ran into Henry," Joy said. "He was putting a sale sign on a sidewalk display."

"What did he say?" She snipped her thread.

"*Nett* much. I did most of the talking, mostly about cookies I plan to make for the Second Christmas sleigh ride and the get-together." Joy sandwiched a piece of batting between two blue squares of material.

"He already thinks you work too much. Why did you talk about baking?"

"I thought maybe he would understand why I enjoy creating new recipes." Joy pushed the needle through the material and it poked her finger. "Ouch." She shook her hand. "He's sampled all the desserts and helped me pick which ones to serve with hot cocoa since we started courting." She studied her stitches. "Besides, I thought if I could get him thinking about Christmas, he would remember the first time he held *mei* hand. I offered to make more peppermint cookies for him to try . . . He was indifferent."

"I hope you're *nett* wasting your time."

"Henry isn't a waste of time. Everyone thinks he's a waste of time. People who don't even know him — or me."

"I'm sorry. I meant wasting your time baking for him." Meredith's brows crinkled. "What do you mean, people who don't know you or him? I know both of you."

Joy groaned under her breath. "The other day I mailed a package of cookies to *mei* cousin, but I found out someone else received them."

"What does that have to do with Henry?"

"I sent a letter in that package."

"And . . . ?"

Joy set her sewing aside and stood. "I'll let you read the response he sent." She crossed the room to where her handbag hung on the wall hook and pulled out the envelope. She glanced toward the sitting room where Lois was sitting by the window reading. Joy hadn't told anyone else about the package mix-up. She removed the letter from the envelope and handed it to her friend.

"Cousin J.?" Meredith looked up at her.

"That's how I signed *mei* letter to Emily."

Her friend resumed reading, then smiled. "You're upset about the peppermint com-

179

ment, aren't you?"

"I'm upset that a stranger read *mei* letter. I poured my heart out only to discover Emily never received it."

"I wonder what the cabinetmaker's name is."

"Who cares?"

Meredith wiggled in her seat. "You're *nett* even a little curious?"

"*Nay,* I'm annoyed. And I told him so."

Her friend's eyes widened. "You wrote back to him?"

"Only to point out how rude he was."

Meredith handed Joy the letter. "I think it's intriguing."

"You can't be serious." Joy paused to calm her rising voice. She leaned back in her chair and glanced at Lois in the sitting room. Then she leaned closer and whispered, "The return address on the envelope is a cabinet shop. I'm sure every man in the building read *mei* letter."

"At least it's in another town."

Maybe so, but ten miles away wasn't far enough.

Noah read the letter a second time. The woman's feathers were as ruffled as a hen in the butcher's hand. Perhaps writing to her hadn't been a good idea. He tossed the let-

180

ter on the shop table, picked up a screwdriver, and tightened the hinge on the cabinet door. Mrs. Dowker expected delivery of her kitchen cabinets today, which meant he had to stop thinking about his pen pal and finish attaching the door hinges and knobs.

But redirecting his thoughts was impossible. The woman's accusations pelted his subconscious like a round of buckshot pellets. Poor mannered, narrow-minded . . .

The shop door opened and his younger sister, Stella, entered. "I just spoke with an *Englischer* who wants an estimate on cabinets for her business." Stella handed him a piece of paper. "It's a motel."

"Did you show her the board with the wood samples?"

"*Jah,* I wrote down the ones she wants quotes on."

"*Danki.*" He glanced at the information. Scenic Hill Motel was at least fifteen miles away. "What day did you tell her I'd be by to take measurements and give her a quote?"

"Monday."

"Okay." He liked that his business was expanding, but to the next county? Traveling fifteen miles by buggy would take two hours one-way. By the time he arrived, gathered measurements, and drove home, he wouldn't have much time to do anything else.

Stella eyed the cabinets. "The fancy stained glass sure is pretty. Mrs. Dowker will be pleased."

"I hope so." He stepped back and admired the way the glass gleamed from the morning sun filtering through the window.

"*Mamm* wanted me to ask you to pick up flour when you go into town. We're going to make an apple pie."

"*Jah,* sure." He preferred blackberry, but he'd be crazy to pass up any pie his mom made. His mouth watered as he lined up the next hinge. He turned the screw into the wood and paused. "Do you think I'm narrow-minded?" The moment her brows lifted, he wished he hadn't asked. He waved his hand dismissively. "Never mind."

"To answer your question," she said, walking to the door, "*jah,* you are."

That was Stella — always agreeable with regard to his flaws. Noah tightened the screw into place.

"I heard Ruby is coming home. Her sister received a letter from her the other day."

"She must have run out of money," he said without looking up from his work.

"Are you going to see her?"

"You said yourself I'm narrow-minded. *Nau* stop interrogating me. I need to get *mei* work done."

Joy whipped the red frosting into a creamy consistency, then dipped her pinky into the bowl for a sample. Perfect. She didn't know why the man's comment about too much peppermint bothered her, but ever since she received his unwanted evaluation, she hadn't been able to erase it from her mind.

She spread a thick layer of icing over each cookie and spaced them out on the parchment paper. Now that the ones she'd baked for Henry were finished, she could get started on the list of items she needed to bake for the customers. Mondays were always busy. In addition to the regular bread orders, the display cabinet needed restocking. On Saturdays she brought everything home for the meal after church or to serve to visitors on no-service Sundays, like yesterday. Only, the visitor she had wanted to serve cookies to never arrived. She tried all afternoon to dismiss thoughts that Henry was probably sitting on Priscilla's porch swing.

Joy hurried and mixed a double batch of bread dough, then set the loaf pans near the oven so the dough would rise faster. Meanwhile, she made a trayful of pumpkin whoopee pies, fried several dozen doughnuts, and prepared a pot of coffee before the first customer arrived. Joy was ready to sit down and rest a few moments, but instead she flipped the sign in the front window to Open and unlocked the glass door.

An hour passed before the first customer arrived. The *Englischer* made his doughnut selections quickly, his thumbs working a cell phone at the same time. Joy boxed up the order. The man was so preoccupied that she had to announce the total twice before he dug into his back pocket for his wallet.

Not long after the man left, Mrs. Yoder came in for a muffin and coffee. She brought up her grandson needing a wife again, and Joy said a silent prayer for the woman's mind. The remainder of the morning crawled by. She had the kitchen spotless and the cookies for Henry boxed when Sarah rushed in the back door.

"I won't be able to work today. Abram's *mamm* asked if I would help with canning." Her sister set the mail on the counter and sashayed from the kitchen into the store.

Joy clenched her jaw.

"You don't mind, do you?" Sarah reached under the counter for a pastry box, assembled it, and then filled the container with an assortment of doughnuts.

Her sister shirked responsibility every chance she could when it came to the bakery and dumped the work on Joy. Now she wouldn't be able to deliver the cookies to Henry. Just once, she wished she could put her foot down with her sister. But forcing Sarah to work at the bakery was like forcing cement through a pastry bag.

"Fine." Joy motioned to the door. "Go. Have a *gut* time."

Sarah poured coffee into a to-go cup and capped it. *"Danki,"* she said, adding, "You're the best sister."

The easiest to push work off on, you mean. Joy grabbed the mail off the counter and plopped down on a stool. Sorting the mail, she stopped on the envelope addressed to "J."

Chapter Four

October 20

Dear J.,

Maybe I do have poor manners. As you pointed out, the cookies weren't mine to eat. But I like to think of myself as practical. The cookies would have gone stale waiting for the postman to figure out the smeared ink on the mangled box. Next time you send a package, you may want to use more tape.

As for labeling me a man who is narrow-minded, you're probably right. But I spoke the truth as I saw it (from a narrow-minded man's perspective). Have you ever heard of someone looking through rose-colored glasses? Everything looks pretty — even when it's distorted. I'm sorry to say that was how you sounded in your letter.

You seem to have taken offense to the

advice I "doled" out. But after reading your TEN-page letter, how could I not know you? Are you as chatty in person? You're hurt, and understandably so. But maybe Henry's lack of commitment after a year should have been a clue. Even so, is your life really in shambles, as you say? I know you don't want to hear any more of my advice . . . but I'm giving it anyway. You can choose not to follow it. Love isn't something you can hold in a vice grip. Releasing your hold is the only way you'll know if it's meant to be — and if it returns — well, praise God. Otherwise, dry your tears.

I probably shouldn't have said what I did in the last letter. I just got the impression you might be a pushover. Before your feathers ruffle, know that I don't mean that as an insult. Just the opposite. I like your ability to trust. It's a good quality.

Sincerely,
Cabinetmaker

P.S. If you care to correspond again, would you please send more of those peppermint cookies?

Joy cringed. Thinking back, she realized

her letter to Emily probably did sound like a crazy woman's ramblings. She was angry, hurt, and yes — at that moment — her life was in shambles. She reread the letter. The cabinetmaker knew too much about her. He was right about her being a pushover, too, especially when it came to Sarah. But she was not wearing rose-colored glasses.

Joy poured a mug of coffee, then sat down with pen and paper.

Dear Cabinetmaker,
My eyesight is perfect. I've never worn glasses — even the rose-colored ones you spoke of.

The bell over the door jingled. Meredith shuffled inside and plopped down on a chair opposite Joy. "It's getting colder out."

Joy shoved the letter aside and stood. "I'll pour you some *kaffi.*"

"Where are all the customers?"

"It's been like this all day." Joy filled the mug and carried it to the table. "I'm *nett* complaining. I've been here since four a.m. and if it stays like this I might close early."

"Where's Sarah this time?"

"Canning with Abram's *mamm.*"

Meredith leveled a teaspoonful of sugar and stirred it into her coffee. "Have you thought about hiring someone else?"

Joy shook her head. "This has always been a family business. *Mei mamm* loved the bakery. She taught me everything I know." Joy ran her finger around the rim of the mug.

"So what are you working on?" Her friend eyed the pen and paper.

"It's just a letter." Joy's face heated.

"Then why are you blushing?" Meredith smiled. "It's from him, isn't it? From Mr. Too-much-peppermint-in-the-frosting Man, *jah*?"

Joy nodded. "It came today."

"Don't leave me guessing. What did he say?"

Before she could answer, a customer entered the shop. Joy slid the letter across the table to Meredith and stood. She took her position behind the counter and, waiting for the woman and young child to make their selections, kept her eye on Meredith's growing smile.

"We'll take two of the pumpkin whoopee pies," the woman said.

Joy placed the items in a small pastry box, then thanked the customer as she handed back her change. Once she and Meredith were alone again, Joy hurried back to the table.

"He seems to know a lot about you," Meredith said.

"*Jah,* thanks to *mei* long-winded rant to *mei* cousin."

Her friend chuckled. "Ten pages, according to Peppermint Man."

Joy rubbed her forehead. "I don't even remember what I said in that letter." She shook her head. "I still can't believe he read it."

"So are you going to send him more cookies?"

"I may, just to prove *mei* peppermint cookies are *gut.*" She cracked a smile. "I made a batch this morning, but those are for Henry." She glanced up at the door as it opened again. Joy stood and shoved the empty chair back under the table. "Hello, Henry."

Meredith brushed past them to the door. "I'll talk with you later," she said, leaving.

Henry slid his straw hat off and smoothed his hand over his chestnut hair. "I was hoping you would have a few minutes to talk."

Noah spotted the Scenic Hill Motel once he rounded the bend on Old Route 39 a few miles outside of Sugarcreek. With so much rain this year, a vast majority of the leaves had already fallen, and the rolling hills were not as vibrant with color. He pulled into the motel's driveway. The sign out front read: CLOSED FOR REMODELING. He didn't think anyone would need the handicapped parking, and since there was no buggy post, he tied Cracker to the parking sign pole.

A woman met him as he stepped into the office. She looked over the pink rims of her glasses and smiled. "I'm Samantha Paddock." The salt-and-pepper-haired woman extended her hand and shook his firmly. "You must be from the cabinet shop."

"*Jah,* I'm Noah Esh." He scanned the empty room. The walls were bare, the floors stripped down to the cement, and a makeshift table held a coffeepot and phone.

"Well, as you can see, we're under construction." Hammers pounded in an adjoining room. "The area I want to put cabinets is in this room." She led the way into a larger room where several workers were hanging drywall. "The last owners used this area for their living quarters, but I want to create a sitting and breakfast area." She pointed to the far wall. "I'd like lower cabinets to line the entire wall." She leveled her hand a little higher than her waist. "And higher than standard."

"That won't be a problem. Are you putting in a sink?"

"Yes, that will go on the end."

"What about upper cabinets?"

"I was thinking stained glass. Maybe a horse-and-buggy design. I want to incorporate some of the Amish lifestyle in the remodel since the majority of our guests will be interested in Amish farmland tours and sightseeing."

He forced a smile. Many of the *Englischers* in the area took advantage of the Amish living in the region to promote their businesses. He just hadn't come across any who were so blatant about their intentions.

"I can do stained glass, but I'm not an artist. I've never attempted anything so elaborate."

"Hmm . . ." She chewed her bottom lip.

"Maybe you should contact some of the other cabinetmakers in the area."

She shook her head. "That's how I got your name. You're the only one who does stained glass in the area. I suppose I could order it online, but that would defeat having everything done locally. And I'm putting a lot of money into this remodel for that purpose."

"Perhaps I could look for a template. If I had a pattern to follow, I could probably come up with something." He liked a challenge, and he didn't have any major projects lined up at the moment, so he could use the money. But creating a horse and buggy out of glass might be impossible.

Joy's hands turned clammy the moment Henry pulled off his hat and clutched it against his chest. "I made you some cookies earlier. I'll get them." She rushed into the kitchen, needing a moment to settle her galloping heart rate. She swiped the box off the counter and returned. "These are the new peppermint ones I told you about," she said, opening the flap. "I'm thinking about serving them after the sleigh ride. You know how I like to make —"

"Joy."

She swallowed hard.

"Are you always going to put the bakery first?"

She glanced at the open box of cookies. "I thought you might like to try one *nau* is all."

"I bought a piece of property today. I plan to build a *haus* in the spring." He looked down for a moment, then lifted his eyes to meet hers. "I think you know how I feel. I don't want *mei fraa* working outside the home."

Is that his way of proposing?

"I need to know if you can give up your job."

She cleared her throat. "It's more than just a job." Had Henry forgotten what the bakery meant to her? She had shared with him before how it made her feel close to her parents. How could he expect her to give up the place that kept her parents' memories alive? The fire had destroyed their family home. The bakery was all she had.

"That's what I thought." He turned from the counter and walked toward the door.

"Wait." She chased him to the door with the box of cookies. "Would you like to take these with you?"

He shook his head, then pulled the door open and tromped out.

Joy gazed around the room, her vision blurred. *Lord, I thought if Henry tasted one, he would remember how much baking means to me.*

CHAPTER FIVE

"His proposal was conditional." Joy picked up a bolt of fabric and followed Meredith down the flannel material aisle. "He doesn't want his *fraa* working. *Nett* even at *mei* family bakery."

"What did you tell him?"

"I tried to explain how it was more than a job. He didn't listen." She lowered the bolt of fabric next to where Meredith placed hers.

"I thought you wanted to win him back." Meredith removed a pen from above her ear, jotted the yardage on a pad of paper, then tucked the pen back into her *kapp*.

"I thought I did too." She followed Meredith to the cutting table. "He said I've changed and I'm sure I have, but so has he. He never discouraged me before about working. He used to love everything I baked." She lowered her head and stared at the metal yardstick attached to the cutting

195

table. "He didn't want any of the cookies I made him. I guess that should tell me something."

"You know who does want them." Meredith elbowed Joy's side. "You should mail them to the Peppermint Man."

"At least they wouldn't go to waste," Joy muttered.

"Do it."

"I was joking."

Meredith pulled the pen from behind her ear and handed it to Joy. "You have his address, right?"

"*Jah,* it's in *mei* handbag."

Her friend nudged the handbag draped over Joy's shoulder. "If nothing else, you'll feel better once they're out of sight." Meredith nodded. "You will. If you keep them, they'll only remind you of Henry."

A customer entered the shop and Meredith crossed the store to greet the woman.

Maybe her friend was right. She didn't want the blaring reminder of Henry's lack of interest, and if she took the cookies home, her brother-in-law might eat them and that wouldn't be good for his diabetes.

Joy removed the envelope and the note she had started from her handbag. She slipped the note inside and addressed the box. She chuckled while wrapping the box with clear packaging tape. This time he couldn't complain about her not using enough tape.

Another customer entered the shop. The man's gaze scanned the room. Studying the quilts hanging on the wall, he nearly stumbled over the braided rug on the floor. Joy pretended not to notice. She looked toward the back room, hoping to get Meredith's attention.

"Excuse me," the man said.

Joy turned.

He stared at her a second as if he'd forgotten what he'd wanted. "I was wondering if you could help me."

"I can try." She studied him a moment. Dark, wavy hair flipped out from under his hat. He rubbed his clean-shaven jaw and looked again at the wall hangings.

"How do you *kumm* up with your designs?" He pointed to a wall hanging of a quilted peacock.

"I'll find out for you." Joy lifted to her toes and spotted Meredith helping a customer near the shelved bolts of cotton fabrics. She approached the two women. "Excuse me," she said. "There's a man wondering about the bird quilt on the wall. He's interested in the pattern."

"Patterns in general," he said, coming up

beside Joy. "I'm *nett* really interested in the bird."

"Most of them are on a rack near the pegboard of thread," Meredith said. "There are some over by the quilting magazines too. Do you mind showing him?"

"Sure." Joy led him over to the larger section first. "What are you thinking about sewing? Maybe I can help you."

"Nothing." He pulled one pattern off the rack, turned it over, then returned it. "I'm looking for a horse-and-buggy pattern."

"What size?"

"I don't know." He rubbed the back of his neck. "I guess about so." He stretched out his arms.

She smiled. "The size of a place mat."

"Even a potholder would do." He continued searching.

The man certainly appeared to be in a hurry. Either that or he was very uncomfortable in a fabric store. He was probably the first male customer since the store opened five years ago. She glimpsed his profile. Tall. Midtwenties. He wasn't from Sugarcreek. She would have recognized him from Sunday services or as someone she had gone to school with.

"I don't see anything that could work," he said. "Do you?"

"I, uh . . ." She shouldn't have been staring. Now her cheeks heated as though she were in front of a roaring woodstove. "I'll check by the magazines."

"Having any luck?" Meredith called out from the cutting table.

"*Nett* yet." Joy glanced at the man. "Sorry. I don't see any here either."

"*Danki* for your help."

He turned to leave when Meredith said, "If you give me a minute, I'll look through our catalogs. There might be a pattern we can order."

"Okay." He circled the perimeter of the room, gazed at the quilts on display, and probably wished he hadn't agreed to wait when it didn't seem like the customer Meredith was helping would leave.

Once Meredith rang up the customer's purchase, she retrieved several thick catalogs from behind the desk. "What pattern were you looking for?"

"A horse and buggy," he said.

Meredith flipped the pages.

The man leaned against the counter and practically twisted sideways to eye something. After following his line of vision to the pastry box, Joy cleared her throat.

He motioned to the box. "I live in Berlin. *Nett* far from the cabinet shop," he said. "I could deliver that for you."

Meredith looked up from the catalog and smiled.

Joy shook her head. "That —"

"That's very kind of you." Meredith set the book aside and swiped the box off the counter before Joy did, then handed it to him.

"Would it be easier if I stop back tomorrow to see if you were able to find a pattern?"

"If it isn't too much of a bother," Meredith said. "That would give me time to look through them all. Otherwise you might be here for a while yet."

"Then I'll see you tomorrow." He smiled and tapped the box. "And I'll be sure to get this into the right hands." He strode to the door.

Joy groaned under her breath as the man left the shop. "I wish you hadn't done that."

"I just saved you postage, and the hassle of having to mail it."

"I go to the post office every day. Besides, I wasn't even sure I was going to send it."

Meredith smiled. "You don't have to worry about that *nau.*"

"*Jah,* you practically thrust it at the man."

"I didn't force him. He offered."

Joy scurried to the front window. The man

200

was just getting into his buggy. She still had time to stop him.

Noah set the pastry box on the bench beside him. Noticing the package addressed to his cabinet shop was a pleasant surprise. He wasn't sure if he would hear from the woman again.

Noah's mouth watered. He grabbed the white box, but it was taped in such a way that he couldn't pry it open. She'd gone overboard with the tape this time. He reached under the bench for his jackknife and had the box open before pulling away from the fabric store.

Noah took a bite of the peppermint cookie and chewed it slowly, allowing the sweetness to melt in his mouth. And she enclosed a note. He wished he knew which of the two women was his new pen pal.

The dark-haired woman who handed him the box or the woman with ivory skin and wheat-colored hair who helped him sift through the rack of patterns. He wouldn't expect a baker to be petite, having to work around sweets like these, especially since she'd mentioned in the first letter how she'd eaten so many that they all tasted the same. Then again, the dark-haired woman seemed to know more about the fabric store.

As he pulled away from the store, he unfolded the note.

My eyesight is perfect. I've never worn glasses — not even the rose-colored ones you spoke of.

Short and to the point. Maybe she wasn't as chatty as he first thought. He selected another cookie. Tomorrow he would make sure he made it to the bakery before they closed.

CHAPTER SIX

The following morning as Noah stepped into the Stolzfus Bakery, the scent of cinnamon awakened his senses. Even though he'd eaten a large breakfast, his stomach still rumbled. He scanned the room. Empty tables. Either the morning rush was over, or a recent mishap with — he took another whiff — burnt cinnamon had driven the customers away.

A woman, squatting behind the glass display case, was busy filling the shelf with pastries.

He bent down. She wasn't the one who handed him the cookies yesterday.

"I'll be with you in —" Her eyes met his through the glass. She stood, set the empty pan on the counter, then wiped her hands on her apron. "Can I help you?"

He stared at the flour dust on her forehead.

She cleared her throat.

"I, uh . . ." Noah couldn't recall the last time he was tongue-tied. He redirected his attention to the glass case and peered at the baked goods. "I thought I smelled cinnamon."

The bell sounded over the door and a woman entered. "Joy, I think something's burning."

"*Mei* cinnamon rolls!" Joy turned on her heel and sped into the kitchen with the other woman following.

Noah leaned over the counter. He didn't see any billowing smoke, but the foul scent and the sound of clanging pans caused alarm. "Do you need the fire department?"

"*Nay, danki.* Everything is fine." Her voice sounded rushed.

He eased behind the counter and poked his head into the kitchen. "Is there anything I can — ?"

The charred substance stuck to the cookie sheet smoked when Joy held it under the running faucet. She fanned the smoke away from her face and coughed. "Will you help the man out front, please?"

"I'm *nett* in a hurry." Noah wanted to wait for her. What did the other woman call her, Joy?

But the younger woman motioned for him to follow her out of the kitchen. "*Mei* sister's going to be detained. May I help you?"

"I thought I might try a cinnamon roll until I saw them smoking." He glanced over his shoulder at Joy scrubbing the pan.

The younger sister laughed. "*Jah,* they're under water *nau.* What else can I get for you?"

"Do you have any of the peppermint frosted cookies?" He returned to the customer's side of the counter.

"Do we have those?" Her brows creased as she searched the display shelves.

"The ones yesterday had chunks of candy on them." He looked, too, but didn't see any.

"Let me check in the kitchen."

He strained to listen but couldn't decipher the mumbling. A moment later, Joy came out from the kitchen, her balled hands resting on her hips. "You requested the peppermint cookies?"

"*Jah.*"

"The ones with crushed candy on the frosting?" Her eyes narrowed.

He nodded. "You sent a box to —"

"I know who I sent it to," she growled under her breath. "So he shared them with you."

He smiled. "Is there something wrong with that?" Even with a stern expression, she was still cute. He dug his hand into his coat pocket and pulled out an envelope. "This is for you."

Her cheeks blushed. She looked over her shoulder before taking the letter, then quickly folded the envelope in half.

"Aren't you going to read it?"

"Nay!"

"The cookies were *gut,*" he said, trying to soften her up.

"Danki." She stared at the envelope. "How well do you know him?"

More than he dared to admit at the moment. She might chase him out of the bakery with a cookie cutter if he admitted to receiving her mixed-up mail. Noah shrugged. "He builds cabinets."

"That much I had figured out. You must know him fairly well if he opened the box and offered you a cookie."

He peered into the glass display. "I was hoping you had more today. But I don't see any."

"Those were a new Christmas cookie."

He grinned. "Well, I hope I don't have to wait until Christmas before I have another one."

She opened her mouth but closed it when her sister sprang from the kitchen. Humming softly, the younger sister went to the

206

coffeepot. "*Ach,* I didn't think we still had a customer." She filled a cup with coffee. "I'll ring him up, Joy. You can go."

"*Jah, danki.* I have a few errands to run." She turned without making eye contact with him and scooted into the kitchen.

The younger woman approached the display. "Did you decide on anything?"

He pointed to a strawberry pastry. "I'll take one of those, please." As she stuffed the treat into a paper bag, he turned and glanced out the front window. Seeing Joy walk past the window, he tossed a few dollar bills on the counter and grabbed the bag.

"Don't you want your change?"

"Keep it." He sped out the door. "Joy." He jogged up to her.

She stashed the letter she'd been reading up her dress sleeve. "How-how do you know *mei* name?"

"In the bakery. Your sister just — I'm sorry. Did I frighten you?"

"I'm *nett* used to customers following me."

He motioned toward the fabric store a couple of blocks ahead. "I was supposed to check today if the fabric store has a horse-and-buggy pattern. Remember?" He eyed her hand clutching the wristband on her dress. "So are you two pen pals *nau*?"

207

"By accident," she muttered. Her blue eyes widened. "Why do you ask?"

He shrugged. "I thought it was nice that you made him Christmas cookies. And you seemed interested in the letter."

Her cheeks flushed. She started to walk. Fast. "Please tell me he's Amish."

"He is." Noah kept pace.

They reached the curb and stopped. She peered up at the traffic light. "How old is he?"

"*Mei* age." He liked that she showed interest. "How old are you?"

She eyed him sharply. "I don't tell strangers *mei* age."

"Sorry." He should've known women were sensitive about their age if they were in their midtwenties and still unmarried. "You've asked about him. What would you like me to say about you?"

"Nothing."

They waited for a pickup truck to pass through the intersection and then crossed the street together. He couldn't remember feeling this awkward around a woman before. "You must *nett* have been a baker long."

She stopped. "Why do you say that?"

"You're *nett* —"

She narrowed her blue eyes.

208

"You're *nett* as big as . . ."

Her jaw dropped.

"I mean — well, you work around sweets all day." *This isn't going well.* "So how long have you been a baker?"

She stared a moment longer, then finally said, "*Mei* parents bought the bakery ten years ago, but I suppose I've been baking since I was old enough to stand on a stool next to *mei mamm* and stir cake batter."

"A family business. That's nice."

Her steps paused, but instead of directing her attention to him, she faced the building.

Now what did he say wrong? It occurred to him then how in one of her letters she mentioned her parents were deceased. He opened his mouth to apologize, but her interest was elsewhere.

She rose to her tiptoes and peered into the front window of the hardware store. Her expression sobered, and she dropped back down and continued walking. "I'm sorry. Did you say something?"

He shook his head. *Nothing important.* He glanced over his shoulder. Gingrich Hardware. Not the typical store where a woman would window-shop, but something in her expression conveyed it wasn't merchandise she was looking for.

■ ■ ■ ■

Joy increased her pace. This man walking beside her asked too many questions. He probably thought she hadn't figured out that he was interviewing her on the cabinet-maker's behalf. She'd already said more than she wished, especially since she didn't even know the man's name. He liked peppermint cookies and wanted to buy a pattern of a horse and buggy. What was she doing walking with a stranger? A shudder went through her.

"Are you *kalt*?"

"Nay." Even if she were, she wouldn't have admitted it. What would he do? Offer her his coat? Once they reached the fabric store, she stopped. "Well, good luck with finding your pattern."

"You're *nett* going in?"

Joy shook her head. "I have to pick up supplies at the dry goods store." Why was she making up excuses?

"Danki for allowing me to walk with you." He reached for the door handle.

Joy nodded, then continued on her route. A few feet away, she retrieved the crumpled letter.

Dear J.,

You didn't say much in your letter. Did I hurt your feelings about the rose-colored glasses?

"Joy?" the friendly man called.

She wadded up the paper and turned slowly to face him. "*Jah?*"

He glanced at her hand and grinned. "If you're going to make cinnamon rolls tomorrow, will you set a dozen aside for me to buy?"

"Sure."

He grinned. "I'll let you get back to reading your letter."

Thankfully he turned before the heat crawling up her neck reached her face.

"Don't keep saying the bakery's in trouble." Joy looked to her older sister to challenge Matthew's statement, but Lois merely nodded with her husband.

"You can't say that you didn't see this coming." Matthew folded his hands and rested them on the table. "We didn't get the fall tourism like we needed. The early rain stripped the trees of their leaves and no one goes on scenic tours when there's nothing to see. I'm sorry. I know how much the bakery means to you, Joy."

"*Nett* just me." She stared at Lois. "This is all we have left of *Mamm* and *Daed.* The fire took everything else."

"They wouldn't want it to become a burden," Lois said.

"A burden! That's *nett* how I see it and I'm at the bakery more hours than everyone." Of course, she hadn't had a paycheck in a year. Perhaps her living with her sister and brother-in-law had become burdensome for them. "Are you upset that Sarah and I are living here and we haven't been able to help you financially?"

"*Nay,*" Matthew said.

"I know having us here must be imposing. You've supported us and bought feed for our horses. I'll pay you back as soon as I can."

"Joy." Lois reached across the table and clasped Joy's hands. "We love having you and Sarah here. But it doesn't change the fact that the bakery isn't making a profit."

"Does Sarah know?"

Lois glanced at her husband, then back to Joy. "We wanted to tell you first."

"We have to be open for the sleigh ride. *Mamm* and *Daed* started the Second Christmas tradition. Everyone in the district makes plans to attend."

Matthew sighed. "It might *nett* be possible."

"I'll figure out things to cut. We don't need to carry the specialty desserts. The ones with pecans . . ." Joy mentally compiled a list. Dates were expensive; she wouldn't reorder them either.

"I don't think that will be enough." Matthew frowned.

"I'll sell more bread."

"You can sell bread even if the bakery closes," he said. "Bake it here."

Apparently the decision had already been made. Tears spilled down Joy's cheeks as she closed her eyes. *Lord, please don't let this happen. Please.*

CHAPTER SEVEN

Joy made a quick inventory of the bakery's supplies the following morning. She had plenty of staples: flour, sugar, butter, and eggs. At least this week she could avoid the market, maybe even next week. If she reduced the batch sizes and was careful not to burn anything, they could put off closing the shop a bit longer. Maybe even for good.

God, will You please send us more customers? As though God prompted her memory, the order for a dozen cinnamon rolls came to mind. She'd mixed the ingredients earlier, so the dough should have had enough time to rise. Joy hoped the man would remember his order. The last thing she wanted was a display cabinet full of unsold rolls.

Once the pan was in the oven, she set the timer. She wouldn't chance a distraction that could cause her to forget. Joy leaned against the counter. It seemed odd not having more to make. Usually as one batch baked, she prepared the next. She grabbed the broom and swept the floor before the timer dinged. Joy removed the rolls from the oven, drizzled them with frosting, and placed them in a box once they cooled.

Hours later, she drummed her fingernails on the counter. *Lord, would You please remind the man about the order he placed? And would You remind Sarah that she's late? Again.* Joy tapped the counter faster. Sarah certainly wasn't upset last night when Lois brought up the possibility of closing the bakery. Joy half-expected her sister to stroll in any moment and announce she'd made other plans for the day.

Joy wandered out of the kitchen. She scanned the display cabinet. If the man didn't pick up his order, she could squeeze them in on the bottom shelf. They probably wouldn't all sell before turning stale. She checked the coffee level in the pot, then sat down at one of the tables with a piece of paper and pen. Without customers to wait on, she had time to write a letter.

Dear Cabinetmaker,

I can't believe I'm admitting this to you, but you were right. My vision isn't as clear as I had thought (long story so I'll spare you having to listen to me ramble). As you said in one of your letters, I'm a pushover. My sister doesn't think anything about coming into work late. She's more interested in securing a marriage proposal than the bakery's success. I'm the only one who cares if it stays open.

I'm sorry. You don't need to hear my problems. But the next time I take an advance order for a dozen cinnamon rolls, I'm asking for the money up front. Well, maybe not — after all, I am a pushover.

The bell over the door jingled and Joy looked up.

"Gut mariye." The handsome man smiled.

"Hello." Joy folded the letter, stuffed it into an envelope, and stood. "I have the rolls you ordered in the back. I'll get them." Taking the letter with her, she went into the kitchen. She set the envelope on the counter and grabbed the pastry box.

"Your morning rush is over, I take it?"

Joy shook her head. "You're *mei* first customer." She placed the box on the counter. "Can I get you anything else?"

"Nett unless you have an idea for a stained glass window design that doesn't involve a horse and buggy."

"So that was why you were looking for a pattern?" She smiled. "I suppose you don't look like a quilter."

"*Danki.*" His cheeks turned a dark beet shade.

"I'm sorry. I didn't mean to embarrass you."

He shrugged. "Why do you think I drove over to another town? I wasn't going to risk one of *mei* friends seeing me enter a fabric store."

"Oh, that would be traumatizing." She chuckled.

"You have no idea."

She sobered and stood taller. "Your secret is safe with me."

He smiled.

"Besides, it wouldn't be much fun to gossip about you since I don't know your name."

"I'm Noah. But I'm still holding you to our secret."

She removed the order slip from the side of the box. "Since you're the best customer I've had all morning, I guess I will." If this was her only sale today, she dreaded having to give the report to Matthew at the supper table tonight. Now that she knew why he was so curious about sales, it made seeing empty tables stressful.

The bell dinged and Sarah poked her head in. "Just wanted to let you know I won't be able to work today." She ducked out.

"It figures," Joy muttered.

Noah's brows lifted.

"I should be used to it. *Mei* sister isn't . . . interested in smelling like a brownie."

"I don't know why *nett.* I'm rather fond of the scent." He motioned to the box next to the register. "I hope *mei Englisch* customer is drawn to the scent of cinnamon rolls. Maybe eating one will help when I tell her about *nett* finding a horse-and-buggy pattern."

"She wants something Amish?"

"According to her, the entire motel is being remodeled to attract tourists seeking a glimpse of our Amish way."

More visitors in the area might increase the bakery sales. Providing the bakery stayed open. She rang up his order. "What about doing the window in a quilt design?"

Noah smiled. "That's a *gut* idea." He handed her cash, then picked up the box. *"Danki."*

"You're *welkom.*"

He took a few steps away from the counter and stopped. "Did you want me to take the letter you were writing to your pen pal?"

"How do you know who I was writing to?

And why do you keep calling him *mei* pen pal?"

He shrugged and contorted his lips into a lopsided smile.

She hesitated. It would save her from buying a stamp. Any savings would help. "Can you give me a minute?"

"Absolutely."

She retreated into the kitchen. After jotting *Cabinetmaker* on the front of the envelope, she took it out front.

Noah reached for it.

"Wait." She withdrew the letter. She'd have a little fun with him. "How do I know this will reach him *un*opened?"

He chuckled. "The letter I brought to you was sealed, *jah*?"

The door opened before she could answer. Lois looked around the empty room and frowned.

Joy handed Noah the envelope, silently praying he wouldn't say anything in front of Lois about her pen pal.

Noah offered a cinnamon roll to the motel owner, Mrs. Paddock, as he used Joy's suggestion of making the glass cabinets look like quilt blocks. "There's a fabric store on Third Street and they have several quilts hanging on the walls. You could pick one out that you want me to copy."

A simple block pattern wouldn't take much to create out of glass. He hadn't ever sweated over a job proposal before this one. Working on the motel cabinets would give him an excuse to drive over here regularly. After talking earlier with Joy, he wanted to get to know her better. He hoped he wouldn't lose his chance once he confessed to writing the letters. Noah wiped his sleeve across his forehead. Just the thought of telling Joy that he was her pen pal made him sweat.

Mrs. Paddock placed her free hand on her hip. The woman took a bite of the roll and smiled. She walked the perimeter of the room, staring at the walls as if she were seeing it for the first time. "I think it could work."

Noah let out a breath.

"I assume they sell the display quilts."

"I can certainly find out."

"Do you have time to look at the displays today? I would like to decide on the pattern so you can get busy. I still want this finished by Christmas. A block of rooms have already been reserved for a group of cross-country skiers."

"Sure, how about now?" He didn't want anything to stand in the way of securing this job. Christmas was less than two months away.

"I have a few phone calls to make before I can leave."

"That's fine. It takes me longer to get into town in *mei* buggy. I'll meet you there." Until she selected the design, he wouldn't know if he had to order any special glass colors and that wouldn't be before Monday.

She nodded and then took another bite of the roll. "This is really good."

Noah smiled. "I think so too." He'd eaten two of them on his way to the motel and would have eaten more had it not been for a sugar rush that made him shaky. Usually too much caffeine affected him that way, not sweets.

Noah headed to the door. He wasn't sure how long Mrs. Paddock's calls would take, but his ol' mare, Cracker, wasn't as fast as she used to be. He didn't want to keep Mrs. Paddock waiting.

He reached for the door as she said, "Did you want to take the rest of your rolls?"

"*Nay,* share them with your work crew." He continued walking outside.

Noah removed Cracker's blanket and folded it. This morning when he hitched the buggy, he wasn't sure if the gray clouds meant rain or snow. So far it hadn't done either. Climbing onto the bench, he noticed Joy's unopened letter. The traffic had been too heavy to read it earlier. He smiled, recalling the flicker in her eye when she playfully snatched the letter back. But once the customer entered the store, it was as if Joy panicked the way she shoved it into his hand.

He clicked his tongue and Cracker's ears perked as she increased the pace. He wasn't on the road long before it started to rain. It turned to sleet as he reached the outskirts of town. A Closed sign hung in the bakery window. He wasn't sure what type of vehicle Mrs. Paddock drove, but he hoped the parking lot at the fabric store was empty so he could sit and read Joy's letter.

He parked next to another buggy and spread the blanket over his horse. The letter would have to wait as several cars lined the building. He pressed his straw hat further on his head, but that didn't keep his earlobes from numbing in the icy rain.

Inside the fabric store a blast of heat met him. So did Joy.

She wiggled her brows. "I must've been wrong earlier. This is two days in a row that you've visited the fabric store. Have you decided you want to learn how to sew?"

"Only if you're teaching the class."

Her eyes widened and she motioned to the opposite side of the room. "Meredith is with another customer. Is there something I can help you find?"

"I gave your suggestion to the motel owner and she's going to stop in and pick out a quilt she likes. They are for sale, right?"

"Yes, but I'll have to find out the price."

"You might as well wait until she selects one," he said when she started to turn.

"Okay. Let me know if you need anything else."

"Can I put a bakery order in for Monday?"

She smiled. "Cinnamon rolls again?"

"Surprise me."

"So you want a dozen of . . . anything?"

He nodded. Anything that would give him a reason to see her again.

"Do you like chocolate? Nuts? Any allergies?"

Occupied by answering Joy's questions, he didn't notice Mrs. Paddock approach until she spoke.

"I think we might get snow tonight," Mrs. Paddock said, her attention already drawn to the quilts.

He made a half shrug at Joy and trailed the *Englischer* to the different quilts. Several of them would be easy to copy. Most were straight cuts arranged in colorful block patterns.

"I like this one." She pointed to the quilt of roses in the shape of a heart.

He studied the design. Not one simple cut.

"Can you do it?"

Noah cocked his head. "That's — a lot of work." A horse and buggy would have been simpler even without a pattern. He would have to start the project immediately. Since tomorrow wasn't their Sunday to host the district services, he would be tempted to skip the afternoon fellowship to work in his shop. But his father, the district bishop, would disapprove. Besides, Noah would never challenge the *Ordnung*. The only work permitted on Sundays was tending livestock. Still, he would have to work night and day to finish by Christmas.

Joy stepped closer. "Is there something I can help you with?"

"Yes," Mrs. Paddock said. "Could you tell me the price of this quilt?"

"Excuse me while I get the information."

"You haven't seen them all." Noah motioned to the back of the store. "There are more displayed on the back wall."

Mrs. Paddock moved in that direction while he held his breath. But in the end, she still liked the rose quilt the best.

Joy returned. "It's seven hundred."

"Okay. I'll take it."

"You do have a pattern for it?" Noah was quick to ask. He wouldn't be able to do the design without one to follow.

Joy nodded. "*Jah,* all the quilts on display have patterns." She turned to Mrs. Paddock. "It might take a few minutes to get the quilt down, and it's probably dusty after hanging several weeks."

"Can I pay for it today and come back on a later date?"

"I'm sure that would be fine." Joy craned her neck toward the register. "I see Meredith is free now. I'll send her over."

Noah followed Joy. "Can I look at the pattern? Also, do you have the fabric in stock?"

"*Jah.*" She stopped at a rack, thumbed through the different patterns, and handed it to him. "I'll help you with the fabric in a minute. I need to tell Meredith about the purchase."

"Okay," he mumbled as he opened the pattern. He hoped the design wasn't as difficult as it looked. A few minutes passed and Joy came up to him loaded down with multiple bolts of fabric. He reached out his arms. "Let me carry those."

She released the stack to him. "You can

set them on the cutting table."

He lowered the bolts and studied the colors. Two different shades of green for the leaves, red, pink, and black for the stems; he should have all the colors in stock.

"How much yardage do you want?" She unrolled the first bolt.

"I'm *nett* sewing anything." His defensive tone caused her to blink. "Sorry." He cracked a smile. "You haven't told me when the classes start."

She cocked her head sideways and wagged the scissors.

"I just need enough to match the color with the stained glass."

She snipped a small section and handed him the pieces.

"Danki." He nodded toward the quilt. "Do you want help taking it down?"

"Probably, but let's wait for Meredith to finish." She piled the bolts at the end of the table. "I'm sure the window will be beautiful when you're finished."

"I hope so." He glanced toward the door as Mrs. Paddock was leaving. "She wants it done by Christmas."

A few moments later, he helped Joy and Meredith take down the quilt, paid for the pattern and swatches of fabric, then walked with Joy out to the buggies.

"You think this rain will turn to snow?" She pulled her cape tighter around her neck.

"It'd be better than sleet." He unfastened her horse from the post, his conscience prodding him to set things straight about the letters. He handed her the reins. "I'll be in earlier than today to pick up *mei* bakery order."

Her eyes narrowed. "You opened *mei* letter, didn't you?"

CHAPTER EIGHT

Noah wasn't sure what prompted Joy to ask about the letter, but she sparked his curiosity. He stared at her a moment, then reached into his buggy and removed the letter. Relieved the traffic had been too thick to read it, he gave her a moment to inspect the envelope.

"Satisfied?"

Her accusatory glare softened. "*Nau* I'm embarrassed."

"*Nay* need to be." He glanced at the letter clutched in her hand. She might change her mind and decide to mail it. Or worse yet, not send it at all.

"I've never had a pen pal. It seems ridiculous at *mei* age."

He smiled. "Since you avoided telling me your age when I asked, I don't find it ridiculous at all."

"I didn't avoid it. I told you I didn't give that information to strangers."

He nodded. "So you did."

"Have you ever had a pen pal?"

"Jah." He scuffed his boot over the wet ground. This was a perfect moment to confess the truth. But he disregarded the inner prompting and lifted his head. "I look forward to receiving her letters. I find her fascinating." His shirt soaked, he had to fight to keep his teeth from chattering. Still, he didn't want to leave.

"We should get out of this weather before we catch pneumonia." She opened her buggy door. "I'll see you Monday."

He stepped closer and gingerly reached for the letter. "You still want me to deliver this, right?"

Her eyes searching his, she tightened her grasp.

He didn't want to wait. If she sent it through the mail, he wouldn't receive it until after work on Monday at the earliest.

"Okay," she said, releasing the envelope. "But don't give it to him when anyone's around."

"I didn't before."

"But tomorrow is Sunday. There will be others around him all day."

"I'll be discrete." He opened his door and tossed the envelope on the bench before she changed her mind. The woman was as jittery as a newborn calf standing up for the first time. Maybe she was cold. "I probably need to get on the road. I have a two-hour ride home."

Her eyes widened. "*Ach, jah,* you better. It'll be dark soon."

He chuckled. "Cracker isn't afraid of the dark, but she will be ready to eat."

"I won't keep you another minute." She climbed into her buggy and shot him a quick wave before pulling away.

He chided himself once she left. Sure, his heart was safer getting to know her through correspondence, but the guilt of not coming forth with his identity was something he didn't want eating at him. He had to tell her, and the sooner the better.

Joy smiled most of the ride home thinking about Noah. They hadn't known each other long and yet he already felt like an old friend. The sun was setting when she reached the farm. Matthew's buggy wasn't under the lean-to. She hoped nothing was wrong. Her brother-in-law was always home at suppertime. She unhitched Candy and led the mare into the barn. After feeding, watering, and toweling off the horse's wet coat, she headed into the house, needing to dry off herself.

Joy entered the kitchen. Lantern light flickered against the wall in the otherwise dark room. Usually several lamps would be burning during mealtime. She removed her cape and winter bonnet as Lois rushed into the room.

"I thought you were Matthew," her sister said.

"Is something wrong?"

"When I was in town earlier I told you about the bishop, right?"

"*Jah,* you said he's in the hospital. Is it something more than pneumonia?"

"*Nay,* Martha said he's doing much better *nau* that he's had a breathing treatment and antibiotics. But Brother Hershberger is still out of town and Brother Troyer isn't feeling well himself, so Matthew was asked to send word to the bishop in one of Berlin's districts and see if he could arrange someone to preach at tomorrow's service."

As far as Joy could remember, they'd never had the bishop and both elders unavailable before. "The rain has turned to sleet. Hopefully he won't be out in it too much longer."

Her sister went to the stove and stirred the pot. "I made stew. It'll only take me a minute to warm it up. Philip and I ate earlier since I wanted him to take a bath so he's clean for service tomorrow."

"I'm going to change out of these wet clothes." Joy hurried up the stairs. She said a quick prayer for the bishop's health and Matthew's safety as she slipped into a dry dress, then plodded back to the kitchen.

Lois lowered a ladleful of stew into a bowl. "So how was work?"

Joy cringed. Her sister asked the same question earlier when she came into the bakery. "We had a few more customers."

"That's *gut.*" She set the bowl on the table along with a basket of biscuits.

Joy pulled a chair away from the table and sat. "You do know how important it is to have Second Christmas at the bakery, right?"

Her sister nodded.

"We have to stay open at least until then," Joy said. "Promise me we will."

"I can't make that promise."

Joy groaned. "Can you at least *try* to convince Matthew? This is *our* family's bakery."

Lois drew a deep breath. "I understand why you're upset. Please understand *mei* position. I must be submissive to *mei* husband. He is the head of this *haus.*"

The baby's cry summoned Lois's attention and she left the room.

Joy pushed the chunks of stew beef around in the bowl with her spoon. Her appetite was gone.

Noah didn't like to run Cracker over black ice, but thankfully the icy rain stopped, and he made good time getting home. After tending to Cracker, he tucked Joy's letter into the quilt pattern envelope, along with the snippets of material, and trekked across the yard to the house.

"Something smells *gut.*" He stepped inside and inhaled. Roast.

His sister stopped pouring milk and glanced at him sideways. "You're wet. What did you do, walk home?"

He tugged on his shirt. "I was standing outside in the sleet talking with a friend. I didn't have a towel in *mei* buggy to dry off."

"Anyone we know?" Stella mouthed *Ruby* then raised her brows.

He ignored his sister and turned to his mother. "How long before supper?"

"You have time to change your clothes before we eat," *Mamm* said.

Noah darted down the hall. He tossed the pattern on the bed and peeled off his shirt. He looked forward to reading Joy's letter, but he would do that after supper. Noah returned to the kitchen and took his place at the table. His family was seated and waiting on him. He bowed his head, thanked God silently for the food and for his safe trip home.

"Tomorrow I'll be giving the Sunday service for Bishop Byler's district. We'll have to leave early," his father said.

Noah nodded. He didn't know Bishop Byler or where his district was located. Over the years, his father had filled in multiple times when a district lost their bishop. Sometimes the distance was too far to travel by horse and buggy and he'd hire a driver to drop them off and then pick them up later in the afternoon. Spending the entire day in a different settlement was awkward. He wouldn't know anyone. At twenty-six, he didn't really fit in with the married or unmarried men. But he couldn't turn his father down. He was well into his sixties with failing health and he needed someone more than his mother to be near should anything happen. Besides, if he stayed home he would be tempted to start working on the stained glass design.

The table conversation blurred into the background and he thought of Joy's letter on the bed. He ate quickly and even turned down a piece of his mother's pineapple upside-down cake.

Mamm frowned. "You're *nett* getting sick, are you?"

"Nay." He shoved his chair away from the table and stood. "I think I'll read for a while and turn in early." Someone knocked on the front door as he was leaving the kitchen. "I'll get it." He opened the wooden door and stared at the visitor.

"Hello, Noah." Ruby's soft-spoken voice was as sweet as he remembered.

He cast those thoughts aside. "What brings you back to town?"

"It's only been a couple of years."

"Four."

She swept her hand over her cloak. "Well, I'm back home *nau.*"

Noah had waited a long time to hear those words. He had only recently started praying that God would free him of both the love he felt for her and the resentment he harbored toward her leaving.

"I, um . . . I wanted to talk with the bishop, if he isn't busy."

Noah stepped aside. "He's in the kitchen."

"Danki." She drew a noticeably deep breath, blew it out, then proceeded forward. The lilac scent that trailed her indicated she hadn't left all of the *Englisch* lifestyle behind.

As Ruby turned toward the kitchen, he

235

went the opposite direction. Whatever she wanted to discuss with his father didn't concern him. He was free of Ruby. Yet his own words haunted him. *If you love someone, set them free, and if they return . . .*

Noah sank onto his mattress, letter in hand. He reached the part where Joy complained about not getting the money up front for the cinnamon rolls and chuckled. No wonder she was concerned that he may have read the letter. He removed a tablet of paper from the top shelf of his closet and had a full page written in a matter of minutes.

. . . You're not the only pushover. I'm one too. To quote your words, "You, on the other hand, have probably never been in love," is far from the truth. I fell in love with a woman who was a talented seamstress, and like you and Henry, Ruby and I had made plans to marry. Only she never found me with someone else in my arms. Our relationship ended not long after she took a job at one of the dress shops in town. I thought it was a bad idea and it was. Instead of using her talent to serve God and our settlement, she made immodest clothing that the Englischers bought to wear to fancy parties. I still think she attracted the enemy and fell to his flattery. She chose being a seamstress and wearing immoral clothes over the Amish way . . . over me.

After a few months, she grew tired of the worldly living and said she wanted to come back. I was a pushover and wanted to believe her words were true. I'm sure you can figure out the rest.

Hours passed and he was still writing, spilling every thought that came to mind. Noah paused. He had never written a six-page letter to anyone. After a moment, he shoved the papers aside and pulled out a clean sheet. Focusing on Joy was safer, especially since opening his heart meant taking a risk he'd vowed never to take again. He started the new letter off with "Tell me about you," then asked what her favorite cookie was to make and if she only made sweets.

After a restless night, Noah dreaded the three-hour church service held in another district — another county — even more. Now seated in the back of the barn on the men's side, he did his best to focus on the teaching. But halfway through the Scripture reading, his attention wandered over to the women's section. Noah spotted Joy sitting beside Meredith a few rows up. He lowered his head and stared at the cement floor. He could avoid telling people he was a cabinetmaker, but if the subject arose during his parents' conversations, they wouldn't hesitate to tell someone about his shop. The muscles in the back of his neck tensed and he clamped one of his hands over the area to knead out the tension.

Once the service ended, the members spread out. The women and children meandered out of the barn while the men gathered in small groups and talked quietly. Noah overheard someone say the bishop was in the hospital. The lingering melancholy mood made sense.

A few minutes passed before he roamed away from the crowd. He stepped outside and caught a glimpse of Joy. She was too preoccupied with uncovering food dishes to notice him as he approached the serving line.

"I hope you brought some cookies today," he said.

Joy looked up from placing a dish of macaroni and cheese on the table and smiled. "What are you doing here?" she said in a hoarse whisper.

"*Mei daed* is the fill-in bishop today." The tip of her nose looked red and irritated from constant wiping. "Did you catch a *kalt* from standing in the rain yesterday?"

She glanced from side to side. *"Nay."* Her face turned the same scarlet shade as her nose.

Noah scanned the area. "I'm sorry. Should I *nett* have said anything?"

She leaned closer. "People might think . . . they might wonder —"

"If we're courting?"

Her eyes widened. "*Nay.* I was worried that someone might ask how we know each other and I don't want you telling anyone about . . . me having a pen pal." Her face turned a rosy shade.

Inquisitive as to why she was embarrassed, Noah opened his mouth, then bit back his question, not wanting to discourage future letter exchange. "I don't want that subject to *kumm* up either." Noah smiled. "But since it has," he said, lowering his voice, "I have a letter for you."

"With you?"

He motioned toward the parked buggies. "It's stuffed under the bench." He hadn't wanted to leave it lying around in his room. At the time, he didn't know his father's buggy needed repair and that he planned to

239

use Noah's today. "Would you like to take a walk with me?"

"It's almost time to eat. I should probably finish getting things ready."

"Is that your horse on the end?"

"*Jah,* why?"

"Look under your seat when you leave." Noah turned when more women walked up to the table with plates stacked with sandwiches. He agreed with her — it was best no one find out how the two of them met.

Standing at the bakery's counter the following morning, Noah opened the pastry box and smiled. Inside, the decorated cookies looked identical to the roses in the quilt pattern. "You decorated these?"

Joy nodded.

"I suppose you could have drawn me a horse-and-buggy pattern."

"Maybe the buggy, but —"

Noah glanced over his shoulder to see what had drawn her attention. A man crossed the room and approached Joy.

"Why didn't you tell me?" the man said to Joy.

She moved closer to the register where he stood. "Tell you what?"

"Yesterday, Matthew said the bakery will probably close by the end of the year."

Joy wiped her hands along her apron. *"Mei bruder*-in-law shouldn't have discussed business on Sunday."

"So it's true." Henry smiled. "After Christmas we won't have anything standing in our way."

The door opened and Joy's sister sashayed across the room. *"Gut mariye."*

"Sarah, if you don't mind ringing up Noah, Henry and I need to talk outside." Joy didn't give her sister a chance to refuse. She bounded out from behind the counter and led the man out the door.

Noah stared at the empty space.

Sarah cleared her throat. "Will it be just the cookies today?"

"Nay," Noah said. "I think I'll have a cup of *kaffi."*

"For here or to go?"

"For here." He motioned to the far table. "Do you mind if I sit next to the window?"

"Sit wherever you like." Sarah poured a mug of coffee then followed him to the table. "Let me know if you need anything else."

Noah nodded. He wished Joy's back wasn't facing him. He would much rather watch her facial expressions than the man with her.

He hadn't taken more than a few sips

before the conversation outside ended and Henry walked away. Joy half-turned, glanced teary-eyed in the direction Henry had gone, then lifted her gaze to the sky.

Noah pushed his chair back and grabbed the box of cookies. At the register, he strained his neck to look into the kitchen. Not seeing Sarah, he called out, "I'm leaving the money by the register." He rushed out the door.

Joy stood in the same spot, face tilted toward the sky, eyes closed.

"Is everything all right?" Noah stepped closer.

She wiped her hands over her face and smiled, but her lips trembled. "*Mei* parents opened this place." Her gaze lifted above him. "I remember watching *mei daed* paint that sign . . . *Nau* the paint's fading."

He peered at the Stolzfus Bakery sign attached to the building. "It wouldn't take much to touch it up."

She tightened her lips into another strained smile. "I should get back inside."

Noah motioned to the box of cookies. "I'll take two dozen tomorrow. *Nay,* make it three."

His mother had asked more than once that he stop by his great-aunt's house. He would honor his *memm*'s wishes and keep some of the calories off his waist. Although it would require he sit long enough to have a cup of her diluted tea and listen to her convoluted stories of the past. Or he could leave them at the motel. If his cabinets were going to be finished on time, he needed to concentrate on work.

CHAPTER NINE

Joy carried the can of white paint up the ladder. Today was the first day of favorable weather in the two weeks since she noticed the faded bakery sign. She dipped the brush into the gallon, then applied the paint with even strokes. It wasn't long before her hands turned numb and her cheeks tingled from the cold wind. At least the sign would dry quickly. She worked her way from one side of the board to the other, painting each letter. Joy took a moment from her elevated position to scan the town. Thanksgiving wasn't until next week and the town had already put up the Christmas decorations. The evergreen wreaths and garlands always looked nice on the lampposts. She spotted Henry outside the hardware store and lifted her hand holding the brush in a wave. He stared at her a moment, then shook his head and went back into the store.

Joy dipped her brush into the can and

continued painting.

"Aren't you afraid of falling?" Meredith's voice startled her.

The ladder shook. Joy glanced down at her friend. "You almost got showered in paint."

Meredith's face cringed. "Sorry."

"I'll be down in a minute." Joy finished the *y* in *Bakery* and then eased down the ladder. "What do you think?" She gazed up at her work.

"Looks brand new."

"*Nett* from up there." Joy shrugged. "The background is peeling in spots, but I didn't have any red paint."

"You should probably wait until spring. They're forecasting snow."

"I haven't seen you in two weeks," Joy said. "How is your little sister?"

"She's finally over the contagious stage. I don't remember having so many spots when I had chicken pox."

"At least she won't be quarantined at Thanksgiving." Joy walked to the back of the building where she squatted at the water spigot with the paintbrush.

"Does your painting the sign mean the bakery isn't closing?"

"It's been *mei* prayer, but Matthew hasn't changed his mind. I noticed the paint peeling a couple of weeks ago and I didn't want it to look run-down when . . ." A puddle of white paint collected at Joy's feet.

"I know this is hard for you."

"Did I tell you Henry stopped by? He thought once the bakery closed there wouldn't be anything standing in the way of us getting married." Joy shook the brush. "He seemed pleased about the closing."

"I'm sorry."

"I could never marry someone who wouldn't allow me to work outside the *haus*. I want to have some say over *mei* life." Unlike Lois.

"*Ach,* I missed a lot taking care of *mei* sister."

"I almost wrote you a letter to slip under your door, but I was afraid one of your *bruders* or sisters would find it and read it."

"*Jah,* and they probably would've thought it was funny to read it out loud too. What about the cabinetmaker — have you heard from him?"

"I've gotten a letter every day." Joy smiled. "Noah drops it off when he picks up his order."

"Hmm . . . Maybe I should ask which one created that smile, the cabinetmaker or Noah?"

"I know what you're thinking." Joy headed

to the front of the building.

"Well?" Meredith followed.

"Noah's a nice guy." She grasped the ladder leaning against the building and gently lowered it to the sidewalk. "He seems concerned about the bakery. I should clarify, I talk about the bakery and he listens."

"Hmm . . ."

Joy said too much. She picked up one end of the ladder while Meredith grabbed the other.

"He sounds like a sweet man."

"He certainly has a sweet tooth." Joy chuckled. "I don't know how he can eat so much."

"I'd say he's a perfect match for someone who loves to bake."

Joy ignored her friend's comment and continued toting the ladder to the storage area at the rear of the building. She wasn't ready to admit how much she looked forward to seeing Noah each day.

"I made a variety pack of some of *mei* Christmas favorites," Joy said to Noah as she brought the box out of the kitchen.

"That sounds interesting." He opened the box at the counter and peeked inside. "Wow, these look really *gut.*"

"I figured if this was the bakery's last

Christmas to be open, I wanted to make all *mei mamm*'s recipes. The ones she taught me over the years."

Noah motioned to an empty table. "Can you sit down and have a cup of *kaffi* with me?"

"Sure." They sat together most mornings for a few minutes when no other customers were in the shop. The *Englischer* at the table reading a newspaper had only wanted coffee and a bagel, and no one else was waiting to be served. She filled two mugs with coffee and followed Noah to their usual table next to the window.

He opened the box and tipped it toward her.

"Nay, danki." She smiled. "I sampled enough of them when they were hot out of the oven."

He picked out a jelly-filled pastry ball coated with powdered sugar. "So these are all your favorites?"

She nodded. "I call that one a sweet snowball surprise."

He took a bite and raspberry jam covered his lips. "I found the surprise," he said, reaching for a napkin. He wiped his mouth. "Those could be addictive."

"I hope everyone at the Christmas sleigh ride likes them."

"You should probably worry more about having enough snow."

"*Ach,* don't say that. We must have snow."

"The sleigh ride is really important to you, isn't it?"

"*Jah.*" She looked out the window and watched a few passing cars. "*Mei daed* proposed to *mei mamm* on a sleigh ride. They were the ones who organized our bakery hosting cookies and cocoa every year on Second Christmas."

"It sounds like a lot of fun."

A man and woman entered the shop and Joy left the table long enough to wait on them. The woman's indecisiveness kept Joy at the counter longer than she wished. By the time the people paid for their purchases and left, Noah's coffee cup was empty.

"Can I refill your cup?"

"*Nay.*" He stood and picked up the box. "All this talk about Christmas reminded me of how much work I have to do yet." He frowned. "I probably won't be in to buy cookies for a couple of weeks."

"I understand." She smiled. "I was going to tell you that with Thanksgiving this week, the bakery will be closed on Thursday and Friday." An odd sensation washed over her. She wasn't sure if she would miss the daily letters he delivered from the cabinetmaker, or spending time with Noah. Over the past month and a half, she'd developed a fondness for his company, as well as for her new pen pal.

"I'll see you . . . hopefully soon." He headed to the door.

"Noah," she called.

He spun to face her. *"Jah?"*

"Happy Thanksgiving."

"You too." Smiling, he touched the brim of his hat and proceeded outside.

Throughout the afternoon, Joy tried to push aside her feelings, but by closing time, she was more confused than ever. She jotted a note to the cabinetmaker.

. . . Have you ever been confused about your future? About life in general? I am. I've told you things that I haven't shared with anyone else. You know about Henry, my parents dying in the fire, and my sister never showing up for work on time. What about you? Have you always known what you've wanted to do in a situation? Have you ever been confused about anything? I wish I understood why things happen. Like you receiving the box I mailed to my cousin and how we've become pen pals.

Noah scored the piece of rose-colored glass

following the petal-traced markings, then rinsed, dried, and covered the glass edges with copper foil. The intricate process required a great deal of patience and most of the day just to complete one rose. This portion of the project couldn't be completed soon enough for him.

He missed Joy and it had been only three days.

Noah finished the rose section and set his tools down. He needed a break. The shading on the leaf took more focus than he had at the moment. He strolled out to the mailbox.

Noah smiled and tore open the envelope on his way back to the shop. But he didn't read past the opening greeting before a buggy entered the driveway.

Ruby stopped the horse at the hitching post next to the shop and climbed out. "I was hoping you would be home today. I *kumm* a few times last week and didn't find you in the shop."

"I had a job out of town." He folded the letter and shoved it into the envelope.

"*Jah,* that's what Stella told me."

His younger sister hadn't mentioned Ruby's visit. Just as well. He didn't wish to discuss Ruby with his sister.

"I hear your cabinet business is really

251

growing."

He nodded. "I need to get back to work *nau.*" He pushed open the door to the shop, but stopped in the threshold when she started to follow him.

"I'm sort of a little surprised you didn't get married," she said, batting her lashes.

Her syrupy voice, which he'd once found so attractive, now grated his nerves. It had taken him four years to get past his hurt. Marriage hadn't entered his mind. "It took me longer to get over you running out on our relationship."

"I'm sorry." She lowered her gaze a moment, then looked up. "Maybe *nau* that I'm back we can try again."

Noah shook his head. "I prayed for months asking God to mend *mei* broken heart. I'm thankful He did." Her sudden tears had no effect on him now. "I wish you well, Ruby. But I'm no longer in love with you."

She turned, took a few steps, and glanced over her shoulder. "I guess I deserve that. If you change your mind . . ."

"I won't." Noah praised God as he entered the shop. If God hadn't healed his heart when He had, Noah wouldn't have formed a friendship with Joy. He sat in the rocking chair and read Joy's latest letter.

Have you ever been confused? Her words lingered until he left the shop and jogged over to the house. He rummaged through the drawer of his bedside table and found the long letter he had started a few days ago. The one where he'd poured out his heart about Ruby. As he added to his letter, he whispered a prayer that his heart would be safe.

Joy read the cabinetmaker's eight-page letter twice, both times stopping at the same spot.

. . . I prayed that I could stop loving Ruby for months. Everyone told me she was wrong for me, but I didn't want to believe she would choose pursuing her dreams over being with me. She didn't share the same hopes of building a plain home and raising a family, and yet it still took me four years to let her go completely.

Pray about what God wants for you, J. Once you discover His plans, you won't be confused.

Joy blotted a hankie over her eyes. She wasn't even sure why his letter had such a strong effect on her, but it did. The cabinetmaker and Henry were alike. They both didn't want to marry someone who had a job. Obviously, the cabinetmaker made the woman choose. Just like Henry had given her an ultimatum. How foolish she was to have talked so much about the bakery. In her last letter she'd even suggested he come to their district's Second Christmas gathering so they could meet.

She tucked the letter with the others in her chest of drawers. She had to help her sisters prepare the Thanksgiving meal. She had no time to dwell on a man she could never be right for, who would never be right for her.

CHAPTER TEN

Noah paced the floor of his shop. How could he work on finishing the cabinets when all he could think about was Joy? He'd sent her four letters since Thanksgiving and hadn't heard anything. Something was wrong. She had always been quick to respond.

He set the glass cutter on the table and went to the shelf where he kept her letters in a wooden box. He'd reread her letters a dozen times since she stopped writing. He must have missed something.

Noah scanned the page. Other than writing about being confused, she talked about new recipes . . . His eye traveled back up the page to the line about being confused. An image of Joy and Henry outside the bakery knotted his stomach. Henry had said after Christmas there wouldn't be anything standing in their way. Christmas was only three weeks away. Noah paced the length of

255

his shop. Why hadn't it dawned on him before that she and Henry might have gotten back together? But in her last letter, she invited the cabinetmaker to the Christmas sleigh ride. Noah reread the invitation part of the letter again.

Our district's annual sleigh ride is on Second Christmas. I'm sure I told you that was why I've been making Christmas cookies. Every year, we all get together at the bakery for cookies and hot cocoa. It's a tradition my mother and father started after they bought the bakery. I would love it if you could attend. That is, if you are interested in meeting your pen pal in person.

Even though he immediately wrote her back to say yes, she never responded to his letter or any of the ones that followed. Had she changed her mind? Was that why she stopped writing?

All this second-guessing would drive him crazy if he didn't talk with her soon. He had to see her. She needed to know *he* was her pen pal. He'd ignored his pricking conscience too long.

Joy refilled Mrs. Yoder's coffee mug, then

moved over to the table next to the window where Meredith was seated. "It's starting to look like a blizzard," Joy said, topping off her friend's mug with more coffee.

"I think it's already snowed a foot."

"We need it to stick."

"I'm sure we'll have plenty of snow." Meredith motioned to the chair opposite her. "Can you take a break?"

Joy glanced at Mrs. Yoder, the only other customer in the shop. A few tables over, the elderly woman nibbled on her pastry and stared out the window. Joy motioned to the pot. "Give me a minute to put this up and then we can chat."

"Just think," Meredith said after Joy sat down. "The sleigh ride is only three weeks away."

Joy sighed. Only three weeks before the bakery closed too. She hated to think about turning the key for the last time. What would she do once it closed? And would she ever see Noah again?

Meredith elbowed Joy. "Have you heard from the cabinetmaker?"

Joy shook her head.

"You two were sending letters back and forth every day. What happened?"

Joy ran her finger around the rim of her mug. "I stopped writing him."

"Why?"

Joy shrugged.

"I thought you were beginning to like him," Meredith said. "I mean *really* like him."

"He told me about his old girlfriend. She wanted to be a seamstress and he made her choose between him and sewing. Henry made me choose between being a *fraa* and working too."

"So you stopped writing to him?"

"I had to." Joy leaned closer. "I was beginning to have feelings for a man I had never met — how *narrisch* is that?" She held up her hand. "Don't answer that. I know it's crazy." She plopped her elbows on the table and buried her head in her hands. "I have feelings for two men."

"Two? Please tell me one of them isn't Henry. I saw him with Priscilla again."

She drew a deep breath and looked up. "Noah."

Meredith's brows rose. "I figured something was up the other day when we were talking about his sweet tooth. Remember, I said he was a perfect match for someone who liked to bake?"

Joy bowed her head. "*Jah,* I remember."

"Why are you so glum?"

"I've never been drawn to two men at the

same time. Noah is kind and fun to be around. But I'm also drawn to the cabinet-maker. The letter about his old girlfriend was eight pages long. He really opened up to me. I got the impression he'd never shared those feelings with anyone."

The doorbell dinged. Joy craned her head but didn't see anyone. She looked around the room. Mrs. Yoder's chair was empty. Joy glanced out the window. Mrs. Yoder was standing on the sidewalk, looking more confused than ever. "I'd better see if I can help her. She's apt to wander into traffic." Joy pushed her chair back and stood. "Sarah should be here any minute. Do you mind watching the bakery until she arrives?"

"Sure. I'd offer to walk Mrs. Yoder home, but she was upset with me the other day in the Quilter's Corner and I'm *nett* sure she would take kindly to it. She didn't even acknowledge me a few minutes ago when I came in. Poor woman. It must be hard when your mind is confused."

Noah tugged his coat collar up higher on his neck. When he left for Sugarcreek, the scattered flurries weren't blinding, but now the snow-covered road made it difficult to tell the pavement from the gravel shoulder. He had no choice but to go slower. He wasn't even sure the bakery would still be open when he reached town. But he couldn't turn around now. Not without seeing Joy.

Noah reached the edge of town, and when he got a block from the bakery, he spotted two women, arms outstretched and turning circles with their faces turned upward. He chuckled, recognizing Joy. She appeared to be trying to catch snowflakes.

Noah maneuvered the buggy next to the curb and sat quietly, enamored by Joy's simple pleasure in chasing snowflakes. When the elderly woman standing with her looked his way, he sat up straighter in the seat. His great-aunt must have said something to Joy because she stopped making circles and turned to look in his direction.

Noah climbed out of the buggy and crossed the street. "*Hiya, Aenti* Lavern."

His aunt peered up at him as if trying to register his face. Then she turned to Joy and smiled. "This is Noah. He's the one I've been telling you about," she said. "He needs a *fraa.*"

He turned and coughed into his fisted hand.

His aunt tapped his arm. "You're Noah, right?"

"*Jah, Aenti* Lavern. I'm Noah, your

nephew. Rachel Esh's *sohn.*" Her dull eyes only stared at him. She hadn't looked this bewildered since the last time she stopped taking her medicine. He motioned to his parked buggy. "How about we get out of this *kalt wedder,* and I give you two a ride."

"I should get back to the bakery." Joy leaned toward his aunt and patted her shoulder. "I'll see you another time." She glanced at him. "It was nice seeing you again, Noah."

"Did you want a ride?"

"*Nay,* I like walking in the snow."

He would like to leave his buggy and go for a long walk with her. "Will you be at the bakery for a while?"

"For a little while."

He smiled.

Joy pointed over his shoulder. "Your *aenti* is crossing the street. You'd better go."

"I'll see you later," he said, hurrying to catch up with his aunt. He reached for her elbow and kept her steady as she climbed into the buggy.

After the short ride to *Aenti* Lavern's home, she turned to Noah, whom she now seemed to recognize. "*Kumm* inside and have a cup of tea with me."

He didn't want Joy closing the bakery before they had a chance to talk, but his mother would be pleased if he spent some time with his great-aunt. He groaned under his breath as he jogged around the buggy to her side.

"Please stay," she said. "I rarely get visitors."

"Sure. I'll shovel your walkway while you heat the water for tea." He'd tried calling on her two weeks ago only to discover she had gone to stay with family members for a while. Noah helped her off the bench and into the small clapboard house.

Noah cleared the path and returned the shovel to the shed. By the time he entered the small kitchen, Aunt Lavern had the water poured.

"So you were talking about me to Joy?" Had his aunt told Joy that he was a cabinetmaker? Was that why she declined the ride?

"Who?" The lines around his aunt's eyes deepened.

"The woman who works at the bakery. The person you were walking . . ." His aunt's short-term memory would cause her to wonder who he was in a few minutes. "Have you been taking your medicine every day?"

"The blue ones make me dizzy and the white ones are too hard to swallow."

"Have you told your doctor?" His mother

would make sure the doctor was aware once she found out about *Aenti* Lavern's deteriorating condition.

"I don't know if I have." She handed him a cup of warm water.

She'd forgotten to add the tea bag, but he took a sip anyway. "This is *gut, danki.*"

"Just the way your *grossdaadi* liked it."

He wasn't about to try to explain that her deceased husband was his uncle and not his grandfather. He took another drink and glanced outside at the falling snow. His aunt's conversation wandered into the past, while his mind drifted to one of the last conversations he had with Joy.

"If this is the last Christmas in the bakery," Joy said, *"I want to make all of* mei mamm*'s special recipes for the annual sleigh ride."*

At the time, he wanted to ask if that included the peppermint ones, but then realized she'd only invited the cabinetmaker to their district's celebration.

Joy loitered longer than usual at the bakery. She sprayed and wiped each table down, still amazed at how her heart fluttered when she saw Noah. She'd certainly missed his dimpled smile.

Meredith refilled her own mug. "Are you sure he was stopping by today?"

263

"That's what he said." She had already prepared a box of cookies for him to take home.

The doorbell dinged. Noah stomped his feet on the floor mat. "It's snowing hard *nau*."

"*Jah,* it is." Joy set the cleaning rag aside and wiped her hands on her apron. "Can I get you a cup of *kaffi*?"

"That would be nice." He nodded at the window. "We should have a white Christmas this year."

Meredith cleared her throat and pulled her cape off the back of the chair. "Have you invited Noah to the district's Christmas sleigh ride yet?"

"I, um . . ." Her friend had a way of putting her on the spot. "Would you like to *kumm*?"

He smiled. "*Jah.* What time?"

"We meet here at dusk, caravan through the woods for a couple of hours, and then return here for cocoa and cookies."

"Sounds like fun."

Meredith swung her cape over her shoulders. "Second Christmas is the highlight of the year around here." She wiggled her brows at Joy. "Ain't so?"

Joy nodded, but with the bakery set to close the day after the sleigh ride, she wasn't sure this year would feel as merry.

Her friend strolled to the door, then paused. "Noah, if you don't have blades for your buggy, you two can ride with me and Walter. But you'll have to wear something warm — he has an open buggy," Meredith said, leaving.

"Did you get your *aenti* home all right?" Joy asked.

"I didn't realize her mind was — scrambled. She must've stopped taking her medicine again. I'm *nett* sure she knew who I was."

Joy smiled. "She thinks you're one of her *kinskind.*"

"Who needs a *fraa,* I know." He shrugged. "Does she *kumm* every day?"

"Usually. I'm surprised you haven't run into her. Although she's often waiting by the door when I arrive to start baking."

"So do you walk all your customers home?"

"Only *mei* faithful ones."

His brows lifted. "I'll keep that in mind."

Joy grabbed a mug and filled it with coffee. "I hope Meredith didn't make you feel obligated to say yes about the sleigh ride."

"She didn't. Are you going to make the peppermint cookies?"

"If you're making a special request, I suppose I will." She handed him the mug. "I have some treats to send with you *nau.*" She whirled around and snatched the cookie box from the counter.

"These are for me?" He eyed the top of the box.

"Jah." She smiled.

Noah reached into his coat pocket and removed his wallet.

"Nay," she said, holding up her hand. "They're from me."

He motioned to the table near the widow. "Do you want to sit and have *kaffi* with me?"

"Okay." She didn't need more caffeine, but she didn't want to say no to the opportunity to talk. Joy poured another mug and sat with him at the table next to the window. "So how are you doing on your stained glass design?"

"The pattern is tougher than I thought."

"I'm sure it's beautiful." She traced the handle of the mug with her finger.

"How's business?"

She shrugged. "*Mei bruder*-in-law still plans to close the bakery after Christmas."

"I'm sorry."

She forced a smile but had to look away. Despite the lengthy prayers for peace, she hadn't fully accepted Matthew's decision.

"I'll pray for you."

"Danki." She cringed. "Pray that I don't harbor resentment. I haven't been as close to *mei* sisters since the issue of closing the bakery came up."

He reached across the table and took her hands in his, then closed his eyes. "Father, we ask for Your perfect will in this situation. You know Joy's heart. You see her pain. Please mend any differences between her and her sisters, and if there's a way, please let the bakery stay open. Amen." Noah squeezed her hand then released it.

Joy dried her eyes with a napkin. In the brief moment he'd held her hand, she had never felt closer to anyone, including Henry. "*Danki* for praying."

He smiled. "You don't have to thank me."

A moment went by when neither of them spoke.

"So," she said, fiddling with the corner of the paper napkin. "Do you think we'll have snow for the sleigh ride?"

"I hope so. I want to see you twirl around trying to catch snowflakes on your tongue again."

She crinkled her brows. "How long were you watching me?"

He shrugged, then picked up his mug and took a drink.

Two cups of coffee later, he glanced out

267

the window. "I suppose I should head home before I get snowed in." He slid back his chair and stood. "Did you have a letter you want me to take back?"

"Nay."

"Oh." He pushed the empty chair under the table.

"You look disappointed."

"I thought you two were getting along *gut.*" He shoved his arm into his coat sleeve. "You always seemed excited about exchanging letters. Are you *nett* pen pals any longer?"

"I'm just taking a break, is all."

His eyes steadied on hers. "If you don't mind me asking, was there something said that offended you?"

"*Nay,* but why are you so curious? And even if something was wrong, I wouldn't tell you." Now she understood why he'd stopped by. It wasn't to see her — it was to spy on her.

"Why wouldn't you tell me?" His expression hardened.

True, she had shared just about everything else about her life with him. Still, he was merely the messenger. She picked up the dirty dishes and crossed the room with him following.

"Joy, what's wrong?"

268

She set the dishes on the counter and spun to face him. "Those letters are personal."

"So something was said that upset you." His eyes bored into hers.

"Noah, don't pry. This isn't your business."

Based on his raised brows, her sharp words had gotten his attention. He opened his mouth as though he was going to respond, then closed it. He turned, shaking his head. When he reached the door, he stopped. "I didn't mean to *kumm* across as prying. I was only curious." He watched her a brief moment, then turned and left.

CHAPTER ELEVEN

Guilt pelted Noah's conscience during the ride home. He had the opportunity to tell Joy that he was her pen pal and he couldn't bring himself to do it, not when she seemed so adamant about stopping the letter exchange. He dare not think about how she would react when she found out.

Lord, in the short time I've known Joy, my feelings have grown. I believe she might be the woman I've been waiting for. I can't keep this farce going. I have to find out why she stopped writing the letters.

Noah's mind churned over the conversation with Joy the remainder of the ride home, as he completed the barn chores, and even while he worked in his shop on a special project.

The door opened, and his sister entered carrying a plate. "*Mamm* wanted me to bring you some supper." Stella set the plate on the worktable. "Is everything okay?"

"*Jah,* why?" He continued scoring the rose-colored glass with the cutter.

"I think the last time you missed supper you were spending a lot of time with Ruby."

He set the blade on the table and glanced sideways at his sister. "You can tell *Mamm* that I'm *nett* courting Ruby. I'm trying to finish a project before Christmas."

"*Mamm* sent me out with chicken potpie, *nett* to pester you for the name of the girl you've been seeing." Stella leaned closer and smiled. "So what's her name?"

Noah molded the metal around the piece of glass and soldered the end.

"Is she Amish?"

His sister wasn't coy, nor was she easily persuaded to mind her own business. He finished joining the pieces together, then held it up to inspect his work.

"What are you making?"

"A pair of glasses."

"Rose colored?"

He set the glasses on the table, then moved over to the plate of food she'd brought and picked up the fork.

Stella slipped on the glasses. "These are strange. Everything looks different."

"That's the point." Noah took a bite of the potpie. He was hungrier than he thought. A few minutes later, he scraped the last forkful off the plate. *"Danki."* He handed his sister the empty dish and walked her to the door. "I have more work to do."

"You've been spending a lot of time in Sugarcreek. She isn't the motel owner, right?"

"Nay." He opened the door, and as Stella was leaving, he said, "You can reassure *Mamm* that I'm only interested in courting a God-fearing, Amish woman." Who just happened to bake the best peppermint cookies he'd ever tasted. Although his stomach was full, his mouth watered for a taste of Joy's homemade treats.

Noah closed the door behind his sister, then returned to his worktable. He inspected the glasses once more, then slipped them on. His sister was right. Everything did look different.

Noah installed the cabinet's last stained glass window, then stepped back to admire his work. It still amazed him that he was able to finish the motel job a week early.

"The stained glass matches the quilt perfectly," Mrs. Paddock said.

"Thank you. I'm glad you're pleased."

"I'm more than pleased." She bit into a cookie and her eyes widened. "This is good."

"It's called a snowball surprise."

"I have to say, I'll miss the baked goods you always bring."

"Stolzfus Bakery is local — and Amish," he said, watching her brows rise. "I'm sure your guests would enjoy Amish breakfast muffins or desserts." He wouldn't try to sell the Amish lifestyle to anyone if it wasn't to help Joy.

Joy normally didn't like working with sticky substances, and she wasn't fond of the flavor of maple syrup, but the candy recipe had a star next to it in her mother's cookbook.

"These are *gut*." Meredith licked her fingers.

"*Danki*." Joy scrubbed the maple syrup off the counter, then set the dirty pan into the hot, sudsy water to soak. Every day this past week, she worked hard to prepare a large assortment of sweets for the Christmas get-together. But mostly she worked hard to push her feelings for Noah aside and to tame her lingering thoughts about the cabinetmaker. How could she have allowed herself to fall for them both?

"You never answered *mei* question," Meredith said. "What are you going to do when Noah and the cabinetmaker both *kumm* to the sleigh ride?"

"I doubt that will be an issue." Joy shrugged. "I never heard any more from the cabinetmaker, and Sarah waited on Noah two days ago when he came into the bakery. He didn't even ask if I was here or stay for *kaffi*. He just paid for his order and left."

"I'm sure he knows you're busy. Didn't you say he had a project due by Christmas?"

Joy nodded even though she was sure Noah's avoidance meant something more. "The last time we talked, Noah pressed me about why I stopped writing to the cabinet-maker. He isn't interested in me. He was on a mission for someone else."

The back door of the bakery opened and Lois entered, holding baby Stephen in one arm and leading Philip on her left. *"Gut mariye."*

"Hiya." Joy lifted Stephen out of her sister's arms so Lois could remove her cape. "What brings you to town?"

"Someone wants to talk with us about the bakery." Lois tugged on Philip's coat sleeve and released his arm.

"Who?"

"Sarah didn't get her name. Apparently a woman stopped by the other day asking to see the owner. She expressed interest in buying the bakery."

"But Matthew said he wasn't going to

advertise it until after the sleigh ride."

"He didn't. I'm *nett* sure how she found out about the sale."

"So where's Sarah? She's part owner." Stephen fussed and Joy tried to soothe his crying by bouncing him in her arms.

Lois reached for her son. "She said she would go along with whatever we decide."

"You mean whatever Matthew decides," Joy muttered.

Lois glanced at her older son, who was eyeing the maple candy, then glared at Joy.

Meredith took Philip by the hand. "How about we go see what's in the display case."

Lois thanked Meredith and waited until they were out of earshot. "We couldn't have kept the bakery open this long if it wasn't for Matthew managing the finances. He's done everything —"

The front doorbell jingled. A moment later, Meredith poked her head into the kitchen. "There's someone asking to speak with the owner."

Joy and Lois looked at each other, then went out front.

The salt-and-pepper-haired woman glanced up from the display case.

Recognizing the woman as the one who bought the heart of roses quilt at the Quilter's Corner, Joy and Meredith exchanged glances while Lois greeted the woman.

Mrs. Paddock introduced herself as the owner of the Scenic Hill Motel and mentioned how one of her workers had supplied them with baked goods from their shop every day. "When I inquired about your bakery, I was told it might be for sale."

The air left Joy's lungs in a whoosh.

Had Noah leaked the news?

Her sister's voice faded into the background of Joy's reeling thoughts as Lois and Mrs. Paddock went into the kitchen.

Meredith elbowed Joy's side. "Aren't you going to go with them?"

She shook her head. "I need a few minutes."

"Isn't she the one who bought the rose quilt?"

Joy nodded. "She's the woman Noah was making the stained glass for. And he must be the worker who told her about the bakery possibly closing."

"You really think so?"

"He's the only one who has bought pastries and cookies every day. Three dozen at a time."

"*Aenti* Joy." Philip sidled up beside her. "May I have a doughnut?"

Joy looked into the pleading eyes of her nephew and smiled. "Sure, pick which one you want."

The young boy pointed to the one with sprinkles on the frosting.

Joy placed the doughnut on a napkin and led him to one of the tables. After instructing him not to get crumbs on the floor, she turned to Meredith. "Do you have a few minutes to watch him?" Now that she'd had time to compose herself, she wanted to find out more about the motel owner.

"I have all afternoon," Meredith said.

Joy swept her hand over imaginary wrinkles on her apron and took a deep breath. Then the sound of the bell above the door caught her attention.

Noah smiled. "*Gut* afternoon." His gaze darted from her, over to Meredith, then Philip, and back to Joy. His smile dropped. "Is something wrong?"

Joy marched toward him. "Do you have a few minutes to talk?" She pointed at the door. "Outside?"

"*Jah,* I wanted to talk with you about something too."

She pushed the door open.

Noah hesitated. "Don't you want to put a coat on? It's *kalt* out . . . here."

She continued out the door. "This won't take long." Leaving the shop, she crossed her arms as the icy breeze sent a chill down

277

her back.

"What's going on?" he said.

"That's what I want to know." She fought to control her shivers. "The motel owner you're doing the stained glass for is here."

A low growl escaped his mouth. He stared at the ground, his jaw twitching.

"Apparently one of her workers has been bringing in sweets from here and talking about this place."

He lifted his head. "Is that why you're upset?" Relief washed over his face as though her concerns were trivial.

"So it was you. You took the motel bakery items."

"To share with everyone. What's wrong with that?"

She looked up at the bakery sign attached to the building and her throat tightened. "You're right. It is *kalt* out here."

A long stretch of silence fell over the supper table that evening. Even Matthew, who was in favor of selling the bakery, didn't say much after Lois shared the details.

Joy pushed the uneaten peas across her plate. She had prayed for God's will and had tried to prepare herself to accept God's decision, yet she was still struggling to understand.

"Mrs. Paddock said she would have her lawyers draw up an official offer," Lois said. "She wanted to send an inspection team in to look at the appliances and an accountant to review the records, but I told her she would have to make arrangements with you after our Christmas sleigh ride."

Matthew nodded.

Lois's idle chatter continued until she must have realized no one was responding.

A few moments passed. This time Sarah broke the silence. "Well, I think it's great news." She paused as if waiting for someone to agree. When even Matthew didn't, she said, "I'm glad I told her that we might close the bakery."

"*You* told her that?" Joy said.

"*Jah,* the other day. She wanted to talk with someone about opening an account with us, and said something about serving our pastries in the motel breakfast room. I told her we probably wouldn't be open much longer."

A ball of fire rose to the back of Joy's throat. She closed her eyes as an image of Noah's confused expression crossed her mind.

"Joy, I don't know if you were in the room when Mrs. Paddock mentioned hiring you to run the bakery," Lois said, buttering a biscuit.

"I heard her."

"At least *nau* you'll be able to receive a paycheck for all your hard work." Her sister handed a sourdough biscuit to Philip.

"And I'll probably have someone interested enough in the bakery to show up on time to relieve me too," Joy scoffed. If her sisters cared, they could figure some way to save the bakery. *Together.* As a family.

"I know what you're trying to do," Sarah said. "You want me to feel guilty for being happy. I can't help that I never liked working there."

"It was *Mamm* and *Daed*'s dream," Joy said through gritted teeth.

"*Jah,* and after they died, you coveted the place."

Matthew cleared his throat and furrowed his brows. "Can we finish this discussion after supper?"

Joy poked at her food.

Once Philip finished eating and was dismissed from the table, Matthew resumed the conversation. "I realize selling the bakery is an emotional topic, and understandably so. But we should all be mindful of one another's feelings. Your parents wouldn't have wanted the bakery to cause division in the family."

Joy bowed her head. As painful as it was, her brother-in-law was right. Despite her sisters' acceptance of the sale, Joy couldn't help but wonder if they had done everything possible.

"Joy," Lois said softly. "Matthew has talked the power company into extending credit two months in a row. The water bill is behind too."

"I didn't know."

"I didn't think it would come to this," Matthew said. "Last year the fall color tours carried us through the winter. I assumed this year they would again, but the rain destroyed the season."

"I didn't know either." Sarah frowned. "I should have been more sensitive. I'm sorry."

Joy reached for her younger sister's hand and gently squeezed it. "Me too."

Tears streamed down Lois's cheeks. "I wish there was some other way." She clasped her hands with Joy and Sarah. "We can get through this together, right?"

Joy gave Lois's hand a gentle squeeze and nodded. They kept each other strong after the fire. They would make it through this difficult time as well. Just as Joy accepted the bakery's fate, another thought caused

an unexpected heaviness to fill her chest.
She might never see Noah again.

CHAPTER TWELVE

Joy weaved through the packed crowd of late arrivals while silently wishing Noah would walk through the bakery door. The sleigh ride was about to start. She hoped he hadn't changed his mind, but after the other day, she would understand if he never wanted to see her again.

Joy spotted an empty cookie tray on the long refreshment table and carried it into the kitchen to refill it.

Meredith trailed Joy. "Your dress is beautiful. I love that shade of green."

Joy gazed at her dress fondly. "*Mamm* made it for me . . . our last Christmas together." She busied herself with restocking the serving dish. "She knew *mei* favorite color was evergreen."

Her friend motioned to the tray. "Everyone loves the fudge cookies."

"*Jah,* they seem to be the favorite this year," Joy said, adding, "the last year," under her breath. She arranged the cookies, into rows.

"I see you made peppermint ones too." Meredith wiggled her brows.

"I've always planned on serving them tonight."

"I'm sure the hazardous roads have kept Noah away, otherwise he would be here."

"Nay." Joy shook her head. "After I accused him the other day and didn't even give him a chance to talk, I don't blame him for *nett* wanting to see me."

Meredith's eyes widened. "I think I heard the bell over the door."

Joy hadn't heard anything but the sound of lighthearted laughter from the other room. Yet when Meredith rushed to the kitchen's entrance and stood on her tiptoes to peek at the newcomers, Joy's heart raced. "Is it?"

"Nay." Her friend frowned. "It's Henry."

"Oh." She turned away to shield her disappointment.

Sarah poked her head into the kitchen long enough to deliver the news about the sleigh ride starting.

Meredith laced her arm around Joy's elbow. "You're still riding with Walter and me, right?"

"I think I'll wait here for everyone to

return. There are still a few things to get ready."

"Please *kumm.* I'll help you when we get back."

Joy shook her head. "With the bakery closing after tonight, I'd like to spend some time alone anyway."

"Are you sure?"

"Jah." Joy nudged her friend forward. "You and Walter have a *gut* time. I'll see you in a couple of hours."

The crowd thinned as people went out to the parked buggies.

Lois wrapped a knitted scarf around Philip's neck, then sent him out the door with Matthew. "I think everything is all set for when we get back," Lois said, tying the ribbon of her winter bonnet under her chin. "Aren't you going on the ride, Joy?"

"I thought I'd stay here and straighten up." Her words caught in the back of her throat. She smiled, hoping her sister didn't notice.

"Do you want me to stay with you?"

"I'll be all right. Besides, you stayed behind the last two years." She walked her sister to the door. "Have fun and stay warm."

"We won't be long," Lois said, shuffling out into the blowing snow.

Joy stood at the window and waved as the buggies pulled away one at a time. The special sleigh runners allowed the buggies to glide with ease over the snow. She recalled the previous years when she rode with Henry and how she'd hung on his every word, anticipating his proposal. It all seemed so silly now. Especially since he'd left with Priscilla tonight and seeing them together hadn't stirred even a morsel of envy. Her only regret now was how things ended with the two men she'd come to have feelings for. She wished she could find the words to explain why she had stopped writing, but she couldn't do that without telling him she'd developed feelings for him.

Her gaze dropped to the floor. Muddy from foot traffic and wet from melting snow, it needed mopping. Besides, she didn't have much to do besides prepare the hot cocoa. She filled a bucket with sudsy water and soaked the mop. Careful not to spill water on herself, she mopped the area and took the dirty water outside to discard. The cold wind sent a shiver down her spine. Everyone would want hot cocoa tonight.

Joy pulled one of the oversized soup pots down from the wire shelf. It was probably too early to start warming the milk, but she wanted everything ready. She set the container of cocoa next to the stove as the bell over the front door jingled. She glanced at the wall clock. Where had the time gone?

Joy grabbed a dishrag and, wiping her hands, walked into the front room. "Did the *kalt wedder* force you — ?"

"I hope it's all right that I'm late." Noah swept his hand over the snow-covered shoulder of his coat.

"*Jah* . . . I, um — you must be *kalt.*" She motioned to the kitchen. "I was getting ready to make cocoa. I'll make you a mug. It'll only take a minute. Do you like marshmallows? I have both large and small." She hated that her words had tumbled out so quickly, and she tried to calm her excitement. "The small marshmallows would probably —"

"Joy." He crossed the distance between them. "We need to talk."

Joy's fretting wouldn't concern Noah if it wasn't for how things were left the last time they were together. She'd offered him cocoa, but why was she fumbling over her words as though they were strangers? His stomach soured. "I, ah — I have something to tell you."

Voices flooded the bakery.

"They're back." She might as well have

flicked a rein for the way she vaulted into action.

Why did everyone have to return now? Just when he'd finally mustered the courage to confess.

"The milk for the cocoa is outside in a snowbank." She whizzed by him toward the back door.

He caught her arm as she reached for the handle. Heat ignited his core. "I'm *nett* the person you think I am."

"I know."

He swallowed hard. "You do?" How long had she known? He opened his mouth just as several women swarmed the kitchen.

Meredith raised her brows while the others held a stoic expression.

He dropped his hand from Joy's arm and took a few steps away.

"I don't think we've met," one woman said. "I'm Joy's sister Lois."

Unlike Joy's younger sister, who looked nothing like Joy, her older sister had the same small nose, big blue eyes, and sweet smile as Joy.

It wasn't until someone cleared their throat that Noah realized he hadn't responded. "It's nice to meet you. I'm Noah."

Joy's cheeks turned a rosy shade. "I should get the milk," she said.

"I'll bring it in." He bolted outside. The cold air caught in his throat and he coughed. Noah located the metal milk can and carried it inside.

The women's chatter hushed when he reentered and set the container on the counter. Joy thanked him without making eye contact. He motioned to the front room where the men were visiting and backed away from the group. "I don't want to be in your way." He rounded the corner as the women's chatter rose and paused. Noah stood among the aprons dangling from a wall hook to listen.

One woman's voice above the others asked Joy how she knew the young man.

"He's Mrs. Yoder's great-nephew from Berlin."

That was it? *Aenti* Lavern's nephew? At least Joy could have referred to him as a new friend. Noah waited to hear if Joy said anything else, but the topic shifted to his absentminded aunt. Noah joined the men loitering around the refreshment table.

He grabbed a plate from the stack and stood in line. Most of the cookies were ones he had tried. He selected his favorites — the frosted peppermint cookie, a brownie nut fudge bar, the oatmeal cranberry walnut cookie, and the one Joy called the snowball surprise — then meandered over to the window. Not too many people wanted to stand next to the drafty window, so it gave him a place to escape the crowd.

As he munched on a cookie, he stared out the window. It was too dark to see outside, but the reflection off the plate glass gave him a glimpse of the room. He noticed Joy's reflection walking toward him before she spoke.

"I brought you a cup of cocoa."

He turned to face her and accepted the warm mug. *"Danki."*

"After the other day, I wasn't sure if I would see you again," she said in a melancholy tone that touched his heart.

"You thought I'd pass up a chance to eat your cookies?"

"It's just that —" Joy turned when her friend and a man slightly taller than Noah approached.

"Walter, this is Noah. Noah lives in Berlin."

"I think I saw you at our Sunday service a couple of weeks ago," Walter said.

Noah nodded. *"Mei* father was the visiting bishop."

"It's nice that you could *kumm* back. So how were the roads?"

"A few patches of ice, but *nett* too bad."

Walter talked about the expected snowfall.

Noah liked meeting new people, but tonight he found himself distracted — dazed by Joy's nonchalant reaction. On his way here, he'd rehearsed how he would break the news of being her pen pal. That part was easier than he expected, but he still didn't know how she felt — why she stopped writing.

Cold air blasted into the room as the door opened and closed. He caught a glimpse of Meredith elbowing Joy's ribs and motioning with her head toward the door. Noah looked over his shoulder.

The newcomer's hat was snow-covered. He stretched his neck to look over the crowd. Noah might not have thought much of it, but Joy stepped away from their group and drifted over to that side of the room.

Noah turned to his side, coughed into his hand, then made up a flimsy excuse about needing a glass of water. Then instead of getting a drink, he slipped out the door. He couldn't stand by and watch her with another man. Noah trekked across the snowy parking area to his horse and buggy under the lamppost. He removed the horse's wool blanket and folded it in half.

"Noah, will you wait a minute?" Joy plowed through the drifts from the back side of the building and jogged to his buggy, carrying a pastry box. She placed one hand on her chest as if to calm her heavy breathing. "I didn't know — you were leaving — so soon."

Another time he might have taken it as a compliment that she rushed to catch him before he left. But he had just witnessed her scurrying across the room to meet someone else.

"It's late. Besides, the weather isn't that great and I have a long drive." He would drive in a blizzard if she gave him reason to.

"So you were going to leave without saying good-bye?"

"You were busy." He opened the buggy door and tossed the horse blanket inside.

She sighed. "That was rude of me to walk away, but —" She lowered her head.

"But what? You wanted to thank someone that you invited for coming?"

"*Jah,* sort of." She lifted her head. "I didn't recognize him as someone from our district. I thought — I thought he was the cabinetmaker."

"What . . . ?" He choked.

She drew back her head in visible surprise. "*Narrisch,* I know. We're *nett* pen pals anymore —"

"Excuse me," he said. "You stopped writing. *Nett* him."

The glow from the streetlamp flickered in her eyes as she stared at him.

His mind reeled. What was the conversation about in the kitchen? "When I told you earlier that I'm *nett* the person you think I am, what did you think I meant?"

She lowered her head. "I falsely accused you of telling Mrs. Paddock about the bakery closing."

"I only suggested she might consider ordering doughnuts to serve the motel guests. I had hoped it would bring you more business."

"I know. I found out Sarah told her about us closing." She burrowed the toe of her boot into the snow. "I'm sorry. I've been wrong about a lot of things lately."

"Does that include stopping your correspondence with the cabinetmaker?"

She shook her head.

So much for trying to reopen the subject. "Why did you stop writing?"

"You've asked that before. It's none of your business."

Noah untied the reins from the post. It was time to leave.

"It wasn't right to keep letters going back and forth with a man I didn't know," she blurted. "Our correspondence was due to a mistake from the beginning. He received a box of cookies and a letter I had written to *mei* cousin. He wrote me back and from there we started exchanging letters." She looked down. "I stopped because . . . well, I'm confused."

"A few weeks ago I was in the bakery when a man came in. He said after the Christmas sleigh ride, nothing would stand in your way."

"That was Henry. We were courting at the time *mei* parents died, and when I took on the bakery after their death, Henry and I drifted apart. He blamed the bakery for taking too much of *mei* time, so when he heard it might close, he thought nothing would stand in the way of our getting married."

It pained Noah too much to listen to more talk about Henry and her confusion. He couldn't offer any advice. He hadn't heeded his own advice. He'd fallen in love again.

Noah cleared his throat and motioned to the box in her hands. "Is that for me?"

She smiled. "*Jah.* I saved all the peppermint cookies for you."

"*Danki.*" He set the box on the buggy bench and reached for the gift he'd brought her. "This is for you."

Her eyes widened like a child's as she stared at the small brown wrapped package with its twine-tied bow. "I don't know what to say. I only gave you cookies."

"*Mei* favorite ones and that means a lot." He grinned. "Are you going to stare at it or open it?"

Joy pulled the twine and unwrapped the package. Her eyes welled with tears as she slowly lifted the glasses from the wooden box. "They're rose colored," she said.

"Read the note."

She removed the piece of paper he had tucked inside the box.

For a beautiful woman who sees things more differently than anyone I know. You said once that your vision was perfect and you didn't need glasses, but I wanted you to have these anyway. I hope one day you'll wear them when you look at me. Maybe then you won't see all my flaws.

Sincerely, Your Pen Pal

She sniffled. "Will you tell him *danki* for me?"

"You can tell him yourself." He motioned to the glasses. "Let's see how they look on you."

She shook her head. "It's late and it'll probably keep snowing and you have a long

295

drive ahead of you and —"

"Joy," he said.

She swiped her hand over her tear-streaked cheek. "I have to go back inside."

He nodded, opened the buggy door, and looked over his shoulder at her. "I hope you work out whatever it is standing in your way."

CHAPTER THIRTEEN

Erasing the daily specials board on the wall of the bakery was like erasing a big section of Joy's life.

Lois sidled up beside her. "I'm glad we decided to do this today instead of last *nacht.*"

"Me too." Joy had lost her desire to stay at the get-together after Noah left. She hid in the back room behind the storage shelves most of the night.

"Are we loading the *kaffi* cups?" Sarah asked.

"*Jah,* apparently Mrs. Paddock plans to buy mugs with a horse-and-buggy design on them." Lois rolled her eyes. "She thinks she's going to make the bakery more Amish by having fancy stuff." She motioned to the wall with the specials board. "She said something about taking down the slate board and putting up one that's lit."

The front door opened despite the sign in

the window that read Closed. Mrs. Paddock sashayed inside with a man dressed in jeans and a gray leather jacket.

"I hope you don't mind," she said. "I brought my assistant with me so we can discuss the changes."

"That's fine. We'll try to stay out of your way," Lois said. She turned to Sarah and Joy. "Matthew's *mamm* is watching the children and I told her I wouldn't be long. If you two don't mind finishing, I'll take this load of crates home."

"There isn't much more to pack," Sarah said. "I'll help you get it loaded." She took a step and paused. "Are you coming, Joy?"

"*Jah,* I'll be there in a minute."

Joy eyed the woman dressed in a short skirt and open-necked blouse and wearing bracelets that jingled like sleigh bells. Had this woman baked anything in her life? The man she introduced as her assistant jotted notes as she dictated. Every so often, he stopped writing to adjust his purple-rimmed glasses higher on his nose.

"I think we should consider expanding the front," she told the man. "We can change out the display cabinet. I'll have the cabinet-maker build something more rustic." The woman whirled around to face the window. "What do you think about all of this being

298

stained glass?"

The man nodded and wrote something on his pad.

"Yes," the woman said, agreeing with herself. "If the name was worked into the glass design, we could remove that hideous sign on the building."

"Excuse me," Joy said.

The woman turned. "Did you need something?"

Joy swallowed hard. "Did I hear you right? You want to take down the sign?"

"It's old and it doesn't fit the décor." The woman eyed Joy from *kapp* to shoes. "Are you the baker?"

"*Jah.*"

"Good. We can discuss the menu changes I want to make." She glanced at her assistant. "Make a note to check on uniforms. Something bright and cheerful."

Joy shook her head. "I don't think I can work for you."

"But that was part of the agreement."

Until the woman stepped closer, Joy hadn't realized how short she was compared to Mrs. Paddock.

"I plan to line up tours by the busload to see an authentic Amish bakery in operation."

Joy ran her hands down the sides of her

dress. "I do my baking at four in the morning."

"That's easy enough to fix. Everything nowadays can be shipped frozen."

"Frozen!" Joy's stomach knotted. "Then you're not interested in the homemade breads and pastries?"

"We might make one or two items. The majority will be brought in so we can cut waste and run more efficiently."

The man nodded. "You'll get used to commercialization."

"But I won't ever get used to being the product you're trying to sell."

"I know this is all new and it'll take some time to adjust. Take a few weeks off and relax. Go somewhere on vacation. It'll take that long to get the remodeling finished."

Joy stormed into the kitchen to give her sisters an earful, but they were gone. She yanked her cape off the hook and marched outside.

Standing near the driver's side of Abram's buggy, Sarah waved. "I'll be in shortly."

"It doesn't matter." Joy untied her mare from the post.

Sarah rushed to Joy's side and caught her arm as she was about to climb into her buggy. "What's wrong?"

"None of this is what *Mamm* and *Daed*

would have wanted. It's one thing to sell the building, but selling ourselves?" She shook her head. "I can't watch it happen — I can't partake in the . . . the phoniness of it all." Joy blew out a breath. "I have to get away from this place."

"Where are you going?"

"Don't worry. I'll be back to finish packing." Joy sat on the bench and flicked the reins. She figured she would waste a few hours at the fabric store, but noticing the letter and glasses she planned to put in the mail, she decided to take a longer drive.

Joy found the cabinet shop without much difficulty. The long drive gave her time to calm down. Now she wasn't sure dropping in uninvited was a good idea. But she climbed out of the buggy and scanned the area. The shop was almost as large as the barn set back on the property. A white two-story house with a large porch and forest-green flower boxes hanging under the windows shared the same driveway.

Joy wasn't expecting a woman to open the shop door.

"Can I help you?" the young woman said.

Maybe driving over here was the wrong thing to do. She could pretend to be lost and ask for directions back to the main road. But she couldn't let things go unsaid any longer. "I'd like to see the cabinet-maker." Joy walked closer to the shop.

The woman opened the door wider. "He isn't here right *nau,* but I can show you some samples." She walked over to the far side of the room and pointed to a board displaying different types of wood. "Are you doing a kitchen? *Mei bruder* can build anything."

"Your *bruder*?"

She nodded. "He's a very *gut* cabinet-maker." The girl's gaze dropped to the wooden box in Joy's hand. "What's that you've got in your hands?"

"I, um . . ." Distracted by the warmth that flooded her cheeks, Joy was unable to respond.

The woman smiled. "I shouldn't be so nosy, but I take it you're *nett* here to see any kitchen cabinet samples, are you?"

"*Nay,* I was hoping to talk with your *bruder.* But I can do it another time." Joy turned toward the door.

"It's close to suppertime, he won't be long." The woman motioned to another door on the opposite side of the office. "You can wait in his shop. It'll give you a chance to see some of the projects he's working on."

"Are you sure he won't mind?" Joy didn't

want to impose, but she was curious to see his craftsmanship.

"He won't." She opened the door. "I'd give you a tour, but I have a few things I need to do first. By the way, I'm Stella."

"It's nice to meet you. I'm Joy Stolzfus."

Stella smiled, backed out of the shop, and closed the door.

Joy scanned the room. Piled lumber took up the far wall while an assortment of tools hanging from pegs took up another. In the corner sat a wooden chair next to the potbelly woodstove. A few miscellaneous cabinets with customer tags dangling from the handles were off to the side. She circled the long wooden worktable in the center of the room, not intentionally snooping, but too curious not to look at some of the paperwork. She spied a copy of the heart of roses quilt pattern and a small box of stained glass pieces and gasped.

The door opened and Noah appeared, a blank expression on his face.

"*You're* the cabinetmaker." She lifted the pattern. "I thought you did stained glass."

He stepped closer. "I do both."

"I've been such a fool!" Joy tossed the pattern on the table, stormed past him, and shot out the door. She untied Candy from the post and climbed onto the bench.

"Joy, wait!" Noah leaped in front of the horse, but his foot slipped on a patch of ice and he fell. He rolled out of the way of Candy's hoof at the same time Joy was commanding the horse to stop.

Joy jumped out of the buggy. "Noah!" She gasped, dropping to her knees at his side. "Say something, please." She placed her hand on his shoulder, but when he rolled to face her, tears blurred her vision.

"I'm all right."

"How bad are you hurt?" She brushed the tears away.

"Don't cry." He groaned as he pushed off the ground. Unable to put weight on his ankle, he teetered. "See, I'm fine."

She placed her arm around his waist and steadied his wobbling. "Let me help you to the *haus*."

"*Nay,* help me into the shop, please." Noah cupped his hand on her shoulder and drew her closer to his side.

Noah hobbled into the workshop with Joy's help. Attempting to stop a moving horse was ridiculous, but at least he'd kept Joy from leaving. Having his arm around her waist made the shards of pain worth it.

He reached the worktable and leaned against it, taking the weight off his foot.

That was a mistake. She moved out from under his arm, placing too much distance between them. He groaned.

"I'll bring your chair over to you," Joy said. "You need to sit and elevate your leg."

Not the response he wanted. Was it bad to moan in order to elicit her guilt? She had practically run him over.

Joy slid the rocker from the corner of the shop, helped him into the chair, then grabbed a wooden bench next to the table and placed it before him.

Noah grimaced as he lifted his leg up on the bench. He didn't have to fake his re-action. His ankle throbbed.

"You're in a lot of pain. I'm so sorry."

"I'll be okay." He blew out a breath — exaggerated, but he was desperate.

"Do you need anything? A cup of *kaffi*? I could have your sister bring out a pillow."

"I need your forgiveness." He reached for her hand, but she stepped out of his reach.

"I'll ask Stella to check on you," she said, avoiding eye contact. She turned to the door. "Good-bye, Noah."

The air left Noah's lungs when the door shut and Joy was gone. His throbbing ankle wasn't nearly as painful as his broken heart. He should have listened to his inner voice and told her the truth weeks ago.

Now he'd lost her forever. Noah closed his eyes.

Deceived and made to look like a fool by Noah, Joy felt like her life had crumbled like a dry piecrust. At least with a bad crust she could add a dash of milk and fix the problem. Her problems were unfixable. Her heart ached for Noah, for the bakery, for her parents. She wasn't sure how to start over, but working for Mrs. Paddock wasn't the answer.

She pulled into the bakery and took a few moments to dry her eyes. Both Lois's and Sarah's buggies were there as well as the *Englischer*'s car. Joy straightened her shoulders, lifted her chin, and marched into the bakery through the back door. The building was cool without the ovens on. Her throat tightened as she looked around the lifeless kitchen. She made her way to the storefront and stood behind the counter one last time. Joy spotted fingerprints on the display cabinet and grabbed the bottle of cleaning solution. She couldn't let the business change hands with the display smudged. She sprayed the cleaner and for half a second watched the liquid run down the glass. She wasn't looking through rose-colored glasses now — everything was distorted. "There you are," Lois said. "*Kumm* sit with us. We're going over a few details."

Joy finished wiping the area, then set the cleaner and rag aside. She nodded at Mrs. Paddock and her assistant as she pulled a chair out from the table and sat between Lois and Sarah.

Joy caught sight of the bakery sign leaning against the wall. Her parents' dreams — her dreams — now lay in a heap. She pushed back the tears.

"We should have the final paperwork drawn up by next week," Mrs. Paddock said to Lois. She turned her attention to Joy. "I look forward to you working for me. It should be easier since the line of baked goods will be streamlined and you'll have less baking."

"I've decided not to accept the job."

"Oh." Mrs. Paddock turned to Lois. "This wasn't what we discussed."

Lois reached under the table for Joy's hand. "I thought you wanted to continue working here."

Joy shook her head.

Mrs. Paddock shifted in her chair. "The offer I made was contingent upon being able to assume the Stolzfus business name and retaining a Stolzfus baker."

307

"Who doesn't need to bake," Joy added. "That isn't me. Maybe Lois or Sarah will work for you, but I won't put my name behind frozen baked goods that are shipped in." She stood. "I'll sign whatever paperwork you need me to, Lois, but I won't be part of this new bakery. I don't need this storefront to continue selling my baked goods."

"We can talk about this later at home," Lois said.

"We need to talk about this now." Mrs. Paddock adjusted her reading glasses and flipped through her paperwork. "I think you'll find on page eight a noncompete clause." She tilted her head to look over her glasses. "Do you understand what that means? You cannot sell baked goods within a ten-mile radius for five years."

Joy smiled. "Then I'll sell potholders. I think people will buy a potholder if it comes with a free baked good."

Mrs. Paddock shuffled her papers. "You don't own your recipes either."

"I already have ideas for new ones." Joy left the table. She refused to be a pushover any longer. Her sisters would have to decide which of them wanted to become Mrs. Paddock's new baker. She grabbed her apron from the kitchen hook and went outside.

The setting sun cast a warm glow of pinks

over the snow. A strange sense of peace washed over her.

Noah limped to the door and met Stella as she was coming inside the house. "Did I get any mail?"

She shook her head. "You've asked the last three days. Are you expecting something urgent?"

"*Nay,* I suppose *nett.*" He shoved his foot into his boot. The swelling in his ankle had gone down enough that he could finally wear them again. Noah removed his coat from the hook beside the door and hobbled outside. Cooped up in the house for three days, he needed fresh air. He ambled over to his shop, not to work, but to be alone.

Noah noticed the rose-colored glasses he'd given Joy on the table and picked them up. He sure messed things up. An envelope with her writing scrawled on the front caught his eye for the first time. How had he missed it? He tore it open.

Dear Cabinetmaker,
The rose-colored glasses are beautiful, but I'm afraid I cannot accept them. My eyesight is no longer clouded. When you didn't come to the Second Christmas sleigh ride, I realized God had placed

you in my life for a short season — until
I could see clearly. You should be happy
to know, because of you, I no longer see
the world distorted as before. I've enjoyed our correspondence and friendship and I thank God for you. I might
have married Henry if you hadn't written me back and said all those things.

Sincerely,
Your Pen Pal

Noah folded the letter as Stella entered
the shop. "I hitched your buggy for you,"
she said.

"Why?"

She planted her hand on her hip. "Can
you really let someone you love go?"

"I've always believed that if it's meant to
be —"

"If you're going to listen to that foolish
advice, then Ruby's the *maydel* for you. You
let her go and she returned, right?"

"Stella, I told you before —"

"I know you're *nett* in love with Ruby. But
you are in love with the woman from the
bakery. The one you made the glasses for."

He opened his mouth to speak, but she
cut him off.

"I hitched the buggy for you. You have ten

miles to figure out what you're going to say to her."

Could he risk rejection — again?

Mrs. Paddock sat at Lois and Matthew's kitchen table, pen and contract in hand, along with a plate of Joy's peppermint cookies positioned before her. "Have you given any more thought to working for me, Joy?"

"I haven't changed my mind." Joy lowered her head. She couldn't bring herself to look at Matthew or see the disappointment in her sister's eyes.

"I came prepared with a cashier's check," Mrs. Paddock told Matthew. "But under the current conditions . . ."

"We understand your reservation," Matthew said. "And we're having second thoughts as well."

Joy stared at her brother-in-law in disbelief. The topic of selling the bakery was hardly mentioned over the last three days.

Matthew continued. "I think it's in both of our interests to not go through with the sale."

Mrs. Paddock stared at him a moment, then gathered the contract off the table. "I'm sorry it didn't work out," she said, tucking the papers into her briefcase. Mrs. Paddock stood and Matthew walked her to the door.

Joy leaned closer to Lois. "What just happened?"

Lois smiled. "We agreed with you. Mrs. Paddock wanted to make too many changes." She wiped her eyes with a hankie. "It didn't hit me until I saw the bakery sign leaning against the wall."

Joy's eyes welled. "Has Matthew *kumm* up with a way for us to keep it?"

"We'll have to trust God for either the financial means or the *right* buyer."

"With *nay* clauses forbidding me to bake." Joy removed a cookie from the plate and took a bite. She'd released the bakery into God's hands and He'd prevented the sale. If only she could release her feelings for Noah as easily.

Several minutes passed before Matthew returned to the kitchen. When Joy looked up, her eyes connected with Noah's.

"Hiya." Noah wiped his hands on the sides of his pants.

Joy blinked several times.

Lois nudged her arm. "Joy, you have a visitor."

"Wh-what are you doing here?"

Noah gulped. "I, ah . . . I was hoping we

could talk." He motioned to the door. "Outside?"

"Okay." She stood and swept her hand over the wrinkles in her dress. "I need to get *mei* cloak," she said without looking him in the eye. She grabbed her cloak from the wall hook and followed him.

"I thought we could go on a sleigh ride." He motioned to his buggy.

She hesitated. "Noah, I don't think —"

"Please." He smiled.

Joy looked down.

"A short ride." He needed to talk with her. God hadn't made a mistake when her package was delivered to him.

Joy climbed into the buggy.

Noah hurried and untied the reins, then climbed onto the bench. Sitting this close, a sweet scent of peppermint filled his senses. He tapped the reins before she changed her mind about going.

Pulling onto the main road, the buggy's blade runners scraped the pavement until he turned down the first snow-covered trail.

"Are you warm?" he asked.

"*Jah,* I'm fine. How's your ankle?"

"This is the first day the swelling went down enough to put my boot on."

"I feel awful. Are you still in pain?"

"*Nay, nett* anymore." At least not his

ankle. His heart was another matter. Silence fell between them. Noah focused on the white puffs of air lingering around the horse's head as his thoughts went a million directions. Anxiety was boring a hole through his stomach; he had to find a place to stop. At the first narrow path wide enough for a sleigh, he stopped Cracker.

"I brought some hot cocoa." Noah reached behind the seat for the thermos. He poured a mug of steaming hot chocolate and handed it to her, then poured another mug for himself.

"*Danki.*" She sipped the drink, leaving a film of milk chocolate on her upper lip.

He smiled.

"What?"

He gently wiped the chocolate off with his thumb. Her eyes widened and he jerked his hand back. "I'm sorry. I shouldn't have taken the liberty." She blushed.

Noah shifted on his seat so that he faced her. "I tried to tell you I was your pen pal the *nacht* of the Christmas gathering."

"Why didn't you?"

"I lost *mei* nerve. I thought if you knew I was the cabinetmaker, you would stop talking to me — like you stopped writing." He paused. *Say you understand . . .* "I read the letter you left with the glasses in *mei* shop.

It said you were following *mei* advice and letting me go."

She nodded. "*Mei* feelings were torn between two men."

His heart twisted. "Henry and who?"

Joy shook her head. "The cabinet-maker . . . and you." Her eyes welled with moisture.

She blinked and tears rolled down her face. He set his mug on the floorboard of the buggy, then lifted his hand to her face and dried her tears. Their gazes locked. He leaned closer — slowly — giving her a chance to resist. But overtaken by the powerful scent of cocoa and peppermint, he lowered his lips to hers, taking possession of her soft, sweet lips in a consuming way. He slipped his hand behind her shoulder and pressed her closer, deepening his kiss.

Her mug of hot chocolate tipped in her hand and hot liquid soaked into his pant leg. He broke from the embrace long enough to set her mug on the floor, then he took her back into his arms and kissed her with even more boldness.

She broke from the kiss, breathless. "Noah!"

He leaned back so he could look her in the eye. "I'm sorry. Did I go too far?"

"It won't work between us," she whispered

hoarsely.

"*Jah,* it will. I know ten miles seems like a long ways, but —"

She scooted closer to the door. "I stopped writing because of what you said about Ruby. You didn't want her to become a seamstress — just like Henry didn't want me to work at the bakery."

Noah shook his head. "It wasn't because Ruby wanted to work. She allowed the world to persuade her to leave the faith. She wanted the *Englisch* lifestyle — not our way." He brushed his hand against her wet face. "You're *nett* thinking about becoming a fancy baker and leaving for the *Englisch* world, are you?"

"*Nay,* of course *nett.*"

"*Gut.*" He inched closer. "Because I didn't just fall in love with your peppermint cookies, I fell in love with *you.*" He leaned down and kissed her softly on the forehead. "*Mei* pen pal."

Joy sighed. "In your letter it didn't sound like you loved *mei* cookies. You said I put too much peppermint in them."

He grinned. "Do you forgive me?"

"That depends." She smiled. "Are you still going to be *mei* pen pal?"

"*Jah.* Are you going to keep making me cookies?"

"Hmm . . ."

Noah pulled her into his arms. He trailed kisses from the tip of her nose, across her cheek, and over to her earlobe. "I have a new cookie idea," he whispered in her ear.

She giggled. "Oh *jah*?"

"Cocoa" — he trailed kisses along her jaw to her lips — "and peppermint. They taste *gut* together."

"I'll have to mix up a batch." She nestled into his embrace as large snowflakes fluttered to the ground.

"Joy," he whispered.

She lifted her head and gazed into his eyes.

"Didn't your *daed* propose to your *mamm* on a sleigh ride?"

"Jah." Her voice quivered.

"I'm in love with you . . . and —"

She sat up straighter. "Are you proposing?"

Noah winked. "You'll have to watch your mail."

READING GROUP GUIDE

1. Joy is so excited about the Second Christmas sleigh ride that she begins planning what refreshments she will serve in October. Do you have Christmas traditions that you look forward to every year?

2. Joy's sister accused Joy of coveting the bakery since their parents' death. Can you see how easily it could happen? Have you found that you've been guilty of coveting something in your life?

3. Could you relate to Joy's pain when the soon-to-be new owner wanted to change the bakery? Did she make the right decision when she refused to take the job?

4. Noah struggled with telling Joy he was her secret pen pal because he had been hurt in a past relationship. Was his failure to tell her who he

was the same as lying? Would you be able to forgive someone as Joy was able to forgive Noah?

5. Joy was upset when she found out that the new owner planned to bring in frozen products and wanted to modernize the bakery while at the same time use the family name. Was there ever a time in your life when you felt as though you were expected to conform to an idea or practice you didn't believe in?

ACKNOWLEDGMENTS

Without my Lord and Savior, Jesus Christ, my thoughts would be paralyzed — so to Him I give the highest praise!

To my agent, Mary Sue Seymour, and my editors, Becky Philpott and Natalie Hanemann, you are all so wonderful and supportive. Thank you for believing in me.

To the team at HarperCollins Christian Publishing, your dedication is truly amazing! Thank you so much for giving me the opportunity to fulfill my dreams.

To my husband, Dan, and my children, Lexie, Danny, and Sarah, your support and encouragement are such a blessing! I love you all so much.

To my critique partners and brainstorm buddies (you know who you are), I am so honored to have you as friends and prayer partners. My virtual sisters, your help is more valuable than words can express.

ABOUT THE AUTHOR

Ruth Reid is a full-time pharmacist who lives in Florida with her husband and three children. When attending Ferris State University School of Pharmacy in Big Rapids, Michigan, she lived on the outskirts of an Amish community and had several occasions to visit the Amish farms. Her interest grew into love as she saw the beauty in living a simple life.

A GIFT FOR
ANNE MARIE

KATHLEEN FULLER

To Zoie, my writer-in-training. I love you!

GLOSSARY

ab im kopp: out of the head
ach: oh
aenti: aunt
appeditlich: delicious
boppli: baby
bruder: brother
buwe: boys
daag: day
daed: dad
danki: thanks
dochder: daughter
familye: family
frau: wife
geh: go
grossmutter: grandmother
grossvatter: grandfather
gut: good
gut nacht: good night
hallo: hello
haus: house
kaffee: coffee

kapp: head covering
kinn: child
kinner: children
maed: girls
maedel: girl
mamm: mom
mann: man
mei: my
mudder: mother
nee: no
nix: nothing
onkel: uncle
perfekt: perfect
schee: pretty
schwester: sister
sehr: very
sohn: son
ya: yes
yer: your

CHAPTER ONE

Paradise, Pennsylvania

Anne Marie Smucker pulled back the light-blue curtains and peered outside into the darkness. On her rural street, the only available light was the tall streetlamp a few houses down. She tapped her fingers against the window frame and squinted. *Where is he?* Her best friend Nathaniel was never late for game night.

She let the curtains fall and breathed in the scent of wintergreen and cinnamon. The spirit of the holiday was in the air. Her mother had started decorating for the season — placing pine boughs, cinnamon sticks tied with winter-white ribbon, and dried orange slices in a small arrangement on an end table near the front window in the living room. Like all her decorating, she kept it simple, yet lovely.

A few minutes later she went into the kitchen. Her mother stood by the stove, peeling off the foil from a pie plate. "What's that?" Anne Marie asked.

"A new pumpkin pie recipe I tried yesterday. I'm hoping it will be *gut* enough for this year's Christmas cookbook." Her mother looked at her. "Would you like to try some?"

Anne Marie frowned. "Pumpkin? *Nee.*"

"I thought you liked pumpkin."

"That must be your other *dochder.*"

"I only have one *dochder,* and she's handful enough."

Anne Marie chuckled as she moved closer to her mother and peeked at the pie. Flawless, as usual, with a golden, high-edged crust. It looked appetizing — to someone who liked pumpkin.

Mamm picked up a knife and sliced a small wedge. She put the piece on a nearby saucer. "Nathaniel's not here yet?"

"Nee." She frowned.

She heard a light tapping sound on the window of the back door. She turned and saw her friend Ruth Troyer waving a mitten-covered hand.

Anne Marie opened the door and let Ruth inside. "This is a surprise."

Ruth smiled, the tip of her nose red from the cold air. "I hope you don't mind me dropping by for a minute." She looked at

Anne Marie's mother. "*Frau* Smucker."

"*Hallo,* Ruth. Would you like a piece of pie?" *Mamm* asked.

"*Nee.* I just need to speak with Anne Marie for a minute." Ruth came closer to her and leaned in, her honey-colored eyes wide with curiosity. "Is Nathaniel here?"

Anne Marie shook her head. "He's a little late tonight."

Ruth let out a breath. "*Gut.*" She lowered her voice. "Is there somewhere we can talk?"

"We can *geh* into the living room."

Once they entered the room, Ruth walked to the coffee table where Anne Marie had laid out the Scrabble board and tiles. "I see you're ready for your game night." She looked at Anne Marie. "I wish you'd come to the singing with me and Hannah tonight. You used to like them."

"I did when I was younger. I don't really see a reason to *geh* anymore."

Ruth frowned. "Because you're busy with Nathaniel?"

It seemed like the temperature in the room dropped twenty degrees. Anne Marie blinked. "Is something wrong, Ruth?"

Her friend paused. "Not really. It's just . . ." Ruth clasped her hands together, her mittens making a soft clapping sound as they met. "I need your help."

"Of course."

"But I need to know something first."

Anne Marie nodded. "What's that?"

"Are you and Nathaniel together?"

That was the last thing she expected Ruth to say. "What? Of course not."

Ruth blew out a breath. "*Gut.* Then you can help me get Nathaniel's attention."

"Attention? Why?"

Ruth cocked her head and rolled her eyes. "I have to explain it to you?"

Anne Marie paused. Then her eyes widened. "You like Nathaniel?"

She rolled her eyes. "You're just as oblivious as he is."

"What?"

Ruth put her hands on the back of the chair near the coffee table. "I don't know what to do to get him to notice me. I've dropped so many hints on him the past couple of weeks, I'm surprised he doesn't have a headache. I even asked him to tonight's singing. But then he reminded me about Sunday game night, which *of course* he couldn't miss."

Was that a touch of bitterness in Ruth's tone? "I didn't know you felt that way about him," Anne Marie said.

"Now you do. So, will you help me?"

Anne Marie turned up the damper on the

woodstove in the corner of the room. "I'm not sure what I can do."

"You can give us your blessing."

She whirled around, confused. "Ruth, I'm not Nathaniel's keeper. He's free to court anyone he wants to."

Ruth dug her hands into her coat pockets. "You know how shy he is, so if you'll just give him a nudge in *mei* direction. A small one. Then I'll take care of the rest." Before Anne Marie could respond, Ruth added, "I have to *geh* or Hannah will have a fit." She touched Anne Marie on the arm. *"Danki."*

"You're wel—"

But Ruth had disappeared before the words left Anne Marie's mouth.

She stood there in the living room, feeling the warmth of the woodstove and looking at the Scrabble board, trying to absorb what her friend had told her. Ruth liked Nathaniel. She hadn't seen that coming. She also hadn't thought her friend would be so forward about it. And she wouldn't consider Nathaniel shy. Reserved, sometimes. But not shy. As she walked back to the kitchen, she tried to picture Ruth and Nathaniel as a couple. But she couldn't see him with Ruth. She thought about other young women in the district. Who would she pair up with Nathaniel? For some reason, she couldn't imagine him with anyone.

"Ruth blew out of here in a hurry." *Mamm* wiped down the counter to the left of the white cast-iron sink. "Is everything all right?"

"*Ya.* I guess."

Mamm lifted a questioning brow. "What does that mean?"

"Sorry I'm late." Nathaniel appeared in the kitchen doorway. "Jonah let me in." He'd already removed his jacket and hat, his thick, dark-brown hair popping up in hanks all over his head. He tried smoothing it down, but it was no use. He'd always had trouble taming his hair. When they were sixteen he had come over to help her spread sawdust on the floor of the barn. Before they started, he'd tripped into the huge pile. She remembered how the small chips of wood and dust had stuck in his hair, how she'd run her fingers through the thick strands to help him get it out . . .

"Something smells *gut.*" He lifted his nose as he stepped into the kitchen.

Anne Marie shook her head, clearing her mind of the memory, and the tingly sensation suddenly coursing through her.

"What are you making, Lydia?" Nathaniel asked.

"Pumpkin pie." *Mamm* cast a sharp look

at Anne Marie. "Keep your comments to yourself."

Anne Marie held up her palms. "I wasn't going to say a word."

"Are there samples?" Nathaniel asked.

"Of course." Her mother cut another slice. "I'm glad *someone* appreciates my cooking."

"Now that's not fair," Anne Marie said. "You know I like everything you make. Everything that doesn't contain pumpkin, that is. Plus, your cookbooks are in such high demand, we can barely keep up production. Clearly, many people in Paradise love your recipes." She moved away from the counter. "That reminds me, I can help you bind the rest of the cookbooks and fill the Christmas orders. It's just a couple weeks away."

"I think you have enough to do with your candle orders," *Mamm* said.

"I can handle both."

"Always thinking about work." *Mamm* shook her head. "We have time." She looked at Nathaniel, then at Anne Marie. "Now *geh* play your game."

When they entered the living room, he moved one of the chairs closer to the coffee table and sat down. He leaned over and started selecting tiles. But Anne Marie's mind wasn't on Scrabble. She was still thinking about Ruth's request. How should she tell him that Ruth liked him? Just blurt it out? Hint at it? She had no idea what Ruth meant by nudging Nathaniel in her direction. She'd never played matchmaker before.

He glanced up. "You going to sit down?"

She looked at him. Saw the competitive gleam in his eye. Ruth could wait — they had a game to play. She grinned and sat down.

He wiggled his dark brows. "Ready to lose?"

"Um, *nee*. When was the last time you beat me at Scrabble?"

"A month ago."

"I let you win."

He smiled and clasped his hands behind his head. "Keep telling yourself that."

Determined to prove him wrong, they began to play . . . and she forgot all about Ruth.

Nearly two hours later, the game was almost tied. Nathaniel didn't know how she did it. But with stealthy play and a lot of thought — sometimes so much thought he had to prod her to take her turn — she'd racked up the points. She twisted the end of one of her *kapp* strings as she surveyed the board. Her thin finger traced a line across the top of one of her tiles leaning against the holder, her blond eyebrows forming a *V* above her pale-blue eyes. He tapped his foot, glancing at the clock hanging on the wall. "Anytime now."

"Don't rush me. I'm thinking."

"Think a little faster. I have to get home."

"Ready for more pie?" Nathaniel looked up to see Lydia walk into the living room carrying a tray with one piece of pie and two glasses of tea. Anne Marie took the glass. She sipped, her attention still on the board. Nathaniel accepted the pie and tea. *"Danki."* He took a huge bite, the taste of cinnamon and pumpkin exploding in his mouth. There was a good reason Lydia Smucker's holiday cookbooks sold out every year right before Christmas. He scooped a smaller portion with his fork and held it out to Anne Marie. "Sure you don't want a little taste?"

She smirked at his offering. "*Ya.* I'm sure."

"You don't know what you're missing." He waved it in front of her. "It's the best pumpkin pie I've ever had."

"That's kind of you to say, Nathaniel," Lydia said.

He moved his fork closer to Anne Marie.

"I know why you won't try this."

She folded her arms. "Why?"

"Because you're afraid you might like it. Then you'll have to admit you were wrong."

"Fine." She grabbed the fork and stuck the tip of her tongue to the pie. She closed her mouth and smacked her lips. "I tasted it. I still don't like it."

"More for me, then." He finished off the bite, looking up at Lydia. He paused at her puzzled look, the fork still in his mouth. "What?"

Anne Marie's mother looked at him, then at her daughter. *"Nix.* Just . . . *nix."* She turned and left the room.

"What was that about?" Nathaniel asked after he polished off the bite.

Anne Marie shrugged, still focused on the game board. With a swift movement she grabbed the rest of the tiles on her stand and placed them on the board. *T A S T Y.* She gave him a triumphant smile.

"More like ironic." He set down the empty dish. "Congratulations. You won."

Her smile widened, the tiny scar at the corner of her mouth disappearing. He remembered the day she'd gotten it. They were both seven, and he'd pushed her a little too hard in the swing at school. She face planted on the ground and the ragged edge of a stone had sliced her lip. Thirteen years later, he still felt bad about it.

After cleaning up the game, he and Anne Marie walked to his buggy. "Same time next week?" He grabbed the horse's reins. "Although I'm picking the game this time."

"Life on the Farm?"

"Of course." He unwrapped the reins from the hitching post underneath the barn awning and took the blanket off his horse. He folded it and tossed it in the buggy.

"Before you *geh* . . ." She moved nearer, rubbing her arms through the thin long sleeves of her dress. "I have something to tell you."

"Okay." He faced her.

"Um . . ." She looked away.

Nathaniel frowned. "Is something wrong?" She had never been hesitant to talk to him before.

"*Nee.*" She faced him again, drawing in a breath. "Ruth Troyer likes you." The words flew out of her mouth like a caged bird being set free.

He leaned against the buggy, his cheeks heating against his will. Ruth was one of the prettiest girls in their district, but he had never thought about her romantically.

"Well?" Anne Marie drew her arms closer to her chest.

"Well what?"

"What are you going to do about it?"

"I don't know. Give me a minute to think."

"You should probably ask her out." Her eyes narrowed in the faint yellow light from the lamppost down the street.

He didn't respond. He'd gone out with a couple of *maed* in the past two years. Yet he wouldn't have called the dates successful. More like awkward. And forgettable.

"Don't be so gun-shy." Anne Marie rubbed his horse's nose.

"Don't be so bossy."

She glanced at him. "Sorry." She faced him. "Nathaniel, if you don't ask her out, you'll never know if you're well suited. Maybe ask her to next week's singing."

"What about our game night?"

"We can miss it for one week. Especially for a *gut* reason."

Nathaniel climbed into the buggy. "I'll think about it." He looked at her. "Why are you so eager for me and Ruth to *geh* out?"

She took a step back and looked at the ground. "Because . . ."

"Because?"

She finally met his gaze. "I just think you two would be a *gut* couple. That's all." She turned and hurried toward her house.

"Gut nacht," he called after her.

She gave him a half wave and ran inside, like she couldn't get away from him fast enough.

Huh. He frowned, wondering why she was acting strange all of a sudden. Things were fine all evening until she brought up Ruth. Was something else going on? Maybe, but knowing Anne Marie he'd have to pry it out of her. Or wait until she was ready to tell him.

He tapped on the horse's flank with the reins and headed home, his mind on Anne Marie, not Ruth Troyer.

CHAPTER TWO

After Nathaniel drove off, Anne Marie walked into the living room, rubbing her hands together to warm her cold fingers. She'd done her duty where Ruth was concerned. Yet something didn't feel right. Ruth was one of Anne Marie's closest friends. She was kind to everyone, one of the more intelligent people she knew, and of course, extremely pretty. Yet despite all of Ruth's wonderful qualities, one question kept nagging at her.

Was she good enough for Nathaniel?

She snatched up the half-empty tea glasses off the coffee table, feeling guilty for even thinking such a thing. Who was she to judge Ruth? Still, she had to wonder. Nathaniel deserved someone special. Someone who could appreciate his quiet nature, his almost obsessive attention to small details, his ability to make sure everyone around him felt comfortable, his —

"*Yer* boyfriend gone already?" Her younger brother Christopher walked into the room.

Anne Marie grimaced. Fifteen-year-old brothers were a thorn. The tea glasses clanked together in her hand. "That joke is getting old."

"Not as old as you." Christopher laughed and left the room.

Anne Marie sighed. Christopher never missed a chance to tease her about Nathaniel. At least her other brother, Jonah, left their friendship alone. She entered the empty kitchen. *"Mamm?"* No answer. Odd, since the pie remained uncovered on the counter and her mother never left food sitting out. Anne Marie placed the foil over the pie plate and crimped the edges. Then she started on the dishes. She had just finished washing the last tea glass when her mother scurried into the room.

"*Danki* for cleaning up, Anne Marie. I meant to do that. I went upstairs for a moment and got distracted." A small smile formed on her mother's face as she grabbed a rag and started wiping down the table.

Anne Marie put the glasses away. "You seem happy tonight. Any particular reason?"

"I'm excited about Christmas," *Mamm* said quickly. She looked at Anne Marie.

"Aren't you?"

"I will be once all the candles are made."

Her mother patted her on the shoulder. "I'm so glad you've taken over that part of our business. I just couldn't do both anymore."

"I'm happy to do it. And remember, I can help with the cookbooks too."

Her mother shook out the rag over the sink. "I don't want you to spend all your time working. You need to *geh* out and socialize more."

"I plan to visit *Aenti* Miriam before she has her *boppli.*"

Her mother lifted her brow. "Anyone else?"

"If I have time."

"We make time for the people who are important to us."

"Which is why I'm going to visit *Aenti* Miriam." At her mother's sigh, Anne Marie held up her hands. "What?"

"Never mind. *Gut nacht,* Anne Marie."

Anne Marie shrugged and completed the finishing touches in the kitchen before heading to her room. She unpinned her *kapp,* giving one last thought to what her mother said. Lately *Mamm* had been making comments about Anne Marie spending more time with her friends. Anne Marie was satisfied with her life — she loved her candle business, and she saw her friends more than her mother realized. Just because she didn't go to singings or date didn't mean she didn't have a social life, or that she wasn't happy.

Yes, things were fine the way they were.

Anne Marie turned off the battery-powered lamp on her bedside table and snuggled under several thick quilts her aunt Miriam had made over the years. She thanked God for all the blessings in her life before closing her eyes and drifting to sleep.

After what seemed like only seconds later, the door to her room flew open. Her mother rushed to the bed. "Anne Marie! Seth is here."

She sat up, bleary eyed. "What?"

"It's Miriam. She's having the *boppli*."

"But it's early yet —"

"Get dressed. We must hurry."

Anne Marie scrambled out of bed, the sense of peace she'd felt before falling asleep replaced by alarm over her aunt going into early labor. She said a short, heartfelt prayer for her *aenti* Miriam's safety, and for the health of the unborn child.

Anne Marie bit at her nails as she paced the length of Miriam and Seth's small living room. Her mother had taken their son, Seth Junior, back to their house. Anne Marie thought it a wise decision. She flinched as Miriam's screams pierced the air.

She glanced at *Onkel* Seth standing by the window. He leaned against his cane. He and her aunt were only a few years older than she was. His handsome face and strong body bore the scars of a reckless youth. Now he was a responsible *mann* and father who deeply loved his family.

"Miriam will be all right," she said, crossing the room to stand next to him. She looked outside the window at the pink-and-lavender-tinged clouds streaking across the horizon, signaling the rising sun.

Another scream. Seth's knuckles turned white. "It wasn't this bad with Junior," he whispered. "I feel so helpless."

She grabbed his hand. "Then let's pray for God's help."

They both stood in front of the window, holding hands, each of them saying their own silent prayer for Miriam. When Miriam screamed again, Seth gripped Anne Marie's hand. She winced. As his wife's cries subsided, he loosened his grip.

"Sorry." He pulled out of her grasp.

"It's okay." She put her hand behind her and flexed her sore fingers.

At the sound of a newborn's cry, they both turned around. Seth's shoulders slumped. "Thank God."

A few moments later, Nathaniel's mother, Mary, entered the living room, a huge smile on her face. A midwife for years, Mary had delivered Seth and Miriam's son. "A girl, Seth. You have a *maedel.*"

"Can I . . . ?" He glanced at Anne Marie. "I mean, we, *geh* see her?"

Mary nodded, her smile widening. *"Ya. She's beautiful, Seth. Both mudder and boppli."*

Anne Marie followed Seth into the bedroom. Her aunt Miriam was propped up in bed with several pillows behind her, her hair still damp from the strain of childbirth. She smiled wearily.

Seth hobbled to the bed and sat next to her. He brushed back a lock of Miriam's hair and glanced down at the newborn. "She's amazing," he murmured. "And *schee.*" He looked back at Miriam, gazing into her eyes. "Just like her *mudder.*"

Anne Marie swallowed. For years her aunt had been insecure about her appearance, which was considered plain, even among a plain people. Yet Seth never hesitated to tell her how pretty she was.

Miriam and Seth looked at their new

daughter. She was perfect, with fair skin and a dusting of dark hair on top of her head.

"We should let them be," Mary whispered to Anne Marie.

Anne Marie nodded and they both slipped quietly from the room.

In the living room, Mary sat down on the hickory rocker near the window, her plump hips wedged between the chair's curved arms. At the same time, Anne Marie's mother walked through the front door.

"*Gut* timing," Anne Marie said.

"Then she's had the *boppli*?"

"*Ya,*" Anne Marie said. "A beautiful girl."

Mamm knelt next to two-year-old Junior and removed his tiny jacket. "Let's meet *yer* new *schwester.*"

The little boy nodded, letting *Mamm* take his hand.

Golden sunlight streamed through the front window. Anne Marie pulled the shade halfway. "Looks like a pretty *daag.*"

"Which is needed after such a long night." Mary took a white handkerchief out of her apron pocket and dabbed her broad forehead. "But Miriam handled it well." She sighed, smiling at Anne Marie. "The women in *yer familye* have little trouble birthing *boppli.* Which is fortunate for you. Whenever you have *kinner,* that is."

Anne Marie glanced away. Mary never hesitated to speak plainly or, in some instances, boldly.

"Miriam and the *kinn* are doing fine," *Maam* said as she walked into the room. "And of course, Seth is relieved."

"He has a wonderful little *familye*." Mary rocked in the chair, scrutinizing Anne Marie. "I've spent years helping women have *boppli*. I wonder when I'll help *mei* future daughter-in-law have one of her own?" She turned to *Mamm*. "It's in the Lord's hands, I know. But *mei* Nathaniel isn't getting any younger. Neither is your Anne Marie."

"I'm standing right here," Anne Marie said, a bit irritated.

Both women looked at Anne Marie. Mary leaned forward. "Do you have something to tell us? Maybe about your Sunday evening 'game nights'?"

"What? *Nee.*"

Mary leaned back in the chair and sighed. "Oh. Well, *nee* harm in hoping, is there?"

Anne Marie looked to her mother. She remained silent but had a sly grin on her face. Why wasn't she saying anything? This wasn't the first time Mary had hinted about Anne Marie and Nathaniel dating, and her mother knew that they weren't. She wished she could tell Mary that Nathaniel had an admirer so his mother would leave her alone. But he wouldn't appreciate it. "I think we could all use some *kaffee,*" she said, scrambling out of the room before Mary could say anything else.

CHAPTER THREE

Nathaniel sat at his bench and repositioned the gas lamp on his worktable, brightening the light and shining it on the watch mechanism he was repairing. As he adjusted the jewels in the pocket watch, he sensed someone looking over his shoulder.

"*Sehr gut,* Nathaniel." His father nodded, peering down at the watch. "That was not an easy repair."

Nathaniel snapped the back on the pocket watch and wound it. He brought it to his ear and listened to the steady ticking. It had been dead when the owner brought it into his father's clock shop earlier last week. "I need to polish it up a bit —"

"Not too much." His father straightened, the tip of his iron-gray beard touching the middle of his barrel chest. "We don't want it too fancy."

Nathaniel nodded. *"Ya."*

Daed clapped him on the shoulder. "You'll

make a fine repairman, *mei sohn.* Like your *grossvatter* and *mei grossvatter* before him." He walked back to his desk in the small repair shop.

Nathaniel smiled, looking around at all the clocks on the walls. His favorite was the century-old cuckoo clock from the Black Forest of Germany. The mechanism had been dismantled because, as his father said, it drove him cuckoo. But it was a fine piece of craftsmanship, like so many of the clocks and watches in the shop.

He pulled out a soft cloth and lightly buffed the outside of the pocket watch. He enjoyed working in the shop, repairing the watches, even trying his hand at carving some of the wood casings containing the clocks. He'd been born into this job, and his father had mentioned how thankful he was for it, Nathaniel being his only child. The business would pass on through the family for one more generation at least.

Just before five that evening, he and his father began closing up the workshop. While he was putting all the tools away in their specific compartments in his toolboxes, his father walked up beside him. He took off his glasses and wiped the lenses with his handkerchief. "You were at the Smuckers' the other day, *ya?*"

Nathaniel nodded. "Game night with Anne Marie."

"How did their wood supply look? I know Lydia's got those two *buwe* to help out, but it won't do for them to run out of fuel during the cold months." As a deacon of the church, his father's responsibility was to make sure the widows of the district were taken care of. Lydia and her family had always been self-sufficient, but his father never took his responsibility lightly.

"They have a *gut* pile laid in, enough to last a couple of weeks. I'll help Jonah and Christopher chop more on Friday after work."

"Take that afternoon off. Don't want you chopping wood in the dark." He put his glasses back on. *"Danki, sohn."*

"Glad to do it." He checked the clock on the wall.

"*Mamm* probably has supper ready. You know how she gets if we're late."

"Last time I checked she was taking a nap. Spent all night delivering Miriam's *boppli.*"

Nathaniel smiled. "That's right. Anne Marie has a new little cousin, Leah. Lydia was finishing up a quilt a couple weeks ago when I was visiting. A gift for the *boppli.*"

"That reminds me. Wait here." His father went to the back room. Nathaniel straightened his chair, wondering why a baby quilt would remind his father of anything. A few moments later, he returned carrying a small, old-fashioned clock. He placed it on Nathaniel's workbench.

"What's this?"

"A *familye* heirloom. *Mei* great-grandfather made it. Gave it to his *frau* for a wedding gift, and *mei grossvatter* gave it to *mei grossmutter* when they got engaged. Then she passed it down to me."

Nathaniel picked it up. It was fairly ornate for an Amish piece. The elaborate silver overlay on the corners of the slate-blue box containing the clock had tarnished over the years. "How old is it?"

"A hundred years, at least. It came from Switzerland. Has been in our family a long time."

"Needs some restoring," Nathaniel said.

"I thought you could handle the job."

Nathaniel set the clock down. "Who's it for?"

"You."

"Me?"

"*Yer* mother said it was past time I gave it to you."

Nathaniel looked at the clock again. "It's not that I don't appreciate it, but I don't need a fancy clock like this."

"Eventually you'll give it to someone special. I'd better check on *yer mamm.* Maybe heat up some leftover soup for her so she doesn't have to worry about supper." He left the workshop, a small bell tinkling as the door shut behind him.

Nathaniel looked at the clock again. Picked it up. Ran his fingers over the slate body, the tarnished embellishments. It was a fine clock, and with a little elbow grease, he could make it as beautiful as it originally had been.

He set the clock down, his hand lingering on the smooth case. It would be a great gift for someone . . . someday. But not anytime soon.

That Friday, Anne Marie sat at the kitchen table and cut candle wicking. She measured each strand at nine and a half inches, cut it with sharp scissors, then tied a small metal washer at one end to weight it. These would be used for simple white taper candles, which she would dip this afternoon in her candle workshop behind the house. She had three dozen to make today if she was to stay on track with her Christmas orders.

After she weighted the last wick, she went to the kitchen sink for a glass of water. She looked out the window as she drank. Dried, crunchy, brown leaves, the remnants of fall, swirled around the gravel driveway. Although it was December, it still hadn't snowed yet. But each day snow threatened, bringing with it dense, overcast skies and brittle wind.

Anne Marie watched her mother stroll across the yard, the strings of her white *kapp* flying out behind her as she made her way to the mailbox. *Mamm* pulled out a few pieces of mail. She thumbed through them quickly, then stopped. Pulled one out. And smiled.

Anne Marie set her glass on the counter and watched as *Mamm* pocketed the letter in her dark-blue jacket and headed for the house. At the same time, Nathaniel's buggy pulled into the driveway. He paused next to her mother, who said a few words to him before he drove toward the barn.

The kitchen door creaked open and her mother walked into the room. "Nathaniel stopped by to help the *buwe* chop firewood."

The gesture didn't surprise her. He was always thoughtful. But Anne Marie was more curious about what her mother had in her pocket. "Anything interesting in the mail?" she asked, leaning against the counter.

Mamm dropped a stack of letters on the table. "Just the usual. A couple of bills. Those never seem to stop coming." But instead of frowning, her mother seemed happy. She looked past Anne Marie for a moment before she started to leave. She made a sudden stop at the doorway and turned around. "Anne Marie, could you do me a favor?" *Mamm* reached into her pocket.

Anne Marie leaned forward, dying to know what was in the letter. "Sure."

Her mother pulled out an index card and handed it to her. "This is a new recipe I planned to try today. Would you mind preparing it for me?"

Anne Marie took the card, trying to mask her disappointment. Chicken and corn soup. "I've never made this before."

"It's a simple recipe. I have all the ingredients in the pantry and the stewing hen is in the cooler on the back porch."

"All right, but —"

"*Danki,* Anne Marie." Before she could say anything else, her mother left.

Anne Marie frowned. What did her mother have to do that was so important she couldn't test a recipe? Anne Marie had always helped her mother cook, but she wasn't as skilled in the kitchen, which was why she took over the candlemaking part of the business.

Anne Marie picked up the pile of mail, shuffled through it, and cast it aside. Why had her mother lied to her? Well, not lied, exactly, but she wasn't being completely truthful either. Something was going on . . . something her mother didn't want her to know.

CHAPTER FOUR

After spending a couple of hours outside with Jonah and Christopher chopping, splitting, and stacking wood, Nathaniel was dripping with sweat, despite the cold temperature. "I think we have enough wood laid to last until next Christmas."

Jonah dropped his stack on top of a neat, towering pile. "We need more. Just to be sure."

"Aw, Jonah. Nathaniel's right," Christopher said. "We got enough."

"I think Jonah's the wise one, Christopher." Nathaniel leaned his axe against the woodpile. "Nothing wrong with laying in a little extra. How about I *geh* inside and get some drinks?"

"I'll *geh* with you." Christopher started toward the house.

Jonah reached out and grabbed his brother by the arm of his jacket. "*Nee*, you're not getting out of work that easy."

Nathaniel headed toward the house, chuckling at Christopher's grumbling. He neared the kitchen, recognizing the scent of chicken and onions stewing. Lydia must be trying a new recipe.

But when he walked in, he saw Anne Marie standing over the stove. She was staring at the pot, absently stirring the contents.

"Anne Marie?" He walked toward her, then tapped her on the shoulder.

She jumped, turning toward him. The wooden spoon flipped out of her hand, hit her forearm, and landed on the floor.

"I'm sorry." Nathaniel grabbed the spoon and set it near the sink. "I didn't mean to startle you."

Anne Marie snatched a dish towel off the counter and wiped the hot food from her arm. "It's all right. I wasn't paying attention."

He watched as a welt formed on her arm. "Here," he said, taking the rag from her and running it under cold water. He pressed it against her arm.

"Really, Nathaniel, I'm okay."

"Just making sure." He pulled the rag away. The redness had calmed. Without thinking, he blew a breath lightly across the burn. He froze, still holding her hand. What made him do that?

Her eyes widened and she pulled away from him. "Uh, see? I'm fine."

She yanked open the drawer and retrieved a clean spoon. "My fault for not paying attention." She focused on stirring what was in the pot. "Did you need something?"

If she could ignore the weird moment between them, he could too. And it really wasn't that strange. He'd tried to cool off the burn, that's all. He forced a casual tone. "I came in to get some water for me and your *bruders.*"

"You know where the glasses are." She glanced at him and smiled.

Now things were back to normal. Relieved, he opened the cabinet door. "I'm surprised to see you cooking," he said, turning on the tap. "Smells *gut.*"

She shrugged. "I suppose. It's a new recipe, so it will probably taste awful."

"Let me try it." He took the spoon and scooped out a small bite of what looked like a thick soup. After he'd tasted it, he said, "Not bad. Needs a little salt."

She grabbed the saltshaker and shook it vigorously. He took it from her. "Not that much."

Anne Marie sighed. "*Mamm* should be making this, not me. But *nee,* she's too busy."

"Doing what?"

"I don't know." She went back to stirring the soup.

Nathaniel knew better than to pry, especially when Anne Marie was in one of her moods. He retrieved two more glasses and filled them with water. "Better get back to chopping."

She didn't respond. He resumed his work, but his thoughts were still on Anne Marie, wondering why she was irritated with her mother.

He had finished stacking another batch of logs when Jonah approached and said, "Nathaniel, can I talk to you for a minute?" Jonah took off his hat and wiped the sweat from his damp bangs. "I wanted you to know how much I appreciate your help with the wood."

"Anytime your *familye* needs something, just let me or *mei daed* know and we'll take care of it."

"I know." Jonah shoved his hat back on his head. "It's just . . ."

"What?"

Jonah looked into the distance. "I'm seventeen, ya know. Christopher is fifteen. We're not *kinner* anymore."

Nathaniel rubbed his cold hands together, seeing where this conversation was going.

364

Jonah had always been serious-minded and mature for his age. "*Yer* doing a *gut* job taking care of *yer familye,* Jonah."

He looked at Nathaniel, his mouth twitching slightly. "You think so?"

"*Ya.* But it doesn't make you any less of a *mann* to accept help."

Jonah nodded. "When we need it."

"Right. And I trust you'll let me know if you do."

"I will. I just didn't want you to think we were helpless."

"I've never thought that." He picked up his axe. "But *mei mamm* says many hands make quick work, so let's get this done already."

Jonah nodded, the sharp wind lifting up the ends of his dark-blond hair. "*Danki.* For understanding."

Nathaniel tipped his head in Jonah's direction. He was glad to see him taking responsibility for his mother, sister, and younger brother. But it also proved that he wouldn't need Nathaniel's help as much.

Even as he continued splitting the wood, Nathaniel's thoughts drifted back to Anne Marie. He hadn't thought about it much before, but eventually she'd find a boyfriend and a husband. She was already encouraging him to date Ruth. What would happen when they didn't need each other anymore? It was something he couldn't — and didn't — want to imagine.

An hour later Anne Marie finished making the soup. Her mother was right — it hadn't been that hard to make. The most difficult part had been the most tedious — picking the meat off the chicken bones. She took a taste and thought it was decent, but nowhere near her mother's standard.

She let the soup simmer on the stove so it would still be warm when her mother came home, whenever that would be. She'd left a few minutes ago without an explanation — and without giving Anne Marie a chance to ask her about the pocketed letter.

She looked down at the red mark on her arm. A shiver ran through her as she remembered Nathaniel's gentle breath on the welt. He was being nice, of course. But that didn't keep goose bumps from forming on her skin at the memory.

Anne Marie entered her mother's bedroom looking for some salve to put on the burn. Her bed was neatly made with her grandmother's quilt and one of Aunt Miriam's beautiful lap quilts folded across the end. The faded fabric of the old quilt contrasted with the sharper colors of Miriam's quilt. But both were beautiful.

She went to her mother's side table and opened the drawer. *Mamm* kept everything from adhesive bandages to sewing needles to ink pens in the messy drawer, the only untidy place in their house.

Anne Marie searched through the deep drawer, lifting objects and looking for the small cylinder that held the homemade salve. She spied it in the far back of the drawer. As she moved the random contents aside to reach for the jar, she touched a stack of papers held together with a rubber band. She pulled it out. Letters.

Unable to help herself, she looked at the return address. Thomas Nissley, Walnut Creek, Ohio. Her brow scrunched. As far as she knew, her family didn't know anyone in Walnut Creek.

She should put the letters back. But curiosity won over indecision and she slipped one of the envelopes out of the pack and lifted the already opened seal. She began to read, ignoring her guilt.

"Anne Marie?" Nathaniel walked into the kitchen. He'd left Jonah and Christopher to stack the rest of the firewood before sundown. Before he went home he wanted to check on Anne Marie's arm. It was a small burn, but he couldn't leave without making sure she was okay.

He faced the empty kitchen and looked at the pot of soup on the stove. His stomach rumbled. He fetched a spoon from the drawer and took another taste. Now it was perfect. Even though she always denied it, Anne Marie was just as good of a cook as her mother. "Anne Marie, do you care if I have some more of this soup?" he called out.

She didn't answer. He headed into the living room. Not finding her there, he started walking through the house, calling her name. When he was midway down the hall, he spied a light peeking through the crack at the bottom of Lydia's bedroom door. He frowned. He had seen Anne Marie's mother leave earlier in the day, so why was the light on in her room?

Nathaniel pushed open the door a little farther and saw Anne Marie sitting on the bed, reading a letter. Next to her, more letters were littered on the pastel quilt covering Lydia's bed. The lines on Anne Marie's forehead deepened. "Anne Marie?"

Her head shot up, and he saw the fury in her eyes. She stood, holding out one of the letters in her hand. "How could she do this?" she said, thrusting the letter at Nathaniel.

"Do what?"

She whirled around, her cheeks as red as holly berries. She started to pace. "I can't believe this."

"Anne Marie —"

"It's one thing to keep a secret. I mean, I've kept my fair share of secrets." She glanced at him. "But to do this?" She held up the letter.

He walked over to her and thought about putting his hand on her shoulder, but quickly changed his mind. "Anne Marie, calm down. It can't be that bad."

"*Ach,* it's bad. *Sehr* bad." She opened the letter. " 'My dearest Lydia,' " she read aloud. " 'I never thought I would feel this way about a woman again. It gives my heart wings to know you feel the same way.' " She pursed her lips in a sour expression. "Gives his heart wings? What kind of romantic nonsense is that?"

Nathaniel didn't think it was too bad. But he did feel like an intruder.

Anne Marie plopped on the bed, her shoulders slumping. "She's been writing to him for months. Apparently she's in love with him." She looked up. "Oh, and he's coming for Christmas. When was she going to tell us? When he landed on our doorstep? 'Oh, by the way, this is Thomas, my secret beau that I didn't bother telling anyone about. Merry Christmas!' "

Nathaniel bit his lip to keep from chuckling. Anne Marie in a snit was entertaining. But he didn't want her anger directed at him. He cleared his throat and sat down next to her. "I'm sure your mother had her reasons for not telling you."

"They better be *gut* ones."

"What's going on here?"

Nathaniel froze at the sound of Lydia's sharp voice. He glanced at her standing in the doorway, her nostrils flaring much in the same way Anne Marie's had moments ago.

Lydia crossed her arms over her chest. "What are you two doing in my bedroom?"

CHAPTER FIVE

Anne Marie jumped from the bed and faced her mother. "Don't be upset with him. He was only checking on me."

Her mother uncrossed her arms, lowering them to her sides. "Nathaniel, I think you should leave."

Nathaniel rose. He glanced at Anne Marie, concern in his eyes. She looked away. He slipped out the door, not saying anything to either of them.

Lydia shut the door behind him. She looked at the letters on the bed. "I see you've been snooping."

"I wasn't snoop—"

"Don't lie." Lydia scooped up the letters.

"I was looking for salve for my burn — the one I got making your recipe, by the way." She lifted her chin. She sounded childish, but she didn't care.

Lydia folded the letters carefully and began putting them in the envelopes. "How did the soup turn out?"

"Soup? Don't you think we have something more important to talk about?"

Her mom turned to Anne Marie, her eyes starting to blaze. "I'm trying not to lose my temper. I'm very disappointed in you."

"Disappointed in me? You're the one keeping secrets."

She averted her eyes. "I was going to tell you and the *buwe* about Thomas."

"Before or after the wedding?"

Lydia froze, keeping her gaze from Anne Marie.

Dread pooled inside Anne Marie. "*Nee* . . . you're not . . ."

Her mother sat down on the bed. She moved the letters to the side and patted the empty space beside her. "Anne Marie, sit down."

"I'm fine standing."

Lydia sighed. "All right. As I said, I was waiting until the time was right. You've been busy with your candlemaking, and I've been trying to get things ready for the cookbook."

It sounded like a list of excuses to Anne Marie. "Who is Thomas?"

"He's a *mann* I knew from my childhood. He used to live in Paradise. When he was twelve, he moved to Walnut Creek. Like me, he married and had children, although now

372

they are grown and have their own families. He's lived alone for several years."

Anne Marie refused to feel sorry for him. But she couldn't help but soften her stance a little. "How did you start talking to him again?"

"He came to Paradise six months ago, to visit his *bruder's familye.* I was delivering some soaps and candles, and when I saw him . . ." Her eyes grew wistful. "He recognized me right away."

"How *romantic.*" Anne Marie nibbled on her finger, unable to keep the bitterness out of her tone. "Love at first sight."

"*Nee,* it wasn't like that. You have to understand, Anne Marie. I loved your *daed* very much. I never thought I'd fall in love with someone else. But something changed these past few months. Thomas started writing me first. Friendly letters, reminiscing about childhood. Then the letters became more personal."

"So I read."

Her mother scowled. "You're not making this easy, *dochder.*"

"You should have said something to me. To all of us."

Mamm raised her voice. "I'm not allowed to have anything of *mei* own? Any privacy?"

Anne Marie opened her mouth, then shut

it. She looked at the letters. Her mother was right. But that didn't change anything.

"Thomas is visiting his *bruder* for Christmas. He'll be coming here to meet you and Jonah and Christopher." Her mother stood, squaring her shoulders as she faced Anne Marie. "You will treat him better than you've treated me today."

Anne Marie pressed her lips to keep from saying something she'd regret.

"Since you want to know everything," *Mamm* continued, "I went to see Miriam today. I needed her advice about Thomas."

"And?"

The hardness in *Mamm*'s eyes softened. "He asked me to marry him." She smiled. "And when he comes here for Christmas, I'm going to tell him *ya.*"

Although the words made Anne Marie take a step back, she couldn't deny the look of love in her mother's eyes. She looked away, guilt gnawing at her. She'd been unfair to her mother. And immature.

"Say something, Anne Marie. Please."

Anne Marie finally looked up, the glistening tears in her mother's eyes melting away the betrayal. "I want you to be happy, *Mamm.*" She took a deep breath, forcing out the words. "If Thomas makes you happy, then that's what counts."

Her mother hugged her. "*Danki,* Anne Marie." She stepped back, wiping her eyes. "I understand why you were upset. It's a lot to take in, especially when we start packing for the move —"

"What move?"

Her mother paused. "The move to Ohio."

Anne Marie's chest felt like a load of baled hay landed on it. "Moving? We're *moving*?"

"Thomas's home is in Walnut Cre—"

"Our home is *here.*"

"And his business is there. I can produce my cookbooks anywhere. Although I probably won't anymore. I want to focus on making a *gut* home for our *familye.*"

"We have a *gut* home." She spread her arms, gesturing to the space around them. "We always have."

"And we will have one in Walnut Creek."

"What about Miriam? *Grossmutter* and *Grossvatter* have already moved away. You'll leave her here alone?"

"I talked to her about that too. She'll miss us, but she understands. And Seth's family is here. She'll hardly be alone." *Mamm* took Anne Marie's hand. "I know it will be a big adjustment for everyone."

She pulled her hand from her mother's. "I won't leave. I can live with Miriam and Seth."

"You can't. You know how small their *haus* is."

"I'll sleep on the couch."

Mamm rubbed her fingers across her forehead. "Miriam and Seth would take you in if you asked, but you know it would be a hardship. And unnecessary, since you would have a home with me and Thomas."

Anne Marie blinked away the tears. Her mother and Thomas. It sounded strange. Unnatural. But her mother spoke of her future husband as if he'd always been a part of her life. She spoke of Thomas with love.

Her heart constricted. What about her life? Her friends, her candlemaking business? She had to start everything over because her mother fell in love?

"Now that you know," *Mamm* said, sounding more cheerful than she had in a long time, "we can start packing. The wedding will be in early January. We'll move right after that."

Anne Marie fisted her hands together. She couldn't do this. She couldn't leave everything she knew. Everyone she loved.

"*Mamm?*" Jonah's voice sounded from the opposite end of the house. "Anne Marie?"

Her mother sighed. "I guess it's time to tell the *buwe.*" She looked at Anne Marie, hope in her eyes. "It would help if you could be supportive and an example for your *bruders.* You're not the only one having to sacrifice."

Anger bubbled up inside her. Unable to speak, she rushed past her mother, past Jonah and Christopher in the living room.

"Hey!" Jonah said, spinning around. "Where are you going?"

"Out." She opened the front door and ran into the cold evening, the screen door slamming behind her.

Nathaniel guided his buggy down the road, tucking his chin into his coat to ward off the chill. Good thing his horse knew the way home, as he wasn't as focused on driving as he should be. Anne Marie consumed his thoughts.

She was overreacting, but he sympathized with her. He couldn't put himself in her place, since his parents had been married for years. Just thinking about one of them being with someone else was impossible. But Lydia deserved to be happy. So did Anne Marie.

A car behind him honked its horn, pulling his attention back to the road. As the vehicle zoomed past, Nathaniel looked in his side mirror. He squinted in the pale light of dusk. Someone was walking behind him. As he slowed his buggy, he could see it was Anne Marie.

He pulled the buggy to a stop, holding the reins as he came to a halt on the shoulder of the road. Although her street wasn't busy, it was best to be cautious. As she neared, he could see her rubbing her hands over her arms.

"Anne Marie," he said, moving toward her but keeping a grip on the horse. If he let go, his horse would head straight home. Anne Marie stopped a few feet away. "What are you doing out here?" he asked. When she didn't say anything, he tilted his head toward the buggy. "Get in."

She shook her head but walked toward the buggy.

"Wait." He slipped off his jacket and handed it to her. "You're freezing. Put this on."

"Then you'll freeze."

"I'll be all right."

She looked at the coat for a moment, then took it. The edge of the sleeves reached past her fingertips. Then she climbed into the buggy. When they were on their way, he said, "Want to talk about it?"

"*Nee.*" Her voice sounded thick.

His heart lurched. Anne Marie was several things: a bit excitable, a little melodramatic, and occasionally annoying. She was also tough. During their long friendship, he'd only seen her cry once, and that was when they were talking after her father's funeral. Whatever happened between her and Lydia after he left was serious.

Without thinking twice, he reached for her hand. She gripped it. Her fingers were cold, but they soon warmed in his palm. Neither of them spoke as he drove to his house. When he pulled into his driveway, he stopped in front of the clock shop. "Are you ready to talk now? We can *geh* into the workshop. *Nee* one will bother us there."

She nodded. Looked at him with tears in her eyes.

And his heart melted.

CHAPTER SIX

"Here. This will warm you a little more."

Anne Marie took the mug of coffee from Nathaniel. "I never knew you had a coffeepot in here."

"It's in the back. We use a camping stove to percolate it. *Daed* can't *geh* more than a couple of hours without his *kaffee.*"

She took a sip of the hot, strong brew as she sat on Nathaniel's workbench. He pulled a chair over and sat across from her, holding his own mug. "Now are you ready to tell me what's going on?"

Anne Marie paused. She didn't want to say the words out loud. But Nathaniel would find out soon enough, as would the rest of the district. She wanted him to hear it from her. "We're moving."

He frowned. "Who's moving?"

"My *mamm, mei bruders* . . . me." She explained everything to Nathaniel.

He became very still, as he usually did

when he was deep in thought. But his expression remained unreadable. Finally he leaned forward. "I know you're upset, Anne Marie, but this isn't the end of the world."

The warmth she'd felt from the coffee and his coat dissipated. "That's easy for you to say." Her eyes narrowed. "Your world hasn't been turned upside down."

"Look, I don't like the idea of you moving either." He stared at his coffee. "I really don't like it," he mumbled.

"What?"

He looked at her again, a muscle twitching in his left cheek. "At least you're not moving too far."

"Nathaniel, it's Ohio. That's a day's ride on a bus."

"*Ya.* Just a day's ride. It could be worse. You could be going to Florida."

"It doesn't make any difference." She set the mug on his spotless workbench, next to an old clock. "What if I lose touch with everyone here?"

"That won't happen. There are letters —"

"You know I don't like writing letters. I don't even mail out cards."

"Then you'll have to come back to visit. And I'll come visit you."

She looked at him, trying to judge if he was serious. He glanced down at his mug so she couldn't read his expression. Then he looked up, smiling. "And until you move, I promise we'll spend as much time together as we can."

She shot up from the bench. "But what if it isn't enough?" she said, shoving her hands into the pockets of his coat. She wasn't cold anymore, but for some reason she didn't want to take it off. "I feel like I'm losing everything. My home. My friends . . ." She looked at him. "You."

He stood and faced her, his deep brown eyes meeting hers. "That won't happen. I promise."

The words were easy to say with only a few inches between them. With a few months and several hundred miles separating them, there was no guarantee they would stay close. "I want to believe you."

"Then do."

She kept her gaze locked on his, and for the first time since her world had been flipped over, her pulse slowed. His steady presence had that effect on her. She forced a small smile. "I should *geh*. I don't want to worry *Mamm*."

"I thought you were mad at her."

"I am."

He half-smiled. "You know how contradictory you sound?"

She shrugged. "That's me, one big contradiction."

"*Nee,* you're not." He moved toward her. "I'll take you home. You'll feel better tomorrow."

She shook her head. "I'll walk. I need to clear *mei* head before I get home."

He pulled open a drawer underneath his worktable and gave her a flashlight. "Then at least take this. And keep *mei* coat. I'll get it from you later."

She nodded and took the flashlight. She spied the clock again. "This is unusual," she said, examining the tarnished silver. She loved old things. Every scratch, dent, and imperfection carried a memory. "It's very *schee.*"

"You think?" He picked it up. "Looks neglected to me."

"Not neglected. Full of history." She glanced at him. "Are you restoring it?"

He nodded and placed the clock back on the bench.

"Then it will be even more beautiful when you're finished." Able to genuinely smile now, she ran her hand down his arm and linked her pinkie with his. "Thanks again, Nathaniel. You're always here when I need you."

"It's what friends are for, *ya?*"

"Ya." Her smile dimmed as she released his finger. A thick lump formed in her throat. She couldn't believe that in less than a month they would be saying good-bye. Before the tears started and she embarrassed herself, she turned to leave.

"Anne Marie?"

The softness in his voice stopped her. When she saw his outstretched arms, she didn't hesitate to walk into them. How did he know she needed this? *Because he knows me better than anyone.*

"We'll figure this out." He rubbed his hand over her back. "Promise."

She closed her eyes and leaned against him, hearing the beat of his heart through his home-knitted sweater, waiting for the steady rhythm to comfort her. But despite his promises and the comfort of his strong embrace, she couldn't be hopeful. After tonight, nothing would ever be the same — including their friendship.

Almost an hour later, chilled to the inside of her bones, Anne Marie walked into her house. Through the darkness, a pale yellow gaslight shone from the kitchen.

She paused, weary but steeling herself for the scolding. But when she entered the kitchen, *Mamm* jumped up and ran to her.

"I was just about to send Jonah and Christopher to find you." Her mom hugged her. "Please, Anne Marie. Don't do that again."

Anne Marie plopped down in the chair and nodded, snuggling into Nathaniel's coat, relieved that her mother wasn't angry, even though she deserved to be. Anne Marie inhaled, breathing in his scent that infused the wool and remembering the hug they'd shared.

"Do you want *kaffee*?" *Mamm* asked. "Maybe some chamomile tea?"

"You're not mad at me?"

Mamm joined her at the table, shaking her head. "I understand why you left."

"I shouldn't have been gone so long."

"You were at Nathaniel's, *ya*?"

She nodded.

"That's why I wasn't that worried." Her mother laid her hands in her lap and looked down at the table. "I told Jonah and Christopher about Thomas."

Anne Marie fingered an empty peppermint candy wrapper in Nathaniel's coat, not saying anything.

"Christopher seems okay with it, but you know him. He's always been easygoing. Jonah, on the other hand . . ." She looked up at Anne Marie and sighed.

Anne Marie didn't know what to say. Had

she expected all of them to be happy to leave the only home they ever knew? "Where's Jonah?"

"In the barn. He needs some time, just like you." Her mother looked tired. "I know you all are upset. But I really want you to give Thomas a chance. You don't understand what it's been like . . . I've been lonely since your *daed* died. Thomas has brought a light to *mei* life that I thought was snuffed out long ago. He's an answer to prayer. Not the way I expected because I never thought I'd leave Paradise. But God doesn't work according to our plans."

What about my plans? Why do I have to give up everything? Guilt stabbed at her again for being so selfish. Yet she couldn't help it. She stood. "I'm going to bed."

Her mother gave her one last look, then nodded.

Anne Marie went upstairs to her room and lay down on the bed, not bothering to take off her *kapp* or Nathaniel's coat. She fingered the wool lapels, drawing them closer to her face. Her mother was right about so many things. Anne Marie could have her candle business in Walnut Creek. She could come back and visit her aunt Miriam and her other friends. Her life wouldn't end if she left Paradise. She knew that to be true.

So then why did it feel that way?

Nathaniel tried to concentrate on repairing the simple alarm clock in front of him, but he couldn't focus. He kept remembering the way Anne Marie felt in his arms — fragile, vulnerable, yet comforting. He gripped a small screwdriver. He had tried to cheer her up by talking about letters and visits. But he'd lied. The idea of her leaving, of her not being a part of his life . . . how was he supposed to accept that?

The alarm clock went off in his hands, the shrill noise making him jump. He searched for the switch to turn it off. When that didn't work, he pried the batteries out — something he should have done beforehand.

"Nathaniel? Are you all right?"

He glanced over his shoulder at his father and forced a nod.

"You seem distracted."

"I'm fine."

"Does it have something to do with Anne Marie being here last night?"

Nathaniel turned to face his dad. "How did you know she was here?"

"*Yer mamm* told me. Somehow she manages to know everything." His father stood, slowly straightening his back. He slid a thumb underneath one of his suspender straps. "Why didn't you invite her inside?"

Nathaniel turned his attention back to the alarm clock. "We needed to talk."

"How about you? Do you need to talk?"

Nathaniel stared at the alarm clock. What good would it do to talk about it? Anne Marie was leaving. Nothing he could say would change that. And nothing could fill the emptiness that started to grow inside him the moment Anne Marie told him she was moving.

"Let me know if you do." The tread of his father's work boots thumped on the floor as he left the workshop.

Nathaniel went back to fixing the clock. After the third time the screwdriver slipped off the screw, he gave up and shoved the alarm clock away.

CHAPTER SEVEN

"I'm sorry," *Aenti* Miriam said over her daughter's squalling. "The *boppli* is always hungry. Junior's appetite was never so big." She lifted the corner of her mouth. "Nor was his cry."

"She has a strong pair of lungs." Anne Marie faced Junior in his high chair and tried to get him to eat a piece of cubed ham.

Miriam sat in a chair in her kitchen and settled into feeding the baby. When Junior finally started eating and the baby stopped crying, Anne Marie glanced at her aunt.

"You didn't come over here to feed *mei sohn,*" Miriam said.

"I need to spend as much time with him as possible. And with you." She looked at her tiny cousin. "I don't even know her," she whispered.

"Anne Marie." Miriam touched her hand. "It will be all right."

"That's what everyone tells me." She

sighed. "Did you know about Thomas?"

"*Nee.* Lydia has always been a private person. We didn't know she was dating your *daed* until they had announced their engagement."

Anne Marie nudged the sippy cup toward Junior. Keeping an engagement secret wasn't all that unusual in their community. The reminder made her mother's secretive behavior make more sense. But it didn't make the situation any easier to accept. Junior picked up the sippy cup full of milk and started to drink. "*Mamm* says you're fine with us moving," Anne Marie said.

Her aunt frowned. "I wouldn't say *fine.* I understand, though." She looked at Anne Marie, her expression sympathetic. "I'll miss all of you. But we can write to each other —"

"And visit. I know." She turned to her cousin and touched the brown hair that flipped up from Junior's bangs. He shoved a cheese-flavored cracker in his mouth. "It won't be the same."

"True, it won't. But I haven't seen your *mamm* this happy in a long time."

Neither had Anne Marie. Since telling them about Thomas, her mother was more productive and chattier than ever, even humming while she was putting the bindings on her cookbooks.

Anne Marie couldn't say the same thing for herself. She had stacks of Christmas candle orders to fill, a few for specialty carved candles that took extra time to make. Yet instead of working on them, she was here with her aunt. She had to cherish every minute she had left in Paradise.

She had thought she would have seen Nathaniel over the past couple of days, but he hadn't been able to come to their usual Sunday game night and he hadn't stopped by. She still had his coat, although she knew he had another one. Still, she should have dropped it off at his house but she'd taken to snuggling with it at night. Part of her felt foolish for doing something so sentimental. Yet she couldn't bear not to have something of his with her as she tried to sort out her feelings.

She would miss Aunt Miriam and her family. She would miss Ruth and her other friends. But the ache in her heart that appeared every time she thought of leaving Nathaniel . . . that was new, and more painful than anything else.

"Anne Marie?"

She turned to look at her aunt again. "Sorry."

"Are you okay?"

"Just distracted, thinking about everything."

"There's a lot to think about." She removed the blanket covering the baby. Little Leah was sound asleep, her pink, heart-shaped mouth still puckered in a tiny *O* shape. "Your grandparents are happy living in Indiana. They say it's a new chapter in their lives."

"I don't want a new chapter." She sighed. One look from Aunt Miriam confirmed what Anne Marie already felt — she was being immature. "I do want *Mamm* to be happy. I just don't want to leave Paradise."

"I understand."

Everyone kept saying that, but Anne Marie had her doubts. She started to bite her fingernail, caught herself, and put her hands in her lap. "If you had moved away, you wouldn't have married Seth."

She adjusted the baby in her arms. "*Ya.* But I would have trusted that God had someone else for me."

"So it's that simple?"

Miriam paused. "*Nee,*" she said softly. "I would be lying if I said it was." Her aunt's eyes grew wistful. "I wasn't sure I'd ever get married. I never thought I would be with someone as wonderful as Seth."

"But why? You and *Onkel* Seth are perfect

for each other."

"I know that now, but at the time I didn't think so." She glanced down at her infant daughter. "I didn't think I deserved him, or anyone else." She looked back at Anne Marie. "But that was *mei* own insecurity, *mei* own lack of trust and belief. So, *nee*, I wouldn't have trusted God. Not that easily, not at that time."

Anne Marie wiped the crumbs off Junior's face, feeling touched by Miriam's admission. At least her aunt was being honest.

"Are you upset about leaving Nathaniel?" Aunt Miriam asked.

"Nathaniel?" Anne Marie lifted Junior out of the high chair. For some strange reason heat crept up her neck. "Why would you bring him up?"

"We were talking about Seth and I just assumed . . ." She shook her head. "Never mind." Aunt Miriam smiled. "I know you can't see it now, but this might be part of God's plan. I'm sure He has *gut* things in store for you in Ohio. Maybe you'll meet your future husband there."

Anne Marie frowned. "I'm not looking for a husband."

Miriam leaned closer, her gaze intense. "Maybe because Nathaniel's in the way?"

Anne Marie settled Junior in her lap, not

looking at her aunt. "What do you mean?"

"It's one thing that you were friends with Nathaniel when you were children. But you're adults now. And if there's nothing romantic between you, then it's time to let each other *geh*."

She smoothed a wrinkle out of Junior's shirt. "It's not like I have a choice anymore."

"That could be God's point."

Anne Marie's head snapped up. "He wants to break up a lifelong friendship? How is that *gut* for me?"

"To make you move from childhood to adulthood. You need to put childish things behind you. Nathaniel, nice *mann* that he is, is part of that. It's time to grow up, Anne Marie."

Anne Marie rested her chin on Junior's head. Was her aunt right? No one could argue she'd been acting like a child about the move, and she was ashamed of that. She was twenty years old. An adult. Yet she couldn't see how sacrificing her friendship with Nathaniel was in God's plan. How could she give up the most important person in her life?

That evening, Anne Marie helped *Mamm* with supper. Neither one spoke as they prepared the pork chops, creamy noodles, and sweet potatoes. When the pork chops were almost done, her mother finally said, "Did you have a nice visit with Miriam?" She began to slice a half loaf of bread.

Anne Marie tensed, her mind still filled with her aunt's advice. *"Ya."*

"Leah is doing well?"

"Everyone is fine." She continued scrubbing the bowl she'd mashed the sweet potatoes in.

"Anne Marie." Her mother put her hand on her daughter's shoulder. "You're going to clean the finish right off that bowl."

"What? Oh, sorry." She rinsed it and put it in the drainer to dry.

Mamm stepped to the side, picked up the bowl, and ran a dry towel over the outside. "Christmas is in less than a week. Could you at least pretend to enjoy the holiday? I can't have both you and Jonah moping around."

A heavy weight pressed against her chest. Miriam and *Mamm* were right. She had to accept the wedding, the move, everything. She handed her mother a large metal spoon. "Don't worry. I won't put a damper on Christmas." She managed a smile. "You know it's my favorite holiday."

Her mother set down the dish and hugged her. She stepped back and wiped the tears from her eyes.

"Why are you crying?"

"I'm happy, Anne Marie. It tore *mei* heart out that you were so upset."

Anne Marie was surprised. Her mother hadn't seemed upset the past couple of days. Then again, lately she'd hidden her feelings well. A lot better than Anne Marie had.

"I'm so glad to have your support. And I know Jonah will come around." *Mamm* smiled through her tears. "You'll come to love Thomas. He's a wonderful *mann.*"

Anne Marie hugged her *mamm.* "If you love him, he must be."

Later that night, Anne Marie entered her room to prepare for bed. She removed her *kapp,* unclipped her hair, and let her braid fall over her shoulder. She turned and saw Nathaniel's coat lying on her bed. She'd slept with it for the past couple of nights, drawing warmth and comfort from it. She picked up the garment and ran her fingers over the stitching. She noticed the small dark stain on the edge of one cuff, and realized the elbows were starting to wear a little thin. She squeezed the fabric one more time before taking a breath, then hung the coat up in her closet and shut the door. Tomorrow she would make sure Nathaniel got it back.

It was time to move on.

CHAPTER EIGHT

The next morning, Anne Marie had just finished cleaning up the breakfast dishes when she heard a knock on the back kitchen door. She opened it to see Nathaniel standing there. "Can I come in?" he asked.

Her body tensed. What was wrong with her? She'd prayed last night for God to help her let go of the past, her close friendship with Nathaniel at the top of the list. She asked Him to help her see the move as a fresh start. An adventure, like *Aenti* Miriam said. She thought she'd succeeded. But seeing him after they'd been apart for a couple of days brought unexpected feelings — both old and new — flooding over her.

There was no denying he was attractive. He always had been, even as a little boy. And he'd grown into a cute — no, make that handsome — *mann.* Yet Nathaniel's looks were the last thing she noticed about him — until now. Her heart fluttered as she looked at his lips. She glanced away, her face heating.

"I, uh, came to get *mei* coat," he said. He shifted from one foot to the other, not looking at her.

He was acting as awkward as she felt. So this was how it was going to be between them? She already missed their closeness, and she hadn't even moved away yet. "I'm sorry. I shouldn't have kept it so long."

"It's okay. I have this one." He tugged on his jacket, which was a thinner version of the one she was borrowing. "You know the real cold weather doesn't set in around here until January anyway."

She wouldn't be here in January. The frown on his face showed that he was thinking the same thing.

"Anne Marie, I'm sorry —"

"I'll get your coat." She fled the kitchen and ran to her room, opening the closet door where she'd left the coat last night. She didn't linger over it. She grabbed it off the hanger and dashed back to the kitchen.

"Here," she said, thrusting the garment at him.

"*Danki.*" He took it from her but didn't move. A moment later he sat down at the kitchen table. She threaded her fingers together and rocked back and forth on her heels.

"Can we talk for a minute?" he asked.

She sat down across from him. "What about?"

He leaned forward. "I didn't come here just to get *mei* coat. I wanted to see how you were doing."

"I'm fine." She straightened and forced a smile. "I'm seeing this move as an adventure." She gritted out the last word.

"Oh. *Gut.*" He rubbed the palm of his hand back and forth on the table. "I'm glad you're okay with it."

"Ya."

"And like I said, our friendship isn't going to change."

But it already had, and they both knew it.

"I'll write to you, even if you don't write back," he added. "And I promise I'll visit."

Until he forgot about her. She nearly choked on the bitter thought.

"I'm also serious about spending more time together. I took the *daag* off from work."

Her eyes widened. "Your *daed* let you do that?"

"When I told him I was coming to see you, he didn't have a problem with it."

Anne Marie's heart tripped a beat. She'd

400

never known him to put anything ahead of work. That he would set it aside to spend time with her . . .

But she had vowed to let him go. She grabbed a dishrag from the sink and started rubbing down the already clean counter. "I'm really behind on work. I have a lot of candles to make."

"I can help you."

She glanced over her shoulder at him. "It's pretty boring work."

"You don't seem to think so. You love it."

True. She paused. What would it hurt for them to make a few candles together? It wasn't like she could refuse the help. "All right. As long as you don't mind."

"I never mind being with you, Anne Marie."

She turned and put her hand over her quickening heart. Letting him slip out of her life wasn't going to be easy.

"Nathaniel, you're a terrible candlemaker."

Anne Marie thought she'd given him the simplest job, dipping red tapers, but he dipped them either too fast or too slow. The last ten he made were lopsided and had drips down the sides. She glanced at him, his brow furrowed in concentration. At least his terrible candlemaking had made her finally relax around him. "For all the delicate work you do on watches and clocks, I'm surprised."

"Watches and clocks are easier to deal with, trust me." He smirked as he looked at her, holding a hoop of candles over the wax-dipping can. "You should give me a break. This is *mei* first time, remember?"

Anne Marie took the warped candles from him and set them on the counter. Two years ago when she'd taken over the candlemaking business from her mother, she converted a small garden shed into her own workshop. A gas-powered heater kept the workshop warm, along with several metal tubs of colored, melted wax warming over three camping stoves. She'd recycle the wax later and make proper candles, but right now she needed to give Nathaniel a different job.

She looked up at the two fancy carved candles on a shelf by the door. She used them as samples of her more intricate work, which she made for *Englisch* customers. She'd just made a red-and-white-layered cylinder candle. It was warm and pliable and ready to be carved. With his skilled hands, maybe he'd do better with a more complex job.

She picked up the sample candle and set it on the small round table in the middle of the workshop. Then she pulled out the chair. "Have a seat."

"For what?"

"To carve this." She put the freshly dipped candle next to the sample and handed him three carving tools. "Make this plain one look like the fancy one."

"You're kidding." He eyed the sample. "I can't do this. I messed up your simple candles."

"Nathaniel, I know how well you draw. I've also seen the nice work you do on those wooden clock cases. I think you can handle carving the candle. It doesn't have to look exactly like that one. Just make it pretty."

"Pretty." He sat down, still looking dubious.

"All right, then. Make it nice."

"Nice I can do." He studied the sample, picked up a round-tipped tool, and started to carve.

"You have to work quickly," she said, watching him cut and pull down thin strips of the candle, revealing the stacked red and white layers beneath. "If the candle cools it will be hard to work with."

"That won't be a problem." He wiped beads of perspiration from his forehead with the back of his hand.

"If it is, tell me, and I'll warm it —" But

she could see he had already tuned her out. She should have had him do this to begin with. The candle was already looking better than pretty, with curlicues that surpassed her sample.

She turned to the pots of wax and started working on more red tapers.

"This is a nice workshop," he said from behind her. "I should have come in here before."

"Uncle Seth helped me fix it up. It was easier to work out here while *Mamm* perfected her recipes in the kitchen."

"Smells pretty *gut* too. Like . . ."

"Vanilla and cinnamon?"

"Ya."

"Those are the most popular scents for Christmas." She forced the wicks out of the candles he'd ruined and folded the soft wax in her hand. "I make scented ones for the candle jars. They're already finished, thank goodness, or I'd be really behind." She dropped the ball of wax in the red wax can.

When he didn't say anything, she turned and checked his progress. Her eyes widened. The candle was beautiful, better than she could have ever made, even with years of practice. Nathaniel had put his own design on the candle. The base was a solid red, which would be shiny after she dipped it in the final setting wax. The strips of wax were curled over and under each other, with some rolled at the top to resemble tiny candy canes. The top of the candle was pure white, with small hearts carved in a wavy pattern a few inches from the rim.

"Oh, Nathaniel." She sat perched on the edge of his chair. "It's so *schee.*" She carefully touched one of the delicate candy canes. The wax was still warm, but hard enough that it didn't give under the light pressure of her finger.

"You think so?" He peered at the candle, turning his head to look at it from different angles. "I think the hearts are crooked."

"The hearts are stunning. Mrs. Potter will love this candle."

He looked at her, his chin nearly touching her shoulder. They were so close she could see the light shadow of dark-brown stubble on his face. "We make a pretty *gut* team, *ya?*" he said, smiling.

But she couldn't speak. All she could do was stare at him, taking in his golden eyes. Why had she never noticed they were the color of honey before? Or that his breath smelled sweet, like the peppermints he was fond of chewing when the weather turned cold? They reminded him of Christmas, he always said.

And why hadn't she ever noticed how badly she wanted to kiss him?

"Anne Marie —"

"Nathaniel —"

They both stopped speaking. She thought his mouth was moving closer to hers. Or maybe she was hoping it was. It didn't matter, because her heart was certain that in a few seconds, she would know for sure.

A moment ago, Nathaniel wanted to bite off his tongue. He shouldn't have told Anne Marie what a good team they made. Just like he shouldn't be sitting this close to her.

But when she sat down on his same chair, he couldn't bear to move. It didn't matter that there was only one chair in the room and she had nowhere else to sit. He liked it. He liked everything about her — the way her lips pursed, the rosy color appearing on her cheeks, her pale-blue eyes that were so clear and vulnerable, his pulse thrummed. His heart ached at the thought of her leaving. He knew letters and visits wouldn't be enough for him.

Things had changed between them. He could feel it, and he didn't want to resist. Unable to stop himself, he leaned forward, closer . . . closer . . .

"Knock, knock!" said a female voice.

His head jerked from Anne Marie's. He looked over her shoulder and swallowed. Ruth Troyer walked inside.

CHAPTER NINE

"There you are!"

Anne Marie shot up from the chair and turned around, almost knocking over Nathaniel's perfect candle. "Ruth?" She struggled to catch her breath. "What are you doing here?"

"Trying to find you." She walked farther inside and pulled a piece of paper out of the pocket of her coat. "I know it's late notice, but *Grossmutter* decided she needed more candles to put in the windows for Christmas. I told her it might be better if she got them at the store, but she wouldn't think of it."

Anne Marie took the paper from Ruth, hoping her friend didn't see the flames of embarrassment rising in her cheeks. "She's always been a loyal customer."

"*Ya.*" But Ruth wasn't looking at Anne Marie. Her gaze was planted on Nathaniel, who was putting finishing touches on the carved candle, his hand as steady as ever, while Anne Marie's insides were quaking.

Maybe she'd imagined the whole thing. And the thought of kissing Nathaniel never should have entered her mind. But now she couldn't think about anything else.

Ruth leaned close to Anne Marie. "What's Nathaniel doing here?" she whispered.

"Helping me. I'm behind on my orders."

"Oh." She kept staring at Nathaniel, but he didn't seem to notice. "Did you tell him?"

"What?"

"About . . . you know." Ruth tilted her head in his direction.

"I think I'm done." Nathaniel put down the tool and leaned back.

"My goodness!" Ruth clasped her hands together and walked over to the table. "Nathaniel, I had no idea you were so talented. It's the most *perfekt* candle I've ever seen."

Anne Marie rolled her eyes. Then she realized she had said almost the same thing. But hearing it from Ruth irritated her.

Nathaniel looked at Ruth. "I'm glad it turned out all right."

"It's better than all right." She bent down, as if she was inspecting the candle with great concentration. She leaned over a bit too far and put her hand on Nathaniel's shoulder.

"Sorry. Lost *mei* balance." But she didn't remove her hand.

"It's fine." He glanced at her, and didn't move either.

Anne Marie crumpled the piece of paper in her hand.

"Is this candle for sale?" Ruth asked Nathaniel. "I'd like to buy it."

"Nee." Anne Marie swooped up the candle and put it on her workbench. "It's already spoken for."

"Oh. Well, maybe I can order another one. As long as Nathaniel carves it."

He shrugged. "I don't know, I'm just helping Anne Marie out for a little while."

"Actually, I don't need any more help." She glared at him. He seemed to be enjoying Ruth's touch a little more than necessary. Just a few days ago she was encouraging him to ask Ruth out. Now the thought of them together made her sick.

But it was for the best, wasn't it? Hadn't she come to that conclusion herself last night?

"I don't know about you, but I'm hungry," Ruth said. "We should have some lunch." She looked at Anne Marie. "Don't you think so?"

Anne Marie didn't miss the pleading message in her friend's eyes. She couldn't be mad at Ruth, who didn't know about the turmoil going on inside of Anne Marie. "I'm not really hungry. But you and Nathaniel can get something to eat."

He finally moved from underneath Ruth's grasp. "That's okay, Anne Marie," Nathaniel said. "I can stay and help."

"Like I said, I don't need any help." She stared at him, crossing her arms.

"But I thought you were behind on your orders."

"I just got caught up."

Ruth moved in between them. "She said she wasn't hungry, Nathaniel. But I'm starving. Do you mind sharing lunch with me?"

Bewildered, Nathaniel looked at Ruth, her light-brown eyes practically begging him to say yes, and Anne Marie, whose pale-blue eyes seemed colder than chipped ice. What was wrong with her? She'd gone from being her usual happy self to being snappish. No, not just snappy. She was angry. Was she mad that he tried to kiss her? Or did he do something else wrong?

"Going to lunch with Ruth is a great idea," Anne Marie said, unfolding her arms and going to the door. When she opened it, a welcome blast of cool air swept through the small workshop. Sweat rolled down his back as Anne Marie's cold gaze landed on him. "You two *geh* have lunch."

His brows pulled in. Usually he could figure out what she was thinking. Anne Marie wasn't exactly a closed book. But she'd shut herself off from him, and he didn't like it.

"Come on, Nathaniel," Ruth said. "We'll *geh* to *mei haus.* I'll make you the most *appeldicht* roast beef sandwich you've ever had. Plus apple pie for dessert."

"You don't have to *geh* to so much trouble." He kept his gaze on Anne Marie. She looked away, then finally turned her back on him and started dipping candles, as if both he and Ruth were invisible.

Fine. If she wanted to play games, so be it. She could be so childish it drove him *ab im kopp.*

But she was also funny. Talented. Intelligent. Beautiful.

"Nathaniel?" Ruth was already halfway out the door.

He paused, then turned. "Coming." He walked out the door with Ruth, but his mind was still on Anne Marie.

"Ouch!" Anne Marie peeled off a small

splash of melted wax from the back of her hand. She'd been careless since Nathaniel and Ruth left a short while ago. Her last batch of tapers looked worse than his. She put her hands against the edge of the counter and closed her eyes, praying for focus and patience.

The door opened, and for a second, her heart flipped over, thinking Nathaniel had returned. But it was only her brother. "What do you want, Jonah?"

He held up his hands. "What are you snapping at me for?"

"Sorry." She squeezed the bridge of her nose with her fingertips. "I shouldn't have done that."

"It's okay." Jonah came over to her workstation. "The candles look great."

"Liar." She picked up the warped tapers and held them in front of him.

"I didn't mean those." He pointed to Nathaniel's candle. "That's the best one you've done."

"It's not mine. It's Nathaniel's."

"Ah."

She looked at him. "Okay, Jonah. Why are you here? You never come in the workshop." He'd always complained it was too hot, smelly, and cramped.

"Just checking on you. We haven't had

much time to talk about . . . you know."

She sat down. Jonah was rarely in a talking mood, and she could see he needed her undivided attention. "How do you feel about it?"

He shrugged. "I think I'm okay with it now."

"You sure?"

"*Ya. Mamm*'s happy. That's what I want." He picked at the bumpy dots of hardened wax on her worktable. "How about you?"

She tossed the useless candles to the side, not in the mood to fix them. "I've already told *Mamm* I'm happy for her. The rest will work itself out."

"Ah."

"Would you stop that!" She faced him. "Jonah, I'm okay with *Mamm* getting married, I'm okay with moving to Ohio. Everything is absolutely fantastic. Couldn't be better."

"Now look who's lying."

She hunched her shoulders. When did her brother suddenly grow up? He was acting like an older brother, not a younger one. "Okay, maybe not fantastic. But it's well enough." She picked up a candle rack. "If you're done drilling me with questions, I have to get back to work."

"Your sour mood wouldn't have anything

to do with Nathaniel leaving with Ruth Troyer?"

She kept her head down. "Why would I care if Nathaniel is with Ruth?"

"I don't know. Do you?"

This sibling chitchat was making her head pound. "Jonah, I'm the one who suggested he *geh* out with her. It was a coincidence that they were both here at the same time, and she invited him for lunch. End of story."

"Okay. As long as you're not upset or anything."

"I'm not! Now get out of here so I can finish these candles!"

Jonah backed away. Then he paused, as if wanting to say something.

Her patience was paper-thin. "What now?"

"Nix." He shook his head and hurried out the door.

She put her head into her hands, frustrated. She'd been rude to her brother, she was upset with Ruth, and she resented Nathaniel. "*Ya,* everything is just perfect," she muttered.

She lifted her head and took in a deep breath. Her face heated, and not because of the hot wax in the pots on the camper stoves. How could she have been so foolish to think Nathaniel would want to kiss her?

And why, after all these years of friendship, was the thought of him being with Ruth almost unbearable? So much had changed between them in such a short time. She'd never been so confused.

She stepped away from her workbench and closed her eyes. *Lord, help me.*

"I hope you like the pie." Ruth set a plate in front of Nathaniel, filled with the largest piece of pie he'd ever seen. She must have given him almost half of it. But after a huge lunch of an open roast beef sandwich smothered in gravy, pickled eggs, and cabbage slaw, he wasn't sure he could eat another bite. For sure, Ruth could cook.

She could also talk. And talk and talk and talk. Sitting in front of her, he could see her mouth moving but had no idea what she was saying. He'd tuned her out halfway through the meal. Apparently she'd never heard the old saying that silence was golden.

He and Anne Marie could spend hours together. Fishing, playing checkers, sitting on the grass at the edge of a pond — it didn't matter where they were. Neither of them ever felt the need to fill the silence between them.

He frowned. If Ruth hadn't walked in, he would have kissed Anne Marie. The thought of kissing his best friend should unnerve him. Instead, he was irritated he didn't get the chance.

But clearly she had a different idea. She couldn't wait to shove him out the door with Ruth.

"Is there something wrong with the pie?" Ruth asked.

He blinked, her face coming into focus. "*Nee.* Why?"

"You haven't tried it yet." She folded her hands on the table and smiled, her posture as straight as a fence post. "I picked the apples myself, from the Bakers' orchard. I know they're an *Englisch familye,* but they grow the best apples in the area. Do you like their apples?"

"I guess." He took a bite of the pie. The flaky crust dissolved in his mouth. Wow. He could probably choke this down, even with his full stomach.

"Are you going to the singing at the Keims' on Sunday? It's the last one before Christmas."

"*Nee.* I'll be at Anne Marie's."

Her bottom lip poked out slightly. "Why?"

"I always *geh* over there on Sundays."

"Don't you think it's time you stopped?"

He put down his fork and looked at her, dumbfounded.

She unclasped her hands. "Nathaniel, she's leaving."

"Which is why I'm going over there on Sunday." He ran his hand across the back of his neck. They wouldn't have too many Sundays left.

Ruth tapped her fingernail against the edge of her plate. "You're spending too much time with her. You always have."

He clenched his hand. "You're not one to judge how I spend *mei* time. Or who I spend it with."

"I don't mean it that way." She sighed softly and reached for his hand. He wanted to pull away, but she held onto it with a tight grip. "I care about you, Nathaniel. A lot." She smiled and squeezed his hand.

He leaned back. When Anne Marie had encouraged him to ask Ruth out, he'd briefly considered it. But so much had changed in a few short days.

"I know you and Anne Marie are *gut* friends," she continued, her voice sticky sweet, like the pie he couldn't finish. "But you have to be realistic. Your relationship with Anne Marie can't last forever. You can't spend your Sundays playing games, pretending you're still *kinner.* You're a *mann* now." She leaned forward and licked her bottom lip. "You need to be thinking about the future. Maybe one with me."

He squirmed, finally able to pull his hand away from hers. "Ruth —"

"If you're worried about Anne Marie, she told me she doesn't think about you that way."

"You don't know that." The words flew out of his mouth.

Ruth folded her hands in her lap, her smile tightening. "I see."

"See what?"

"That you have feelings for her." She shook her head, as if she felt sorry for him. "I can't say I'm surprised. You wouldn't be with her so much if you didn't."

Her superior tone irritated him. "You don't know what you're talking about."

She tilted her head. "It's okay. I've talked to Anne Marie about us." Ruth stood and walked around the table. She moved close to him, then leaned against the table edge. "She's already given us her blessing." She touched his shoulder, then bent over and whispered in his ear. "I can help you get over her, Nathaniel. What you feel for her will fade in time."

He looked up at Ruth but didn't move beneath her touch. He didn't appreciate the way she acted like she knew him. She was too pushy, and bolder than he was comfortable with. Yet he could see she was genuine.

And she was right. Anne Marie would always think of him as part of her childhood. Not part of her future.

Ruth reached out her hand. Nathaniel looked at it. Paused. Then hesitantly put his hand in hers.

CHAPTER TEN

On Sunday evening, Anne Marie paced the living room. She kept peeking out the window looking for Nathaniel. An hour after his usual arrival time, she decided he wasn't coming.

She turned to the coffee table in the living room. She'd already set up the game. Life on the Farm, his favorite. She knelt down and started gathering up the pieces, trying to stem the despair welling up inside. She hadn't seen him since he'd left with Ruth a few days ago. Today they didn't have church, so she hadn't expected to see him until tonight. Hadn't he promised they'd spend as much time together as possible?

But that was before she'd pushed him and Ruth together. Before she decided to let him go. Before she realized her feelings for him ran deeper than friendship.

Still, she had hoped he would come. Even though she pushed him away, tried to get him out of her mind and heart, she had wanted to see him tonight.

"Why are you putting up the game?" Her mother walked into the living room, holding several white taper candles in plain brass candleholders. She went to the window and placed one on the sill. "Where's Nathaniel?"

"He's not coming."

"Oh?" She turned around. "Did something happen?"

"I guess he couldn't make it tonight."

"That's strange. He never misses game night." She crossed over to the other window in the living room and put a candle in it. Tomorrow she would tie back the curtains, and in the evening, she and Anne Marie would light the candles for the few nights leading up to Christmas.

"I'm going to Miriam's tomorrow to talk about wedding preparations." Her mother smiled, her eyes sparkling. "Would you like to join us?"

Anne Marie fiddled with the lid of the board game. She had promised to be supportive. And she wanted to be. But she couldn't take discussing wedding plans, especially right now. "I'll let you know."

"Oh. Okay." Her mother's smile faded a bit.

Anne Marie stood, chastising herself for

being selfish. "I'm sorry. Of course I'll *geh.*"

"Miriam and I can take care of it."

"I know, but I want to help. I wasn't thinking straight when I answered the first time."

Her mother touched her arm. "*Danki,* Anne Marie. I'm glad you want to be a part of this." She started to leave the room.

"*Mamm?*"

She turned around. "*Ya?*"

"How did you know you were in love with Thomas?" The question wrested free from her thoughts, like a bird escaping its cage. She hadn't meant to voice the words or to pry. But suddenly she really wanted an answer.

Her mother sat down on the couch. "I'm not sure how it happened. I can't really pinpoint a moment when I realized I loved him."

Anne Marie sat on the floor at her mother's feet. She wrapped her arms around her knees, the skirt of her dress touching the tops of her stocking-covered feet. "What if you change your mind?"

"What do you mean?"

"When he gets here. What if you regret saying you'll marry him?"

Mamm crossed her legs at the ankles. "Anne Marie, even though this is sudden to you, it's not to me and Thomas. We've prayed about this. I've never been more sure about anything in my life . . . except when I married your *daed.*" She touched her knees and leaned forward. "Remember, Thomas and I were friends when we were younger. We rekindled that friendship when we started writing each other. One thing I've learned is that friends are life's treasures. But sometimes when you least expect it, a friendship blossoms into love." Her mother stood. "I hope that eases your mind."

Anne Marie nodded. It did about *Mamm* and Thomas, but confused her further about Nathaniel.

"I still have a couple of cookbooks to finish binding. Nothing like doing things at the last minute."

Popping up to her feet, Anne Marie said, "I'll help you."

"I can do them." She looked at the game on the table. "You shouldn't put that on the shelf just yet. Nathaniel is sure to come."

She nodded, but didn't agree.

After her mother left, Anne Marie sat down on the couch and stared at the game, willing Nathaniel to come as the minutes ticked away. Half an hour later she gave up and put the board game away.

Her mother's friendship with Thomas started a new beginning, but it appeared that Anne Marie and Nathaniel's friendship was coming to an end.

Nathaniel stood outside Anne Marie's house on the edge of the yard by the road. Instead of driving, he had walked, hoping the cold air and exercise would straighten his thoughts. They didn't, and the closer he got, the more confused and nervous he became. When he arrived, he couldn't bring himself to go inside.

For the first time in his life, he had no idea what to say to Anne Marie. Should he tell her about his changing feelings toward her? Or follow Ruth's advice and end their friendship? The thought pained him. Still, he couldn't deny they both needed to be free of each other in order to move on.

The problem was, he wasn't sure he wanted to move on.

The light in the window disappeared. Nathaniel exhaled, his breath hanging in cloudy puffs in front of him. A full moon filled the clear sky. He pushed his hat lower on his head, shoved his hands in the pockets of his coat, and headed for home.

"Nathaniel."

He turned at the sound of Jonah's voice. The kid was walking toward him from the barn. He didn't stop until he was a few feet away, close enough that Nathaniel could see the spark of anger in his eyes. "What are you doing?" Jonah asked.

"Leaving." He hated the dejection in his voice. "Anne Marie's gone to bed already."

"Because you didn't show up for your game." Jonah put his hands on his hips. He wasn't wearing a coat, and his stance emphasized his broad shoulders. "I don't know what's going on with you two," Jonah said. "Normally I stay out of things. But when *mei schwester* is upset, then it becomes *mei* business."

Nathaniel faced him. "She's upset?"

"Of course she is. You left with Ruth Troyer the other day. Then you don't show up for your weekly game night that's been going on forever." He frowned. "Except you did, but you didn't tell her you were here. I don't get that at all."

"It's complicated."

"I don't care." He stepped forward and looked Nathaniel in the eye, the straight, serious line of his brow illuminated by the silvery moonlight. "If you have something to say to Anne Marie, you need to say it. If not, stop wasting her time." Jonah turned and started to walk away. "Don't be a coward, Nathaniel. You're better than that."

His ego stinging, Nathaniel opened his

mouth to rebuke him. He didn't have to take advice from Anne Marie's little brother. Or from Ruth Troyer, for that matter. He could make his own decisions. And it was time he did just that.

CHAPTER ELEVEN

"Anne Marie, did you polish the furniture in the living room?"

Anne Marie stilled the broom she was holding and rolled her eyes at the sound of her mother's frantic voice from the other end of the house. She'd been like this for the past two days, fluttering around, making sure everything was ideal for Thomas's first supper with them tonight. "*Ya, Mamm.* I polished it."

"All of it?"

"*Ya.*" She went back to sweeping the kitchen as her mother rushed in. Anne Marie looked up and saw the gleam in her eyes, the rosy tint of her cheeks. She put her hand on her mother's arm. "Everything is fine, *Mamm.* Don't worry."

"I'm not worried." *Mamm* hurried to the stove, wiping her hands on her clean apron. She opened the oven, releasing the scent of garlic and peppercorns in the air. "Almost done," she said, closing the door.

"*Gut.*" Christopher looked out the kitchen window. "Because he's coming up the driveway."

"He's what?" Her mother turned to Anne Marie. "But supper's not ready, the table isn't set —"

"Christopher can set the table," Anne Marie said.

His jaw slacked. "What? That's a *frau*'s job."

Anne Marie shot him a glare before turning back to her mother. "*Geh* ahead and let Thomas in. Once you're settled in the living room, I'll bring you both a glass of tea."

"Okay." Her mother nodded, but seemed anything but okay. Anne Marie smiled. She wasn't used to seeing her *mamm* this flustered. She turned her mother by the shoulders and shooed her out of the kitchen.

"Jonah doesn't have to set the table," Christopher grumbled.

"I'm sure he's helping Thomas with his horse." Anne Marie tasted the mashed potatoes, which were warming on top of the stove. Scrumptious, as usual. She hoped Thomas knew how lucky he was to be marrying a good cook. If he didn't know, he was about to find out.

A plate landed on the table with a clatter.

Anne Marie left the stove and took the rest of the dishes from her brother. "Never mind, I'll do it."

Christopher grinned and retreated from the kitchen.

She tried to focus on setting a pretty table, not on the nerve-wracking fact that her mother was in the living room with her future stepfather. As she placed the last plate on the table, she guided her mind elsewhere. It immediately went to Nathaniel, as it had done since Sunday, despite trying to keep herself busy making her candles.

She gripped the edge of the table at the image of Nathaniel and Ruth. Jealousy twisted inside her like an ugly weed winding around her heart. She'd never had a reason to be jealous, and she didn't like the feeling. For the first time she was looking forward to the move. She couldn't bear the thought of seeing Nathaniel and Ruth together.

She finished setting the table, calming her frayed nerves with a silent prayer. She set the candle Nathaniel had carved in the middle of the table. Her customer had canceled her order, and Anne Marie decided to keep the beautiful wax creation. Just then her mother walked in the kitchen.

"That's lovely." She put her hand on Anne Marie's shoulder, her face glowing. "Your skills have improved."

"*Danki.*" She didn't bother to explain the truth. It didn't matter anymore. "Where is Thomas?"

"Talking to Jonah outside. That *bu* is giving him a thorough questioning."

"I'm not surprised." She felt a little sorry for Thomas.

The distant thud of heels against wood sounded right outside the kitchen. "They're coming. Are you sure everything is okay, Anne Marie?"

She nodded and gave her mother a quick hug. "It is. I promise."

Jonah and Christopher walked in the kitchen first, followed by a stocky man with a mop of ginger-red hair threaded with gray. His blue eyes were wide set, and he held onto his hat, gripping it by the brim as if it were his lifeline. He looked nothing like her father, who had been taller, thinner, and darker. But he was handsome in his own way.

She glanced at her mother, who couldn't keep her eyes off him. They both seemed frozen in their own moment. Watching them, Anne Marie realized how deeply her mother loved him, and that he truly loved her.

She relaxed and gave Thomas a genuine smile, beckoning him into the kitchen. "I hope you're hungry," she said, pulling out the chair at the head of the table. "*Mamm* made a feast."

Anne Marie put away the last clean pot, then drained the dirty dishwater from the sink. Her mother and Thomas had disappeared into the living room after eating. Jonah and Christopher went to the barn, leaving her to clean the kitchen alone.

She wiped down the counter, then turned to the table. The candle was still in the center, unlit. She walked to it, touching one of the delicate white and red curls. The empty kitchen instantly felt too small. She grabbed her coat off the peg by the back door and went outside.

The light of a lantern shone from the barn, where her brothers were probably taking care of the animals for the night. She breathed in the cold air, crossing her arms over her chest. It still hadn't snowed, unusual for this time of year.

"You're not too cold out here?"

She turned to see Thomas approach. He had his hat on but wasn't wearing his coat.

"Sure you're not?" she asked as he arrived at her side.

"I'm a human heater." He smiled. She could see his slightly crooked teeth gleaming in the darkness. "That's what my late wife told me." He paused. "She would have liked you."

Anne Marie tilted her head and looked at him. *"Ya?"*

"She appreciated hardworking people. Lydia told me about your candlemaking business. How successful it is. You don't have success without hard work."

A knot formed in her throat. It felt good to have someone acknowledge her efforts.

"I know the move will be tough, Anne Marie. I wish it could be different."

"It's as God wills." She turned to him, a sense of peace slipping over her. "I never thought I'd leave Paradise. But that seems to be what God wants of me. Of our family."

Thomas's shoulders relaxed. "There's a busy tourist business in Holmes County," he said, his deep voice sounding less tentative. "You won't have any problem finding customers for your candles."

"That's *gut.*" She turned to him and gave him her warmest smile. "We should *geh* back inside. I'm sure *Mamm* is waiting for you."

He faced her and swallowed. "Your *Mamm* said you were something special. She was right."

"She was right about you too."

As they walked back inside, Anne Marie realized everything would be okay. While she was still unsure about Nathaniel and the part he would play in her life in the future, she was sure about one thing. Thomas Nissley was a *gut* man who made her mother happy. She couldn't ask for more.

CHAPTER TWELVE

While Christmas Day was a time of contemplation and quiet celebration of Christ's birth, the day after Christmas was anything but.

The Smucker house was filled to bursting with people. Jonah and Christopher were playing Dutch Blitz against Seth and Thomas, who in a few short days had fit seamlessly into the family. *Mamm* was holding a sleeping Leah while *Aenti* Miriam played blocks with Junior on the floor. Anne Marie watched her mom and Thomas sneaking sweet glances at each other when they thought no one was looking.

Anne Marie stood to the side, breathing in the scent of fresh popped corn, buttered and seasoned to mouthwatering perfection. Flames flickered on several of her vanilla and cinnamon candles, their sweetly spiced aroma mixing with the mugs of warm apple cider. She heard the laughter, saw the smiles. And wished she could share in their happiness, instead of being on the sidelines.

She hadn't forgotten that Nathaniel had a standing invitation for Second Christmas, but apparently he had. He was probably with Ruth and her family today. Or maybe with his own.

She went in the kitchen to fix herself a cup of hot cocoa. Her mind wandered back in time, to all the memories she held close over the years. She thought about when she and Nathaniel were eight and they'd lie in the grass, counting the stars, only to end up covered in mosquito bites. When she was twelve and he and her brothers had hidden in the loft of the barn and dumped a bucket of cold water on her head when she walked in. But she had gotten him back when she stuck a frog in his coat pocket before he went home.

She peered out the kitchen window. Large, fluffy flakes of snow floated down from the dark sky. A white Christmas after all. She took her hot chocolate and stepped out on the back porch. Stuck her tongue out and caught a snowflake. Another memory with Nathaniel. She'd never realized until now that most of her sweetest memories included him.

She didn't know how long she stood

outside, sipping lukewarm hot chocolate, wrapped in a cloak of the past, until she noticed her own shivering and the snow that had blanketed the ground.

When she went back into the kitchen, her aunt was putting two mugs in the sink. She looked up at Anne Marie. "I wondered where you went off to." She grimaced. "Have you been outside long? You must be freezing."

Anne Marie set the half-full mug in the sink. "I just needed some fresh air."

"I'm pleased with how you're handling this, Anne Marie. I know you were troubled at first, but I'm glad you've come to terms with everything."

Not everything. She exhaled. "I'm sorry for the way I acted when I first found out. I should have been more supportive."

"You don't need to apologize. Everyone understands, especially *yer mamm.*" Aunt Miriam walked toward the mudroom off the kitchen. "Seth and I are heading home before the snow gets too deep." She disappeared for a moment and returned with coats, hats, and her black bonnet. "Merry Christmas, Anne Marie."

She hugged her aunt. "Merry Christmas."

Thomas left shortly afterward, also not wanting to get stuck in the snow. Her brothers were already upstairs and her *mamm* had started tidying up the living room. "I'll get that," Anne Marie said.

"You sure?" Although her mother looked happy, she also seemed tired.

"I'm sure. Get some rest. *Gut nacht, Mamm.*"

Moments later Anne Marie put the card game in the drawer of the side table. She cleaned out the popcorn bowl and the corn popper and put them away. Folded the green-and-red quilt Aunt Miriam had given them for Christmas ten years earlier and laid it over the back of the couch. And tried not to cry.

She looked around the living room. The wedding was planned for two weeks from today, and a couple of days later she would be on her way to Ohio. *God, help me. One minute I think I'm okay with moving, and the next I'm not. I think I'm okay with Nathaniel not being in my life, and then I'm not. I can't get through this without Your help, Lord.*

She blew out the candles in the windows, then walked to Nathaniel's candle, the flame dancing and illuminating his exquisite carving. Her mother had wanted to light it, still not knowing Anne Marie hadn't carved it. She watched red wax drip down the side, altering the curves and curlicues, changing

438

it forever. The candle, like her life and her relationship with Nathaniel, would never be the same.

She leaned over to blow it out when she heard a knock at the back door. Who would be coming over this late and with heavy snow falling? When she answered the door, she froze. "Nathaniel?"

"I . . ." Snow covered his black hat, the shoulders of his coat. The coat she'd slept with for several nights. She leaned against the doorjamb, weary of being confused, upset, hurt. She was tired of it all.

"It's late, Nathaniel. Christmas is over." She started to close the door when he stopped her.

"Don't." He locked his gaze on hers. "Don't send me away . . . even though I deserve it."

Nathaniel's knees buckled at the pain in Anne Marie's eyes. Pain he'd caused. He shouldn't have stayed away so long. He shouldn't have waited until now to see her. To let her know how he felt.

Before she could push him away, he walked inside. He set down the paper bag he was carrying and put his arms around her. He heard her gasp as he pressed her against him, burying his face in her neck.

Yes, he should have done this a long time ago.

When she relaxed against him, he closed his eyes. When he heard her sob, he looked at her. "I'm sorry," he whispered.

She pulled away and wiped the tears from her face. "We need to talk."

He nodded as she turned on the gas lamp near the window. He followed her to the couch and sat down. She rubbed her hand over her eyes one more time before looking away.

He'd practiced the words all the way over here, hurrying his horse through the newly fallen snow that had turned to slush on the roads. But now that he was here, the words wouldn't come. He couldn't tell her how he'd spent the past few days in prayer, had talked to his father, and had told Ruth that they were over before they'd even started. He didn't doubt his decision. But he did doubt his ability to convince Anne Marie.

"I'm glad you're here," she finally said. "I have something to tell you." She took a deep breath. "Nathaniel, it's time we both moved on."

His breath hitched. "What?"

"I know we talked about writing letters and visiting, but that won't last."

"Anne Marie —"

"And I'm glad you and Ruth found each other." Tears pooled in her eyes again. "You'll both be very happy together."

He couldn't stand to listen to this anymore.

"Maybe I can come for the wedd—"

He took her face in his hands and kissed her.

Anne Marie couldn't stop Nathaniel from kissing her, and she didn't want to. The kiss was sweet and gentle and he parted from her too fast. When he drew away, she fought for words. "What about Ruth?" she asked when she was able to catch her breath.

He shook his head. "There's nothing between me and Ruth." He took her hand.

Her palm tingled in his. Then she came to her senses. "Wait a minute." She pulled out of his grasp. "You stood me up on Sunday."

He rubbed his right temple. "About that —"

"And then you're late tonight." She crossed her arms over her white apron. "Now you're kissing me. What's going on, Nathaniel?"

"I'm sorry about last Sunday and about being late tonight. But I needed time."

"Away from me?"

He cupped her chin in his hand. "I had to

sort things out. Most important, I had to pray about us. I've always cared about you, Anne Marie. You're *mei* best friend. I didn't want to do anything to ruin that. But I knew things couldn't stay the same between us."

"Because I'm moving." She looked away.

He tilted her face toward him. "*Nee.* Because I love you."

She stilled, letting his words wash over her in a warm wave. "You do?"

He chuckled and let his hand drop to his side. "That shouldn't be a surprise. Everyone else has known. Even before I did. And I think from the way you kissed me back, you do too."

She couldn't deny it. "So? We love each other." It felt strange and right at the same time to say the words out loud. "There's not much we can do about it now."

"We could get married."

Her eyes widened. "Are you serious?"

"Very. I don't want you to leave. I don't want to be separated from you. I know I said letters and visits would be enough." He drew her to him. She laid her cheek against his chest, feeling him rest his chin on top of her head. "But we both know it won't."

He was right. Being in his arms, feeling his heart beating in time with hers . . . how could she be apart from him? *"Ya."*

"Does that mean . . . ?"

She looked up at him. "It means I'll marry you."

He pulled her to him and held her. A moment later, he sat back. He grinned, his expression holding a mixture of happiness and relief. He stood, went to the door, and picked up the brown paper bag. He opened it and pulled out the antique mantel clock she'd admired in his workshop. "Merry Christmas."

She took it from him, touching the polished silver decorations, every trace of tarnish removed. The smooth blue box that encased the simple clock looked fresh, but still showed its age. "It's beautiful."

He sat down next to her. "I'm glad you like it."

She looked at him. "And all I did was make a plate of your favorite brownies."

"Can't wait to eat them." He grinned.

She looked at the clock again. "I can't believe you're giving this to me. Doesn't your *daed* want to sell it in the shop?"

"He gave it to me, to give to someone special." He took the clock from her and turned it around. A small brass plate was attached to the back. She read the engraved words: *Out of friendship grew love. Nathaniel and Anne Marie.*

Tears came to her eyes. Goodness, she'd never been this weepy in her life. But they were tears of joy. "You were that sure I would say *ya*?"

"I was pretty sure." He rubbed his thumb over her knuckle. "Okay, I was praying. Really hard."

She leaned over and kissed his cheek.

"It's about time."

Anne Marie pulled away from Nathaniel and found Jonah standing on the steps. "How long have you been there?" she asked, cutting her eyes at him.

He waved her off and continued down the stairs. "Don't mind me, I'm just getting a brownie."

"Those are Nathaniel's."

"Okay, some pie, then." He headed toward the kitchen. "So when's the wedding?" he asked over his shoulder.

Her mouth dropped open. "How did you know?"

He gave her a wily grin. "Like I said, it's about time."

CHAPTER THIRTEEN

January

"I wish I wasn't so nervous."

Anne Marie smiled at her mother. She straightened the shoulders of *Mamm*'s wedding dress, the dark-blue fabric complementing her deep brown eyes. "You look *schee, Mamm*. And happy."

"So do you." She hooked her arm through Anne Marie's. They turned and looked in the mirror above the dresser. "Are we ready for this?"

Anne Marie studied the two of them in the mirror. In a few minutes their lives would be altered forever. Several weeks ago she'd fought against change. Wondered about God's plan. And along the way, fell in love with her best friend. She placed her hand over her mother's. "*Ya*. We're ready."

They walked out of *Mamm*'s bedroom and into the living room. Anne Marie instantly locked eyes with Nathaniel. He grinned, and the butterflies dancing in her stomach calmed. Her mother moved to stand next to Thomas. Anne Marie took her place next to Nathaniel. Between them, the bishop started the double wedding ceremony.

As he spoke, Anne Marie glanced around a room filled with family and close friends. Her grandparents, her aunt Miriam and uncle Seth, her brothers. Then she saw Nathaniel's mother wipe a tear. She'd been the most overjoyed of all when she heard the news. Like Jonah, she had simply said, "It's about time."

She glanced at her mother and Thomas. Soon enough she'd have to say good-bye to them and her brothers. While they started a new life in Ohio, she would start her new life as Mrs. Nathaniel Mast. The thought added a touch of bittersweetness to her heart.

But she didn't have to think about good-byes right now. Today was her wedding day, and she was rejoicing over the greatest gift she'd ever received — friendship that turned into love.

READING GROUP GUIDE

1. Anne Marie knew she shouldn't have read her mother's letters. What would you have done in the same situation?
2. Do you think Nathaniel was fair to Ruth? Why or why not?
3. Anne Marie questioned God's plan when she found out she was moving. Have you ever wondered why God has led you down a certain path, especially if it caused disappointment or discomfort? How did you deal with it?
4. Do you think Anne Marie and Nathaniel would have fallen in love without the threat of her moving away?

ACKNOWLEDGMENTS

Thank you to my family — my husband James, my children Mathew, Sydney, and Zoie, and my parents Jim and Eleanora Daly. I love you all so much!

ABOUT THE AUTHOR

Kathleen Fuller is the author of several bestselling novels, including *A Man of His Word* and *Treasuring Emma,* as well as a middle-grade Amish series, The Mysteries of Middlefield.

■ ■ ■ ■

THE CHRISTMAS
APRONS

TRICIA GOYER

■ ■ ■ ■

*Dedicated to my daughter, Leslie Goyer,
who sees everyone as a friend and
creates community wherever she is!*

GLOSSARY

aenti: aunt
boppli: baby
dat: dad
danki: thank you
demut: humility
Englisch: not Amish
ja: yes
kapp: prayer covering
kinder: children
maedel: girl
maude: nanny
mem: mother
ne: no
onkel: uncle
rumspringa years: running-around years
vat: what
vell: well

CHAPTER ONE

Esther Glick looked out the ice-frosted window of her cousin's house, noting the traffic that jammed up the narrow road leading to the West Kootenai Kraft and Grocery. It had been a mild winter until two days ago when the sky dumped fresh snow. Outside, two Amish bachelors rode bicycles over the layer of packed-down snow, their tires occasionally sliding on the icy surface. The bike riders moved with great effort, almost in slow motion, but you couldn't tell it bothered them by the bright grins on their faces. They were passed by an *Englisch* boy — no older than ten years old — on a four-wheeler. Two young Amish women, both with red hair neatly tucked under their starched white *kapps,* also strode by, the frosty air from their breaths leading the way.

Esther enjoyed watching them. More than once when she'd been outside — bringing in kindling or feeding the horses — she'd seen someone from the Amish community walk by. Each time she considered walking out to the road to greet them, but she always changed her mind. Unlike her twin sister, Violet — who was very outgoing — Esther always held back. She worried about what to say. She worried about taking up too much of someone's time, and so she usually just waved instead.

An Amish wagon followed the bicyclists. It was the lumber wagon that she'd seen driving back and forth to Montana Log Works, but today it carried a different type of load. Three more Amish bachelors, and a dog that paced back and forth and barked a friendly greeting to the two young women as they passed.

"Why, I've never seen such commotion for some pies," Esther mumbled to herself. Inside her cousin's kitchen, heat radiated from the wood-burning cookstove, and the smell of her own pie cooling caused her stomach to rumble.

She stepped back from the window, breathing in the sweet aroma of the vanilla crumb pies she'd just baked. It was a pie that her *mem* was well-known for, and one Esther had never made on her own . . . until now.

For all her life *Mem* had closely guarded the secret recipe. It wasn't written down — just in *Mem*'s head — and she hadn't even let her daughters stay in the kitchen as she stirred the ingredients together. Once, Violet had tried to hide and watch, but she got caught. Her punishment? No pie that day. Not even a sliver of a slice. And that's why the letter *Mem* sent was such a mystery.

An envelope had arrived from her mother just yesterday. Inside were two things. First, to her complete surprise, a recipe card with the pie recipe, and second, a quick note written on the back of a faded grocery receipt.

Good luck with the silent auction. Our prayers are with you. Love, Mem. P.S. Guard this recipe with your life. Don't tell a soul.

Esther hadn't remembered telling *Mem* about the silent auction. It must have been her cousin Hannah who'd shared the news. Or maybe one of the scribes mentioned it in the *Budget.* Then again, *Mem* had other friends in the area too. It always surprised *Englishers* how ladies from different Amish communities kept tabs on one another. They didn't need cell phones or computers

461

to share news. Letters and personal visits did a fine job all on their own.

Esther's fingers had trembled the first time she held the recipe in her hands. As she read through the ingredients and directions, she couldn't believe how simple it was, yet she knew *Mem* had offered a great sacrifice by offering it up. But why now?

Esther could hardly sleep last night, and this morning, she'd been up bright and early to get started. Now, two pies sat cooling on the kitchen counter. If she'd only made one, it never would have made it to the auction. Vanilla crumb pie was Hannah's favorite too.

As if on cue, footsteps drew near as if wisps of vanilla had lured her cousin in. Esther had swaddled Mark, the newborn baby, and had set him in the kitchen cradle right before putting the pies into the oven. Thankfully, he still slept. She'd come to be Hannah's *maude,* caring for the new baby and assisting the new mother. Guilt trailed after her for taking this Saturday off for the fundraiser.

Esther swatted a potholder toward her cousin, who walked with hesitant, careful steps. "Hannah, you know you're not supposed to be on your feet yet."

"The *boppli* is two weeks old, Estie." Han-

462

nah chuckled. "Giving birth didn't leave me completely helpless. Besides, I had to make sure for myself that you made an extra pie for me . . . My stomach's been growling the whole time they've been in the oven."

"Of course. I knew you'd tackle me if I dared to make only one vanilla pie and then leave with it." Esther stroked her chin. "Yet what I don't understand is why *Mem* sent me the recipe — why now? Heaven knows I've been begging her for it for years."

Hannah's eyebrows peaked. She quickly looked away but not before Esther noticed the sparkle in her cousin's gaze.

"What was that look?" Esther picked up the almost-cooled pie from the counter and placed it in a wicker basket.

Instead of answering her, Hannah hurried to the second pie, moving faster than Esther had seen her move in two weeks. She took a knife from the knife block and cut herself a generous piece. "I don't know how your piecrust always comes out so evenly, so perfectly browned."

"I use a heavy pie pan. A dark finish is best. My *mem* —" Esther paused. "Wait, you're trying to change the subject." She dipped her rolling pin into the sink of hot, soapy water and washed it. Another reason why her pies turned out so well was that

Esther took care of her baking tools. Her father was a mechanic, and he worked on small gas engines. He kept his shop as neat as her *mem*'s kitchen — she'd learned well from both of their examples.

Hannah leaned closer to the countertop and took a bite of pie. "I'm not trying to change the subject. I honestly want to know. There has to be a few secrets to pie as wonderful as this!"

"Secrets?" Esther chuckled. "I like to think of them as family treasures."

Hannah took another bite, and a smile curled her lips. "Aren't we supposed to share from the storehouse? It's about time your *mem* shared. If I've heard one woman ask her for this recipe, I've heard a hundred."

"*Ja,* well, she finally just shared it with me and urged me not to tell a soul. I just hope this pie will fetch a *gut* price to help the new fire department." Esther crossed her arms over her chest. "I tossed a little last night, worried that mine would be the last one on the auction block. After all, the people in these parts know each other . . . I'm sure they'll bid on each other's pies first."

Hannah swallowed her bite. "I wouldn't worry yourself about that. Folks make friends quick around here. And look at your offering. Look how beautiful it is. There's nothing you should be worried about. And maybe" — Hannah had a twinkle in her eye — "maybe you'll make a new friend."

Esther nodded. How many times had people told her that?

"Come to our picnic . . . maybe you'll make a new friend."

"There is a sewing frolic on Saturday . . . maybe you'll make a new friend."

She liked what her *dat* used to say, "Finding a new friend is easy, but finding a *true* friend is a gift from God."

The truth was, she didn't think either was easy. A friend was about reaching out and connecting with people, but that was hard for her to do when she constantly worried about people's opinion of her — of her family. Especially when she was too shy to approach them in the first place.

She'd grown up in an area known for its thriving Amish community, but during her growing-up years, it had been hard to fit in. Her family had been part of the Amish church, yes, but they were lowest in the pecking order — for many reasons.

While most Amish men farmed, her father had a small gasoline engine shop that struggled financially. Her *mem* worked, too, to help support the family, which meant she often couldn't attend the sewing frolics or help neighbors with their canning. Her father also smoked cigarettes, which the elders in the church looked down upon. No one talked about it, but she could tell by the look in their eyes that others disapproved. If it wasn't for her *mem*'s vanilla crumb pie, her family may not have been accepted at all.

But they were invited to socials and weddings often, and hosts always asked the same thing. "You wouldn't mind bringing a pie or two, would you?" No one had to mention which pie. Esther didn't have to wonder why *Mem* didn't like sharing the recipe. It was her key to staying accepted in their community.

Esther noticed this at a young age. While Violet had flitted through life, not caring too much what people thought, Esther tended to worry. She was more comfortable keeping to herself.

Hannah finished off her piece of pie and then cut a second one. "As much as I'd like to chat, you'd better get over there. The silent auction will be starting in an hour, and you need to make sure your pie gets a prominent spot."

"A prominent spot? It's a pie, that's all."

She rose and moved to the back door, slipping her feet into heavy snow boots. "It's a fund-raiser, *ja*?"

Hannah didn't answer. Instead she took another large bite, closed her eyes, savoring it, and then nodded, opening her eyes again. Her cousin had a look in her eyes that Esther didn't understand — eagerness and . . . was it mischief? She slipped her arms into the heavy jacket. Just what had her cousin gotten her into?

Whatever it was, *Mem* seemed to be in on it. Esther picked up her vanilla crumb pie. Was *Mem* trying to use her pie's appeal to help her reserved daughter make friends? It was just something her mother would do.

CHAPTER TWO

Ammon Schwartz noted that even though the sun was up, the heavy, dark clouds made it gloomy outside. He'd be heading over to the West Kootenai Kraft and Grocery soon for the silent auction. He had to admit he was looking forward to some pie. What kind didn't matter. The fact that he'd be sharing it with a single Amish lady wasn't too bad of an offer either. All of the Amish bachelors had been talking about it — win a pie and a date. What could be better than that? They'd have twenty minutes to bid and an hour to share a meal and conversation.

Ammon hadn't heard of this type of auction before, but the other bachelors quickly filled him in. It seemed a few of the ladies had come up with the idea of a Bachelor Pie auction as a fund-raiser for the local fire department. Although from the way his sister talked, the ladies were far more interested in the bachelors than the money.

Personally, Ammon wasn't interested in finding his true love . . . at least not today. He had enough on his mind caring for his *mem*.

"Maybe I should just head over there now, before the sky spits more snow." He said the words out loud even though his *mem* couldn't hear them. Or if she could, she couldn't respond. *Mem* rested in a hospital bed against the far wall. She lay still on the clean, blue sheets with a quilt smoothed over her. She'd made that quilt and dozens of others over the years. Now her frail hands curled in soft fists, idle. Her skin paper thin, yet the veins just below the surface pumped life through her body. Life and breath without words and laughter. Ammon hated seeing her in such a state.

Mem was still there, tucked away within the shell of her broken-down body. She could open her eyes. She could sit, and with help, she could eat. But she couldn't communicate. She followed him with her eyes as he moved around the cabin. He talked to her about all kinds of things. But Ammon missed hearing her response.

The doctor had told them that she could last about a year in this state. The stroke had made communicating impossible, but it was the cancer growing inside her that would likely take her life. She'd been so vibrant before. The only thing that gave Ammon peace at all was that her broken body wouldn't hold her captive forever. *Mem*'s faith in Jesus, and the good life she'd led, gave them hope of her eternity in heaven.

Heat radiated from the stove in the corner of the cabin. He rose from the wooden chair and moved to the window. How had he ended up here? Actually, he knew *how,* but *why*? Could being in this small community be part of God's plan? He didn't see how.

He'd come to Montana on his way back from Mexico. He'd taken his mother down there for a cancer treatment. Since the Amish counted on each other and not insurance to cover their medical bills, treatments in Mexico were a much cheaper option. His brother-in-law, Will, had talked them into "swinging by" Montana on their way home to Missouri.

They'd gotten here in September — just as the Indian summer was giving way to the cool fall breeze. They'd spent a day up in Glacier Park and were packing up for a day trip to a place called Kootenai Falls — hiring a driver to take them there — when his *mem* collapsed. She'd already been weak from cancer treatments. Maybe they'd tried to do too much, too soon.

It took forever for the hired driver to get her down to Eureka, and when they arrived the doctor said she'd had a stroke. After weeks in the hospital, they'd allowed *Mem* to come home, into the care of her family. Ammon didn't know how it was possible that almost three months had passed since then.

He glanced over his shoulder, as the walls seemed to close in around him. It was a small vacation cabin with a bathroom, a kitchenette, and a queen bed. They'd moved the western-print sofa out to make room for *Mem*'s hospital bed. They'd tried at first to stay at Will and Polly's house, but the active kids had made *Mem* restless.

She was conscious at times but couldn't speak. When the kids were around, running and calling out, *Mem* wore a scowl. Once they moved into the quiet cabin, she relaxed more. Her doctor had told them she needed rest. The question was, for how long? Would it ever be possible for him to take her home? Would she ever be able to talk again? Walk again? If it wasn't for the cancer, they could have started physical therapy. But he knew what *Mem*'s answer would be if she could voice her choice. Her broken body was a reminder that a new one awaited. She'd told him that once before. She'd only done the cancer treatments because so many people had urged her to, but even before the stroke, *Mem* had longed for heaven, for *Dat,* for Jesus.

And so their short stopover had become a temporary home. It didn't seem right that he'd seek out love and then leave. After all, his farm waited back home.

Most Amish men came to the area to hunt, but Ammon had never considered leaving his farm in Missouri. After his *dat*'s passing, he took over running the farm. It was being rented out indefinitely until they knew more about what the future held for *Mem.* Where did that leave him?

His sister Polly was the one who cared for *Mem* during the day, but she couldn't do it full time, not with ten kids under the age of sixteen. But Ammon couldn't stay here forever either. Their brothers were all married, and his single sister, Ilene, was a full-time schoolteacher. It was hard enough for him to think of being here until the time for spring planting. Not having the large farm to tend was like a whale being confined to a creek. On the farm, things slowed down over the winter months, but Ammon always had work to do.

Sitting around the cabin all day had drained him of joy, and so after those first few days, Ammon had made a decision. He'd build friendships and offer assistance where he could. Tonight, that meant heading over to the Kraft and Grocery early to help set things up.

Ammon slid on his jean jacket lined with flannel and pulled a stocking cap over his head. With one more glance over his shoulder, he saw that *Mem* was sleeping well. No need to light the lantern. There was still enough morning light streaming through the window, and no doubt Polly would be over soon to feed *Mem* lunch, even before she fed her own family.

He pulled on the heavy iron door handle and stepped outside. With three steps he crossed the porch. With three more steps he descended the log steps onto the snowy path. The cold air bit at his cheeks, and his work boots squeaked on the snow. Back in Missouri the snow was wet and thick. The air was much drier here in Montana, making the snow light and fluffy. It sparkled like glitter. He kicked at the ground and it fluttered up like a dust cloud.

It wasn't more than fifty yards to Will and Polly's place. Even before he reached their front porch steps, he heard the shrieks of the *kinder.* He paused to distinguish if they were laughing or crying. Thankfully, today it was laughter.

The steps were icy. He held the handrail as he climbed them. Then he entered without knocking. Before the door could be shut behind him, a chorus of voices rang out.

"*Onkel* Ammon. *Onkel* Ammon!" A flurry of arms, legs, and hands flew his direction. Like a passel of puppies, his nieces and nephews tumbled toward him. One set of arms wrapped around one of Ammon's legs and then another. Small hands gripped the front of his jacket and yanked, wanting to be pulled up. Another pair of arms wrapped around his back and shoulders from behind, like a big bear hug. As the second-to-youngest child, Ammon knew what it was like to be surrounded by nieces and nephews. Polly's kids were drawn to him as much as the bear cubs around these parts drew the attention of tourists.

"*Onkel* Ammon, did you come to play checkers? Or marbles?" seven-year-old David asked.

"*Vell*, it sounds like fun, but not today . . ."

"*Vat?*" Little Miriam lifted her face to his, showing off a pouty lip. "But I miss you so much when you're not here."

"Can you tell us a story yet?" Ruthie stood to the side. She was ten years old and the studious one of the group. She had enthusiastically listened at the Thanksgiving table just a few days ago as he told them about their Anabaptist ancestors who left everything in Europe to move to the New World in search of religious freedom.

"I'd love to tell you more stories. My grandmother — your great-grandmother — was a storyteller and I have plenty to share. But . . ." He peeled off one set of arms and then moved to unclench two more sets. "But not today."

Polly approached, wiping her brow with her kitchen apron. Her face was flushed from cooking, but her smile was wide. "*Ja, vell,* your uncle has a date."

"A date!" The oldest of his nieces, Katie, called out from her place at the kitchen table. She lifted her head and turned to him. From the spread of paper and colored pencils before her, Ammon guessed she was busy making Christmas cards to send back to friends in Missouri. Out of all the children, Katie was the only one old enough to remember what life was like back in the Midwest. He noted disappointment on her face at the mention of a date, and he knew why.

Katie wanted Ammon to return to Missouri as much as he did, mostly because her *dat* had agreed that when Ammon returned,

Katie could go with him. With their large extended family, there were enough needs for a *maude* to keep her busy, and the young woman declared that Montana was the worst place ever to experience her *rumspringa* years. With only a dozen youth, there was little to do. Even the craziest adventures often included ice skates and snowballs, neither of which interested Katie.

Ammon peeled off two more sets of hands from his limbs and stepped forward. "It's not a date —"

"*Ja,* what do you call it then? You are going to be sharing pie with a beautiful Amish woman . . . staring across the table into her doe-eyed gaze. You'll feel awkward. You'll work hard at making small talk." Polly winked. "It sounds like a date to me."

Ammon puffed out his chest. "It's a fundraiser for the fire department. And I plan to do my part. I hear they're going to be buying some medical equipment too — to train some of the volunteers."

He didn't have to explain the importance of this equipment. Would things have been different with *Mem* if they'd had an emergency medical technician closer? If they'd gotten *Mem* medical help sooner, would she be up, walking around, and ready for the return trip home instead of lying in bed?

The doctor had said it would not have made much of a difference since the damage had been done in an instant. But Ammon wanted to support the fire department as much as he could. One never knew when someone in his family would need their services next.

"Speaking of the *silent auction,* I'm heading over," he said, emphasizing the words. "I got *Mem* to drink half a glass of water today, and she ate much of the thin oatmeal from breakfast."

"Oh, *gut.*" Polly clasped her hands in front of her. She looked like *Mem* in so many ways. The same stocky frame. The same wide smile. The same small ears that perfectly cupped the side of her head.

Ammon was the only one with their father's lighter coloring. Out of all the children, he alone had light-brown hair and blue eyes. *Mem* said to look at him was like seeing his father thirty years ago.

Ammon didn't consider himself handsome, but his looks had been fine enough to gain the attention of Grace Yoder. They'd even gone to a few summer picnics before his mother's medical needs had taken him to Mexico. Grace said she liked his light eyes and skin tanned from working in the fields in the summer. Not that that mattered now. In his absence Jeb Hooley had stepped in and taken his place. Ammon had heard they were seriously courting, which made him even more insistent that tonight wasn't a date. He would leave West Kootenai, hopefully before spring, without his heart getting wrapped up in a pretty girl. His farm waited. His old life waited. He couldn't plant roots here.

"You'd best get going now." Polly waved her hand, shooing him out. "Katie will feed the little ones, and I'll head over to feed *Mem.* Last night when you were helping Abe Sommer fix that fence, I was reading *Family Life* to her and I was sure she smiled. Maybe I'll do that again tonight."

"*Ja.*" Ammon nodded, but he wasn't getting his hopes up. Something inside told him that *Mem* wasn't going to make much of an improvement. He was sad about that, but not as sad as he would be if he didn't have hope in the life after. His *mem* had lived a *gut* life. He didn't know anyone who'd loved better. The question was, how long would he have to wait before he could get his own life started?

CHAPTER THREE

Esther squeezed through the gathering of people — mostly men — near the front door of the Kraft and Grocery as she made her way to the kitchen. Usually, this time of day was busy enough, but today the jingle of the door's bell rang constantly as more and more bodies piled in. She looked around, sure she'd never seen so many people packed into this small store and restaurant. There were hardly any people in the far corner by the windows. If she didn't have a pie in her hand, she would have rushed over there and found a seat out of everyone's way. But she had a pie to offer, and she guessed the ladies in the kitchen would need help. Maybe *Mem*'s plan was already working.

Esther sucked in a breath and then blew it out slowly, telling herself to be brave. She moved through the sea of men to the kitchen.

As she moved past, she was surprised to see that most of those waiting were the Amish bachelors. She also saw a few families and some tourists, but she had no idea that pie was such a draw to the single men. It made sense, she supposed. All of them were far from home, missing their *mem*'s baking.

She'd also seen the sign-up on the front bulletin board advertising the need for volunteers to man the fire station. More than one Amish man had added his name to the list. Back home in Ohio some of the Amish men she knew volunteered. More than once she found humor in the sight of an Amish man running down the road or across the field toward the fire station in order to catch the fire engine as it headed out.

Once she'd even seen two Amish buggies parked in front of a burning building while the volunteers joined the others in their work. She guessed that was why so many Amish bachelors were here. Supporting this silent auction would make the volunteer fire department a reality, and they'd have a chance to join in the adventurous, risky work.

Entering the kitchen, Esther placed her pie on the counter with the others and then quickly pulled off her jacket. She'd only been in the West Kootenai area for two months, helping her cousin to prepare for her new addition, but she'd also spent a lot of time in the bakery at the store. Once word got out about Esther's baking skills, Annie, the owner of the Kraft and Grocery, had come to Hannah's house for a visit — her long, blond ponytail swishing as she talked. Cousin Hannah and her husband, Matthew, had agreed to share Esther with her until the *boppli* was born. Esther enjoyed the early morning hours when she was able to bake. She loved listening to others share about their lives, and she was always quick to help with the less popular chores, such as shoveling the walk or getting wood for the fire before the customers turned too much of their attention to her.

"I'm so glad that the community agreed to try this new fund-raising event." Jenny Avery, one of the bakers, removed her soiled apron and threw on a new one. The apron was white with red polka dots and a heart-shaped top. The pockets were green with tiny red reindeer. She tied the back and bustled around the kitchen, checking out the pies that all the women had dropped off. Jenny didn't get into the bakery until midmorning, after her daughter, Kenzie, was at school, so Esther hadn't gotten to

481

know her too well. The *Englisher* was a single mom and the five-year-old spent every afternoon at the West Kootenai Kraft and Grocery while her mom worked.

"Does anyone want to help with the place cards while I finish up the dining room?" Jenny asked.

"I will," Esther said. She had spoken without thinking and now she was kicking herself for having offered to do something so visible.

"Of course you will." Jenny cast her a warm smile. Heat rose to Esther's cheeks.

"I can always count on you . . . and I'm pretty sure we're all going to lock the doors if you ever even mention returning to Ohio."

Esther looked to her apron and then to her shoe, hoping they'd turn their attention on someone else next. She didn't want to argue with them about staying. Her plan was to come for the winter and early spring to help Hannah and then to return home. As wonderful as this place was, she felt too exposed here. It was easier to hide among hundreds of other Amish than to be the new person whom everyone noticed. To be noticed was to be evaluated. And in a small community it was harder to find a place to slip away alone.

Esther created small place cards with the

names of each pie: apple, banana cream, blackberry, huckleberry, buttermilk, and vanilla crumb.

"Would you like me to put the baker's name on the card too?" Esther asked.

"No!" The word shot from Jenny's lips. "That would take the fun out of it." She chuckled, shaking her head.

Esther forced a smile, knowing the back of her neck was growing red under Jenny's gaze. She colored too easily.

"Take the fun out of it?" Esther was going to ask what that meant when the scraping of a chair leg across the floor interrupted Esther's words. Jenny's little daughter, Kenzie, was pushing a chair over to a miniature table that one of the bachelors had made a few weeks ago. Jenny's face had glowed when Ammon brought it into the store. Kenzie had danced a little jig upon seeing it because now she had her own table to do her homework and crafts on.

Jenny hummed as she hung up the damp dish towel on the towel rack. The window above the kitchen sink was cracked open slightly and a cool breeze filtered in. A chorus of men's voices filled the air. Even more bachelors were making their way to the store. Butterflies danced in Esther's stomach, but she quickly pushed them away.

As many times as she'd been interested in a young man, she'd never had the interest returned. How could she when her twin sister was one of the most outgoing women in Sugarcreek?

Their *Englisch* neighbor Pearl Stevens often told her the quickest way to a man's heart was through his stomach. She'd believed that was true during her growing-up years, but during her *rumspringa,* it was Violet who was always given buggy rides after the youth singings. And it was Violet who was unpacking her things at her new home with her husband, and it was Esther who was in West Kootenai, Montana, caring for their cousin's *boppli* and making pies in her free time. She was happy for Violet, and making good pies could fill a person's stomach, but they wouldn't guarantee a lasting friendship.

At least her pie would bring a smile to someone's lips today.

The aroma of fresh-baked pies mingled with the scent of baked bread as Ammon entered the restaurant. Voices rose and fell from the kitchen, women busy in conversation. Some bachelors had already huddled up by the door, as if afraid to step any farther into the establishment until the start of the silent auction. They eyed Ammon as he dared to move past them. One of the bachelors shook his head as if giving Ammon a silent warning, but Ammon paid him no heed.

The West Kootenai Kraft and Grocery was part store, part gift shop, and part restaurant. Made of logs, it looked like a building from the Old West. Even the store shelves were crafted from rough lumber.

It wasn't until he heard someone clearing his throat from the other side of the front counter that Ammon realized the front counter clerk, Edgar, sat there eyeing them all. The older *Englisch* man glanced up and offered him a smile.

"You know the silent auction doesn't start for thirty minutes yet," Edgar said.

"Oh, I know, sir." Ammon removed his stocking cap and tried to comb down his hair with his fingers. From the humor in Edgar's eyes, Ammon knew he wasn't doing a good job.

"I just came to see if the women needed help with anything. Taking out trash? Setting up tables . . ." He didn't admit that it was easier doing something — anything — other than sitting next to *Mem* reading or holding a one-sided conversation.

Edgar smiled. "I do suppose those pretty young women might need some help."

Ammon nodded, but he wasn't going to explain that the last thing he'd allow himself to do was catch the eye of a young *maedel*. Montana wasn't a place to farm, and he wasn't interested in changing careers and becoming a logger. Their farm back in Missouri was more than a job — it was a lifestyle. He felt as if he was an extension of God's hand as he helped to grow food that nourished his community. He felt God's pleasure when his body ached from hard work, and dreamed of someday having sons to work by his side, in the simple ways of his ancestors. It was a lifestyle that his heart ached for.

"All right then . . . they might need help moving tables," Edgar said. Ammon was sure Edgar didn't believe him, but he let him pass with a nod. Ammon strolled into the kitchen, and as he did, the women's voices stopped. They eyed him with suspicion and the woman standing closest to him moved her pie around to her back so quickly he worried it would topple from her hands. All of them wore cooking aprons over their Amish dresses. Most aprons were white, and a few were gray, nearly all of them with flour or splatters of ingredients on them. Only the *Englisch* woman's apron was festive.

"Ladies, I'm sorry to startle you. I just

x

486

came early to see if you might need help."

"Help?" The *Englisch* baker stepped forward. She was young, no older than twenty-five. Her dark hair had a streak of hot pink, and it was pulled back into a ponytail. The name tag on her apron shirt read Jenny. "Oh, I'm sure you'd like to help with some of these pies — find out whose pie belongs to which woman." She placed a hand on her hip and jutted it out. "But there is really no need for that type of help —"

"Tha-that wasn't my intention at all!" Ammon sputtered. He didn't come to scope out the women or their pies. Instead of trying to explain, he pointed to the dining room area behind him. "But the tables . . . don't you need help moving tables? Maybe I could push some of the extra chairs out of the dining room to make room for the crowds?"

"You'd do that?" Jenny asked.

"Better than twiddling my thumbs. I get so tired of just sitting . . ." Ammon let his voice trail off. Did any of these women know about his *mem*? She had only been in the area a few days when she fell ill, and she hadn't even made it to church yet. "I just like to help, that's all."

Jenny nodded and showed him what tables to move. The women in the kitchen resumed their conversation.

As Ammon lifted a large, heavy table, he considered what his *mem* would say if she knew about the silent auction and was able to talk. Like Polly, she'd be excited about this so-called date. *Mem* would encourage him not to hide his heart, not to worry about the "what coulds" and "why nots." All his siblings had been married by his age. And even his youngest sister, Ilene, who was working as a schoolteacher back home in Missouri, was being courted. Ammon had no doubt that by Christmas they'd have their upcoming wedding published.

"You can try to have fun tonight," Ammon mumbled to himself under his breath.

Jenny paused and glanced over at him. Her hands were filled with salt and pepper shakers that she was putting into a plastic bin, freeing up the tables from clutter.

Ammon offered a shy smile. "Oh, I was just saying it should be fun tonight. There's nothing better than pie."

"Or beautiful single women," Jenny commented, pausing to brush a strand of dark hair from her cheek. Her brown eyes sparkled with excitement.

"Apple pie is my favorite, but I've never tasted a piece of homemade pie that I didn't like," he said, making it clear where his focus was.

Jenny seemed disappointed that he wasn't begging her to know whose pie was whose. Not that he knew the young women well enough to have a preference. He'd seen them at church, but he'd kept his distance, preferring to spend time with the men, asking if there were any odd jobs around their places that he could help with. He'd made a lot of friends that way.

Sometimes at night he'd sit next to *Mem*'s bed and tell her about all he did. He had hopes that she could still understand him, even if she couldn't respond.

The tables were heavy, solid wood. It took great effort to lift and move them. He set the first table where Jenny indicated and then moved to the next one, telling himself he would get through this night just like he handled everything else in West Kootenai, by being the one others could count on.

Tonight, Ammon would pay attention to who needed help — who needed a bid on her pie — and offer it. Since help — not his heart — was what Ammon had to offer, it didn't matter whose pie he bid on. He just hoped that someone would return home that night with a happy heart.

CHAPTER FOUR

Within a span of ten minutes, the tables had been arranged and the pies were set out — one on each table. Also on each table was a clipboard. The name of the pie was written down and clamped to the clipboard. A starting bid of five dollars was on every sheet. One newly sharpened yellow pencil was situated next to each bid sheet.

Esther watched Jenny pace in the wide doorway between the kitchen, where the women were gathered, and the dining room, where the men were starting to filter in. Esther paused and focused on the bakers — all of them young. All of them single. Why hadn't she realized that before?

Jenny clapped her hands. "The doors are opening . . . Bakers, please stay out of the main dining room until the bidding is over in twenty minutes," she called. "And whatever you do, don't give any indication of which pie is yours."

"No indication?" Esther mumbled under her breath. "I don't understand . . ."

Eve Peachy, the redheaded woman who stood next to Esther, leaned forward. "Didn't you know that it's a silent bidding for a pie and a date?" Eve's hair had been pulled back under her *kapp,* but a few red curls had escaped and framed her face. Her cheeks were bright. Her eyes sparkled. Eve sucked in a breath as the men continued to fill the dining room. "Whoever puts the highest bid down in the next twenty minutes wins the pie and the right to share it with the baker."

"Share it? When?"

"Today . . . Didn't you know what this was about?"

Esther shook her head. She looked down at her dress and the flour and splatters of egg on her cooking apron. She couldn't believe she'd forgotten to change before heading out. Then again, she'd assumed she would just be in the kitchen, watching from a safe distance. Or tucked away in some corner, like she always was.

She'd never been a neat cook. She must have gotten that from her mother. Of course, her father and brothers never complained, and when it came to church socials, folks had come to know what her mother's serving dishes looked like and hers were the first cleaned out.

The men formed a line as they strode in, their usual playfulness gone. They walked between the tables of pies, examining each one.

The women around her didn't speak, but she sensed their nervous excitement.

"I hope Amos spots my dish," Eve said, leaning close. "I used the blue pie dish that my *mem* always uses at church gatherings . . . Is it too much to hope he'll remember?"

Eve watched as one of the bachelors spotted her blue dish. He had a stocky build and dark hair that nearly covered his ears. He hurried over to the paper next to the blue dish, wrote down a bid, and then turned and moved to the coffee that had been set up on a far table.

Esther glanced over at Eve. Joy radiated from her face. The bachelor was indeed Amos.

Esther cleared her throat and forced a smile. "He must have placed a pretty good bid. Do you see how the other bachelors are walking right by and not even attempting to top it?"

Eve placed her hands over her mouth, as if she'd just been given a gift.

"Oh, I hope that's the case. We've been friends for so long . . . over a year . . . but I didn't dare hope . . ." She let her words trail off, and Esther noticed Eve's cheeks brightening to a pretty shade of pink. Yet as Esther watched, it was Eve's sister, Hope, that Amos kept glancing at.

Amos must have known that the pie had come from the Peachys' kitchen. But he'd guessed the wrong sister.

The emotions came stronger than Esther expected. Her heart ached for Eve. Her eyes burned as if someone had blown cinnamon into them. Beside her, Eve smiled, staring at the bid sheet, eager to note her worth. When would she find out that Amos had eyes for the other Peachy daughter? Esther's breaths escaped her as if someone had lassoed a rope around her chest and cinched tight. She, too, had been the sister who had hoped and dreamed for so many years, only to be disappointed.

Esther watched Amos closely. He stared at Hope, who was standing just five feet away. She was talking about her quilting project with a friend and had no idea about the unspoken drama that was playing out around them.

Some people were easy to love, she supposed. And some people longed for it and still came up wanting — like her. Like Eve.

Esther placed a soft hand on Eve's arm. "Would you like some coffee? I'll get you some."

"Tea — just hot water and the tea bag if they have it . . ." A smile filled Eve's face. "Oh, and as you're passing by the table with my pie on it, can you check the bid sheet? I'm not sure if I can stand not knowing for another minute."

"I would," Esther said, sighing, "but don't you think I'd be giving something away?"

"True, if you give too much attention to my bid sheet, then Amos might get confused and think it's yours . . ."

"*Ja,* of course." Esther walked over to the table that held the hot drinks. She didn't even have to look at her bid sheet.

Even as she chatted with Eve, she'd watched from the corner of her eye, and not one person had placed a bid.

Should she just leave now? She opened a hot cocoa packet and dumped it into a Styrofoam cup, adding hot water. Then she stirred it slowly with a plastic spoon. Remembering Eve's request, she filled another cup with hot water and added a single tea bag, letting the paper tag dangle from the side of the cup. Voices chattered around her. Even harder than being alone was being in a room full of people and feeling alone.

Esther picked up the two cups and then turned just in time to see a man approaching her table. It was Ammon, the same man who'd come early to set up the tables. The one who'd also made the little table for Kenzie.

She'd heard many people talking about him, and he'd greeted Esther once or twice. He'd arrived in West Kootenai the same week as her, but instead of hiding away, as she had done, Ammon had volunteered to help in the community.

It seemed that every time someone came into the store, their voice would carry to the bakery section, and she'd hear another story about Ammon helping to chop and stack wood for a widow, or helping to patch a hole in the roof of the small Amish schoolhouse, or helping to pull an automobile out of a ditch with his brother-in-law's team of horses.

Esther's stomach quivered with anxiety as Ammon stood there, gazing at her sheet. She pulled her lower lip into her mouth and bit down gently. Should she approach Ammon to warn him that it was her pie? He no doubt wanted to spend the evening with a local woman. It was clear that even though he wasn't from West Kootenai, he cared about the area — and the people. He was going to be so disappointed when he realized that the baker of the pie wasn't from around these parts.

Movement toward the kitchen caught her attention. Jenny was wagging a finger at her. Knowing Jenny would be thoroughly displeased if Esther gave herself away, Esther walked right back to Eve with the two cups in hand. Her footsteps quickened as she passed Ammon. Her gut tightened down, and it hurt so much that all she could think about was sitting down, being still. But out of all the people who could have bid on her sheet, deep down she was thankful that it was him. Ammon was a kind man. And friendly, she knew that to be true.

Besides, it wasn't a date. Just pie and conversation.

CHAPTER FIVE

Ammon had scanned all the tables and there was only one that didn't have an opening bid. From the way men hovered around certain tables, he guessed that they knew better than he whose pie was whose. Yet someone in this room must be feeling bad that her pie wasn't bid on. Ammon approached the table, gazing down at the pie, and then moved his attention to the bid sheet. He thought about the money that Abe Sommer just gave him for working on their guest cabin. He didn't need the money, not really. He picked up the pencil and, with a smile, placed a very nice bid.

The room buzzed with excitement as the timer, set on the table nearest to the kitchen, ticked down.

"Two minutes left," he heard someone next to him say.

An older woman, who was mingling through the crowd, laughed as she walked from sheet to sheet. "Why, I'm certain this just might be the best fund-raiser for the fire department yet! Some of these pies are going for as much as a quilt at the summer auction." She elbowed Amos who was standing next to her. "That only means one thing . . . some of these bachelors came to the area for a buck and bragging rights in hunting, but they'll be taking home much more."

Ammon chuckled along with the rest, but while other guys may have had that on their minds, that was not his intention.

The timer buzzed, and Jenny jumped to her feet and waved her hands to get everyone's attention. Her daughter, Kenzie, stood by her side.

"Okay, men, if I call your name, you won the highest bid. Go and sit on one side of the table, and the baker will join you."

Then, table by table, Jenny went down the line, picking up the papers and looking at them. "Amos, William, Jebediah, Jonathan . . ."

When Jenny got to the table with the pie that Ammon had bid on, Jenny's eyes widened. "Oh, Ammon . . . You're always so helpful around the community. Just know that from what I hear, this pie is worth every penny."

"I'm sure it is." He approached the table and sat. It was only after all the men were seated that the women from the kitchen stepped forward.

For a packed restaurant, there was silence as one by one the young women moved to the tables and sat. His heart pounded as he sat motionless. His hands were spread open on the table and both excitement and worry pushed around for space in his heart. What if the young woman took his high bid the wrong way?

He watched as one Amish woman looked as if she was nearing his table and then walked past. Another woman followed in her footsteps, then quickly sat in the chair across from him. Ammon recognized her as one of the bakers who was often here in the early morning. Her head was bowed low.

She looked as shy and skittish as a young colt back on his farm. Ammon drummed his fingers on the table, afraid that if he said the wrong thing she'd dart away. "Hello. This pie looks wonderful," he managed to say.

She lifted a face that was brilliant scarlet and the first thing he noticed was her blue eyes. There was nothing especially beautiful about her. Her nose and mouth were a bit large, but he imagined she looked pretty when she smiled. Conversations started up around them. Most people from this area knew each other. And Ammon guessed they were the only ones who were complete strangers.

As he watched her face, her eyes darted to the bid sheet. They widened slightly and then narrowed again. She turned her attention to the knife, two plates, and two forks sitting beside it.

"I hope you like the pie," she said.

He nodded and grinned. "I haven't met a pie I didn't like. Would you like me to cut two slices?"

"Oh, I can do it," she said in a rush.

"I'm thinking I should let you . . ." Ammon paused. "But can you cut me an especially large piece?"

She looked at him again, and the smallest smile lifted the corners of her lips. She studied him for one long moment, then whispered, "I appreciate this . . . I mean, being new here, I thank you kindly."

"I'm new here too. I know most of the other bachelors have been here since spring, but I've only been here three months yet."

She cut him a large piece, placing it on a plate, and then slid it over to him.

Before taking a bite, he picked up the small note card that said Vanilla Crumb Pie and turned it over in his hand. "I'm not sure I've had this kind before."

"It's my favorite." Her shoulders relaxed as she talked. "I always ask for it for my birthday."

"I'm sure it's wonderful then."

Without hesitating Ammon picked up a fork and took a bite. The subtle sweetness melted in his mouth. The crunchiness of the crumb topping was a nice surprise. His eyes widened and he glanced up at Esther. On her face was a smile she couldn't hide.

"This is wonderful. I've never tasted anything like it!" He took another bite, and his eyes closed slowly as he concentrated on the taste.

At the table next to him, his friend Amos was enjoying a piece of buttermilk pie. Amos was chatting with one of the red-headed sisters who'd baked it. He never could remember which was which. Ammon leaned over and placed a hand on Amos's arm. Amos jumped slightly but seemed almost relieved for the interruption.

"I know you have a pie of your own, but you have to taste this," Ammon said.

"I won't say no to a bite of great pie," Amos said. Without a moment's hesitation he took his fork and scooped a big chunk out of Esther's pie. He put the bite into his mouth, and his eyes widened. "That has to be some of the best pie I've ever tasted!" Then, as if remembering who sat across from him, Amos turned his attention back to the Peachy sister and her pie.

"And you, my dear, should also win a ribbon for the best pie ever," Amos said, squirming slightly. "My stomach is going to be happy today!" He took another bite of his own pie and smiled broadly at his date. Some of the others in the room must have seen Ammon's and Amos's reactions, because a few more bachelors approached, asking if they could have a taste. It went fast — and soon it was gone.

It wasn't until Ammon looked at the empty pie plate that he had a sinking feeling. He hadn't even saved a bite for his *mem*. And the baker never did get a piece for herself.

He also hadn't talked much with the young woman. Instead he'd been focused on sharing the pie. Other couples around him seemed deep in conversation, but the woman across from him still looked as if she was sitting on tacks.

Ammon opened his mouth, his mind racing for the right words. He looked into the woman's eyes, and he expected to see her pleasure over the fact that her pie was so popular. Instead he saw a look of defeat. It was as if she'd given it her all and still felt as if she'd fallen short. How could she feel that way after her pie was obviously the most popular?

He forced a smile. "I'm so sorry. I just realized that you didn't even get a piece."

"Oh, it's all right." Her words came out with a soft breath. "It's nothing really to worry about. That pie is my *mem*'s specialty." She wrapped the string from her *kapp* around her finger. "I've had it more times than I can count. And I made two pies this morning — one for here and one for my cousin." She offered a slight smile. "Of course, it's Hannah's favorite pie, too, so I'm not sure if there will be any left when I get back."

Her laughter sounded like the soft tweeting of a dozen winter finches and it made Ammon grin.

The woman went on to tell him about coming to Montana, about being a *maude,* and a little about her family back in Ohio. The woman was talkative enough, but something was missing. She talked to him as if that's what she was supposed to do, as if she was going through the motions instead of trying to connect.

"You make too much of things and always

try to read between the lines," his sister Polly had often chided him, but in this case he had a feeling he was right. Maybe God had given him the gift of being perceptive. Still, he had to wonder, why was Esther so nervous? What was she afraid of?

"So, tell me about *your* family," she said after several minutes. She turned the fork over in her hand, and he wondered if she was hungry. He offered to buy her lunch, but she insisted she couldn't eat a thing. From the slight trembling of her voice, he was sure that was true.

Ammon told her about the farm and their trip to Mexico. For some reason he didn't tell her about *Mem*'s current condition or the stroke. And as they sat face-to-face, Ammon realized he was doing the very thing he'd just privately accused her of — denying her access to the life issues that mattered most to him.

Around them some of the couples were starting to leave, and before he could figure out what else to say, the woman stood. "I suppose I should get back. Baby Mark had a restless night last night. I need to be around to walk the boards if he's still fussy for his nap."

"Ja." Ammon stood too. "I understand."

She turned to leave and Ammon reached

out, gently brushing his fingertips on her arm. "I'm so sorry. I feel foolish I didn't ask . . . Can you tell me your name?"

The woman turned back and nodded. "Esther. Esther Glick."

"That's a lovely name, Esther. I'll make sure and use it next time we do this."

"Next time?" She cocked her head and studied him. Her face softened, appeared less guarded. And something else was there. Was it a glimmer of hope?

Seeing that caused a strange feeling to come over him. His simple words had meant so much to her, and an overwhelming desire to protect her surged through Ammon.

And then, without thinking too much about it, he said, "*Ja,* Esther, I'd love to have pie with you again . . . and maybe lunch. Would you be interested? I promise I'll pay more attention to you next time, instead of sharing what I have with everyone within arm's reach."

She waited so long to answer that he was sure she would say no. And then she nodded once. "*Ja,* I think I'd like that."

And as she walked away, a surprising excitement soared in Ammon's heart.

Hannah and Matthew were sitting at the

table eating sandwiches when Esther entered. Both sets of eyes were on her as she took off her coat and hung it. Baby Mark was asleep in his kitchen cradle. Hannah smiled, hearing his gentle snore.

"Did you have a good time, Estie?" her cousin asked. "Who won the bid? What is his name? Do we know him?"

Esther turned and lifted an eyebrow. "So why didn't you tell me the auction included a *date*?" She placed a hand on her hip.

Hannah tried to hide a smile. "*Vell,* your *mem* said not to . . ."

"My *mem!*" Esther pointed a finger into the air. "I knew she had something to do with it."

"*Ja!*" Matthew jutted out his chin, stepping in for his wife. "She left a phone message with the neighbor and asked me to relay a message. She told me to tell Hannah she was sending the recipe. Your *mem* thought you needed a friend around here."

"A friend?" Esther crossed her arms over her chest. "It seems a bachelor auction is a little bit different yet than trying to make a friend."

"Oh, Estie." Hannah waved a hand in the air. "It was a kind gesture, that's all. Your *mem* cares about you. She thinks you spend too much time alone. Besides, now you have the recipe for the pie. That's worth some-thing, *ja?*"

"I'm not alone. I care for baby Mark. I'm with you . . ." Esther let her voice trail off. By "friend," *Mem* meant people outside their family.

Hannah shook her head. This wasn't go-ing to be a fight Esther would win, but she couldn't let it drop that easily. She'd write to *Mem.* She'd tell her that while her gesture had been kind, Esther could make friends on her own . . . and she knew how to do it without pie.

Esther sat in a wooden chair and removed her boots. Her mind replayed the evening, and when she looked up her cousin's eyes were on her.

"Vell?" Hannah asked.

"Ammon. Ammon Schwartz."

Esther looked away, hoping the heat rising to her cheeks didn't betray her. But not fast enough. Hannah's smile widened as she noted Esther's face turning two shades of red.

It wasn't so bad, though, she had to admit. *I liked getting to know him.*

But she'd never admit that, of course. It was easier to be mad than to be hopeful.

And yes, Hannah was right, the bonus was she also now had the recipe for the pie.

CHAPTER SIX

In the week after sitting across the table from Esther Glick, Ammon knew that he was in trouble. Something about Esther made Ammon want to spend more time with her — to give her attention and listen to her. But the more he thought about that, reality sank in. He couldn't allow his heart to get wrapped up in someone. He needed to get back to Missouri. He had a farm to tend.

Yet how could he leave? *Mem* wasn't doing any better, and Polly couldn't manage everything alone. More than once Ammon had considered asking Polly if he could go back home, but guilt plagued him and he never got up the nerve. He couldn't leave his sister with so much responsibility. Leaving West Kootenai would be leaving Esther too. He wanted to see her, but he didn't. He longed for someone to share his heart with, but at the same time he was scared.

Unwilling to let his emotions override common sense, Ammon filled his time with activities. He kept himself away from places he might see Esther.

More than that, the work was a privilege. Unlike working on the farm, Ammon could venture out each morning without a clue of how he'd spend his day and then meet up with someone to help out.

He'd cut wood for the widow Millie Arnold. He'd patched a porch floor good enough to last through winter for that single mom, Jenny. He took care of David Carash's horses when Dave and his family journeyed to Chicago to visit relatives for an early Christmas. Each day he'd get so busy with work that he was able to push thoughts of Esther into the back of his mind, until one morning when he came upon her at the Kraft and Grocery.

They'd chatted about simple things, but he had made her laugh, and seeing that had brightened his whole day. And then he found himself forgetting all his own warnings. After delivering a load of firewood to Edgar's house, he passed right by the home where Esther was staying.

Before he had a chance to talk himself out of it, Ammon tied up his horses on the hitching post and then hurried up the steps.

Esther answered with a baby swaddled in her arms. His heart leapt at the sight of it.

"I'm sorry to bother you. I'm sure you are busy."

"I was just getting ready to give the baby a bath. The water is warm, but if you want to come in —"

"No, I won't keep you." He took a step back. "I was just wondering if you'd like to go on a sleigh ride with me. Abe Sommer said I could use his sleigh anytime."

"*Ja!*" The word spouted from her lips and then she looked away, as if embarrassed by her eager response. "I would like that very much."

Esther wished she knew what to do with her hands as she sat in the high-backed log chair in Hannah's kitchen. The chair gave her a view of the road leading up to Matthew and Hannah's house. A view of Ammon coming to pick her up for a sleigh ride.

She folded her arms and then unfolded them. She clasped her hands and then wiped her sweaty palms on her skirt. She knew *Mem* would have disapproved of her fidgeting, but how could a gal not be unnerved by a man like Ammon? He was so kind and helpful. But as much as the helpfulness drew her, it also bothered her.

He'd only been here months, not years, but with the friendships he'd built and the projects he was involved in, it seemed he'd lived here his whole life. Did that mean he wanted to stay? To build a life here? As nice as this place was, she never imagined herself living in such a small Amish community. She'd also said her piece to God more than once in the hours leading up to this date — this real date.

Oh, sure. Now there is someone who wants to spend time with me but it looks like he wants to plant roots here.

A sleigh ride had seemed ridiculously romantic. Violet never had been on a sleigh ride, and Esther could picture *Mem*'s curious smile when she heard the news. *Mem* just might attribute this date to the pie. But there was no pie in Esther's hands now, and that's what had kept her from getting much sleep last night.

In the dark, quiet stillness of her bedroom, Esther had enjoyed thinking about Ammon. Only the hoot of an occasional owl had interrupted her pondering, but every time she considered getting to know him beyond sharing a piece of pie, or going on a sleigh ride, her chest would clench so tight she'd think she was having a heart attack. To get to know someone well would mean she'd have to open up.

Esther didn't allow those thoughts to go too far before she pushed them out of her mind. Who was she to think that Ammon would *really* be interested in her?

Just last Sunday at church in the Sommers' home, the Amish preacher had spoken about allowing one's heart to become still with the quiet winter season. Just like the earth needed time to rest under a layer of snow, he said that each of their hearts needed those seasons too.

"A time of new life, of growth, and of harvest come in their due season," he'd said. Yet even though the world outside was shrouded in cold, in snow, a stirring of new life — of hope — dared to poke out of her heart at Ammon's friendship. She'd been quiet and still for most of her life. And now, Esther had a sense within that it was time to grow. To bloom.

The sound of a sleigh approaching caused her to jump, and Esther prayed that she would be able to have a conversation and not make a fool of herself.

The sound of horse hooves crunching on the snow paused. Ammon must be parking the sleigh. Esther refused to look out the window as she listened to the horses' whinnies and a man's voice saying he'd be right back. There was a knock on the door, and Esther hurried to it. She opened it and waved Ammon inside. She swallowed down her emotion. Even worse than not feeling that attraction was to allow hope in, only to have it stripped away.

"Warm yourself by the fire before we head out."

He nodded once. "Thank you, I will."

Ammon's cheeks and nose were bright red from the cold, but it made him even more rugged looking. He was tall, with light hair and blue eyes. He was handsome . . . so much so that her breath caught in her throat and her hands grew clammier.

Esther reached for her coat and then saw she was still wearing her dirty kitchen apron . . . some impression she was making.

She untied the back and then pulled it over her head. "I'm so used to wearing this old thing, I forget to take it off."

"I like the look of an apron. You should have left it on."

Ammon watched her every move as she dumped the apron into the small wicker basket by the back door where she'd tossed the dirty kitchen towels earlier.

"That's kind of you to say." Esther smoothed her blouse and cape and then reached for her thick wool coat. "But my mother would scold me for certain if she knew that's how I'd met you at the door. I'm thankful that Matthew and Hannah are at his parents' house today so word won't get back."

"I'm not just saying that — I mean it." Ammon stepped forward and took the coat from her hands, holding it up so that she could slide her arms into it. She buttoned up, put on her gloves, and then turned to him.

"My favorite people spent most of their days in their kitchen aprons: my grandmother, my *aentis* and *mem* . . ." His voice hiccuped as he said that. "An apron is a sign of serving others. It's a symbol of feeding the hungry. Even Jesus tied an apron around His waist and lowered Himself as He cared for His disciples, kneeling before them to wash their feet."

Esther couldn't help but be puzzled by this man. He looked similar to so many other Amish bachelors, but there was a tenderness to his words that surprised her. Without another word Ammon opened the front door and led her out.

"Have you ever been on a sleigh ride before?" He took her hand and helped her up into the sleigh.

"No, I can't say that I have. I'm sure that it's common around here, but not where I'm from — Sugarcreek."

"Sugarcreek." His lips pursed. "That's a nice area. Nice farms there."

"*Ja.* We lived in town, but every time we'd head into the country for church or a sewing frolic, I'd look at the farms and try to pick which one I'd want to live on someday."

He climbed in beside her and took up the reins. "It sounds like you have a great imagination."

"It's silly, I know." She waved a gloved hand in the air.

"It's not silly. It's a *gut* dream, Esther. In fact . . ."

The rumble of a large diesel pickup truck interrupted his words. It made its way down the driveway and parked beside the house. A short, older woman hopped down from the driver's side and Esther recognized Millie from the store.

"Esther, Ammon, I'm sorry to interrupt your day out, but I see that Jenny's idea for the fund-raiser is reaping many rewards!" Laughter spilled out with her words. "But that's not what I've come to talk about." Millie jingled her keys in her hands. "I'm supposed to bring a pie to our prayer group's Christmas gathering, and I'm the worst baker ever. I was wondering, Esther, if you'd be willing to bake a few pies for me? I didn't get a taste of that vanilla crumb pie, but I heard it was amazing."

Esther looked to Ammon, who was nodding vigorously, and then back to Millie.

"I'd be happy to pay you," Millie chirped.

"Oh, I don't need any money," Esther rushed to say. "All my needs are provided for with my work as a *maude,* and I really do enjoy baking."

"Well, dear, I can't have you do it for free. What if you donated the money to the volunteer fire department? I'm sure they won't mind."

Esther clasped her gloved hands together. "Oh yes, that's a wonderful idea!" Esther nearly bounced in the buggy seat. "I'll have to ask Hannah if I can use her kitchen, but I'm sure she won't mind."

"Oh, that's another thing." Millie pointed her finger into the air. "I asked Annie if you could bake them over at the Kraft and Grocery. It would be easier for you, I'm sure, and she didn't mind at all."

Esther chuckled, and foggy breath escaped. "That's kind of you, Millie, but I don't think I need to borrow the large kitchen of the Kraft and Grocery for a few pies."

A sheepish look crossed Millie's face, and she shuffled from side to side, leaving boot prints in the snow. "Yes, well, maybe I should have mentioned that first. When I was at the store, talking to Annie, she said that she'd like a few pies, too, for Christmas."

"*Ja,* I'm sure that will be fine."

"But then, well, a few customers overheard us. Word had already gotten around about your baking. So others asked if you'd be interested in baking Christmas pies for them as well."

"Others?" Esther's eyebrows shot up, and she no longer felt cold. Instead, heat radiated through her. "How many others are we talking about, Millie?"

Millie reached her hand into her parka and pulled out a slip of paper, handing it up to Esther in the sleigh. Esther unfolded it. Her eyes widened as she saw that there were no fewer than twenty names on the list.

Laughter spurted from Ammon's lips. She gave him a quick elbow to the ribs, which only made him laugh again.

"All of these folks want a pie for Christmas?" Esther didn't know whether to be happy or horrified.

Millie rubbed her chin and paused, as if

afraid to say the next words. "Actually . . ." She drew her words out. "Actually, some of them want two."

The horses pranced, getting impatient, and Esther's stomach sank as she tried to consider how many pies she'd need to make each day to reach her goal by Christmas. She couldn't start until a few days before then. She needed to make sure they were fresh for Christmas Day.

"Well, I'm not sure —" That was a lot of work, and she still had to help with Mark. He was a *gut boppli,* but it wouldn't be fair to Hannah. Unless . . . unless she was able to bake during his morning nap.

"Millie, just how much money would that bring in for the fire department?" Ammon's words interrupted her thoughts.

Millie stepped closer, as if pleased that he seemed to be on her side. "Well, it's just some quick calculations in my head, but after the cost of supplies, I suppose it would be enough to buy a dozen of those fire emergency blankets they've been looking at."

Neither spoke, waiting for Esther's response.

Laughter slipped from Esther's lips, knowing that she'd been cornered, but feeling happy about the prospect of her donation.

"*Ja,* well, how can I say no?"

For the first time in her life she felt like she didn't have to hide. She wasn't comparing herself with her sister, and she'd carried on a conversation with two new friends without worrying about what to say next. And more than that, they trusted her with their Christmas desserts, and that thought settled happily in her soul.

CHAPTER SEVEN

The horses danced over the snow as they pulled the sleigh along, and the swish of their tails lulled her. Esther tried to concentrate on the sounds of the runners sliding and the crunch — almost a squeak — of the horses' hooves on the snow, which sparkled like glitter, but her mind was buzzing with thoughts about the pies she'd just agreed to bake. And also buzzing with thoughts of Ammon, who sat nestled beside her.

As Millie had driven off, Ammon had taken a thick fleece blanket and laid it over both of their legs, tucking it in. The heat radiating from his legs warmed hers, and as a cold wind blew, she resisted the urge to snuggle closer.

With Ammon by her side, the world seemed different than it had just days ago. It seemed warmer, more inviting. A strong sense of community lightened her heart.

She felt as if she belonged and had value. Maybe Esther would have realized sooner that she had value if she hadn't spent so much time comparing herself to Violet. She could talk without having to be chatty. She could make a few good friends without having to be a friend to everyone in the community.

Her mother said that in time, Violet's looks would fade, while Esther's skills in the kitchen would never stop being appreciated. But maybe the greatest asset either of them had was just being a friend.

"I remember when we first moved to Montana," Ammon said. "I was certain I'd never seen a bigger sky. Nor a darker one at night. The stars look brighter here, don't you think? Like sparkling pins on a pincushion made of black velvet."

"Ja." Esther tilted her head up, but that single act caused one tear to slip from the corner of her eye. The tears came as she considered how much of her life she'd spent hiding. And also because she knew that it wouldn't be easy to change overnight. She quickly wiped her cheeks, but not before Ammon noticed.

"Esther, is anything wrong?"

"Not really —" Her words caught in her throat like a giant snowball, and she attempted to swallow them down. "I just worry that I'm not going to be able to fill all the orders, and I'll let so many people down . . . especially on Christmas."

"If you need any help, let me know. I'm not much of a baker, but I can carry bags of flour and such. And I could sit in the kitchen and chat with you as your pies baked."

She looked at him. "You-you'd do that?"

"Of course I would. I'd love to . . ." Ammon cleared his throat. "I'd like to get to know you better."

She let those worlds filter down on her soul like fresh-falling snow. Ammon laughed. "And I could hope that one of those pies wouldn't set right or the crust would get too brown, and then I'd have to help destroy the evidence — one bite at a time."

She pretended to laugh along, but again, worry filled her mind.

"Yes, well, I'm sure you'd like more pie. You sort of gave all yours away." Esther blew out a breath and then told herself to smile. "To be truthful, I don't remember much of that day either. I was so flustered. I'm not sure how I didn't get the message, but when I showed up, I had no idea that a *date* was included in the bidding." Then she glanced up at him. "I'm just so thankful that it was you." His eyes fixed on hers for a moment, and she looked away, feigning anger. "I'm still a little mad at Jenny over that one."

A soft laugh slipped from Ammon's lips. "Leave it to Jenny to come up with that. Ever since she returned to West Kootenai, she's taken it upon herself to play match-maker, or that's what others around the area have told me. I suppose with seeing all the Amish bachelors and all the single Amish young women, she can't help herself."

"It seems strange, though, that an *Englisch* woman would be so concerned about Amish romance." An ache grew in the pit of Esther's stomach, and she remembered how things had been back home. There was a greater distance between the *Englisch* and the Amish. Or at least that's what she'd observed.

"From what I've gathered, there's nothing typical in West Kootenai. Jenny worked at the Kraft and Grocery for a few years, and she became friends with many of the Amish cooks and bakers. She was gone for a year or so — taking care of her mom, who was ill. But I hear that her mom's doing better so Jenny came back."

"That's *gut* about her *mem,*" Esther said, unsure why Ammon knew so much about the *Englisch* baker. To her, all this match-making just seemed as if the woman was putting her nose where it didn't belong.

"Of course, I think it has more to do with a longing than just being nosy," Ammon commented, as if reading Esther's thoughts. "Jenny's a single mom. Since she's not finding love, maybe she's content in helping others find it." He cleared his throat, and he looked over at Esther. The word "love" hung in the air between them.

The horses plodded along and they chatted about their families back home and Christmas traditions. Ammon seemed to take an especially long route, and it took over an hour to get back to Matthew and Hannah's place. By the time Esther climbed down from the sleigh, her cheeks and nose were practically numb.

"Esther, before you go, I have a question for you."

"*Ja,* okay." She blew warm breath into her cupped, gloved hands.

"First of all, do you have to work tonight?"

"Work, as in caring for baby Mark?" Esther shook her head. "No, my cousin's family will be gone all day and evening."

"Oh, good. In that case, I was wondering if you'd join me for a family dinner at my sister's place. My nieces and nephews happened to overhear my plans for today and they insisted on meeting you."

"Really?" Esther placed a hand over her heart. "I'm honored. That sounds like fun."

"Well, just so you know, they are very active . . . and there's a lot of them. If you get overwhelmed, I'll whisk you away."

Esther nodded, but she loved children. They were easy to talk to.

"Good. I'll return the sleigh and be back in an hour or so. It's just a short walk to my sister's house."

Esther placed her hand on the doorknob and turned, but then she remembered something. "And your mother? Will I get to meet her too?"

Ammon stopped in his tracks. He turned slowly and lifted his gaze to meet hers. "Excuse me?"

"Well, I thought I'd heard someone say that you came here with your mother. They thought she was still in town. Can I meet her?"

The color drained from Ammon's face, and a boulder settled in the pit of Esther's gut. She didn't know what she'd said wrong. Ammon's face was as white as the snowy ground beneath his feet. Her heartbeat quickened.

"I-I'm not sure. Perhaps. Let me talk to

my sister about it, and we'll see what we can do." With that, Ammon turned and strode to the sleigh.

Esther walked into the house, quickly shutting the door behind her, hoping she hadn't messed up her words too badly. She didn't understand why he had even asked her to go on a ride with him. She surely didn't know why he'd invited her to meet his family. Those were all signs that he thought fondly of her. Signs of commitment. And if that was the case, then why was he so clearly hiding something from her?

Oh Lord, what is happening between Ammon and me? Please help me understand. Help me to know what to do, what to say.

Chapter Eight

Ammon led Esther down the snowy street to his sister's house. He glanced down at her gloved hand. Would it be too bold to reach out and take it? He hadn't meant to have feelings for her. He hadn't even known whose pie it was when he placed that bid, but he knew that God knew. Was it possible that God had brought them together?

Ammon had spent much of the night trying to figure out what drew him to Esther, and he decided it was her *demut*. Humility was given a high value among the Amish, but sometimes it was just a show. Esther, on the other hand, seemed truly surprised when someone acknowledged or appreciated her. She seemed tongue-tied and unsure of what to say.

He was still trying to decide whether or not to hold her hand when Esther's feet went out from under her on an especially icy spot. Ammon reached out and grabbed her, holding her up by her shoulders.

"Whoa!" She reached out and clung to his arms, pausing to regain her footing. "Thank you."

"You're welcome — it is slippery out here. You can hold on to my arm if you'd like."

She stepped closer and tucked her arm under his, holding tight. "*Ja, danki.* I appreciate that." The night was still and the snow glowed in the fading moonlight. Yet, as they neared the home, they heard voices . . . of children.

He paused at the door and glanced over at Esther. Both surprise and humor shone in her eyes at the commotion. "Are you ready for this?"

"Ready as I'll ever be!"

He opened the door and stepped in. Within seconds, a passel of children gathered around them. Ammon was surprised that the younger children hardly paid any attention to Esther. Instead, they grabbed his arm and dragged him to their *mem*'s rocking chair that was set in front of the fire.

"Tell us a story! Tell us a story!" they called out.

A woman hurried from the kitchen, wiping her hands on her apron. "I'm sorry that they didn't even say hello." She nodded to

Esther. "I'm Polly." She swooped her hand in an arch. "Welcome to our home and our chaotic life."

Esther laughed. "Your children are beautiful . . . and . . ." She tried to find the right word as she watched Ammon sit and a half dozen children clamor for space on his lap.

"And active, I know." Polly blew out a heavy breath and then tucked her hair up in her *kapp.* She motioned to the kitchen and Esther followed. Polly moved to a large pot of stew that was simmering on the stove and stirred it.

"Do you want a big family someday, Esther?" She placed the spoon on a spoon rest and turned.

Esther pulled back slightly at the direct question. How serious did Polly think her relationship with Ammon was?

"*Ja,* of course. I love children. I've been a *maude* for many years. I love caring for *bopplis* and . . ." Esther didn't know what else to say. Why did she suddenly feel as if she were being interviewed?

The serious expression on Polly's face softened. "Yes, me too." She approached and leaned against the counter. "What Amish mother doesn't want a big family? But it's different — harder — than I ever expected. My children are active. They take after their father, I think. Matthew loves to hike and swim. He loves playing baseball in the summer with the young bachelors, and I'm afraid that most of my children have inherited that energy."

Polly moved to the wooden cutting board. She removed a red-and-white-checkered dishcloth from the top of a freshly baked loaf of bread and began to slice it.

"They are active." Esther chuckled as she watched two of the children give up on their uncle and begin to chase each other around the living room.

"I've never been able to keep them quiet or still in church. Well, not as quiet and still as they should be. They get bored. They squirm around. Sometimes they talk." Polly shook her head, and then she broke off a small piece of bread and put it into her mouth. "I've heard the other moms talk . . ."

"So, is it hard?" Esther asked.

"Raising kids? Yes, it's hard."

"No, I don't mean that." Esther paused and looked down at her hands. "Do you ever worry what others think of you?"

Polly tapped her fingertip on the counter. "Sometimes. It has helped moving to West Kootenai. Folks are more relaxed here. I don't feel as if I have such big expectations to live up to. Also, I'm older and hopefully wiser. When I was young I was much more concerned about what others thought. I seemed to fret over everything when I just had two and three kids. Now that I have ten, I'm too busy chasing them to worry much about it."

Esther listened. She was surprised — pleasantly surprised — that Polly was so easy to talk with. Polly told Esther about their move to Montana, and Esther talked about her train ride here from Ohio, and the little boy who'd asked her if she was a pilgrim. They both laughed over that, and the laughter felt good.

"I heard about your pie," Polly said, changing the subject. "And I heard about how word got around. It seems you're going to be quite busy baking between now and Christmas. And" — Polly pointed a finger into the air — "Ammon also said that the money he spent on that pie was worth it. He's really enjoyed getting to know you, Esther."

She leaned close and lowered her voice. "In all his years you're the only young woman that Ammon has ever brought home. You should have seen the glow on his face as he entered the house tonight with you at his side. And I caught the way he looked at you . . ." Polly let out a sigh.

Esther didn't know what to say. Instead, she tucked Polly's words deep in her heart and let the smallest smile play on her lips.

"Now, I've hogged you enough. Why don't you get over there and spend some time with my brother."

"No, let me help." Esther took a step forward.

Polly waved her away. "The biggest help is keeping those kids out of my hair for the next ten minutes so that I can get dinner on the table. Shoo, shoo." Polly patted her *kapp,* as if making sure it was still in place with all her busy movement.

Esther walked over to where Ammon was sitting with the kids. He'd just gotten them settled down for a story.

"*Onkel* Ammon, will you tell us again about our great-great-grandpas who came across the ocean so they could worship God?" a little girl with bright blue eyes similar to Ammon's asked.

"They didn't come on the *Mayflower,* did they?" another girl, a few years older, asked.

"*Ne,* it was one hundred years later," Ammon said. "You're very smart, Mary Beth, to remember that."

"That was the Thanksgiving story. *Onkel* Ammon is going to tell us a new story," the oldest boy insisted.

"*Ja,* your brother is right." Ammon's gaze scanned the children. "I do have a new story. It's about a group of people who lived far away and tended sheep. Just like on your grandfather's farm back in Missouri.

"Out of all the people on the whole earth, the birth of God's Son, Jesus, was told to them first. They lived in the fields and cared for lowly animals. They were looked down upon by the townspeople, yet God saw their hearts. *Demut* doesn't make us godly, but humility is evidence of holiness. They depended on God to help them, and because of that, God came to them first." Ammon paused for a moment and looked at Esther. There was a tenderness in his eyes that took her breath away. She placed a hand over her heart, urging it to cease its wild beating.

"Humility is a wonderful trait," Ammon continued. "It's one that God highly values. It's considering others before yourself. It's putting on your apron and serving — like my friend Esther here — even in the smallest ways."

Esther's throat grew hot and thick. Tears filled her eyes. She'd struggled her whole life with not feeling good enough, with not measuring up, and Ammon's words were like a balm to her soul. She quickly wiped away the tears as Ammon fielded questions from the children about the type of sheep that the shepherds cared for, and if it was really, really cold out on those hills.

Seeing Ammon's simple care for her reminded her how much God must care for her. The thought penetrated her soul. *You love me just as I am, don't You, God?*

In the quiet of her heart, she heard, *I do.*

It wasn't an audible voice, but a deep knowing. *Look at these children. Consider how they are loved. This is how I love you too.*

Esther looked around and noticed the wonder on each face. She felt a simple love for them even though she'd just met them. She was sure that as she got to know them better, she'd love them more. Some were loud, and at least one of them was reserved . . . just like her. But that didn't make them less valuable.

"Onkel?" An older boy lifted his hand to get Ammon's attention. "Sometimes I feel as if I'm looked down on by townspeople. They look at my clothes and hat and stare. And once —" His voice caught in his throat. "And once when I was walking to school, some people stopped and were laughing at me. I didn't wear shoes that day — not because I didn't have them, but just because

I didn't want to wear them. And they laughed."

"If you read the Bible, and if you listen to the preacher, you'll discover that what God thinks is important is often opposite of what the world thinks."

Esther rocked back and forth in the rocking chair and thought about her own life. Everything in her family, community, and church was set up to make God the focus, but had it? Had knowing about God and His ways penetrated her heart?

"What do you think about that, Esther?"

It wasn't until Esther heard her name that she realized Ammon had been talking to her.

"I'm sorry, what was that?"

"Who do you think God values?" Ammon asked, his eyes fixed on hers. His gaze was intense and intimate, as if he saw a part of her that she'd never seen herself — a worthy part.

"I think that what you said earlier was right. We don't serve God to earn His love — it's never worked that way. But because of love we should be honored to serve, and I think that God values a willing heart. He values someone who's not fighting for first, but who's happy just doing the task set before him or her."

"I like that answer." Ammon rose from his

chair and motioned to the dining room. "And it looks like dinner is ready. Esther, I'm sure you're hungry."

Esther nodded. She rose and followed him into the dining room. She should be hungry, but amazingly she felt full. Ammon's words, and God's echoes in her heart, had made her very, very full.

CHAPTER NINE

Esther breathed out a contented sigh, and her chest still felt warm, happy from the previous evening spent with Ammon and his family. It was the second time she'd been over there in a week. It was hard to believe that a week had passed since she'd gone on the sleigh ride with him. They'd seen each other every day since then.

She moved into the living room of her cousin's house and realized that she hadn't heard baby Mark cry all night. He was plump enough to be able to sleep through the night now — she always loved when babies reached this phase. The question was, what was *she* doing awake?

The air inside the cabin was chilly, but she wasn't about to start a fire in the woodstove and wake her cousin. Instead she hurried to Hannah's thick wool shawl that was lying folded over the back of the rocking chair. She wrapped it around her shoulders and then settled onto the chair, swaying with a gentle motion.

Esther took a deep breath and could still smell the wonderful aroma of last night's pot roast and the bacon that she'd fried up for the broccoli salad before leaving for her date with Ammon.

This was Esther's first Christmas away from her family. For the last few years, she'd lived away from home as often as she'd lived at home because of the positions she took to be a *maude* in different surrounding counties, but during all that time, she'd always made it home for Christmas.

For the Amish, Christmas was the most celebrated holiday, even though they didn't put up Christmas trees and put few decorations out. They didn't purchase piles of presents like the *Englisch.* Instead, the day centered on family and kinship. Some Amish families drew names and purchased or made gifts for each other, but in her family, only the young children received gifts. Well, except for the young women in the family who everyone expected would get married soon. For the last four years, both Esther and Violet had received decorative dishes from their parents. Violet's would be gracing her table this year, at her first home.

Even though she wasn't with her family,

her heart felt happy. In addition to caring for the *boppli* and spending time with Ammon, she had practiced making her pies, but she hadn't started making the ones for the orders yet. Vanilla crumb pie tasted best when it was fresh, and if she was going to do this, she wanted to do her best. Her goal was to make ten or twelve pies a day and deliver them right before Christmas. Ammon had already offered to be in charge of the deliveries.

She liked having him around. Most of the time he'd just come to hang out with her at Hannah's place. Hannah had come down with strep throat, and Esther was needed around the house, cooking, baking, and caring for the baby.

Hannah's husband, Matthew, had been busy at Montana Log Works, crafting log benches to give for Christmas presents, so Ammon had helped by chopping wood and shoveling snow off the porch steps. They'd chatted as she rolled out piecrusts or kneaded dough. As they talked, it was easy for her to pretend that this was her house. That Ammon was her husband. But realizing that scared her as much as excited her. He was the first man to give her so much attention, but how much did she know about him?

As Esther sat and rocked, she thought about how she needed to get to know him better. She couldn't let her heart move past her emotions. Her *mem* had done that, and she lived a very hard life, with their family having little money and feeling as if she had to win everyone's acceptance with her notable pies.

Esther wanted to be appreciated for more than her pies. She wanted to be seen as someone special, even though she wasn't as outgoing as Violet. She wanted to love and be loved, yes. But she also needed to make sure that whoever loved her would also understand her, take care of her, and give her a good life. And she'd always hoped that good life would be on a farm back east. If Ammon wanted that life to be in West Kootenai, then Esther had a lot of thinking to do.

Ammon lit the lantern. A gentle glow filled the room, falling over his *mem*'s sleeping form. He'd spent more time away from her lately. He felt guilty about that, but it was his sister who constantly pushed him out of the door. "Go, spend some time with Esther. Someone like that doesn't come along every day."

He put a pot of coffee on the stove and

then walked over to his *mem*. She appeared as if she was just sleeping, but Ammon knew the truth. She would never get better. There was less and less time during the day that she opened her eyes. She looked thinner too. Thinner than he'd ever seen her. Maybe that was another reason why Polly always shooed him out. Maybe she knew more than she admitted about *Mem*'s condition. As a big sister, she'd always taken care of her little brother — tried to protect him.

He pulled up a chair next to his *mem*'s bed and sat. Tears filled his eyes as he thought about her hustling around her kitchen last Christmas. Even though there were plenty of daughters and daughters-in-law to do the cooking, *Mem* had made sure that she oversaw it all, getting each dish just right. They had no idea then that the cancer was growing in her body. They had no idea that it would be the last time she cuddled the newest grandbabies or tied an apron around her waist.

Last Christmas, *Mem* had teased him about some of the young women at church who she'd heard were interested in him. The interest hadn't been mutual. He wished he could introduce her to Esther. Tears filled his eyes, yet a smile graced his lips as he imagined those two women in the kitchen together. Oh, they would have been good friends.

"*Mem,* I finally found someone . . ." Ammon's voice caught in his throat. He reached forward and took her hand in his. *Mem*'s hands had fed babies, pulled weeds, and kneaded bread. They'd hung more laundry than one could track, but they'd also caressed sleeping children.

"Her name is Esther, and I think she's someone I could build a life with. I want to do something special for her for Christmas."

Ammon had already decided that for Christmas he'd tell Esther about the simple farm animals he carved from wood on the occasional quiet morning. Polly was knitting a small drawstring bag for him to put them in.

He rested his mom's hand back on her quilt, then he ran a hand down his face. "I wish I could think of something to give her now though," he mumbled. Esther was a lot like *Mem.* Selfless and caring. Humble. And she loved to bake.

Ammon sat up with a start. He hadn't opened *Mem*'s suitcase once, but he'd seen Polly go through her things many times, and he knew what was in there.

Ammon knelt on one knee and unzipped the top of the suitcase. Opening the lid, he saw what he'd been looking for right on top.

He heard footsteps from outside and quickly stood. Polly hustled in and then quickly closed the door behind her. She stopped short when she saw Ammon standing by the suitcase. She eyed the object in his hand curiously.

"Since Christmas is only three days away, Esther's going to begin baking all those pies that folks around here have asked for. I was going to run over there in a little bit for moral support, and I thought that by giving her this . . ." Ammon let his words trail off. Was giving this simple gift silly? Did he want her to know that he appreciated the way she served others, or was it something more? He shrugged. "I thought it would be a nice gesture."

Suddenly heat poured down his limbs, and he worried that he was moving too fast. They'd spent a lot of time together over the last few weeks, but was it enough of a foundation to build more on?

He looked to *Mem* and then to Polly. His sister clapped her hands together. "I think giving something of *Mem*'s to Esther is a wonderful idea. She's sweet on you, you know. I can see it in her eyes."

Ammon smiled. His sister wouldn't tell him that unless it was the truth. Those words gave him the confidence he needed. Ammon moved toward the front door. He put on his boots and then slid on his heavy jacket, tucking the item inside one of his pockets. "I hope Esther knows how much I am starting to care for her."

When he looked back he saw tears rimming his sister's eyes. "She'll know, little brother, she'll know. Now get out there and win her heart."

CHAPTER TEN

There was a lightness to her step as Esther approached the Kraft and Grocery. She reached the porch and noticed a layer of ice on the steps. She clung to the wooden handrail and did some math in her head. Just three more days until Christmas, but she calculated that if she could make twelve pies a day for the next three days, she'd be able to get them all done. That would leave Sunday as a day of rest and Christmas Eve for getting them delivered.

Esther paused at the front door and took out a key that Annie had given her. It was just a short walk from Hannah's house to the store, and she'd assured Annie that she could let herself in. No need for the store owner to get up extra early.

They were new friends and yet the fact that Annie trusted Esther with the keys to the store amazed her. Esther felt guilty that even though she enjoyed it here, she still couldn't picture herself making it her home. A stirring deep in her gut told her she needed to talk to Ammon about that soon. Did he see West Kootenai as his forever home?

The first thing Esther noticed when she stepped inside the store and flipped on the lights was the wooden nativity scene set up on the front counter. Fresh balsam pine branches also decorated some of the short shelves. In the dining room white lights twinkled against the wood beams of the ceiling. Annie had been busy.

Not five minutes later she had the woodstove going and all the ingredients for the pies lined up.

In a large mixing bowl, she began to mix up a piecrust. She felt at peace in the kitchen. It was a space to think and to pray, and the person heaviest on her mind — and in her prayers — was Ammon. What were his dreams? His goals for the future?

Her own *mem* came to mind. If *Mem* told her once about her need to know the man she was to marry, she'd told Esther a hundred times. Her mom loved her dad, yes. But they'd met and married quickly. She didn't understand before they wed how some of his bad habits would negatively affect their whole married life.

Esther had just finished preparing six of the pies and had placed the first two in the oven when she heard a slight knock on the front door.

She glanced at the clock. It was only six thirty. The bakers weren't supposed to come in until seven. Surely they wouldn't get here this early . . . unless it was Annie and she needed to get in because she'd lent Esther her keys.

Esther wiped her floury hands on a dish towel and then peered out the side window. It was Ammon standing there. Esther rushed to the door and unlocked it.

He greeted her with a huge smile.

"What in the world are you doing here?" The morning sun hadn't risen over the mountains yet and the morning was still dark. "Are you the only one in there?" Ammon said.

Esther nodded.

"Well, it probably wouldn't look right for us being alone in there. Do you mind stepping out? For only a minute."

Esther followed him to the front of the store. He held her hand as he led her down the slippery steps.

"Esther, I don't know where to start. I've enjoyed these last few weeks. It's been so *gut* getting to know you. I never planned on

547

staying here in Montana, but taking care of my *mem* has been hard."

"Wait . . . you're caring for your *mem*?"

"Yes, she had a stroke. We're staying in the small cabin by Polly's house."

She wanted to ask more. She wanted to know how his *mem* was doing. She wanted to ask if she could meet her, but instead she waited for Ammon to finish.

"When I was telling my nieces and nephews about the story of the shepherds, I couldn't help but think of you. I appreciate the way you don't walk around proud. Your humility and service to others has made me want to get to know you better."

She studied his face, trying to figure out where this was going, and wondering why it was so important that he tell her this now. The air was cold and it numbed her cheeks. Esther hugged her arms tighter to her chest and wished he'd hurry it along.

"I have something for you, Esther." He pulled something white from his pocket and unfolded it. "It's my *mem*'s apron. I wish she could meet you — just wake up for a little while and see your smile. But I want you to have this as you begin your pies. To wear it. I want you to know how much I care."

"Wait." Esther held up her hands. "Let

548

me be sure I understand. Your *mem* is not conscious. She had a stroke, and you've been caring for her. I am concerned for her. We've been together every day for the last week and you're just now telling me about this?"

She took a step back. Ammon's eyes grew round. "*Ja,* but we've been talking about happy things. It's too hard talking about my *mem,* so . . ."

"I-I wish you would have told me sooner." She looked down at the apron. She should be honored, but a cold chill swept through her. What else had he not told her?

"As much as I'd love to take this, Ammon, I can't. This is happening too fast. There is so much I need to learn about you. Accepting that — accepting your *mem*'s apron — seems like it's a commitment I'm not ready to make."

A frown furrowed his brow. "It's not like I'm ready to publish our wedding, Esther. I just wanted you to know that I'd like to consider you more than a friend."

She looked up at the dark sky and all the stars, wishing the words were written in them, words to give him hope but not to make too big of a commitment.

"Listen," she finally said. "I enjoy you. I enjoy your family, but there is so much more I need to know — about your plans, about your life and where you want to live . . ."

"I'd love to tell you. Any questions feel free —"

She held up a hand, halting his words. "Not now. Not today. I —" And then she remembered. Her pies! She had to finish them before the regular bakers came and took over the kitchen.

Esther glanced back over her shoulder at the front door, as if expecting smoke to be pouring out. How long had she been out here? Long enough for the pies to burn for certain.

"I have to go back in. I have two pies in the oven." She turned away and moved toward the restaurant, leaving him standing with the apron still in his hands. Her heart thumped in her chest as she moved with quickened steps.

"Esther, wait," his voice called out, echoing through the still, quiet morning.

"I can't!" she called just as her first foot touched the wooden step. Too late she remembered the thin layer of ice. Her foot spun out, propelling her body forward. She tried to catch herself. Her right hand hit first, and she heard a loud cracking sound at the same moment pain shot up her wrist and arm. It sounded like the crunching of eggshells. Her body tumbled to the ground as a moan escaped her.

"Esther!" Ammon's voice echoed in her ears. A wave of nausea fell on her as she felt the first stabs of pain. Her whole body was cold, but all she could think about were the pies. "You have to get in there, Ammon. You have to go get those pies out of the oven . . . before they burn down the place."

He gingerly walked up the icy steps and then moved to the door. "I'll be right back, Esther! I'll be right back!"

CHAPTER ELEVEN

Thankfully Annie's personal number was listed by the phone inside the store. Ammon had called her and without hesitating, Annie had picked them up and driven them down to Eureka. Even in the warm car, Esther's face was white. She trembled from the pain and Ammon wished he could do something — anything — for her.

They made it to urgent care and the doctor ordered an X-ray. By then her wrist was purple and swollen. There was no question that it was broken. The doctor was just checking to see how badly.

Esther had Annie call the store and ask about the pies that still needed to be baked.

"Yes, Jenny took care of them." Annie patted her hand. "There is no need to worry."

"But even with those baked, that's only six done, just a fraction of what I need for the orders." She looked down at her wrist. "There is no way I can finish them now."

Ammon blew out a sigh, and he held back his words. Did she know how ridiculous she sounded? "I'm just glad that you're going to be all right, Esther," he said. "That's what matters most."

She nodded but he could tell that she didn't believe him. Not entirely.

The door opened and the doctor came in. "I'm sorry to say, miss, that it's worse than I thought. It's fractured in two places. I'm going to put a cast on and you're going to have to wear it for two months."

"Two months?" Esther gasped. She didn't say anything more, but Ammon could read her thoughts. Two months without cooking, baking, or taking care of the baby. Two months of idleness was a curse to an Amish woman.

Ammon and Annie sat with her and watched as the doctor put the cast on. He gave her medicine for the pain, and Esther slept the whole drive back to West Kootenai.

"Don't worry, I'll take care of her," Hannah had said as Annie dropped her off. Esther's only response was a frown.

Ammon stopped by the next day, but Hannah said that Esther was napping. Two days later, when he came by again, Ammon could see her through the kitchen window as he strode up the front porch steps. Esther let him in but it seemed like there was a wall around her heart. They talked about his *mem*. He told her more about the stroke. They talked about baby Mark and about the six pies that were delivered.

"At least some of the people on the list got one," she said.

Ammon was just about to leave when something inside told him there was more they needed to talk about.

"Esther, can I ask you something?"

She must have seen the serious look on his face because her eyes widened. "*Ja*, I suppose."

Ammon returned to the kitchen chair where he'd been sitting, thankful that Hannah and the baby had left for the day.

"It seems you are reluctant to share your heart with others. Has someone hurt you?"

"What do you mean?" She cradled her casted arm.

"*Vell*, I've asked you a few times to tell me about your life in Sugarcreek, and your family, and you give me just a few details. But whenever the questions go deeper, you turn the attention back to me."

"I suppose it's because I love hearing your stories, that's all. You never did finish telling me about Mexico and what you saw —"

"See!" Ammon pointed his finger. "You're

doing it again."

Esther's mouth circled into an O. Her eyes widened. "*Ja,* I suppose I did." She lowered her head slightly, peering down at her cast. "I guess that means you're not going to tell me more about Mexico."

"Not until I hear more about you."

She nodded and he waited. He'd wait all day if he had to. He just hoped it wouldn't come to that.

Esther didn't deserve a man like Ammon. He'd been so tender when she'd fallen on the ice. He'd stayed by her side when she'd gone to urgent care, and he was here now. His consistency gave her hope. Maybe she had seen enough of his character to open her heart. *Lord, show me. Help me to trust.*

Ammon wanted to know more about her. She could tell him trivial things, but from the look on his face, he wasn't going to allow that. She might as well go to the heart of the matter.

Esther looked to the wood-burning stove, as if it was holding her secret, and then she turned back to him. "I have a twin sister," she finally said. "She was my best friend during most of our growing-up years."

"Was?" Ammon tilted his head slightly.

She realized, then, she'd been hiding

plenty too.

"She still is a *gut* friend, but she's busy spending time with her new husband. Violet is pleasant and kind. She has a wonderful sense of humor."

"It sounds like someone I know." He smiled.

"Me?" Esther asked. Her heartbeat quickened slightly.

"Of course."

"Everyone in Sugarcreek will tell you that I'm nothing like my sister." She swallowed down a mixture of pleasure and worry. She wanted him to keep thinking of her like that, but was afraid there'd come a time when he saw her as she truly was.

"I wouldn't know, Esther, but I do believe you have all those wonderful qualities. I enjoyed getting to know you over that first piece of pie, and each time I learn more, I appreciate the woman you are."

Esther didn't know what to say to that. She'd never had anyone speak to her in such a manner, and definitely no one as wonderful and interesting as Ammon. The light from the lantern brightened his face, his smile.

A greater heat than that of the lantern and fire lighted inside her. Adoring eyes looked at her, and she squirmed under his gaze.

Esther told herself to release the breath she was holding. She didn't know how to respond to his kind words.

"Violet does the most beautiful stitching, and she's often invited to sewing frolics. She was just married a few months ago. Her beau was from Berlin, but they bought a small place in Walnut Creek, halfway between his town and ours."

Ammon nodded and there was humor in his gaze. She was doing it again, getting the attention off of herself, but old habits were hard to break.

"I never thought I lived up to my sister, but I think I'm beginning to understand what *Mem* has been telling me my whole life. We are different people, but neither is better. She is not better than me . . . and I am no better than her."

Ammon smiled. "And what has you believing that? What's changed?"

Esther wanted to tell him that he'd helped — seeing the care in his eyes, but she couldn't be that transparent. Not yet. So instead she tried to share the other part of the truth.

"Well, everyone was so caring, even after I had to cancel their pie orders. Hannah's been so good to me, and you too. I like to think that you all care for me as I really am."

"We do." His voice lowered. "I do."

Butterflies danced in her stomach. "I guess that it's taken me sitting still — not using my hand — to learn that."

"And I have to say I like that too. Not only that you're letting God's truth sink deep into your heart, but I like having you all to myself." He reached over and took her left hand. "I like seeing you be still."

"I don't sit still very often." Esther laid her casted arm over her chest.

He chuckled. "You think I don't know that?"

CHAPTER TWELVE

They had a simple but wonderful Christmas dinner at Hannah's house. Ammon had stopped by and then he asked if she'd like to meet someone special.

The small cabin was warm and the older woman lay in a hospital bed by the windows. Esther approached and smiled, tears filling her eyes. "I wish I'd had the chance to know you. I wish we could have baked together." Ammon stood next to her, silent, but she could tell from the look in his eyes that he was thankful for this moment.

"I'm not sure how much time she'll have with us, but it helps to remember the woman she was. The woman who loved to bustle around the kitchen, just like you, Esther."

"You'll have to tell me more," she said. "When it's not so hard — not because I want to change the subject, but because I really want to know."

Ammon nodded. "*Ja,* I would like that, but I have one more Christmas gift for you. It's over at the Kraft and Grocery."

"At this late hour?" Esther looked at the clock on the wall. It was almost eight. "And on Christmas?"

"Yes, come. I think you're going to like it."

It was a short walk to the store, and Esther was surprised to see a few buggies still parked outside. Ammon held her good arm as she walked up the steps, but when they got inside, he motioned her toward the kitchen. "Go on, go ahead."

Esther walked into the kitchen and paused. Not only were all the lights on, but the kitchen was full of people. Her cousin Hannah, Deborah Shelter, Jenny and her daughter, Kenzie. Annie, along with a few other *Englisch* women Esther had met a few times. Hope and Eve Peachy were there, along with Marianna Stone, whose baby belly had grown seemingly overnight. Each wore a Christmas apron — the frilly red and green kind.

But the most surprising of all was when Ammon walked into the kitchen and put on an oven mitt. "I'm all ready for service, ma'am." He grinned.

Her mouth dropped open, and she looked

from face to face, finally settling on Ammon's.

"Ready for service? What do you mean?"

"Well, I know we missed getting all of those pies ready for Christmas, but don't we Amish celebrate Second Christmas?" he said. "We're here to help you complete those orders. We know how hard it was for you to feel as if you let so many people down."

She opened her mouth to say something and then closed it again. "You-you'd do that for me? All of you? On Christmas?"

"We won't do it for you, but we'll do it with you, if you tell us what to do," Jenny piped up. "Around here, we're always happy to help a friend."

"I-I, well, I don't know what to say."

"I know how you feel about sharing your *mem*'s recipe and all," Annie said, concern in her eyes. "If you don't want to tell us, then we can work a system out. One person can measure one ingredient over and over. Just tell us what we need to do —"

Esther thought about the recipe card. She'd left it back at Hannah's house, but the recipe was simple and she knew it by heart. She thought about what *Mem* had told her, *"Please don't share this recipe."* She also knew the reason why. *Mem* needed that recipe — those pies — to secure her place in their community. But things were different for Esther. The friends who God had brought into her life were different.

She looked around, paused at each face, each smile. She didn't need to work to earn their love. Instead they gave it freely. These friends didn't care for her because of what she could do for them. Instead they cared from the bottom of their hearts and wanted to assist her in doing what she couldn't do herself.

"That's awful kind of you, Annie, for wanting to help me protect my recipe, but really there's no need for that. Just all of you being here tells me that you care, and that you're trustworthy. At first I didn't know that. I need to explain to you . . . to all of you . . ." She turned her attention to Ammon. "I need you to know why I have pushed everyone away."

He nodded and waited for her to continue.

"Back in Sugarcreek — as in every other Amish community — there are those who are most well-loved and those who are not. My dad never made much money in his business, and some of his shortcomings were well-known in the community. My sister overcame all of that with her beauty and her outgoing nature, and my mom was always known for her pies. No, actually for one certain pie. It made her special, and I felt it made me special too. Yet when I fell — when I failed — when I fell short, you all loved me just the same."

"Of course we did — you're our friend." It was Jenny who spoke.

"It's not your pies that make you special, Esther. It's you."

"And that's why I'm going to share the recipe. I trust all of you. And I know . . . well, it's because of you that I shine bright."

"You'll really shine when we all have pieces of that pie in our bellies." Marianna Stone patted her large pregnant stomach. "I hope you don't mind, Esther, if we make a few extras to share at the end of the day."

"Of course not." Then Esther hurried to the chalkboard that the bakers used to write their work orders on, and she wrote down the recipe for vanilla crumb pie. And as she stepped back from the board, she felt a freedom she'd never felt. She felt valued and important, not because of what she offered, but because of what God had given her — undeserved favor. Friends.

The women set to work then. They rolled up their sleeves and got busy preheating, measuring, and mixing.

Esther was standing next to Jenny, explaining how she and *Mem* always added a dash of vinegar to the piecrust — even though the recipe didn't call for it — to keep the crust flaky, when Ammon approached.

He held something behind his back. "Can I, uh, talk to you for a minute?"

He shuffled from side to side and his brow was slightly furrowed. She pulled her casted arm to her chest, hugging it close as he led her into the dining area. Ammon paused beside the first table and motioned for her to sit.

"Is something wrong?"

"No." The word shot from his mouth. "Well, I don't think so. I do have something for you."

Esther remembered the last time he'd said that. He'd offered her his *mem*'s apron and she'd refused his gift — refused him. She'd been such a fool to push Ammon away like that. Was he going to make the same offer twice?

Ammon pulled something from behind his back. Esther's heart sank to see that it wasn't his *mem*'s apron. Instead it was a red and green one that matched those of all the women in the kitchen.

"I know it's fancy for an Amish woman, but Susan Carash made them for everyone. If you don't want to wear —" He started to pull it back toward him.

"Wait," she interrupted. "It's fancy, yes, but even more importantly, it's a symbol of this community. When I leave here someday, I'll have something to remember everyone by."

Ammon's eyebrows lifted and he leaned in closer. He was no longer looking at the apron. Instead his eyes were focused on her face. "What did you say?"

"I said it was fancy but —"

He waved a hand. "No, not that. The other part."

"I said that it'll be nice to have this to remember —"

"After you leave?"

"Yes, after I leave."

Ammon tilted down his chin, fixing his eyes on hers. "So you're not planning to make this your home?"

"*Ne*. I mean, I don't think so. It's a nice place, but I miss the larger communities. I miss the expansive fields I passed in my buggy back east. I miss the farms."

"You — you'd like to live on a farm someday?"

Esther nodded slightly. "Isn't it the dream of every Amish woman to have a spot for a nice garden? To raise her children to know the value of hard work? To see her husband in the field, working to provide?" She could have added that it was also a dream for that husband to come in from the fields hot, tired, but happy to see her. Maybe she would share that with him someday.

"For some reason I didn't know that." Ammon jumped to his feet as if unable to hold in his eagerness. "I thought you'd moved here for good, that you left Ohio for a reason."

A laugh burst from her lips, seeing his excitement. "The only reason I came was to be Hannah's *maude.* To help care for baby Mark for a few months. He's a sweet baby, but Hannah's almost at the place where she doesn't need me."

Ammon blew out a heavy breath and then sat down. "There is something I need to tell you then. I don't want to stay here either. I've been here to be a support for *Mem,* but Polly just told me that my youngest sister, Ilene, will be coming to take my place. She's broken off her engagement and she's moving here in the summer. She's going to fill in as a teacher since Lydia Wise — the current teacher — will be married next year. Her wedding isn't published yet, but she wanted to give the school board plenty of notice."

Esther tilted her head, trying to make

sense of all he was saying. "And this means?"

"This means that I'll be heading back to Missouri soon. And . . ." He reached into his pocket and pulled out a small knitted bag. "And I have something else for you."

Instead of handing it to her, Ammon opened the bag and spilled the contents on the table. There were four carved wooden animals.

She gasped and picked up a small horse. "Did you make these? They are so cute." She picked up the others one at a time. A cow. A chicken. A sheep. Esther remembered the story of the shepherds and said a silent prayer, thanking God for a man who loved to serve.

"They're not just for decoration. I've been wanting to tell you something, but I've been worried."

"*Ja,* what is it?" she asked.

"I have a farm in Missouri. I love it and I can't wait to return. I also . . . can't wait for you to see it."

"And what made you worried about that?"

"Well, I thought you wanted to stay here."

"Oh no!" Esther chuckled. "I'd much rather live on a farm someday."

She didn't say "your farm." She didn't have to. By the look in Ammon's eyes, she

567

knew he understood.

"There is a lot of work that needs to be done on the farm to prepare for spring planting. It's going to be a busy year, especially if I'm going to be courting a young woman from Ohio."

Esther's heart leapt in her chest. "Courting?"

"If you will have me."

"*Ja.* Yes, I would." Warmth filled her chest and spread to her limbs, and then it cooled slightly as she remembered what happened a few weeks ago, and how she'd acted. A sinking feeling settled in the pit of her gut.

"That's wonderful." He reached across the table and took her hand, squeezing it tight. "I-I've never been so happy."

"But I have one condition," she quickly added. "Something I need you to do for me."

She could see Ammon's Adam's apple bobbing as he swallowed. "*Ja,* of course."

"It's just a little thing. I know you've already given me two gifts today, but I'd like a third. It's about your *mem*'s apron. Do you think I could have it? I don't know what I was thinking when I turned it away."

"*Ja.*" Ammon's face glowed as if someone held a lantern light close to it. "I would like that very much."

"*Vell,* in that case, we'd better get in the kitchen." Esther squeezed his hand and stood. "Now that we have a few matters settled with the future, let's see what we can do about those pies."

She picked up the apron and attempted to loop the neck strap over her head with her good hand, but it got caught up in her *kapp.*

"Here. Let me help you with that."

Ammon took the apron from her and looped the strap over her head. She adjusted it the best she could and then he moved behind her and pulled the two strings to tie it. The action was intimate, and Esther held in her breath.

Ammon leaned close so that his mouth was near her ear. She could feel the warmth of his breath and it sent a shiver up her spine. "It's okay to breathe, Esther."

"Okay." She released her breath.

He let her hands drop and she turned. Before she even stopped completely, Ammon placed the softest kiss on her lips and then pulled away. He stepped back, and she saw care in his eyes. Her heart felt full and it wasn't until she noticed pink rising to his cheeks that she realized there was no noise coming from the kitchen.

She turned to the open doorway of the

kitchen. Annie was the only one peeking out, but Esther had no doubt that all of the bakers had been spying.

"Um, we're sorry to interrupt," Annie said, "but you wrote down vanilla extract on the recipe, but you didn't write down the measurement."

Esther fanned her face, feeling heat rise to her cheeks. "Yes, well, that would be three teaspoons. I, uh, I'll be right in."

"Don't hurry yourself." Annie waved a hand. "We have this covered."

"*Ja,* well, I don't want to miss the fun." She looked up at Ammon and he waved a hand to the kitchen. "After you. Your friends await."

"Yes, they do. Don't they?" she said with a sigh, and then she rolled up her sleeves. Esther was sure that this was the happiest day of her life.

Pies for Christmas. And a man who taught her what friendship, service, and love were all about.

READING GROUP GUIDE

1. Esther Glick is a shy Amish woman who's spent her life comparing herself with her sister and trying to see if she measures up. How did this comparison hinder Esther's relationships? Do you struggle with comparing yourself with others?
2. Ammon Schwartz ends up in Montana unexpectedly after his mother's stroke. How did Ammon make good use of his time while in Montana?
3. Both Esther and Ammon had put walls around their hearts. Why was Esther worried about opening her heart to someone? What concerned Ammon about becoming interested in a young woman from West Kootenai?
4. Throughout the story the apron is a symbol of caring for and serving others. What various aprons were

highlighted through the book? What
did each one symbolize?

ACKNOWLEDGMENTS

Thank you to Amy Lathrop and the Litfuze Hens for being the best assistants anyone can have. Many people ask how I do it all . . . thankfully, I don't have to do it all thanks to you!

I also appreciate the HarperCollins Christian Publishing team, my editor on this project, Becky Philpott, plus Karli Cajka, Katie Bond, Laura Dickerson, Daisy Hutton, and Natalie Hanemann. Your insight, help, and enthusiasm have been amazing! I also send thanks to all the managers, designers, copy editors, salespeople, financial folks, and everyone else who make a book possible!

I'm also thankful for my agent, Janet Grant. Your wisdom and guidance make all the difference.

And I'm thankful for my family at home: John, who serves me with love daily. Cory, Katie, Clayton, and Chloe. Leslie, our missionary girl across the world. Nathan, Isabella, Alyssa, and Casey. I love all of you! Grandma Dolores, thank you for all the pies you've made me over the years.

Finally, I appreciate Beth Wiseman, Kathleen Fuller, and Ruth Reid. How blessed I am to share this book and these stories with you!

ABOUT THE AUTHOR

USA Today bestselling author **Tricia Goyer** is the author of thirty-five books, including the three-book Seven Brides for Seven Bachelors series. She has written over five hundred articles for national publications and blogs for high-traffic sites like TheBetter Mom.com and MomLifeToday.com. Tricia and her husband, John, live in Little Rock, Arkansas, where Tricia coordinates a Teen MOPS (Mothers of Preschoolers) group. They have six children.

RECIPES FROM BETH WISEMAN'S *WHEN CHRISTMAS COMES AGAIN*

KATHERINE'S PAPRIKA POTATOES

1/4 cup flour
1/4 cup Parmesan cheese
1 tablespoon paprika
3/4 teaspoon salt
1/8 teaspoon garlic salt (or onion salt)
6 medium potatoes
vegetable oil or cooking spray

Put all the ingredients except the potatoes into a gallon-size plastic baggie. Shake until well blended. Wash the potatoes and cut them into small wedges. Add potato wedges to the bag until one-third full. Shake the bag to coat the potatoes. Place them on an oiled pan and repeat until all the potatoes are covered with the mixture. Bake at 350 degrees for 1 hour.

MARY CAROL'S CHOCOLATE CAKE

2 cups white sugar
1 3/4 cups flour
3/4 cup unsweetened cocoa powder
1 1/2 teaspoons baking powder
1 1/2 teaspoons baking soda
1 teaspoon salt
2 eggs
1 cup milk
1/2 cup vegetable oil
2 teaspoons vanilla extract
1 cup boiling water

Preheat oven to 350 degrees. Grease and flour two 9-inch round pans. In a large bowl, stir together the sugar, flour, cocoa, baking powder, baking soda, and salt. Add the eggs, milk, oil, and vanilla. Mix for 2 minutes on medium speed. Stir in the boiling water last. Batter will be thin. Pour into prepared pans. Bake for 30 to 35 minutes, until the cake tests done with a toothpick. Cool in the pans for 10 minutes, then remove to a wire rack to cool completely. Frost with your favorite chocolate frosting and enjoy!

RECIPES FROM RUTH REID'S
HER CHRISTMAS PEN PAL

HAZELNUT ALMOND BISCOTTI
3 cups flour
1/4 cup hazelnut instant coffee powder
1 1/2 teaspoons baking powder
1 stick butter, softened
1/4 teaspoon salt
1 cup sugar
2 eggs
1 teaspoon vanilla
1 cup slivered almonds (or chopped nut of choice)

Preheat oven to 325 degrees. Combine all ingredients in a large mixing bowl.

Divide dough in half. On lightly floured cookie sheet, shape into two logs about 16 inches long. (Dough will be sticky; coat hands with flour before shaping logs.) Place 2 inches apart on greased and floured cookie sheet.

Bake for 25 minutes or until lightly

browned. Remove from cookie sheet and let cool for 5 minutes.

Cut diagonally and place on cookie sheet 1/2 inch apart. Bake for 10 minutes or until slightly browned.

Makes 2 dozen.

OATMEAL CRANBERRY WALNUT COOKIES

2 sticks butter
1 cup firmly packed brown sugar
1/2 cup granulated sugar
2 eggs
1 teaspoon vanilla extract
2 cups flour
1 1/4 teaspoons baking soda
1 1/4 teaspoons cinnamon
1/2 teaspoon salt
3 cups uncooked oats
1 cup dried cranberries
1 cup chopped walnuts

Preheat oven to 350 degrees.

Combine butter, sugars, eggs, and vanilla; beat well. Add flour, baking soda, cinnamon, and salt; mix well. Add remaining ingredients. Drop tablespoons of dough onto ungreased cookie sheet. Bake for 10 to 12 minutes or until golden brown.

Makes 4 dozen.

PEPPERMINT-CANDY-FROSTED SUGAR COOKIES

1 cup butter
1 1/2 cups granulated sugar
1 teaspoon vanilla extract
1 teaspoon peppermint extract
3 eggs
3 3/4 cups flour
1/4 teaspoon salt
2 teaspoons baking powder
3/4 teaspoon baking soda

Preheat oven to 350 degrees.

Beat together butter, sugar, vanilla, peppermint extract, and eggs. In a separate bowl, mix together flour, salt, baking powder, and baking soda. Fold into first mixture. Refrigerate until firm.

Roll out dough on floured surface and cut with round cutter. Place on greased cookie sheet.

Bake for 7 to 9 minutes or until lightly browned.

Frosting

1 cup powdered sugar
2 teaspoons milk
2 teaspoons light corn syrup
1/4 teaspoon peppermint extract
1/2 cup crushed peppermint candies

Stir together powdered sugar and milk until smooth. With an electric mixer, beat in corn syrup and peppermint extract until icing is smooth.

Spread over cooled cookies and sprinkle with crushed peppermint candies.

*Recipes provided by author.

RECIPES FROM KATHLEEN FULLER'S *A GIFT FOR ANNE MARIE*

VERY GOOD PUMPKIN PIE

4 eggs, separated
1 cup brown sugar
1 cup white sugar
2 cups pumpkin
4 tablespoons flour
1/4 teaspoon salt
2 teaspoons vanilla
5 cups milk, heated (2 cans evaporated milk)
2 teaspoons pumpkin pie spice

Beat egg yolks and brown sugar together until light in color. Add white sugar, then remaining ingredients except egg whites. Beat egg whites and fold in. Pour into two unbaked pie shells. Bake at 425 degrees for 15 minutes, then at 325 degrees for 45 minutes or until done.

* Recipe from Eli Mary in *A Taste of Home,* from the Schlabach family

Never Fail Pie Dough

4 cups flour
1 1/2 cups lard
1 tablespoon brown sugar
1 1/2 teaspoons salt
1 tablespoon vinegar
1 egg, beaten
1/2 cup cold water

Mix flour, lard, sugar, and salt. In a separate bowl, beat together vinegar, egg, and water. Combine the two mixtures, stirring with a fork until mixed. Chill for at least 15 minutes. Dough can be left in refrigerator up to three days or frozen until ready to use.

* Recipe from Mrs. Wayne M. Hershberger in *A Taste of Home,* from the Schlabach family

RECIPES FROM TRICIA
GOYER'S *THE CHRISTMAS APRONS*

VANILLA CRUMB PIE

1 (15-ounce) refrigerated piecrust
3/4 cup light brown sugar
2 tablespoons flour
1/2 cup light corn syrup
1 teaspoon cream of tartar
1/8 teaspoon salt
3 teaspoons vanilla extract
2 eggs, beaten
1 1/4 cups water
3/4 cup flour
1/2 cup light brown sugar
1/2 teaspoon cream of tartar
1/2 teaspoon baking soda
1/8 teaspoon salt
3/4 stick butter

Preheat oven to 350 degrees. Unroll piecrust and place in 9-inch pie plate; flute edges.

In a large saucepan, combine brown sugar,

flour, corn syrup, cream of tartar, salt, vanilla, and eggs. Slowly stir in water and cook over medium heat, stirring until mixture boils and rises. Remove from heat.

In a medium bowl, mix crumb topping ingredients until crumbly.

Pour cooled brown sugar mixture into crust to three-quarters full. (There may be some mixture left.) Use your fingers to sprinkle crumbs evenly on top.

Bake for 45 to 50 minutes or until golden and set.

SUGAR CREAM PIE
1 (15-ounce) refrigerated piecrust
1/4 cup brown sugar
1/4 cup cornstarch
3/4 cup white sugar
1/8 teaspoon salt
2 cups half-and-half
3/4 cup whipping cream
1/2 cup butter
1 1/2 teaspoons vanilla
Cinnamon

Preheat oven to 350 degrees. Unroll piecrust and place in 9-inch pie plate; flute edges.

In a bowl, combine brown sugar and cornstarch. Set aside. In a saucepan, combine white sugar, salt, half-and-half, and whipping cream. Bring to a boil; lower temperature to medium. Gradually whisk brown sugar mixture into the sugar and cream mixture. Add the butter. Stir until butter melts. Add vanilla. Cook over medium heat, stirring constantly, for 3 minutes or until thick. Pour into crust. Sprinkle with cinnamon.

Bake at 350 degrees for 30 minutes.

The employees of Thorndike Press hope you have enjoyed this Large Print book. All our Thorndike, Wheeler, and Kennebec Large Print titles are designed for easy reading, and all our books are made to last. Other Thorndike Press Large Print books are available at your library, through selected bookstores, or directly from us.

For information about titles, please call:
  (800) 223-1244

or visit our Web site at:
  http://gale.cengage.com/thorndike

To share your comments, please write:
  Publisher
  Thorndike Press
  10 Water St., Suite 310
  Waterville, ME 04901